Mc

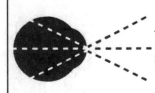

This Large Print Book carries the
Seal of Approval of N.A.V.H.

MOONLIGHT MASQUERADE

JUDE DEVERAUX

THORNDIKE PRESS
A part of Gale, Cengage Learning

GALE
CENGAGE Learning·

Detroit • New York • San Francisco • New Haven, Conn • Waterville, Maine • London

GALE
CENGAGE Learning·

LIBRARY OF CONGRESS CIP DATA ON FILE.
CATALOGUING IN PUBLICATION DATA FOR THIS BOOK
IS AVAILABLE FROM THE LIBRARY OF CONGRESS

ISBN-13: 978-1-14104-5510-9 (hardcover)
ISBN-10: 1-14104-5510-6 (hardcover)

Published in 2013 by arrangement with Pocket Books, a division of Simon & Schuster, Inc.

Printed in the United States of America
1 2 3 4 5 6 7 17 16 15 14 13

MOONLIGHT MASQUERADE

PROLOGUE

Edilean, Virginia

"I quit!" Heather said. "I cannot take any more of that man's bad temper."

She was in the outer office of Dr. Reede Aldredge's medical clinic and she was talking to Alice and Betsy. Alice wanted to retire and she was nearly desperate for Heather, young, recently married, and new to Edilean, to take on her job. But Heather was having a difficult time adjusting to Dr. Reede's sharp tongue. Betsy and Alice referring to it as his "perfectionism" wasn't helping Heather to adjust. "He never says a pleasant word."

"But what he does say is usually right," Alice said, her face encouraging.

"Yes, but it's the *way* he says it. Today I said, 'Good morning,' he says, 'I'm inside so how would I know?' And yesterday, he told Mrs. Casein that her only problem was that she ate too many of her husband's pies."

Betsy and Alice just looked at her. Betsy was in her late forties and had lived in Edilean since she was six. She was glad she wasn't a nurse as Heather was. Instead, she sat at the computer all day and answered the phone — and that kept her away from young Dr. Reede for most of the workday.

Heather understood the looks the women were giving her. "I know, I know," she said. "That's true about the pies, but couldn't he at least *try* to be diplomatic? Hasn't he even *heard* of a bedside manner? Last week Sylvia Garland left here crying. He wasn't at all sympathetic."

The two women again gave her a look.

"What?!" Heather asked, exasperated. She'd moved to Edilean because her husband worked nearby and he said the small town would be a great place to raise kids. And Heather had been thrilled to get a nursing job so close to their new house. But that was three weeks ago and now she didn't know if she could stay there. All this week she'd been saying she was going to quit.

Betsy spoke first. "Everyone in town except her husband knows that Sylvia Garland isn't going out with the girls on Thursday nights. She's sleeping around — and Dr. Reede told her so."

"What business is that of his?"

8

"Communicable diseases, I guess," Alice said. "Besides, he's used to working with people who have serious problems, like elephantiasis and leprosy."

Heather had heard about Dr. Reede's work around the world, but she wasn't going to be put off by that excuse. "If he thinks that small town illnesses are beneath him, why doesn't he leave?"

Yet again the women exchanged looks, then Alice spoke. "He tried to get other doctors to take over the practice for him."

"But doctors today want lots of money," Betsy said. "And they don't want to live in a tiny town and have to care for locals who talk too much, and tourists who get too many mosquito bites."

"Although he did enjoy that rescue last month," Alice said. "He had to climb down the side of a cliff."

"Great!" Heather said. "If everyone jumped off the side of a mountain would that make him happy?"

For a moment Alice and Betsy seemed to consider the idea. They too were worn out by Dr. Reede's never-ending bad temper. In fact, though she'd never admit it, it was the real reason Alice was taking early retirement.

Heather dropped down onto a chair by

the photocopy machine. "Doesn't he have a personal life? A girlfriend? He's a good-looking man. At least I think he would be if he weren't always frowning. Has he ever smiled in his entire life?"

"Dr. Reede used to smile a lot," Betsy said. "When he was a child he loved to come to the office to visit cousin Tristan's father who was the doctor then. Reede was a very sweet little boy who always knew he wanted to be a doctor. But then . . ."

"What happened?" Heather asked.

"Laura dumped him for the Baptist preacher," Alice answered.

"Where?"

"Where what?" Betsy asked.

"Where did this Laura find a preacher so dynamic that she left a hottie like Dr. Reede?" Heather asked.

"A hottie, is he?" Alice asked. "Even though he never smiles?"

"If I just *saw* him I'd think he was gorgeous. But he opens his mouth and I can't stand him. So what about this Laura? Where'd she go to find a man?"

"Nowhere. She lives here in Edilean. Her parents moved here in the 1970s."

"Wait a minute!" Heather said. "You don't mean Laura Billings, do you? The wife of the Baptist preacher here in Edilean?"

"The very one," Alice said.

"But she's . . ."

"She's what?" Betsy asked.

"Drab," Heather said. "She looks like she was always somebody's mother. I can't imagine her being the Great Love of anyone."

"But she was. She and Reede were inseparable from seventh or eighth grade and all through college. Then he went away to medical school and she took up with the new pastor." Betsy lowered her voice. "The rumor is that Dr. Reede was so depressed that he tried to kill himself, but he was rescued by Dr. Tris's wife. This was before they were married and she was still a teenager."

"Wow!" Heather said. "Drama in a small town. Are you saying that Dr. Reede has been sulking ever since Mrs. Billings ran off with another man?"

"More or less," Betsy said. "Although he'd never admit it. For years he was a world hero."

"Everyone falls back on that," Heather said. "Africa, Afghanistan, and countries I've never even heard of, but that doesn't excuse him *now*."

"If you ask me," Alice said, "that boy was

11

trying to go so fast that he'd outrun his past."

"And now he's stuck back here in Edilean," Betsy said with a sigh.

"And he lets everyone know that he doesn't want to be here," Heather added.

"Actually . . ." Betsy said, "he does a lot of good, only he doesn't let people see it."

"I know he does," Heather said. "He's a good doctor. He's efficient anyway."

"No," Betsy said. "It's more than that. He . . . Okay, let me tell you about something that happened a couple of months ago."

Betsy told how she'd been sitting at her desk, typing out invoices of unpaid bills, when Dr. Reede came out of the exam room. She had long ago learned to keep her mouth shut around him, since she never knew if he was in one of his "moods," as she and Alice called them. He varied from a grunt in answer to a greeting to a "Is there no work to do in here?"

But that day he'd stood there in silence until Betsy looked up from the computer. "Can I help you?" she asked.

"When does Mr. Carlisle come in again?"

She brought up the schedule on the screen. "Tomorrow." Since Mr. Carlisle was a hypochondriac who wanted attention more than medicine, she asked if she should reschedule him.

Dr. Reede hesitated. "When are Mrs. Springer and Mrs. Jeffrey coming in?"

Mrs. Springer was a very nice middle-aged woman who usually brought the staff cookies, while Mrs. Jeffrey had a six-year-old daughter and was pregnant with twins. "Wednesday," Betsy said. "Mrs. Springer at nine a.m. and Mrs. Jeffrey at three."

"Change them," Dr. Reede said. "Everybody on Friday. Carlisle at ten, Springer ten-fifteen, and Jeffrey at ten-thirty."

"But —" Betsy began. There was no way that Mr. Carlisle would get in and out in a mere fifteen minutes. And Mrs. Springer was to have her annual physical. This was going to cause a traffic jam — and it would be Alice and Betsy who would have to do the apologizing.

"Just *do* it," Dr. Reede snapped and went back into the exam room.

"So what happened?" Heather asked.

"Everyone was on time and everyone was predictable," Alice said, her eyes twinkling.

"What does that mean?" Heather asked.

"Mr. Carlisle took forty-five minutes in the exam room and during that time . . ." Alice began.

"They helped each other," Betsy said. The

13

two women had worked together for so long they often finished each other's sentences. "Mrs. Springer put down her knitting and played with Mrs. Jeffrey's daughter."

"And when the young mother fell asleep in her chair, Mrs. Springer asked us for a pillow for her," Alice said.

"And when it came time for Mrs. Springer's exam, she said she'd reschedule and she took care of the little girl while Mrs. Jeffrey went in."

"They've been friends ever since," Alice finished. "Mrs. Springer is an honorary grandmother to the kids."

Heather leaned back in her chair. "You think Dr. Reede did it on purpose?"

"If it were an isolated incident, I'd say no," Betsy said, "but there have been other things too."

"Such as?" Heather asked.

"One morning when I came in to work Dr. Reede was just getting off my computer. I was curious about what he was doing so I —"

"She snooped," Alice interrupted.

"I did indeed. He was on Amazon and he was still logged on, so I looked at what he'd ordered. It was a novel by Barbara Pym."

"Never heard of her," Heather said.

"They're sweet little English novels," Alice said.

"I'd think he'd read horror stories, the more gruesome the better," Heather said.

"I know he reads the *New England Journal of Medicine* from cover to cover," Betsy said in the doctor's defense. "Anyway, I thought I'd found out some secret about him."

"She didn't even tell *me!*" April said reproachfully.

Betsy continued her story. "The package came two days later, and I asked if he wanted me to open it. He said no and took it into his office. Three days later when Mr. Tucker left the exam room, he was carrying the book. I wouldn't have noticed but he had a note from the doctor and the poor man couldn't read the handwriting, so he asked for my help." Betsy stopped talking.

"What did the note say?" Heather asked.

"Well . . ." Betsy said, "Mr. Tucker is in his seventies and all his family has moved away. His son lives in England. Or is it Sweden? Or maybe it's Wyoming." She looked at Alice, who shrugged. "Anyway, the poor man was alone and deteriorating fast. He was in here every other week with a new ailment."

" 'Was' alone?" Heather asked. "What happened?"

15

"The note he couldn't read was the date and place of a book club meeting in the basement of the Baptist church. I didn't tell the poor man so, but it was an all-female group."

"Which is why they read authors like Barbara Pym," Alice added.

"Mr. Turner went there to return the book and he —"

"Let me guess," Heather said. "He met someone."

Betsy smiled. "Mrs. Henries. She was sixty-eight and had been widowed two years before. Her two children also live elsewhere. Dr. Reede told Mr. Turner that Mrs. Henries had left the book in his office and would he please return it to her."

"And it was the book the doctor had ordered?"

"Yes, it was. Last week I saw Mr. Turner and Mrs. Henries sitting in the town square, and they both looked very happy — and Mr. Turner hasn't been back in this office since. All his physical complaints seem to have disappeared."

Heather was quiet for a moment. "Because the doctor's done a few good deeds doesn't excuse his bad behavior to most of his patients."

"You mean he should be nicer to the many

females who come here with no real problems but *always* end up inviting Dr. Reede out?" Alice asked.

"Or the men who live on beer and chicken wings but can't understand why they're so tired?" Betsy asked.

"And what doctor today makes house calls?" Alice asked. "Dr. Reede does. If a person is genuinely sick, he goes to them. One time he delivered the baby of a woman pinned inside a wrecked car. He slithered in through the broken back glass while the EMTs cut the door open to get her out. And he'd cut his leg enough to require stitches, but he didn't tell anyone."

"I don't understand," Heather said. "I keep hearing about this Dr. Tristan and how everyone loves him. What would *he* have done in those situations?"

"The same things, but his attitude is different. Dr. Tris would have gone through the back windshield too, but he wouldn't have yelled that the EMTs weren't doing their jobs quickly enough," Betsy said.

"And while he was delivering the baby he would have teased and flirted with the young woman until she was half in love with him," Alice said.

"Would he have put the knitting lady and

the pregnant woman together?" Heather asked.

"Probably, but he wouldn't have done it in secrecy," Betsy said.

Heather looked from one to the other. "Didn't some philosopher say something about it being better to give anonymously?"

Alice and Betsy were looking at her with little smiles on their faces.

"Okay," Heather said, "so maybe I won't quit. Maybe the next time he snaps at me I'll try to remember some of his good deeds. But damn! He's hard to be around. Maybe if he had a girlfriend he —"

"You think we haven't tried that?" Betsy asked quickly. "We have paraded every pretty girl within fifty miles of here past him. Tell her about the party you threw at your house," she said to Alice.

"I cooked for three days, and along with the other guests I invited eight very pretty, young, single women. Betsy and I made a list, then filled it: tall, short, skinny, plump."

"Never married, been married with a child, even a young widow."

"Betsy and I made sure Dr. Reede talked to each of them, but he wasn't interested."

"So what's his sex life like?" Heather asked.

"I have no idea," Betsy said somewhat stiffly.

"And we certainly don't ask," Alice added.

"It seems to me that the only thing that's going to make Reede Aldredge happy is to get out of Edilean," Heather said.

"That's the conclusion we came to."

"Maybe *we* can get another doctor to come here."

Alice pulled a thick file folder out of the cabinets. "These are the letters we've sent."

"And the replies."

As Heather flipped through them and noted the refusals, she said, "There *has* to be a way. I need this job. It's a good salary and good benefits. If I could just figure out what he needs I'd give it to him."

"You're welcome to try," Betsy said.

"We're open to suggestions," Alice said.

"And we'll help you," Betsy said, and they all three nodded.

They didn't know it, but a bond had been formed by the women. They were united in a single purpose: to find out what Dr. Reede Aldredge wanted and to give it to him.

ONE

Sophie tried to control her anger, but it wasn't easy. She could feel it rising in her like bile, traveling upward from her stomach.

She was driving her old car and she was about twenty miles from Edilean, Virginia. The scenery was beautiful, with trees sheltering the road, the fading sunlight playing on the leaves. She'd heard about Edilean from her college roommate Kim Aldredge. The two of them, with their other roommate, Jecca, had laughed at Kim's portrayal of the little town as a cross between heaven and . . . well, heaven. "Everyone knows everybody!" Kim said with enthusiasm.

It was Jecca who'd asked for a further explanation of that concept. Kim told them of the seven founding families who came to America in the 1700s and created the town.

"And they're all still there?" Jecca asked in disbelief.

"Enough of us are descendants of those seven families that we're related to one another and yes, we still live there." There was so much caution in Kim's voice that Jecca pounced. They were told there were "others" in town and they were called "Newcomers." Even if the family had moved there in the 1800s, they were still "Newcomers."

When these lively discussions about the merits — or lack of them — of small town living took place, Sophie stayed out of them. She covered her silence by taking too big a mouthful of food and saying she couldn't speak. Or she would suddenly remember that she had to be somewhere else. Whatever she needed to do so she didn't have to participate in a discussion about growing up, she did it.

The truth was that Sophie had been embarrassed. Kim and Jecca had such normal childhoods. Oh, they complained about a parent or sibling, but they'd grown up loved and protected. Sophie hadn't. Her mother had gone from one man to another. And then there was the little Texas town. Ruled by Treeborne Foods and riddled with poverty.

Sophie wasn't sure how it started, but when the first person asked her where she was from she named a pretty little Texas town with country clubs and golf courses. So many people had fond memories of the town that she never corrected her lie.

But then Jecca and Kim didn't notice, for they had always been so very trouble free, with few worries. It was a state of being that Sophie had tried to imagine, but she hadn't succeeded. It seemed that her life had always consisted of running toward something or trying to get away from a lot of things.

She glanced at the big envelope on the passenger seat of the car, and the Treeborne logo seemed to leap out at her. It was like a flashing neon light going off and on.

The sharp sound of a horn brought her back to reality. Her distraction had caused her to wander across the line and into the left lane. As she jerked to the right, she saw what looked to be a gravel road disappearing into the trees and she took it. She only went a few yards before stopping, her car hidden from the road. She turned off the engine and for a moment bent her head against the steering wheel as her mind filled with images of the last five years.

The death of her mother had changed everything. There'd been a job offer when Sophie graduated from college, but she'd had to turn it down. Taking it would have meant relocating from her little Texas hometown, and since her sister couldn't leave, Sophie had to go to her. Oh how noble she'd felt on that day! She'd called the nice, older man who'd asked her to work for him. "It's not much to begin with," he'd told her, "but it's a start. You're talented, Sophie, and you have ambition. I think you'll go far." When she called him to turn the job down she'd felt like a saint. She was sacrificing herself for others, giving up what *she* wanted to help her sweet, innocent, vulnerable twelve-year-old sister.

The man had made an attempt to change her mind. "Sophie, you're too young to do this. Isn't there someone else your little sister could live with? An aunt, a grandparent? Someone?"

"There's no one and besides, there are extenuating circumstances. Lisa needs —"

"What do *you* need?" the man had half shouted.

But nothing he said dissuaded Sophie from putting her life on hold so she could spend the next five years protecting her sister. Protecting, providing for her, trying to teach her about the world. But somewhere in there Sophie had begun to want things for herself, like love and family. At that she had failed.

Sophie got out of the car and looked around. Through the trees she could see the highway. There wasn't much traffic, just a few pickups, some of them towing boats.

She leaned back against the car, closed her eyes, and held her face up to the light. It was warm out but she could feel autumn in the air. Other people were at home raking leaves and ordering cords of firewood. Maybe they were thinking about Thanksgiving and what candy to give out this weekend at Halloween. But Sophie was on the road.

Would Carter spend the holidays with his fiancée? she wondered. What would he buy her for Christmas? A perfect little diamond tennis bracelet for her perfect little blueblood wrist?

Would they go sledding in the snow?

Yet again, Sophie felt anger surge through her.

Carter had a right to his own . . . Sophie put her hand over her mouth, as she had an almost uncontrollable urge to scream. He'd said, "You must know that you're the kind of girl a man —"

No! She was never again going to let herself remember the things he'd said to her on that last night. But then, it was the

25

way he'd said it all that had hurt as much as the words. He'd acted surprised that she didn't know what to him was a given. His face — that she'd thought she loved — looked at her in innocence, as though no blame could be attached to him. According to him, it was all Sophie's fault because she hadn't understood from the beginning. "But I thought you knew," he said, his brow furrowed in puzzlement. "It was just for the summer. Aren't there books written about summer romances? That's what we had. And the good part is that someday we'll both look back on this with fondness."

His words were so sincere sounding that Sophie began to doubt herself. Had she known but not let herself admit it? Whatever the truth was, she'd felt crushed, defeated. She'd truly believed that she loved Carter — and that he felt the same way about her. He'd made her feel good about herself. He'd listened to her complaints about her jobs, about how she often felt that she'd missed out on life, then he'd kissed her until she quit talking.

It had taken Sophie nearly a year after graduation to figure out that putting her own life on hold to help someone else was easier said than done. She'd gone from being a laughing college student to having two jobs. She was always on her feet, always having to smile at customers, at bosses, at coworkers, then having errands to run after work. Waitressing, receptionist, temporary secretary, part-time sales work, she'd done it all. No one wanted to give her a permanent position because they knew that once Lisa was out of school Sophie would leave. It had all worn her out. When she got home, Lisa would help her with dinner, but she had schoolwork to do. And then there was their stepfather, Arnie, drink in hand, always nearby, always watching, always looking as though he couldn't wait to get away from Sophie's ever vigilant eyes. Sophie had wanted to take Lisa away from that town, but Arnie was the legal guardian so they'd had to stay there. As soon as Sophie returned to town Arnie said he'd injured his back and quit his job as a driver for Treeborne Foods, which meant the financial burden fell to Sophie. She'd contacted a lawyer about getting custody of her sister but was told it would be a legal battle that she couldn't afford. Arnie didn't have a record, and he always said that as soon as his back healed he would return to work. Besides, there was the fact that her mother's will named him as guardian and their marriage was legal. All Sophie could do was wait until Lisa came of age.

All in all, since college, Sophie's life was endless stress — until Carter came into it. For years her life had been about her sister, but then Lisa got an afterschool job, and some of the pressure was taken off Sophie. For the first time in years she had some time of her own — and that's when Carter stepped in. And he had made her realize that yes, she wanted a career in some creative field, but she also wanted a family. Family first, art second.

She stepped away from the car and looked at the wooded area around her. She'd like to think all that was behind her now. Two days ago she'd driven Lisa to the state university, and she'd felt good that she'd put enough money in the bank to cover the first year. There were hugs at good-bye, lots of tears, and Lisa's thanks. Sophie loved her sister and would miss her, but Sophie couldn't help but feel that she was at last free to start her own life. And that life centered around Carter Treeborne, the man she'd come to love.

As she drove the two hundred miles back to her stepfather's house she'd been jubilant, feeling the best she ever had in her life. She would go back to her art, what she'd studied in school, and she and Carter would spend their lives together. That he was a Treeborne would cause some problems at first, but she could adjust. She'd met his father several times, and the man had listened attentively to all she'd had to say. He seemed to be a very nice man, not at all intimidating as people in town said he was. But then the enormous Treeborne plant was where everyone worked. Of course they'd be in awe of him.

Sophie couldn't help comparing him to her alcoholic, lazy stepfather. He was the man Sophie had had to protect Lisa from. That night after she'd dropped Lisa off, as soon as she entered the house — the one her mother had bought and that Sophie had paid the mortgage on since her mother's death — his greeting was to ask her what was for dinner. With a smile, Sophie said he could eat whatever he cooked for himself.

Ten minutes later, she was at Carter's house. After they made love, he told her that next spring he was marrying someone else, that he and Sophie had just been a "summer romance."

There are times in a person's life when emotion takes away your ability to think. Carter had taken full advantage of Sophie's stunned state as he shoved clothes at her, then had half pushed her out the front door.

He'd placed a chaste kiss on her forehead and closed the door.

She'd stood there for what could have been ten minutes or an hour. She couldn't seem to make her eyes focus or her mind work. Somewhere in there she decided that Carter was playing a prank on her, a sort of belated April Fool's joke.

She opened the door of the big house and stepped inside. The huge entrance hall with its curved, double staircase loomed before her, silent, even menacing. Quietly, slowly, she went up the carpeted stairs, her heart pounding in her throat. Surely she'd misheard what Carter said.

She stopped outside his room and looked through his open door. He was on the phone, lounging on the bed, his back to her. The tone he was using, so soft and seductive, was one she'd heard many times. But this time his words were being cooed to someone named Traci.

When Sophie heard a voice from downstairs, she came to her senses. She was sneaking around inside the home, the mansion, of the richest family in town, and coming up the stairs was Mr. Treeborne himself.

Sophie had only time to step behind the open door of Carter's room. She pulled her toes back into her shoes, praying she wouldn't be seen.

Mr. Treeborne stopped in the doorway, and his big, powerful voice — the one his thousands of employees at Treeborne Foods knew well — rang out. "Did you get rid of that town girl?"

"Yeah, Dad, I did," Carter said, and Sophie didn't hear a drop of regret in his voice.

"Good!" Mr. Treeborne said. "She's a pretty little thing, but that family of hers isn't something we can associate with. We have a status to uphold. We —"

"I know," Carter said, sounding bored. "You've said it all from the day I was born. Do you mind? I'm talking to Traci."

"Tell her father hello for me," Mr. Treeborne said, then went down the hall.

Sophie nearly fainted when Carter closed his bedroom door, exposing her to the hallway. Her first thought was to get out of the house as quickly as possible. She was at the first step down when she halted. Suddenly, it became crystal clear to her what she should do. She turned back and confidently strode down the hall, past Carter's room, and into his father's office. The door was open, the room empty, and there on the big oak desk was *it*. The recipe book. Two hours before, Carter had taken it out of the safe in his father's office.

The Treeborne cookbook was legendary in their little town and was used in all the company's advertising. It was said that the entire line of frozen foods was based on the secret family recipes passed down from Mr. Treeborne's grandmother. A stylized drawing of her graced every package. Her face and the Treeborne logo were familiar to most Americans.

When Sophie had arrived at the Treeborne house tonight, she'd been talking so much about her future plans, all of which included Carter, that she'd been unresponsive to his lovemaking. He'd become quite frustrated after just a few minutes. But then he knew that this was going to be their last night together.

Finally, he gave up trying to get her attention and said he'd show her *the* book.

She knew exactly what he was talking about and the thought that he'd show it to *her* made her stare at him in stunned silence. Everyone in town knew that only people named Treeborne — by birth or marriage — had ever seen the recipe book. But Carter was going to show it to Sophie!

He'd been right and even the thought of such an honor took her mind off everything else. Carter held her hand as he led her into

his father's paneled office, moved aside a portrait, and opened the safe. Reverently, he pulled out a large, thick envelope.

Sophie waited for him to open it and reveal the contents, but that didn't seem to be part of the deal. He let her hold it in its envelope on her outstretched palms. When Sophie made a move as though she meant to look inside, Carter took it from her and started to put it back in the safe. He never made it because Sophie began kissing him. To her, being allowed so near something so precious was an aphrodisiac — and it seemed to be an indication that what was between them was permanent. In his urgency, Carter dropped the envelope on top of his father's big desk, then made love to Sophie on the floor.

It was afterward that Carter told her it was over between them and pushed her out the door. But after Sophie heard Carter's and his father's dismissal of her, as though she didn't matter as a human being, she walked down the lushly carpeted hallway, her shoulders back, her stride firm. She picked up the envelope containing the precious recipe book and tucked it under her arm. As she turned, she saw that the door to the safe was still open. Inside was a lot of cash, stacks of hundred-dollar bills. It

was tempting to reach inside and take a bundle, but she didn't. With great insouciance, not caring who heard, she shut the heavy little door hard. The resounding bam! made her smile. Still with her shoulders back and the envelope clutched to her, she went down the stairs and back out the front door.

By the time she got home, so much anger was surging through her that she felt strong and sure of herself. She fell onto her bed and slept heavily. She awoke early the next morning, and she knew exactly what she was going to do. It didn't take her but minutes to throw her every possession into suitcases, plastic bags, and two cardboard boxes.

Her stepfather followed her out the door, already with a drink in his hand. "You don't think you're leaving here, do you? Lisa will be back for the holidays so I'd advise you not to go anywhere," he said with a smirk on his thin face. "So you'd better get back in here and —"

She told him precisely what he could do with his threats. As she opened the car door, her cell rang. The ID said it was Carter. Had he discovered the missing book already? She wasn't going to answer to find out.

34

She tossed the phone to her stepfather. He didn't catch it and it landed in the brown grass in the front of the house. As he fumbled for it, mumbling angrily, it kept ringing. Sophie got in her car and started driving. When she stopped for lunch, she bought a disposable phone and texted Kim. I NEED A PLACE TO HIDE AND A JOB she typed out. She knew her friend well enough to know that the message would intrigue her. And she knew that even though she'd had no contact with her for years, Kim would help.

Instantly Kim wrote back that she was out of town at the moment, but she'd take care of everything. An hour later, Kim called to say that it was all arranged — and it was so good to hear her voice. With her usual efficiency, Kim said Sophie could stay at Mrs. Wingate's house in Edilean, and she could have a temporary job of working as a personal assistant for her brother. "Reede needs someone to manage his life, but I don't think he'll stand for it," Kim said. "I'll find you another job soon because I should warn you that my brother's temper isn't pretty. Nobody deserves what he shells out. The three women who work in his office all want to quit, but Reede keeps giving them raises to get them to stay. I think they make more money than he does."

Kim was happy and chatty, and at no time did she pry into Sophie's problems. In fact, when Sophie started making a weak, hesitant explanation about why she'd been out of contact for so long and why she needed to hide, Kim saved her by interrupting. "I'm just glad you're back in my life. When I get home we can talk and you can tell me as much or as little as you want to. But for now, I think you just need to feel safe."

Her words had been so exactly on target that when she hung up, Sophie allowed herself her first quick tears. But she knew she couldn't indulge herself that way.

She spent the night in a motel, paid for with cash she'd taken from where she'd hidden it from her stepfather — she hadn't even trusted a hometown bank to hold money for her — and was on the road just after the sun was up. By the time she neared Edilean, she'd calmed down some, but not much. She couldn't help comparing herself to Kim and Jecca. They were the same age as Sophie, but both of them now had fabulous jobs and she'd learned via the Internet that both of them were married. Sometimes Sophie felt that her roommates had been given fairy godmothers while Sophie had been overlooked.

She shook her head at the absurd thought. Years ago when her mother had said she was going to marry Arnie, Sophie had seen the future. By then she was in the third year of college and her mother was ill. "He's only marrying you to get custody of Lisa when —" Sophie broke off. "When I die?" her mother asked. "Go on and say it. I know it's happening. As for Lisa, she can take care of herself. It's *you* who has the problems." Sophie resented that statement. Hadn't she fought like a demon to get herself into college? But when she pointed that out to her mother, she'd only scoffed. "You're a dreamer, Sophie. I mean, look at the facts. You go to college but what do you study? Art! What use is that? Why didn't you learn something that could get you a job? Be a doctor or a lawyer, or at least work for one." Again, Sophie had no reply to give her.

Her mother died two days before Sophie graduated from college, and she ran home for the funeral. When she got there, she saw her stepfather leering at her pretty little sister. Sophie decided to stay for the summer, but she never left. Until now.

She walked to the other side of the car and opened the door, but paused before even touching the big envelope. Did she really have it in her possession? *The* book?

The one the whole Treeborne empire was based on? Were there police after her? She had her laptop with her, but she hadn't checked the Internet. Her cheap phone had no Web connection, so she didn't know what was going on. Would federal agents be brought in? If so, how far back would they look to find out where Sophie was? There'd been no contact between her and Kim since college graduation, so they wouldn't find calls to Edilean.

Sophie shut the car door and told herself that she had to return the book. She'd go to Edilean and send the package back to Carter. Maybe if they got the book back he'd drop the pursuit. If there was one.

She got into the driver's side and turned the key, but nothing happened. Dead. "Like my life," Sophie muttered. Whereas before she'd thought the surrounding countryside was lovely, now it looked scary. She was down a gravel road that stopped just a few feet ahead, blocked from view of the main highway. It would soon be dark, and if she stayed in the car she'd never be found.

She looked at her cell phone. No signal. She went outside, walked around, holding her phone aloft, but there wasn't even a hint of a signal.

There was only one thing to do: walk. She

opened the trunk and rummaged through bags and boxes until she found her running shoes. Not that she ever ran. She was not very athletic. In the last few years, the most she did was walk from her desk to the water-cooler.

She removed her pretty gold sandals, put on some ankle socks, and tied on her big shoes. She pulled out a pink cardigan to wear over her summer dress. It was going to get cool before she reached Edilean. She went to the front, got her handbag, and at last picked up the big envelope. She'd left her tote bag hanging on a kitchen chair, so she didn't have anything to carry it in.

She tried starting the car again, but nothing happened, so she locked it and walked back on the gravel road to the highway. The shade of the trees had become deeper so that it was almost dark. A burst of wind rustled the leaves, and Sophie pulled her sweater closer. When she heard a car coming down the road, she instinctively stepped back into the shadows and waited for it to pass. Every horror story of hitchhikers and the mass murderers who picked them up went through her head.

After the car passed, she started walking again and telling herself she was being ridiculous. According to Kim, Edilean was the safest place on earth. Nothing bad ever happened there. Well, except for some major robberies in the last few years that Sophie had read about online, but it was better not to think about those.

Two more cars went by, and each time Sophie stayed under the trees and waited. "At this rate I'll *never* get there," she said aloud and shuddered as she had a vision of walking along the road at midnight. Every few minutes she stepped onto the pavement and checked her phone, but there was still no signal. But then, she hadn't gone even a mile from her car.

She was so absorbed in maneuvering her phone around that she didn't hear the approaching car. It had come around a curve, headlights glaring, and for a second Sophie felt like a deer mesmerized by the lights. The car was coming straight at her! She could clearly see the BMW symbol just a few feet away. Survival was the only thing on her mind. She threw up her arms and like a diver heading into the water, she dove straight for the side of the road. She landed, facedown, in the sharp branches of a clump of scrub oak, her mouth full of dirt. Quickly, she turned to look back toward the road. She was just in time to see a sleek little silver blue BMW drive over both her phone and the book. Thankfully, she'd been wearing her handbag crosswise, so it was still with her. The car kept going; it didn't stop.

All of Sophie hurt as she got up, hobbled onto the road to retrieve the remains of the phone, and picked up the envelope. There were tire tracks across it and one edge had been torn open. There was little light but she could see that the book inside was frayed, the pages bent. She didn't know if it had been that way or if it had been done by the reckless driver in the BMW.

Sophie carried everything to the side of the road and for a moment she fought back tears. Maybe she wouldn't have been prosecuted if she'd returned the book in pristine condition, but now it looked to be nearly destroyed. She was going to prison because of some jerk in a Bimmer.

As she pulled leaves out of her hair, raked dirt out of her mouth, and brushed at bloody scrapes on her arms and legs, she knew her logic was flawed, but if she didn't give her anger an outlet she'd fall down into a ditch and never get out.

She started walking. This time she didn't step aside for the cars, but kept going. Three cars, each with a single male driver, asked if she wanted a ride. The anger in her was increasing with every step and she had

41

glared at the men as she said no.

Her legs ached, the cuts and scrapes on her arms and legs hurt, her feet were blistering. In fact, it seemed that every inch of her was in pain. But the image of the expensive car driving over the book kept her going. In her mind, it was just like Carter driving over her. He'd never looked back either. She put one foot in front of the other, each step so hard it jarred her body. But she kept going, never slowing down — just as the driver had done.

She heard the noise of the tavern before she saw it. It wasn't particularly loud, but when the door was opened the music, a mixture of rock and country, floated out.

Sophie's steps began to slow down. Here at last was civilization. She'd be able to call a cab. Or maybe her landlady, Mrs. Wingate, could come and get her. If this town of Edilean was as good as Kim had said it was, there would be help.

When Sophie stopped and waited for a car to pass, she saw it. In the far left of the parking lot was the silvery BMW that had nearly run over her, had destroyed her phone, and was probably going to cause Sophie to spend a few years in prison. She put her head forward, set her sore jaw in a hard line, the recipe book in its torn envelope under her arm, and strode across the street.

Inside the restaurant, the lights blinded her for a moment, so she stood in the doorway to look around. It was a quiet place, with booths full of people eating huge amounts of fried food. Very American. To the left was a big jukebox, a dance floor, and some tables with men and women drinking beer from pitchers and eating great bowls full of chicken wings.

Sophie had been sure that she'd be able to pick out the person who'd nearly killed her.

Over the last several miles she'd conjured an image of a long face, close-together eyes, even big ears. She imagined him to be tall and thin, and of course he was rich. Carter's family was rich. If he ran over a woman, he'd wonder why she didn't get out of his way. Would he call it his "summer hit-and-run"?

She walked to the bar along the wall and waited for the bartender to come to her. He was a young man, blond and blue eyed.

"Hey! What happened to you?" he asked.

"I was nearly run over."

He looked concerned. "Yeah? Want me to call the sheriff?"

Sophie tightened her grip on the stolen

book. "No," she said firmly. "I just want to know who owns the silver BMW."

The young man's mouth opened as though he meant to say something, but a woman sitting at the bar spoke first. "See the guy over there in the blue shirt?"

"Is that him?" Sophie asked.

"Yes it is," the woman answered.

"Mrs. Garland," the bartender began, "I don't think —"

"Take it from me," the woman said to Sophie, "that guy's a real bastard. Thinks he knows more than anybody else in town. I'd like to see him taken down a peg or two."

Sophie didn't answer, just nodded and walked straight to the table. He had his back to her so she couldn't see his face. There were two other men sitting there, and when they saw Sophie their eyes lit up in appreciation. Ignoring them, she walked to stand in front of the man.

Her first impression was that he was strikingly handsome, but he looked tired — and sad. She might have felt sympathy for him, but when he saw Sophie he grimaced, as though she were someone he was going to have to do something for. It was that look that broke her. All she'd wanted to do was talk to him, tell him what she thought of him, but she'd be damned if anyone was

44

going to look at her as though she were a . . . well, a *burden*. She'd not been a burden since she got her first job at sixteen. She prided herself on carrying her own weight.

"Can I help you?" the man asked, his deep voice sounding as though Sophie was going to demand something dreadful of him.

"You own the BMW?"

He nodded once, and that look that Sophie was a great bother to him deepened.

She didn't think about what she did. She picked up a full pitcher of beer and poured it over his head. Not dumped, but poured it so it took several seconds to empty the contents. While cold beer was running down his face, she was aware that every person in the tavern had stopped talking. Even the jukebox was silenced, as though it had been unplugged.

As for the man, he just sat there, blinking up at Sophie, nothing but surprise on his face. When she finished, the restaurant was totally silent. Sophie glared at him, his face dripping beer. "Next time, watch where you're going." One of the men at the table took the empty pitcher, and Sophie walked across the room and went out the front door.

Outside, she stood still for a moment, not

sure what to do next. Then the door behind her opened and one of the men who'd been sitting at the table came out.

"Hi," he said. "I'm Russell Pendergast and I'm the new pastor in town and I think maybe you might need a ride."

When Sophie heard noise returning to the tavern, she didn't give herself time to think. "Yes I would," she said and got into a green pickup beside the man. They started the drive into Edilean.

Two

They rode in silence for a while before Russell said, "Is it possible that you're Sophie Kincaid?"

Immediately the hairs on the back of her neck stood up. Had he heard her name on the news? CNN maybe?

"Sorry," Russell said as he glanced at her. "I didn't mean to startle you. Kim said you didn't want the whole town to know about you, but she told me you were coming because she married my brother."

Sophie let out a sigh of relief. "And you're a pastor."

"Newly," he said, smiling. He was a very handsome man. "In fact, everything about me seems to be new. New town, new job, newly married, new to being a father."

At the words *married* and *father* Sophie felt a bit of a letdown. It looked like she wasn't dead after all.

"I'm even new to having a brother," he

said. When that tidbit sparked no interest in Sophie, he changed the subject. "How did you get here?"

"Car. I pulled off the road and it quit working. I'm surprised it ran as long as it did."

"I'll call the sheriff and he —"

Sophie drew in her breath sharply.

A quick frown momentarily creased Russell's forehead. "The sheriff's family owns Frazier Motors," he explained. "They'll fix your car or tow it or do whatever it needs."

"My clothes are in it," she said, looking down at her dirty skirt. On her lap, her hands tight on it, was the tattered envelope. When she saw that her knuckles were white, she tried to relax them.

"Sophie," Russell said softly, "if you need someone to talk to, I'm always available."

"Thanks," she said, "but . . ." How could she tell a man of God that she'd stolen something that was the backbone of a very large company?

"Whenever you want to," he said. "How about if I take you to Kim's house tonight instead of Mrs. Wingate's? Kim has closets full of clothes, and maybe it will feel more familiar to you being around her things."

Quick tears of gratitude came to Sophie's eyes but she blinked them away. "I would like that," she said softly. The thought of soaking in a tub full of very hot water and putting on clean clothes made her begin to relax.

"Do you have plans for your visit?" Russell asked cautiously as he glanced at Sophie. She was extraordinarily pretty, with hair that looked to be naturally blonde, big blue eyes, and skin as perfect as a camellia petal. As for the rest of her, he'd seen the way everyone in the tavern had watched her walk. She had a figure that people did double takes on.

But her physical appearance aside, he could see that she was extremely upset. She was holding on to the big envelope with the tire tracks across it, as though it were the key to life. Her clothes were torn and dirty, there was a big smudge on her chin, and one knee was bloody.

Whatever had happened to her seemed to have been caused by Reede Aldredge.

Russell had to work to cover his smile at the sight of this beautiful young woman pouring beer over Reede's head. Russell knew he'd go to his grave with that image in his mind.

Not long before, Reede had entered the restaurant looking like he wanted to murder someone. Russell and Roan had been hav-

49

ing an interesting conversation on the religions of the world, but Reede's bellyaching took over.

"He said it was a heart attack so I went running," Reede said. "Never mind that I hadn't been to bed in two days. It was only indigestion. You know what his eldest daughter did while I was there?"

"Come on to you?" Roan asked. He and Reede were cousins and had a long history together. "She's a pretty little thing and she's not that young."

"Not interested," Reede said as the waitress put a clean glass in front of him and a new pitcher of beer on the table.

"Not interested in her specifically or in any woman?" Russell asked.

"If you're implying what I think you are, be glad you're a preacher or I'd deck you," Reede said.

"I'd like to see that fight," Roan said. "Russell here is younger than you are and from the look of you, healthier. When did you last take some time off?"

"I think that was when I was in college."

"Before Laura dumped you?" Roan asked.

Reede groaned and took a deep drink of his beer. "Don't you start on me too. Everybody in this town thinks I'm pining away for a girl I barely remember."

50

"They like the romance of the story," Russell said.

"Believe me, getting told to get lost is no romance," Reede said.

"And that attitude is the reason everyone still talks about you and the Chawnley girl," Roan said.

"You know how you could stop the gossip, don't you?" Russell asked. He was a new friend to both men.

"I know this is a trick, but what is it?"

"You should get married," Russell said.

Reede nearly choked on his beer.

Roan laughed. "Well said, and I couldn't agree more wholeheartedly."

"What about *you*?" Reede was looking at his cousin.

"I missed out on Jecca."

"We both did, but at least I didn't nearly lose Tris's friendship over her," Reede said.

Roan grinned. "Who would have thought that a city girl like her was actually a *woman*?"

"They grow them in the cities too, you know."

"Maybe." Roan didn't sound convinced.

"If you two are through with your bromance," Russell said, "I'm serious, Reede. You should get a wife. You can't cook and you're losing weight. You live in that awful apartment, and your bad temper is legendary."

Reede gave a one-sided grin. "It keeps the staff in line."

"Ha!" Roan said. "Those poor girls are in the matchmaking business, and you're their only client."

Reede ran his hand over his face. "Do you have any idea what they *do* to me? A few months ago they gave a party and they —"

"Invited every eligible female around," Roan cut in as he leaned toward Russell. "We'd never before seen such a flurry of dress buying in the history of Edilean. I heard that one of the women bought a dress, changed her mind, and took it back."

"Is that bad?" Russell asked.

"She did it six times," Roan said, obviously enjoying Reede's discomfort.

Russell was frowning. "Did you like any of the women?"

"How would I know?" Reede asked. "They were all so disgustingly agreeable that I couldn't figure out any of them. If I'd said I liked to torture baby ducks for a hobby I'm sure all of them would have agreed with me."

"Whoever heard of an agreeable woman being something bad?" Russell asked. "Did you date any of them later?"

"No," Reede said. "I don't have time for dating. Besides, I've tried it and it doesn't work. I get called out on an emergency and have to stand her up and she gets angry. Or I see her as a patient and that *never* works out."

"So you live in lonely solitude," Roan said.

"Look who's talking," Reede said. "You want a woman who can discuss philosophy with you and also repair your chain saw."

"I was sooooo close," Roan said.

"What does that mean?" Russell asked.

"Too long a story," Reede answered. "I'm going home and go to bed."

"Wow!" Roan said as he looked around Reede to the front of the tavern. "Speaking of female bliss, look what just walked in."

The other men turned to look at the woman who'd entered. In spite of the dirt on her, she was easily the prettiest girl in the place, maybe in the town. She was wearing a simple cotton dress with a pink cardigan, and running shoes, but they didn't hide her curvy figure.

"She looks like a young Bardot," Roan said.

"She seems to be looking for someone," Russell said.

Reede turned back around. "With my luck, it's me. She probably bruised her arm

53

and wants immediate medical attention."

"Maybe so," Roan said, "but the exam would be a real joy."

"Not to me." Reede drained his beer. "Is she coming this way?"

"No, she's talking to Mrs. Garland," Russell said.

Reede groaned. "Another person who hates me. She's spreading — That's confidential, but I had a stern talk with her, and she put on such a show of misery for my staff that for two days I had to put up with their eye rolling and huffing."

"They still counting the days until Tris returns?" Roan asked.

"There's a three-year calendar by Betsy's computer. She penciled in *x*'s on every day and she erases one each morning. Each day takes them closer to when their precious, can-do-no-wrong Dr. Tris returns."

"Uh-oh," Roan said, "the little beauty is coming this way. I sure hope it's *me* she wants."

"Some tutoring in Hegel and Kant?" Russell asked. Roan taught philosophy at Berkeley but he was now on sabbatical.

"I'd give that baby whatever she wants," Roan said.

It turned out that Sophie had wanted Reede, but not for any reasons they had thought of.

Both Russell and Roan had sat there, paralyzed, unable to move, while the pretty young woman poured beer over Reede's head. He'd been wearing his look of dread, that yet another woman was going to come on to him, when he got a shock of cold beer.

Her words of "Next time, watch where you're going" seemed to explain it all. Earlier, when Reede had sat down with them, he'd complained about people littering the highway.

"I glanced down in the seat at some paperwork and when I looked up there was a big white envelope in the road. I couldn't help but run over the thing. I don't know what the hell was in it, but it crunched under my tire. I hope it didn't give me a flat."

Russell thought that from the look of Sophie's dirty, ragged state, there was more to the story than what Reede had told them — or that he knew. For one thing Russell doubted if Reede had just "glanced" down at some paperwork. In spite of his complaining, Reede Aldredge was an extremely dedicated doctor. If someone was really ill, he'd do whatever was needed to save the person, even if it took days of his time. Reede had said he hadn't slept in days, then he'd had the frustration of being called to an emergency that wasn't real. It was Russell's guess that Reede had been more absorbed in his caseload than in his driving.

Russell glanced at Sophie as she sat there in silence, clutching her envelope to her, and she looked as though she were at the bottom of her ability to go on. He'd worked with people who had her look, and too many of them came to a bad end.

Yesterday he'd called his brother and Kim, who were on their extended honeymoon, to tell them the good news that he'd been given the job as pastor of Edilean Baptist Church. He'd start in three weeks. Travis had asked him to look after Kim's friend, Sophie Kincaid, saying that she was staying at Mrs. Wingate's and . . . Russell couldn't remember exactly what else his brother had said. Was there mention of a job? "Yesterday was pretty busy at my house but didn't I hear that you have a job in Edilean?"

"Yes," Sophie said. "I'm to be a personal assistant to Kim's brother, Reede. Watch out!"

Her statement had so shocked him that Russell had swerved to the right and nearly run off the road. He got the truck straightened out and tried to think about what to do. Tell her that Reede was the man who'd nearly run over her? He looked back at her. She looked so forlorn that he couldn't kick her while she was down. Maybe if he could postpone the meeting for a few days he could find Sophie another job. He wondered what she was qualified to do.

"So you went to school with Kim?"

"Yes," Sophie said. "College."

"What did you study, if you don't mind my asking, that is."

"All three of us roommates got our degrees in fine arts. Jecca went two dimensional, with painting, Kim only cared about jewelry, and I went three."

"Dimensional? As in . . . ?"

"Sculpting."

Great, Russell thought. How was he going to find a job for a sculptor in Edilean? He smiled at her. "I bet you're hungry."

They had reached the town and Sophie was looking out the window at the beautifully restored old houses that lined the streets. Kim had said that Edilean was a town that time forgot, and it looked like she was right.

"It's pretty," she said to Russell as he pulled into the parking lot of what looked to be a 1950s dinner. "Al's," she said and smiled for the first time.

"Kim tell you about the place?"

"She said it could give you a coronary at one plateful."

Russ smiled. "I'm sure she's right, but sometimes grease heals wounds."

"I'm not exactly dressed to be seen," Sophie began as Russell went around to open her door.

"This is Edilean, not Paris. No one will notice." As he ushered her inside the little restaurant he realized how wrong he'd been. Sophie's prettiness caused everyone to look. Even in her frayed attire, she drew attention.

The real reason he'd stopped at the diner was to be able to make some calls before he took Sophie to Kim's house. As soon as they'd ordered, he excused himself and stepped outside to call his wife, Clarissa. He asked her to please go to the grocery and get enough to fill Kim's refrigerator.

"But I thought her friend was staying at Mrs. Wingate's."

"She was nearly run down by a car."

"Is she all right?" Clarissa asked, alarmed. "Should she go see Dr. Reede?"

"No!" Russell nearly shouted, then controlled himself. "It's a long story and I want to tell you about it — and to ask your advice. The gist of it is that Reede is the one who nearly ran over her and she's to start work for him tomorrow. I'm afraid she may take a baseball bat to his head."

"She'll have to get in line," Clarissa said. "Half the women in this town want to murder him. I heard that the last meeting of the Edilean Book Club spent three hours plotting ways to get revenge on him. I think the Lifetime channel is interested."

Russ didn't laugh. "I think Sophie has reason to chair the club. My brother —"

"Is going to be his usual scathing self," Clarissa said.

"He'll enjoy telling me what I *should* have done."

"And you'll enjoy telling him his faults," Clarissa said. "I'll get groceries and flowers and put them in Kim's house. Come home soon and we'll talk about what else to do."

Russell smiled. He'd fallen in love with her the second he saw her and he still marveled at his excellent judgment. "Did I ever tell you that I love you?"

"Not for an hour or so," she said, her voice soft. "Come home. I miss you."

"Me too," he said and clicked off. He could see Sophie through the window of the diner and he lifted his hand to her. As he walked back into the restaurant, he looked upward. "Give me wisdom," he whispered, then went inside.

THREE

The next morning, Sophie felt much better. Yesterday, over thick cheeseburgers and fries, the handsome young pastor had told her funny stories about him and his brother. He'd made her feel so much better that she'd even had a strawberry milk shake. After they ate he drove her to Kim's house and, at Sophie's insistence, he'd left her there alone. All she wanted to do was get clean and put on clothes that smelled good. Kim's pretty house, with its blue and white furniture, supplied her every need. She soaked in a tub of hot water, washed her hair, used a conditioner that smelled of peaches and almonds, put on a clean cotton nightgown, and fell into bed at 9:00 p.m. She was asleep instantly.

She didn't wake until after seven the next morning, and she was pleased to see that the fridge was full of food. She made herself a big breakfast, raided Kim's ample closet, then set out to find Dr. Reede's office. It wouldn't do to be late on the first day.

But when she opened the front door, she was startled to see a young woman sitting on the porch, waiting for her. "Hi," she said. "I'm Heather Davis, I work for Dr. Reede, and I've come to drive you to the office."

"Oh," Sophie said, "I didn't expect this."

The woman was looking Sophie up and down, as though she were judging her. "Anything to help our beloved doctor. The poor man is so lonely, so needy, that our hearts cry out for him. We've been searching for someone to come along and rescue him."

For a moment Sophie could only blink at her. "Rescue?" she managed to say.

"Well, you know what I mean. Not literally, of course, because he's a hero in his own right, but then you must know that. If you were Kim's roommate, you've probably seen a thousand photos of him."

"Not really," Sophie said. "Kim was more interested in trying to find —" She cut off, not wanting to betray a confidence. "But no, I've never met Kim's brother. I'm sure I've seen photos of him, but that was a long time ago."

"Great!" Heather said, then caught herself. "I mean it's good that you've had some acquaintance with him. So to speak." She waited until Sophie got in, then took the driver's seat.

"I need to get my own car," Sophie said. "Do you know what's happened to it?"

"Junked," Heather said.

"What?"

"Early this morning Mr. Frazier sent a tow truck out to get your car and he said it wasn't worth fixing. I'll have to drive you everywhere and make sure you see only the right people."

Sophie looked at the young woman, who seemed to be talking very fast and with a great deal of nervousness. "I'll need my car to —"

"You'll get one. Russell and Clarissa took care of everything last night."

"Clarissa?"

"Russell's wife. She was married before and she has a little boy named Jamie. They've been married a very short time and when Ellen — that's Kim's mom but I guess you know that — asked our old pastor — not old in age but he'd been here a while — if he wanted to leave, he said yes and Russell was one of the candidates. He gives good sermons, but then we all say we just go there to *look* at him and that he could say anything and we wouldn't care. It was announced yesterday that he and his wife will be taking over the church. Gum?"

Sophie wondered if the woman always talked this fast or if she was just nervous. "What?"

"Chewing gum. Would you like some? We're here." Heather pulled into a six-car lot in the back of some brick buildings and they got out.

Sophie smoothed her hair and her skirt, hoping she was presentable to meet Kim's heroic brother.

Heather was watching her. "The doc's not here. He left early this morning, something to do with tourist problems." She started walking quickly toward the back of a building.

Sophie hurried after her. "What does that mean? What are tourist problems?"

"Oh, you know. They burn down forests, break body parts, run their cars into the lake, fall out of trees, all the usual things."

"My goodness," Sophie said as she followed the young woman into the building. They'd entered at the back of a doctor's suite, and she hurried past three exam rooms. In the outer office two women were standing and looking at Sophie as though she needed to pass inspection. The three of them stared at her in silence.

"I don't really know what my job is," Sophie said. "Kim was rather vague about my duties, and she said it was temporary, so —"

"Oh no! Not at all," said the middle woman. She was pleasantly plump and looked like she laughed a lot. "I'm Betsy and this is Alice. We want to welcome you to Edilean and your job will be to give Dr. Reede —"

"Our dear Dr. Reede," Alice interspersed.

"Yes, our esteemed Dr. Reede, a man loved by everyone, any and all personal service that he needs."

"Or wants," Heather said.

"What exactly does that mean?" Sophie asked. "Are we talking cleaning or handling his finances? Or what?"

"Yes," Betsy said. "I mean no, you don't have to clean, but actually he doesn't have anyone now."

"He did," Alice said, "but she . . . Well she had to quit so, uh, she did."

"Not because of Dr. Reede," Heather said quickly. "She really should have seen the cobwebs, but she didn't, so —"

"What Heather means is that you're his *personal* assistant so you're to do what you can," Betsy said.

"When do I meet him?" Sophie asked.

"Who?" Alice asked.

Betsy elbowed her. "Our doctor works long, hard hours, and sometimes he leaves early and stays late. You might not meet him for days."

"If we can arrange it," Heather said under her breath.

Betsy glared at her. "Heather means that we have difficulty arranging his very busy schedule. It keeps him so busy because he lives for other people, and is always helping them. He never thinks of anyone but his patients."

"He sounds like a remarkable man," Sophie said. She remembered that Kim used to talk of her brother as though he were a pest, and that she didn't much like his hometown girlfriend. "The most boring person on earth," Kim used to say about the woman. "I don't know what he sees in her."

The three women were staring at Sophie as though they expected her to say something, but she didn't know what. "Should I come back later when he's here so he can tell me what he wants me to do?"

"Oh no!" Betsy said. "He won't be back until this evening. Late."

"But what about his patients? Don't they have appointments?"

"We cancelled them," Heather said.

"Because of emergencies," Alice added.

"Why don't you go upstairs and make yourself at home?" Betsy said.

Sophie had no idea what they were talking about. This was a job, not a home. Before she could express her doubt, the three women opened a door and practically pushed her up the stairs. She went through a doorway, a door shut behind her, and she found herself alone in an apartment.

Her first thought was that it wasn't a very nice apartment. There were few windows, little furniture, and what there was seemed to be covered in gray. It looked as if people who wanted to get a new set of furniture had given Dr. Reede their old things. There was a fine coat of dust over everything, and as far as she could see, there was nothing personal anywhere. Motel rooms had more personality.

There was one large room that contained a living area, an old dining table with three scruffy chairs, and a little kitchen that had some basic appliances. At the end of the room was an open door and inside was a bedroom with as little personality as the rest of the place. The bed hadn't been made up, but it wasn't a jumble. The bathroom, with a stack washer and dryer, completed the apartment.

Sophie went back to the living room and called Kim on the landline and right away confirmed that it was all right for her to stay in Kim's house.

"Make yourself at home," Kim said.

Sophie went on to tell her where she was at the moment. Kim groaned. "Horrible, isn't it? It used to be the sheriff's apartment. His office is next door and the apartment is above both of them."

"Where did this furniture come from?"

"Grandma's attic."

"That was my guess. Kim, I don't mean to be ungrateful, but what am I supposed to *do* here?"

"Make him stay."

"What does that mean?"

"Reede agreed to stay in Edilean for three years while the original doctor, Dr. Tris, works in New York to be near Jecca."

"The other doctor is who Jecca married? This Dr. Tris?"

"Sorry. I keep thinking you know everything that's happened. Yes, Jecca married Dr. Tris, but then she got a job in New York and Tris went there to be with her. But that left Edilean without a doctor. When he gets back in about two and a half years, my brother is going to hit the road again. Until then he's staying in that hideous apartment."

Sophie tried to digest this news and her heart went out to Dr. Reede. How many men would do such a noble thing? "Isn't there a house he can rent here in Edilean?"

"The man hardly has time to sleep, much less to go looking for a place to live. Sophie?"

"Yes," she said.

"My brother is miserable. He took a job he didn't want and got stuck with it for years. I'd appreciate anything you can do to make his life more comfortable. And you have carte blanche to do whatever you want to that horrible apartment."

"I don't know . . ." Sophie said as she looked around the place. "I'm not sure . . ."

"You *can* do it," Kim said and began a pep talk.

Sophie had to smile. Kim was a doer, a go-getter. Tell her something was impossible and she went after it. Right now she seemed to believe that Sophie's problem was a lack of belief in herself. That was far from the truth. Sophie was tempted to interrupt Kim's little speech by saying "I'm just concerned that the FBI might be after me," but she didn't. Instead, she said, "You're saying I should be a cleaning woman, a

68

secretary, a cook, and an interior decorator. It sounds like a wife. Tell me, is sex included in this job?"

Sophie meant it as a joke, but Kim didn't miss a beat. "I would imagine that some all-night, mind-blowing sex would cheer both of you up. It's done wonders for me. Speaking of which, Travis is pointing at his watch. I have to go. Oh, and Sophie, help yourself to my clothes. After all I've bought on this trip, I'm going to need the closet space." With that, she hung up, and Sophie stood there, staring at her phone.

" 'All-night, mind-blowing sex,' " she said aloud, and that made her think of Carter. Kim knew nothing about what Sophie had been through since they graduated. For that matter, she and Jecca didn't know the truth about Sophie's life before college.

She set the phone on the kitchen counter and looked around. The women had said Dr. Reede wouldn't be home until this evening, and Kim had asked Sophie to make him stay. Maybe she only had this day before she was found and had to face the consequences of what she'd done, so she was going to use the time to the best of her ability.

She went downstairs and asked if she made a list of things she needed, could someone get everything for her. The three women nearly fell over themselves saying yes. "Including my things from inside my junked car?" Sophie asked. She looked at Heather as she said this, and the young woman's face turned red. Sophie had an idea her car wasn't as bad as she'd been told, but then, it looked as though the women wanted her to help their beloved Dr. Reede. And why not? He was an overworked doctor who thought of other people before himself. He should have the best.

With that thought in mind, she went back upstairs, took off her cardigan, and set to work.

FOUR

Reede didn't think he'd ever been so tired in his life, but then he knew it was an accumulation of things that had made him feel so bad. The young woman pouring the beer over his head had been the straw that was about to break his back. Today he'd called six people he'd been at school with and offered them the job. He'd praised Edilean until it made Nirvana seem like a wasteland.

But the answer had always been the same: no. "You want me to move my entire family to some backwater town for just two and a half years? Then what? Your cousin returns and I have to get out?"

No one was interested. Reede had even called a former professor and asked. Maybe the man would like to retire to a small town and deal with a lot of cases of poison ivy. He'd laughed at Reede. "Give up the comforts of a college city to move into one of those small town closed societies? Thanks for the offer, but no."

No matter what Reede tried, he couldn't get anyone to take his place. Sometimes he felt like packing his car and driving away and saying the hell with all of them. He was sick of being compared to his cousin Tristan. Tired of hearing people say, "Dr. Tris would have —" Fill in the blank.

If Reede hadn't grown up in Edilean he wouldn't have any idea what was going on, but he knew it all. The problem was that "the Tristans" were believed to be destined to be Edilean's physicians. Since the town was established in the 1700s, an Aldredge had been the town doctor. That's what the people wanted, and they weren't settling for something different.

But somewhere along the way, the Aldredge family had divided, and there were now two branches of it. One side inherited Aldredge House, which was just out of town and set on a beautiful lake, and they were the town doctors. But then, there were the "other Aldredges" . . . They didn't inherit the house and they had different jobs.

The problem came when Reede, like his cousin Tris, had been born knowing he was going to be a doctor. In other families that would have been treated as a gift, but in

Reede's case he was looked on as an oddity. "So *you* want to be a doctor too?" they said, looking at him as though he'd said he wanted to grow a third arm.

The only person who saw nothing strange was Tristan. He couldn't understand why everyone didn't want to be a doctor.

The two boys, born the same year and third cousins, were fast friends while growing up, and they'd talked about their professions as something that couldn't change. It had made Reede feel secure knowing what his future was going to be.

So maybe he was a bit jealous of Tristan, but that couldn't be helped. Tris was going to live in town in the same house he'd been born in, and from the way the girls followed him around, he was going to have no trouble finding someone to share it with.

Reede was a very different person. Whereas Tris easily mingled with people, played team sports, and dated every girl who smiled at him, Reede had always been a loner. He had a few good friends and he stayed with them. He'd never been easy in large groups.

As for girls, he'd never been confident in asking them out. Quite a few of them had come on to him, teasing him, some of them even asking him out. But when he was with them, Reede had always bored them by talking of medicine.

When he was fourteen he'd met Laura Chawnley. Her family had just moved to Edilean, and when she was introduced to the class she'd look so scared Reede thought she was going to cry. Later, he saw her from across the hall. She was trying to arrange all her books into a pile and wasn't very successful at it. He smiled at her fumbling; she seemed so helpless. She seemed to need someone to come and rescue her. And Reede did.

He carried her books and made sure she found her classrooms, and he introduced her to people. She was so shy that she'd stood behind him, almost afraid to even look up. From the first, Laura had made him feel good as she looked to him for everything — to introduce her to people, to take her places, and even to do all the talking. He loved telling her of his dreams for the future — and from the beginning he included her in those plans.

His mother had a different view of the two of them. She said that Laura just sat and waited for Reede to come and get her. But Reede had liked that. Having grown up around his dynamic mother and sister, Laura's quiet passivity was refreshing. And most important, she made him feel as though he could see his future. He knew that they'd get married, live in Edilean, and have children. Reede even knew the house they would buy. Like Tristan's Aldredge House, it was a bit out of town, set on two acres, and the old house needed a lot of repair. Reede and Tris would jointly run the Edilean clinic and . . . Well, Reede's life would be set.

As far as he could see, the only bad part in his plan were the little comments people made. Especially his mother. One time she said, "You can't be Tristan no matter how hard you try." When Reede said he had no idea what she was talking about, she'd glanced around his room. There were travel posters everywhere. Egypt, Petra in Jordan, the Galapagos Islands. "How are you going to see these places if you live with Laura here in Edilean?"

"We'll go together," Reede had said enthusiastically. "Laura wants to go places and do things as much as I do. And Tristan can take over while we're away."

His mother had looked skeptical. "From what I've seen of that girl, she's afraid to cross a street by herself."

Reede narrowed his eyes at his mother, and she threw up her hands in surrender.

"I'm sure you know her better than I do, but I do wonder if she tells you what you want to hear because she's so in awe of you."

"Awe? Are you kidding?" Reede lowered his voice. "Mom, I know you have good intentions, but you really don't know Laura as I do. She's sweet and considerate and —"

"A dud," Kim said from the doorway. "She stays with you because you get her included in everything. You think she was put on the yearbook committee because of her great personality?"

"Why you —" Reede began but his mother caught his arm.

"Kim, would you mind? This is a private conversation."

"Whatever," Kim said, shrugging as she went down the hall.

Reede had stood up, signaling the end of all that he was going to listen to.

It was years after that when he'd come home from med school and Laura had dumped him. With a coolness, a detachment, that shocked him, she'd told him that she was in love with and was going to marry a little man with watery blue eyes and spend her life as a preacher's wife. Reede's foundation was knocked out from under him. For weeks afterward, he'd had no idea what he was going to do with his life. If he had no one to share things with, if he was to be alone, should he even become a doctor? During those weeks, all he could do was sit and stare at the TV.

There was one incredibly low point when he'd climbed up Stirling Point and jumped off the cliff into a pool of water. As he'd gone down he'd thought that it wouldn't be a bad thing if he didn't come up. If it hadn't been for Kim's cute little friend, Jecca, jumping in to save him then nearly getting drowned, Reede wondered if he'd still be alive. After that, he'd been so embarrassed by his depression and his reckless behavior, which had almost cost Jecca her life, that he'd packed up and left before she got back to the house.

He'd returned to medical school, but he'd rarely gone back to Edilean. At first all he could think about was that he was *alone*. Truly and deeply alone. But then he began to see some advantages in that. Other women were his first foray into a world-without-Laura. Then there was volunteering for jobs that other people didn't want, such as rescue missions. He was the one who put on fire fighter's gear and went into a burning building to search for trapped people.

It seemed that the more dangerous the

mission, the more he liked doing it. After his residency, he went to Africa — and he found that he fit in there perfectly. The small town life of Edilean had prepared him for village life.

What he didn't want to see is how good it made him feel to be free of the stigma of not being Tristan. He'd not realized that all his life he'd been compared to his cousin — and found wanting. Reede was an Aldredge and he was a doctor but he wasn't Tristan. Tris made people laugh; Reede was too serious. Tris cared about everyone; Reede couldn't abide people who imagined illnesses that weren't there. Tris was sweet and kind, always in a good mood; Reede wanted his time alone, and he let people know it.

The list went on and on. In the Middle East, in the Gobi Desert, anywhere on Earth other than Edilean, Reede wasn't compared to anyone. And maybe it was vain of him, but he liked being appreciated for what he did, what he risked to help people.

Reede stared through the windshield of his car. It wasn't until he'd returned to Edilean to help Tris out after he'd broken his arm, that Reede began to see things more clearly. With the constant comparisons, it's no wonder he wanted to leave and never return. After the first week in Tristan's office he'd begun counting the days until he could get out of town again.

Tris's staff of two women, one ready to retire, had nearly driven him mad. "Dr. Tris always —" began every sentence. They seemed to expect Reede to walk, talk, eat, breathe exactly as Tristan did.

And that Reede wasn't like his cousin made them roll their eyes, give grimaces, and make little comments under their breath. Reede gave up trying to appease them. Besides, when he found out he was going to have to endure all of it for three years while their beloved Tristan was in New York, Reede's ability to smile left him.

One of the women decided to retire early, and to replace her she hired a young woman who jumped at Reede's every word. But then, the truth was that by that time there was so much anger inside him that he probably did snap out an answer to her every question.

But yesterday had been too much. He'd been indulging himself in whining to Roan and Russell about his life when a pretty young woman poured beer over his head. Reede had been so shocked that all he could do was sit there and stare at her. Since he'd been in Edilean he'd become so used to people asking him about their ailments that

that's how he'd come to see them. Some-where along the way his misery had even overridden his ability to appreciate a pretty girl.

The young woman had stalked out of the restaurant and Reede was shocked that some of the people had applauded her. Had Reede been so bad that a physical attack on him was *applauded*?!

Russell, as befitting a pastor, had gone after the girl, but Roan went to the bar and returned with a couple of towels. He tossed them at Reede. "I don't know what you did to that girl but it sounds like a lot of people think you deserve what you got." He waited while Reede sopped up some of the beer, and they left together. Reede didn't meet anyone's eyes, but he saw the smiles.

Tomorrow, he thought as he left the tavern. Tomorrow he would call more people and do anything he could think of to get someone to take over for him in Edilean.

But that was yesterday. He'd spent today at the hospital in Newport, and he'd called people he barely remembered. He'd begged, pleaded, offered to pay, but no one wanted the job. He'd accomplished nothing.

So now he was driving back to that bleak apartment that came with the office. As he parked at the back of the building, he noticed that there was a light on upstairs. His first thought was that a patient was up there waiting for him. Or worse, it was a single woman who saw Reede as a challenge to win.

He slumped up the stairs, expecting . . . He didn't know what would be there when he opened the door.

Everything he'd imagined didn't come close to being what he saw. First of all, the apartment was clean. Not just with the dust moved around as the last two women he'd hired had done. Surfaces sparkled. The ugly furniture looked brighter. There were half a dozen new pillows on the couch, and their colors almost made the room look cheerful. He turned to put his medical bag on the floor by the door, then saw a little table there. There was a chrome bowl on top, and he dropped his keys into it.

Hesitantly, as though afraid that if he moved too fast the dream would disappear, he stepped farther into the room. And that's when the smell hit him.

Was that *food*? He usually ate a frozen dinner, but that smell didn't come from something premade. Like a cartoon character, he followed his nose into the kitchen.

He lifted a lid on a pot on the stove and took a whiff of something heavenly. It was

81

an orange soup. He couldn't help sticking his finger in it and tasting. Divine.

In the fridge he found a plate of chicken and vegetables with a note on top. "Microwave five minutes." Salad was in the crisper, and there was a cold bottle of white wine in the door. As he got them out he noticed a note on the oven door. "Open" it read.

Inside was a small pan that held something that was oozing juice, with a crumbly crust on top. It took Reede only minutes to gather it all and put it on the old dining table — which had been set with a place mat and tableware. He ate everything, every drop of soup, every morsel of the chicken, and he practically licked the bowl of the apple dessert. He emptied the bottle of wine.

When he finished, he leaned back and saw that the room didn't look as bad as it usually did.

When his cell rang, he didn't hesitate in answering it.

"So how do you like Sophie?" Kim asked.

"Sophie?"

"Yeah, your new employee. Remember her?"

"I think maybe I ate her."

Kim hesitated. "Are you drunk?"

"I've been more sober."

"Did Sophie cook for you?"

"I think so," Reede said. "Someone did. Orange soup. Chicken stuffed with something, and green beans, and some kind of mashed something, and —"

"Probably parsnips. She used to make them for Jecca and me. What I want to know is how you liked *her.*"

"Don't know," Reede said, smiling. "Never met her. I got back and the place was clean and I had food."

Kim was beginning to understand. "Not your usual Treeborne dinners? A little wine to go with it all?"

"Exactly." Reede sat down on the couch. "She bought me some new pillows too."

"Did she?" Kim hadn't heard her brother in such a good mood since he'd taken the job in Edilean. Maybe it was good that he hadn't seen Sophie. In college guys sometimes became blithering idiots around her. Her prettiness along with her great figure often made them speechless. "So what are you going to do tomorrow?"

"I'll be in Richmond all day."

"Why?" Kim asked in a way that was a demand.

"Not that it's any of your business but I'm going to observe some eye surgery."

"Wouldn't you send your patients out of Edilean for that?" Kim asked.

"I'm not always going to be in this town. As soon as Tris gets his fill of the big city I'm —"

She cut him off. "Don't forget that the McTern Halloween party is on Saturday. What are you going to wear?"

Reede thought maybe he was falling asleep.

"Reede!" Kim said sharply. "You need to call Sophie and thank her. And this weekend you can invite her out. You do take Saturday and Sunday off, don't you?"

"Ostensibly."

"What does that mean?"

"Outwardly appearing as such. Apparently."

"I know what the *word* means! Why do older siblings always treat us younger ones like we're morons? Reede, I mean what does that word mean to *you*?"

"That I'm on call 24/7. Half this town gets sick on the weekends."

"Well, not this weekend. This one you're going to the Halloween party."

"No I'm not. I hate those things. I spent too much time in countries where they believe in witchcraft. Halloween isn't funny."

"You're just making up an excuse not to go."

84

"I guess you're not dumb after all."

"When you call Sophie, why don't you ask her out? Break the ice at the lavish party. Listen, I have to go. But call Sophie. Do you hear me? Call Sophie."

"I don't have her number."

"Call my landline. She's staying at my house."

"Okay," he mumbled, then clicked off the phone.

FIVE

When the phone on the bedside table rang, Sophie wasn't sure she should answer it. Maybe it was a private call for Kim. But after about the eighth ring, she picked it up. "Hello?" she asked tentatively.

"Is this Sophie?"

For a moment her heart stopped. She'd been found! She glanced at the envelope on the bed, a tire track across it. Beside it was the old cookbook, tattered and frayed. It was made of yellowing papers tied together with ribbon, each page with writing on it. But it was either written in a language she didn't recognize or it was some sort of code.

"Yes it is," she said, her breath held. There was no use lying.

"This is Dr. Reede. Actually, forget the doctor part. After the dinner you made you can call me any name you want."

His voice was nice, deep and rich. Actually, it sounded a bit like melted chocolate.

"I hoped you would like it." She was trying to remember what Kim's brother looked like.

"If it weren't for Treeborne's I —"

"What?!" Sophie said in alarm, then realized that he meant the frozen food she'd seen in his freezer. Opening that little door and seeing the name on the stack of boxes had given her a shock. "Oh. Sorry, I nearly spilled my drink. Yes, the frozen food people."

"What are you drinking?" he asked in a way that was decidedly flirty.

She'd learned to believe the old saying of "Feed a man well and you'll own him." "You drank the whole bottle of wine, didn't you?"

"I ate it all, drank it all. I don't usually get . . ." He searched for a word.

"Tipsy?"

"Spoken like a true Southern belle. Yes, tipsy, but I didn't have lunch, and breakfast was one of those egg and muffin things."

"Not good for you. What time do you want me to come in tomorrow? If I have the job, that is."

"Are you kidding?" Reede said. "I'm going to double your salary. By the way, how much am I paying you?"

Sophie laughed. "I have no idea. Kim

87

didn't mention money." She wondered how much Kim had told her brother about Sophie's situation. "Didn't she speak to you about me and the job?"

"I thought you knew my sister. She called me and said she'd hired you to be my PA, then said she had to go. I didn't even know what day you were going to arrive."

Thank you, Kim, Sophie mouthed. "I, uh, needed a job quickly, and Kim got me one."

"That sounds ominous," Reede said with sympathy in his voice. "Let me guess: boyfriend problems."

Since what Carter had done to her, Sophie hadn't had a chance to tell anyone. In college she and Kim and Jecca had spent a lot of time commiserating with one another about the treachery of men. Since then there'd been no one to talk to. "I . . ." she said and felt a lump forming in her chest.

"What happened?" he asked softly.

There was so much understanding in his voice that Sophie decided to tell the truth, but she did her best to make it sound light. "It's an old story. We had a difference of opinion. I thought we were serious, but he said we were just a summer romance. Turns out that the whole time he was engaged to someone else."

Reede didn't laugh. Instead, he said softly,

88

"I know."

"What did Kim tell you about me?" Sophie asked, alarmed.

"Nothing. Honest. I meant me. Nearly the same thing was done to me."

Sophie tried to remember what Kim had told them about her brother, but it was a long time ago and a lot had happened since then. "Wasn't there something with you and Jecca? Didn't she have a crush on you?"

"Jecca? Naw. Nothing like that. She was a kid. She grew up rather nicely and I envied Tris, but there was nothing between us. Unless you count that I think she saved my life and almost drowned doing it."

"Now you have to tell me," Sophie said as she snuggled down in the bed.

"It's late and you probably want to sleep."

She'd spent the day scrubbing his dark, dingy apartment and was exhausted, but she wasn't going to tell him that. Maybe hearing someone else's problems would make What Carter Did to Me stop screaming in her head. "I'd like to hear of someone else's misery," she said.

"I know the feeling." Reede stretched out on the couch, his cell phone to his ear. "Okay, so Once Upon a Time," he said and began telling about him and Laura. Maybe his need to talk was from his frustration that

89

day at not being able to get anyone to take over for him, or maybe it was because he was sick of keeping everything inside him. He could complain to his male friends about his patient load, but he couldn't tell them about how he hated being compared to Tristan. Nor could he tell the truth about him and Laura. For one thing, everyone in town was waiting to say "I told you so." They'd all known he and Laura were incompatible.

But Sophie hadn't been there. She wasn't a patient or even someone who knew him. She was a stranger, it was night — he could see the moon through the window — and he'd had too much wine. When he began to talk, the story flowed out of him. It took a while to tell.

"From what I've heard you've always liked to rescue people," Sophie said about Laura's shyness.

"I do, rather," he said. She was making him feel better.

"Kim is such an achiever and that's what she values in others. Sometimes I was intimidated by her."

"Yeah?" Reede asked. "I've sometimes thought that I liked Laura because she was the polar opposite of my mother and sister. It was relaxing to be around Laura, as she didn't order me around or give me her opinion on everything."

"What about now?" Sophie asked.

"I think I've learned to stand up to them, although that isn't always good. Mom wanted to send food over and get cleaners for me. I told her I was a grown man and could do it myself. You see how that turned out."

"No," Sophie said. "I meant, what if you had married Laura and stayed in Edilean? You'd be working where you do now. But it wouldn't be for two more years. It would be forever."

"Wow!" Reede said. "I never thought of it that way. I think . . ."

"What?"

"This summer Jecca and Kim made me face Laura, and they said that she may have done me a favor." He told Sophie how his childhood bedroom had been covered in travel posters. "I told Mom that Laura would go with me and that we'd . . . It wouldn't have worked, would it?"

"I guess not," Sophie said. "From what I've heard of you, you're needed by the world, not just Edilean."

"You know how to make a man feel good, don't you?"

"That's just what . . ." She didn't want to

say Carter's real name. "Earl said right before he dropped me flat. He also said —" She broke off.

"He said what?" Reede asked softly.

"It's too new for me to repeat all that." She glanced at the cookbook on the bed. What she needed more than anything in the world was to talk to someone about what she'd done. A lawyer maybe? But she knew that a lawyer would advise her to give herself up. Tomorrow, she thought, she'd return the book. She'd send it from another state so the postmark wouldn't be Virginia. She'd —

"Are you still there?" Reede asked.

"Yes. I was just thinking about what you told me."

"And how to get revenge on Earl?"

"I . . ." She hesitated. How much could she trust this man? She took a breath. "I came away with something that belongs to him and I'd like to return it, but I don't want him to see that it was sent from Virginia."

"Where do you want it sent from? I have friends all over the world. We'll package it, send it overseas, and my friends will send it back to the U.S. They won't even look at it. How does that sound?"

"Won't that take a long time?"

"Express shipping goes everywhere."

Sophie had to blink back tears of relief. Except for the jerk who nearly ran over her, everyone in Edilean had been so very *nice*. She wanted to help make Reede's life easier. "There are some unpaid bills on your kitchen counter. Mind if I pay them? You could sign some blank checks for me — if you can trust me, that is. How's your online banking?"

Reede grinned. "Sophie, I've never set up online banking, but I hear it's very handy. How about if tomorrow I meet you at the office at nine and we set it up together?"

"I'd like that," she said, smiling.

"Okay, so now I'm the doctor, it's about midnight, and we both need to go to bed."

Sophie had to suppress a laugh at the way he said it, but he caught his error.

"Foot in mouth. So you go to bed and I go to bed. I mean . . ."

"I got it," she said. "I'll see you tomorrow."

"And bring your package to send to the very stupid Earl."

"I will," she said, smiling. "Good night and thank you."

"You're the one deserving of the thanks. What was that orange soup?"

"Butternut squash."

"And the mashed stuff?"

"Parsnips."

"That's what Kim said it was. All right. Go to bed. I'll see you in the morning."

She said good night again and hung up.

Sophie lay in the bed for a while, looking up at the ceiling and smiling. Maybe things were going to be all right, after all. If she returned the cookbook to Carter's family they might not pursue her. And if it were postmarked from another country they might not find her.

For the first time since she left her stepfather standing on the sidewalk, Sophie thought she might possibly have a shot at a life. It was possible that the past was done with and that today, this night, was the beginning.

And maybe, she thought as she turned out the light, this moonlit stranger was part of her future.

SIX

"Good morning," Dr. Aldredge said to the three women who worked for him.

Heather was so startled by his pleasant tone that she dropped her folders to the floor. Betsy choked on her coffee, and Alice's chin dropped by inches.

"Beautiful day, isn't it?" he said. When no one answered, he picked up the appointment book. When he saw that it was blank it took him a moment to remember that he'd been planning to spend the day in Richmond. He looked back at the staring women. "Sophie, my new assistant, is meeting me here at nine and we're going to go over her duties. I want to thank you ladies for making her welcome yesterday. In fact, after you say hello, why don't you take today off?"

They were staring at him so hard and in such deep silence that it was difficult for him to maintain his good humor. But then he remembered Sophie and smiled. She was the first person he'd ever told the whole story of him and Laura. He'd made jokes about the breakup to other people and he'd repeatedly said he was over her, but last night he'd realized that he hadn't been. Over her personally, yes, but not over the pain of it all. He'd never fully understood why Laura had wanted a man who was so . . . well, less than Reede. His ego, his masculinity, his belief in himself, had been crushed.

But last night it was as though a weight had been lifted from his shoulders. As Sophie had so wisely pointed out, if he'd married Laura he'd now be trapped in Edilean forever.

"Sophie?" Betsy said at last.

Reede couldn't help himself as he frowned at her. "Yes, Sophie —" He couldn't remember her last name, if Kim had told him, that is.

"Did you like her?" Alice asked tentatively. None of them ever dared to ask Dr. Reede a personal question — at least not after the first time. Scalpels didn't cut as sharply as his replies.

"Yeah, I did," he said, and again there was that smile. "She's interesting to talk to."

"Talk to?" Betsy asked. "You met her? In

person?"

Reede put the appointment book down on the counter and took a deep breath. What in the world was wrong with these women? "No, I haven't met her in person, but I had a lengthy talk with her on the phone. I would like to know what's going on with you three. Why are you looking at me as though I've met a ghost? Is Sophie not real? Did I make her up?"

The women looked from one to the other, then seemed to settle on Heather to tell him the truth.

But when Heather just stood there, Reede had to refrain from snapping at her, but then she was such a timid person. His least little comment that could be construed as less than loving-and-caring and she lost it. But Reede's eyes bore down on the young woman with the intensity of a hawk's. It was the look he'd often used in the field to make people get off their behinds and *do* something.

"She threw beer on you," Heather blurted, then fell into a chair, as though all the energy had left her.

Everything came to Reede at once. The pretty girl in the tavern, beer running down his face, Kim's friend showing up in Edilean at the same time. He'd not thought about it much, but he'd assumed the girl with the beer had been passing through on her way to somewhere else. The tavern was off the main highway; it led to places other than Edilean.

The women were looking at Reede with wide-open eyes, waiting to see what he was going to do. But he had no idea what to say. Without a word, he turned and went down the hall to his office.

Sophie would quit, was his first thought. She'd take one look at him, see who he was, and walk out. Yesterday Russell had called and explained what had happened on the highway.

"You nearly ran over her," Russell said.

"I did no such thing."

"Yes, you did," Russ said. "You came around that long curve, the one five miles east of the tavern, and you were looking down at your papers. The poor girl had to dive into the scrub oaks to keep from being hit."

"God!" Reede whispered.

"You have the right person," Russell said. "He must have been looking after both of you."

"The crunch under my tire . . . ?"

"Her phone. And she had something in an envelope too. You ran over it."

"And all she did was dump beer over my head," Reede said. "A shotgun would have been more appropriate. You don't have her name and address, do you? I'd like to send her my apologies — and a new phone." That's when Russell said he had to go.

Reede sat down in the big leather chair and closed his eyes for a moment. When it came to women he didn't seem able to do anything right. He'd had two serious relationships since Laura, and they'd both —

He ran his hands over his face. This wasn't the time for more wallowing in self-pity. No wonder he felt better when he was swinging from a cable out of a helicopter. Angry oceans were easier to understand than women.

So what was he going to do now? The best thing, the most honorable action, would be to meet Sophie at the door and try to explain himself.

And just how would he do that? Play on her sympathy? Talk of his lack of sleep? Say that he's such a busy doctor that he has to read files while he's driving?

There was no way she'd forgive him — and she shouldn't. He didn't deserve it.

But then, what would be the result of his doing the right thing? At the end of today there'd be no delicious cooked food, the bills would still be waiting for him to pay, and worst of all, there'd be no one to talk to tonight.

Talk, he thought and sat up straighter in the chair. He could still *talk* to her. If she didn't see him, that is, and if some blabbermouth in Edilean didn't run to tell Sophie who had nearly killed her.

He knew that if he spent another ten seconds thinking about this utterly ridiculous, absurd idea that he'd come to his senses. He'd back out. He'd do the heroic thing and wait for Sophie to show up and he'd take the consequences. He'd be a good employer and write her a severance check, and — Oh hell!

He practically ran to the front office. It was fifteen minutes to nine. "Don't tell her," he said to the staring women. "And don't let anyone else in this town tell her. I need time to . . . to . . . ." He couldn't think what he was going to do. "Got it?"

They silently nodded in unison and Reede ran out the back door. He had to get his infamous car out of the parking lot before Sophie arrived. His first stop this morning would be Frazier Motors in Richmond to see if he could get a loaner for a while. The BMW would have too many bad memories for Sophie. As he drove he couldn't help

100

but wish he'd listened to his sister when she'd told him about her roommates. Maybe she'd know of a way to appease Sophie.

But first he had to call his mother and get the gossip line started — or rather stopped. He called her by using the hands-free phone — no more looking down to punch in numbers while driving! "Mom?" he said when she answered.

"Well, well, if it isn't the Beer Boy of Edilean."

Reede grimaced and wished he were back in Namibia, but he said nothing. It was better to let her get it out of her system.

"Kim said her friend Sophie wouldn't last long with you," Ellen Aldredge said. "Between your bad temper and your attempt at murdering the poor girl, Kim was more right than even she imagined. So what did Sophie say when she found out her employer was the hit-and-run driver?"

"Nothing," Reede said. His mind was working hard as he tried to think of how he could get Sophie to forgive him.

"I don't blame her for not speaking to you," Ellen said. "Did she throw things at you? I hope everything sharp was locked up. Roan stopped by and told me the details. He was absolutely delighted and he's going to go after her. He said he likes her spunk. Isn't that a lovely old-fashioned word? As for you, a pretty girl, unattached, was practically handed to you on a platter but you messed it up. Roan said —"

"Mother!" Reede said loudly. "Don't let her know it was me."

"Sophie? Don't let pretty little Sophie know that it was you who nearly killed her, then drove off as though nothing had happened? You who — ?"

"Yes, exactly. I'm going to try to make her forgive me."

That news so startled his mother that for a moment she was silent — something that didn't happen often.

"If I introduce myself to Sophie now," Reede said, "she'll run away screaming. But if I have some time maybe I can . . ." He trailed off.

"Maybe you can what?" she asked.

"I don't know," he said honestly. "I'm sure it's just a pipe dream, but Mom, I *liked* her. I told her about Laura."

"You did what?"

"Last night I talked to her on the phone and I told her about Laura and me. Sophie said that if it had happened as I'd planned, that now I'd be living in Edilean forever and I'd never have been anywhere."

"True," Ellen said cautiously. "But then, if

102

I remember correctly, several other people said that same thing to you."

"Maybe they did, but last night I was full of Sophie's food, a bottle of wine, and . . . I don't know, maybe I've reached my limit of misery. If I'm to be here for another two and a half years maybe I should try to make the best of it. What do you think?"

"Yes," Ellen said in a voice with a quiver in it.

"Mom? Are you crying?"

"Of course not!" she said quickly. "But I do admire your spirit. I'll talk to those silly women in your office and do whatever I can to keep Sophie from finding out the truth for as long as I can."

"This weekend. If you can give me these three days I'd appreciate it."

"Don't forget the big party tomorrow night. Everyone we know will be there. I ordered your costume months ago, and Sara's almost finished with it."

"How about if I wear a stethoscope and ask everyone to remove their clothes for an exam?"

His mother didn't laugh and Reede started to say he had to go, but he stopped. "Why are the women silly?"

"Because they prefer Tristan over *my* son."

"Thanks, Mom." Grinning, he clicked off

the phone. But the next minute his mind was full of asking himself what he could do in just three days.

Reede was standing in the big office at Frazier Motors, waiting for a salesman. His hands were in his pockets and he was staring out the floor-to-ceiling glass wall. Below him was the huge showroom full of sparkling cars, salesmen hovering about, ready to destroy any speck of dust that dared touch one of the vehicles.

Behind him the door opened, but he didn't turn around.

"What is that saying about 'Physician, heal thyself'?"

Reede turned to see his cousin, Colin Frazier, in the doorway, blocking the light with his big body. He'd recently married and his wife was going to have a baby. "How's Gemma?" Reede asked. She was going to an OB/GYN in Williamsburg.

"Great. Healthy," Colin said. "She outeats my little brother. Is that normal?" Colin's youngest brother was a *very* large young man.

"Perfectly," Reede said. "Why are you here?" Colin was the sheriff of Edilean. There'd been some shock in his family and even in the town when Colin decided that he didn't want to go into the family business of wheels. Anything that had wheels on it and the Fraziers were involved.

"Front end alignment on my truck," Colin said. "The guys told me you looked bad, so they sent me up here to hold your hand." He motioned for Reede to take a seat on the chair along the far side. Colin sat down on the couch, and his big body nearly filled it. Leaning forward, he stared at his cousin. They'd grown up together and knew each other well. "Is your gloomy face because of the girl you nearly ran over?"

Reede nodded.

"And I take it you've found out that she's your employee."

Reede nodded again.

"What are you going to do about it?"

"So far, I've turned tail and run away. Mom's bawled me out. Kim has left me three voice mails and those women who work for me —" Reede threw up his hands in exasperation.

"You should fire them," Colin said. "They belong to Tris. They used to give Gemma a hard time when she went in there."

A bit of light came into Reede's eyes. Colin had been very jealous when the woman he loved was friends with Dr. Tris.

"The best thing for you to do," Colin said,

"is to come clean to the girl and tell her the truth. Grovel. Apologize. And get her another car."

"You're right," Reede said as he stood up and looked out through the glass. His hands were shoved deep into his pockets. "What happened to her car? She didn't have a wreck, did she?"

"Naw. It just died of old age and neglect. I don't think the oil had been changed in years. Dad sent a rental over to her last night."

"Sure," Reede said without much interest. "Send me the bill. It's the least I can do."

"And what about you?" Colin asked. "Dad said you wanted to change out your Bimmer?"

"Yeah. I can't very well drive it around and remind Sophie of what I did."

"It's time for service, anyway. I have a Jeep I can lend you." Colin was watching his friend. Part of him had a lot of sympathy for Reede. He'd voluntarily agreed to help his cousin out for a few weeks while his arm healed, then Tris had gone to New York and Reede had been stuck in a job he didn't want. And Reede had been saddled with Tris's employees and his patients — all of whom made it clear that they wished their beloved doctor would return.

106

On the other hand, Colin and everyone else who knew Reede was fed up with his gloomy attitude.

"You like this girl, don't you?" Colin asked.

Reede didn't turn around as he shrugged. "I don't know. I've only had one conversation on the phone with her, but she . . ."

"She what?"

"Cooked for me, cleaned up that apartment. We talked. It was nice."

Colin used to live in that apartment, so he knew how depressing it was. Little light, bad smells that wouldn't go away, noises in the night. Returning to it at the end of the day was sometimes more than he could bear. For it to have the smell of good food, a clean floor . . . Yes, that would almost be an aphrodisiac.

Colin knew quite a bit about wanting things, whether it was a job or the woman he loved. "There has to be a solution to this. Surely, something can be done."

Reede sat back down. "Nothing that I can figure out. I asked Mom to get people to keep their mouths shut, but the beer dousing was too public. The first Newcomer who sees her will be happy to tell her that Dr. Reede nearly killed her."

Colin knew that the residents of Edilean

could keep a secret — but only if the Newcomers weren't involved. Unfortunately, they'd seen it all. That Sophie hadn't yet been told was a miracle.

"If she could get to know you before she's told . . ." Colin trailed off because the Reede he'd been seeing lately wasn't the man he knew. Over the years, Colin had twice flown to other countries to help Reede in his charity work. Reede had been organized, efficient, dedicated, and charming to donors. But that wasn't the man he was here in Edilean. Colin tried to think of a way to change that. Reede had always responded to a challenge.

"Oh well," Colin said. "You and this girl would have been temporary anyway. You're always miserable, so that would have driven her away. And I'm sure she's like all other women and wants a home and kids. If you two were to get together she'd dump you just like Laura did. Besides, I hear Roan is already going after her. She'll probably like him."

"He's a windbag," Reede said, his eyes losing some of their gloom. "And who knows? Maybe Sophie would like to travel. There are women who do, you know." More light was coming into Reede's eyes.

"So you're thinking of marrying her, are you?"

"I just met her! Actually, I haven't even met her. I just enjoyed talking to her, that's all."

"Talking, eating her cooking, sleeping on sheets she's washed. Sounds to me like a marriage."

Reede started to protest the absurdity of that statement, but then he laughed. "Okay, so I get your point. I've made too much out of this, but it was nice for a while to hope. I should go back and tell her the truth. She's —" He looked at Colin. "Today Sophie is sorting out my banking. I left her my debit card number, and she's going to set up online banking for me."

Colin shook his head. "You have it bad. Maybe you can delay the inevitable for a while."

"I told Mom to give me three days. I don't know what I was thinking. That I'd give such great phone calls that when she found out the truth she'd say, 'Oh that's all right, I forgive you'?"

"Women don't forgive, and they sure as hell don't forget. As soon as she finds out, you're dead."

"Thanks," Reede said.

"Maybe you could —" Colin broke off

because the door opened and a pretty secretary entered carrying a big cardboard box.

"Oh, sorry. I didn't know anyone was in here." She put the box on the desk. "Your dad wants these for tomorrow. He said he wanted to hide the faces of the team that had such a bad last quarter."

"Sure," Colin said. "Just leave it there and he'll see it."

She left, closing the door behind her.

"Anyway," Colin said, "maybe you could apologize enough that she would —"

Reede had gone to the box on the desk and was looking inside it. "It's Halloween," he said in wonder.

"Yeah. Dad always gives a little party to the staff and hands out incentive awards, but this year the sales are so bad that —" He broke off because Reede had pulled out a mask of a werewolf and was holding it over his face.

It took Colin a moment to understand. "A mask would hide you."

"Yes," Reede said as he put the furry thing down. "She wouldn't be able to see who I was."

Colin's eyes showed his racing thoughts. "It would take some work, but maybe we could keep the secret for three days. That's today, Friday, then Saturday and Sunday. There's the big party tomorrow night. Everyone will be in costume. My family will be there. Mom is dying to tell the world that Pere's girlfriend, Rachel, is pregnant."

"Everyone knows that," Reede said. "Rachel's bought enough baby clothes for six kids."

"That's all right. Ariel's pregnant too, and with Gemma, all the clothes will be needed."

Reede couldn't help smiling. Everyone knew that what Colin's mother, Alea, wanted most in the world was grandchildren, and now her daughter Ariel, her daughter-in-law Gemma, and probably soon-to-be daughter-in-law Rachel were all expecting babies. A wish come true.

"Hey! I have an idea," Colin said. "What about a private party for you and Sophie tomorrow afternoon? You know the old Haynes house out on McTern road?"

Reede couldn't help drawing in his breath. "What?"

"That's the house I wanted to buy for Laura and me. The pond . . ."

"Yeah, right. It's a clone of Tris's Aldredge House." Between them passed years of understanding. "Anyway, Ariel and Frank bought that house. They closed on it last week, and it's empty until they return to

Edilean."

Ariel, Colin's sister, was in California finishing her medical residency. The plan was that she'd return home and share the practice with Tristan. That way they'd both have time off for their families.

"What if I get Mom to arrange it so you could have a private party for just you and your Sophie at that house? Since it's Halloween it could all be done while wearing masks."

Reede had to blink a few times as he thought about what Colin was saying. Maybe it could work. Possibly. Probably not. Maybe definitely not. What woman would go out with a man in a mask? Then he remembered Tris saying that Jecca, the woman he married, was an artist, so he'd had to be creative in courting her. "Not easy for a man of science," Tris had said, "but I did it." Sophie was an artist too, so maybe she'd like —

Reede looked back at Colin. "Think Sara can find another costume between now and then?"

"I think that if there's any hope to get you out of your gloom and doom this whole town would start sewing and *make* you one. Hell! I'll put on a few buttons." Colin took out his cell phone. "This is your last chance

112

to say no. Once I call Mom and tell her, there'll be no backing out."

"Between her and my mother . . ." Reede didn't want to think anymore. "Sure, why not?"

Colin pushed the key that contained his mother's phone number.

SEVEN

Sophie leaned back from Dr. Reede's computer and smiled at her work. It had taken hours, but she'd set up online banking for him and had put every bill she could find on autopay. She'd even used his AmEx points to order a new vacuum cleaner and a set of white dishes. The ones he had were chipped and cracked and so old she was afraid the glaze contained lead.

She'd downloaded Quicken and put his expenses into categories. He didn't spend much and his checks were mostly for bills, so it hadn't been too big of a job to do the whole year.

As for his income, savings, and investments, she had no idea what they were. Every few weeks a check would be deposited and it would cover his expenses. If what was deposited was his total income or not she didn't know. If it was, he was far from rich.

"And his financial state is none of my

business," she said aloud as she looked around the apartment. This morning she'd been disappointed when she was told she wouldn't be meeting Dr. Reede after all. But she understood about medical emergencies. Yet again, the women in the office had talked at length about what a great guy Reede is, how he thinks of everyone but himself.

"And he's so very sweet tempered!" Heather said. "Just this morning he was smiling in a way that I'd never before seen any human do. Lit up the entire room, didn't it? *I* certainly felt it!"

The other women enthusiastically agreed as they looked at Sophie with wide eyes.

As she went up the stairs to the apartment, Sophie couldn't help smiling. It was obvious that the women had crushes on their Dr. Reede.

It was at lunchtime, just as Sophie had finished the computer work, that he called. He started with a profuse apology for standing her up that morning.

"It's all right," she said. "I understand. My job is to help you, not get in your way."

"That's nice," Reede said hesitantly. "So how are you getting along?"

Sophie took her time telling him of all that she had done since their last phone call, but he didn't seem interested in the banking.

"What about your art? My sister says that she'd die if she couldn't create things — but then Kim is a bit melodramatic."

"I used to feel that way, but it's been so long since I created anything that I don't remember what it's like."

Reede hesitated. "I'm sure Kim told me, but what kind of art do you do?"

"Sculpting."

"Like welding steel structures?"

"I mainly worked in clay. When I graduated I had a job offer of sculpting the heads of the American presidents for a company that made silverware. I was to make them about a foot tall, then they'd reduce them and put them on the handles of teapots. George and Abe and Mr. Jefferson would have profiles put on flatware."

"That sounds . . ."

"Tacky?" she asked, smiling. "I'm sure it would have been, but it was a beginning."

"So why didn't you do it?"

She told him of her mother dying and leaving twelve-year-old Lisa under the care of a disgusting man. "I figured he'd be climbing into bed with her the day after the funeral."

"So you stayed and took care of her." There was awe in Reede's voice.

116

"I did what I had to," she said modestly.

But Reede saw past her attempt to dismiss what she'd done. He well knew what sacrificing yourself took out of you. "Were you ever tempted to run away?"

"Why don't *you* pack up and leave town now?"

"Family obligations," he said, then paused. "I see. It was the same with you."

"Exactly the same." She was sitting on a stool at the kitchen counter, and when she moved she gave an involuntary yelp of pain.

"Are you okay?" he asked.

"Yes and no. I'm bruised from hitting the side of a road. A reckless driver nearly ran me over." She gave him a brief account of what had happened.

"So you don't know who was driving?"

"I know his car and — Wait a minute! Russ was sitting near him at the restaurant, so he knows who he is! I'll have to call and ask him. Maybe I should do that now. The creep should be taken off the road for driving like that. He should —"

"I'm sure he's far away by now," Reede said quickly. "That's an almost major highway, and we get a lot of tourists in this area." He wiped sweat from his brow.

"You're probably right," Sophie said. "If the jerk lives in Edilean I'm sure someone would have told me about him. I did put on a rather public show when I poured beer over his head."

"Did you?" Reede asked. He was in the new Jeep that he'd borrowed from Colin and he didn't know where anything was. He needed something to wipe away the sweat that was beginning to trickle down the back of his neck. "I bet the man was . . . surprised."

"Shocked, is more like it," Sophie said. "I wouldn't have poured beer over him if he hadn't been looking at me as though I were going to ask him for something."

"Like what?" Reede was unbuttoning his shirt as his body overheated.

"Money, I guess," Sophie said. "He looked rich."

"Did he?" Reede pulled his shirt off but his hands got stuck in the cuffs.

"He did. He had that arrogant, bored look that comes from never having to worry about money."

Reede stopped pulling on his cuff and gave his attention to what Sophie was saying. "Surely not everyone who can pay his bills is arrogant."

"Maybe not," Sophie said. "Maybe I'm generalizing based on my recent experience, but the man in the bar looked bored rich."

" 'Bored rich,' " he said and couldn't help smiling at her phrasing. He unbuttoned a cuff. "Was the man ugly?"

"No. He was actually rather handsome. Not as beautiful as Russell, but passable."

Reede smiled broader. "You wouldn't like to go on a date with me, would you?"

Sophie was glad she was on the phone so he couldn't see her grin. After what Carter had said to her about her looks, it was nice to think a man did like her as a person. And Dr. Reede had never even *seen* her. That made her feel even better. "Yes," she said, "that would be nice. When?"

Reede took a breath. "Saturday. In costume."

"What?"

"We'll have a date in costume. For Halloween. At a house owned by a friend of mine. Eleven. We'll have lunch." He knew his sentences were staccato, but he was so nervous he couldn't think clearly. "Afterward we can go to the McTern party. It's big. In costume."

Sophie's first thought was that this wasn't possible. She didn't have anything appropriate to wear, and she had work to do. But then she remembered that she was no longer supporting her sister and stepfather, so she could afford to have only one job.

119

"Bad idea?" he asked softly in her silence.

"No . . . I . . . I rather like it, but I don't have a costume. Maybe Kim has one in her closet."

Reede let out the breath he'd been holding. "It's all arranged. My cousin Sara will make anything you want. Any ideas on that?"

It had been so many years since there'd been any frivolity in her life, that Sophie was having trouble adjusting to the idea. She and Carter had never gone to a party together. He'd always said it was because he hated them and just wanted to be alone with her. At the time she'd been pleased by what he'd said. Now she realized it was because he didn't want people to see them together.

"I'll match you," Sophie said.

"What does that mean?"

"If you go as Edward the Seventh, I'll go as —"

"Queen Alexandra."

"Absolutely not!" she said. "I'll be Lillie Langtry."

"Yeah?" Reede asked, smiling. "So how about Spider-Man?"

"Mary Jane."

"Papa Bear?"

"Goldilocks for sure."

"Is she the one in the blue dress with the headband?"

"That's Alice in Wonderland, and you'd have to go as the Mad Hatter."

"I could do that."

"Well?" Sophie asked. "Who *are* you going to be?"

"I think I'll let my cousin Sara tell you. She makes costumes for all of us." And she can tell me, he added to himself. What could he wear that would put Sophie in something red? And low cut?

Sophie was smiling deeply for the first time in a very long while. "You have no idea what you're going to wear, do you?"

Reede laughed. "I am caught! None whatever. I've had a very busy morning and —"

"Does Sara know your sizes?"

"Six one, one eighty-five," he said. "What about you?"

"Five three and you'd have to put me in a hospital before I told you how much I weigh."

"That doesn't sound bad. I know a place —" He stopped as he remembered the circumstances of their meeting. "So should I pick you up at Kim's house tomorrow?"

"Sure. No, wait. I think I should move into my own apartment at Mrs. Wingate's house. I'm imposing too much on Kim."

"So no one has told you?"

"Told me what?"

"Yesterday, Mrs. Wingate eloped with the gardener."

"Oh," was all Sophie could think to say. "I got the impression that she was an older woman."

"Forties, not too old. Very elegant lady. It seems that while she was married to a man the whole town knew was abusive, she was in love with Bill Welsch."

"And he's the gardener?"

"And a builder. He's a cousin of mine and he's a great guy. Anyway, when she and Bill left, one of her tenants, Lucy Layton, asked —"

"Layton?" Sophie said. "But that's Jecca's last name."

"Nobody told you that either? Kim's husband's mother married Jecca's dad."

Sophie had to think a moment to put that relationship in place. "No, no one told me. So what did Mrs. Layton ask?"

"If she could buy the Wingate house. Travis — that's Kim's husband — wants to open a camp for inner city kids, and they want to use the big Wingate house as part of it."

"I guess this means that the apartment is no longer available."

Reede's first thought was to tell her that she could stay with him, but he refrained from saying it. What in the world was wrong with him anyway? He'd had dozens of offers from women in town, but none of them had interested him, but there was something about Sophie that intrigued him. Maybe it was the fact that she wasn't one of the women who was going after him with the subtly of a submarine torpedo.

Sophie was quiet as she thought about the problem of the apartment. This morning she'd been going through Kim's closet, rummaging about in her kitchen, and she hadn't liked doing it. It was Kim's house, and Sophie needed a place of her own. That she no longer had an apartment waiting for her was a blow.

Reede sensed that he'd inadvertently ruined the mood. "I'll find you a place to live," he said. "My cousin Ramsey owns several properties. I'm sure he has something available." Even if I have to buy it, he thought. "What are you doing today?"

Sophie hoped he was leading up to inviting her somewhere this evening. It would be nice to get to know each other better before the masquerade of tomorrow. "The usual," she said, which made no sense, as the job was so new to her that nothing was "usual." "What about you?"

He couldn't tell her the truth, that he was putting all his time and energy into planning the next two days, so he said he had "medical work."

"It must be wonderful to save lives."

"It was," he said, thinking of his past rescue work and of the clinics he'd set up. "I mean it is now. I better go," he said.

"Yes, go save someone," she said, and they hung up.

Reede clicked off his phone and leaned his head back against the seat. It had been even nicer talking to Sophie the second time. So now he had to drive back to Edilean and see his cousin Sara and talk about costumes. But as he reached for the ignition, his arm caught on his shirt.

"What the hell?" he mumbled, then remembered his guilty conscience when he'd been talking about nearly running Sophie over. When he couldn't straighten his shirt he stepped out of the car, unbuttoned it, and put it back on.

Once he was back in the car, he called Betsy. Since he was asking a favor of her, he reminded himself not to bark at her. But then, for the first time since Tristan had asked him to take over the job, Reede didn't feel like snapping.

"I know I gave you women the day off, but I need for you to get something for Sophie."

"Anything for her," Betsy said.

There was such feeling, almost desperation, in her voice that for a moment Reede was embarrassed. Maybe he *was* a bit too hard on them. "Well, uh, she needs clay."

"Clay? You want me to buy her some clay?" She sounded as though he'd given her a Herculean task, and he had to work to keep his retort to himself.

"Yes. Go to an art store or . . . I don't know where to go, but get her something she can use to make a sculpture."

"Oh, you mean modeling clay," Betsy said. On the back of a water bill envelope she wrote *Call Kim* and underlined it twice. "I'll gift wrap it. Anything you want on the card?"

He hadn't thought that far ahead. "Uh . . . Just write 'Thanks, Reede.' "

"I will. By the way, your mom told us about your costume for the big Halloween party. Do you like it? I think it's —"

This intimacy was more than Reede could take. "Yeah, it's great." He clicked off. If Betsy liked the costume, that meant it was something her beloved Dr. Tris would wear. A James Bond tux? Or would he go as a superhero? Reede could imagine his cousin in a cape and tall boots. The image made him smirk in derision. He'd *never* be caught in a cape! But then, Tristan got the girl he wanted, so maybe . . .

Reede called his cousin Sara and yet again, his tongue seemed to stick in his throat. "I need a . . . a special costume. Something that's . . . For tomorrow."

"I know," she said. "Your mom's already ordered it. I had to get a new leather foot for the 830 to make it." She was referring to her big Bernina sewing machine.

"Sara," Reede said as he tried to recover himself, "I don't know what my mother is up to, but I do *not* want anything in leather. I need something for tomorrow, something . . ." He hesitated. "A costume that . . ."

"Reede!" Sara said, "I have two babies to take care of and a husband to feed, plus six costumes to finish by tomorrow night. I don't have time for you to tiptoe around. What kind of costume do you need?"

"Romantic," he spit out. "Heroic."

"Oh," Sara said, "so it's true about you and this girl? Sylvia, is it?"

"Sophie — as I'm sure you know. She's going to wear a costume that coordinates with mine, so make it nice."

126

"From what I've heard she should go as a barmaid."

"Give me a break!" Reede said. "Can you do this?"

"I have a question."

"If it carries the word *beer* it in, I'm hanging up."

"How long has it been since you rode a horse?"

EIGHT

Sophie was sitting on the stool at the kitchen counter and looking at the big box of clay that Betsy had given her. It was fine, white, and self-hardening, so perfect that Sophie felt sure Kim had had a hand in choosing it. The package had been gift wrapped with a card of thanks from Dr. Reede.

It had been so long since anyone — even she — had thought of herself as an artist, that all those years in school came back to her. How innocent their worries had been back then! Whether their professor was going to like their line quality, if he approved of Kim's silver designs, if Sophie's likenesses of her roommates would gain approval had been their biggest concerns. It had all seemed so very important. She remembered the fear and thrill at her first bronze casting. When it had come out perfectly, she'd had to resist the urge to cry in relief in front of her classmates. Later she'd danced about the apartment in triumph, and Jecca had shown up with a bottle of champagne. It had been a glorious day!

But soon after that Sophie had gone home to her mother's funeral and she'd taken on the responsibility of her young sister. Two years later she'd had to sell everything she'd made in school: paintings, fiber sculptures, even her precious bronze. They'd gone for a pittance, but at the time the money had enabled her to pay the utility bills.

The sight of the clay brought back bad memories, but the feel of it was making them fade. In their place were thoughts of what had made her study art in the first place. She remembered how much she liked to create things, to make something beautiful out of a formless lump.

And something else came to her: the kindness of Dr. Reede for sending her the clay. Her experience of men was that they gave flowers, candy, even lingerie, but she'd always seen those as an invitation to what *they* wanted. No man had ever thought of what Sophie wanted . . . needed. "Thank you," she whispered as she got up and went to his bedroom.

Yesterday while she was cleaning, some photos had fallen out of one of Dr. Reede's jacket pockets. They'd all looked to have been taken in Africa and they were of grinning children reaching up toward the photographer. The fact that some of the children had deformities, missing limbs, and big bandages was overshadowed by their smiles. If the photographer was Dr. Reede, she could see why he wanted to go back there.

The last picture was different. There was a young, dark-haired man in the middle, but his face was turned away as two exuberant children rumbled his hair. A baby was on his lap and three little boys, with their arms around Reede, were grinning at the camera.

All in all, it was a very happy scene, with enough joy in it to lighten a person's heart.

Since it was obvious that Dr. Reede didn't want the photo displayed, she'd put it in his empty bedside drawer.

She got the picture out and took it into the kitchen. As she propped it up beside the block of clay, she looked at it from an artist's point of view: proportion, composition, shadow.

There weren't many cooking utensils in the little kitchen, but she took out a couple of knives, an old fork that she could bend, and toothpicks. When she found an ice pick, she smiled. She used to brag that she could carve the Lincoln Memorial with an ice pick. Pot roast bubbled on the stove and pumpkin pie was baking as Sophie picked up the knife and made the first cut.

By the time Reede got home that night, he was exhausted. He'd spent the day answering questions, being fitted for a costume he was sure he would never have nerve enough to wear, and making plans. At the end of it he'd gone to Sara's husband's gym and worn himself out with weights and in Mike's boxing ring.

As they took off their gloves, Mike teased him about Sophie. "You get a girl and you'll drop twenty pounds of muscle."

"You got one and you didn't," Reede answered.

"Sara wears me out more than any gym."

The two men laughed together.

By the time Reede showered and drove back to his apartment, it was after nine. Sophie's rental car was gone, so she'd left, which meant that it was safe for him to go inside.

As soon as he opened the door to the apartment, he began to smile. She'd added a couple of lamps and they were on, making the light in the room softer, kinder even.

The table was set, and he could smell the food.

It took him only minutes to fill a plate with Sophie's pot roast and carry it to the table. There were two big napkins covering things and he pulled one of them off. Pumpkin pie, freshly baked, and still warm from the oven. He inhaled the fragrance.

Smiling, he removed the second napkin, expecting to see another dish, but what he saw made him freeze in place. There was a clay sculpture of him and the kids in Africa. He remembered the time well. He'd been photographing them, but they wanted him in the picture.

He posed with them but a second before the shutter clicked, they'd pushed him, laughing hilariously, saying he was too ugly to be in a picture.

Reede had kept the photo, as it was one of his favorites. He'd meant to have it framed, but he hadn't found the time. In the last months he'd forgotten about it.

But there it was, in 3D, on his dining table. He was in the middle, the baby who'd nearly died on his lap, his arms firmly around her. The boys were laughing hard as they tumbled about him and kept him from looking at the lens.

The exquisite little sculpture brought back

fond memories of his time abroad — and it made him want to go back.

He picked up the sculpture and turned it around to see all sides of it. It was as beautiful as anything he'd ever seen in his life. What an extraordinarily talented woman Sophie was!

He set it down carefully, then called her, but she didn't answer Kim's landline. He couldn't leave a message because she wouldn't know Kim's voice mail code. And Sophie didn't have a mobile phone because of Reede. He'd crunched it under the wheels of his car.

He sat down and ate while studying the beautiful sculpture. At ten he called Sara and told her he'd be there tomorrow morning to pick up the costume she'd tried to coax him into.

"What about the horse?"

"That too," Reede said.

"What changed your mind?"

"Talent," he said. "The sight of some very deep talent. I'll see you tomorrow."

He put the clay vignette on his bedside table, where it would be close to him while he slept. Tomorrow, he thought, he was going to do anything that was necessary to get Sophie to forgive him.

NINE

They were in Kim's house and Sophie was smiling as she took the box from Heather. It contained the costume that Reede's cousin, Sara, had made for Sophie to wear for her date with him.

"Sara guessed at your size," Heather said. "I think she called Kim, then put it together out of some other outfits she had. That's how she did it so fast."

"If it matches Dr. Reede's that's all that matters," Sophie said.

"You like him?" Heather asked, sounding as though she couldn't believe that. She cleared her throat and said, "You like him, don't you?"

"Very much. See the roses?" She nodded toward a vase of a dozen long-stemmed reds. "He sent them as thanks."

"For what?" Heather asked, looking at Sophie with curiosity.

"I used the clay he sent me to make a

sculpture of him."

"Oh," Heather said, but not understanding at all. Sophie was opening the box she'd brought. Sara had asked that it be delivered in case Sophie needed help getting it on. By that, Heather thought maybe it had a long zipper in the back.

When Sophie pulled a red silk corset out of the tissue paper, both women gasped. It would take two people to pull the cords that fastened it.

"I . . ." Sophie began as she held it up and looked at it. "I don't think . . ."

Heather's eyes lit up. Great. If this pretty young woman wore this very sexy costume maybe Dr. Reede would be so happy he'd stop snapping at everyone. "I think it's perfect!" Heather said energetically. "And I can tell that it'll fit you. Maybe it's a little small on top, but some spillover will be nice."

"Spillover?" Sophie said. "This thing wouldn't cover a preteen. I can't possibly —"

In Heather's mind she was fighting for her future children. If something didn't take away Dr. Reede's bad temper she was going to have to quit, which meant that she'd have to get a job that paid less, which meant that she'd have to postpone having children. If it

135

took coaxing a reluctant woman into a shiny red corset that left most of the top half of her exposed, so be it. It was certainly for a good cause. Maybe she'd name her first daughter after Sophie.

"Is your real name Sophia?"

"What?" Sophie asked as she stared at the corset. "My name? What does that have to do with anything?"

"Nothing, really. Now," Heather said briskly, "let's get you out of those clothes and into these."

"But I don't think it's appropriate for me to wear something like this," Sophie said. "I'm not sure —"

"That's okay. I'm a nurse so I'm used to nudity."

"That's not what I meant," Sophie said. "I —"

"I hear Dr. Reede is going to arrive on a black horse."

Sophie's eyes widened.

"Wearing a cape."

Sophie's eyebrows raised.

"And a black mask."

Sophie blinked a few times.

"Oh look, there's a blouse to cover the corset." Heather held up a filmy garment that was made entirely of black lace. It was so transparent it wouldn't cover anything.

Sophie's mouth fell open.

Heather knew she was going to have to take a firmer hand. "He's wearing boots!" she said loudly. "Tall black leather boots. He's on a horse! He's wearing a cape and a black mask! Now get out of those clothes!"

Sophie got her face under control and said, "Yes."

By the time Sophie was ready, she found she was quite nervous. Heather had left, saying that Dr. Reede wouldn't like for her to be there. From what Sophie had seen and heard, she thought maybe the real problem was that Heather didn't want to see her beloved Dr. Reede with another woman.

Sophie went out to the front of Kim's house, but the cool air gave her goose bumps. The sky had darkened, as though there was going to be a storm, and in the distance she saw a strike of lightning. The mask she was wearing rubbed on her eyelashes, and she adjusted it. Heather had pulled the strings on the corset so tight Sophie could hardly breathe and her breasts were so high above the top she felt that she looked like a poster for the sale of melons. If it hadn't been for Heather's encouragement, Sophie never would have dared wear such a thing.

137

She was dressed as though for a Zorro film. Besides the red corset and filmy black jacket, she had on an ankle-length silk skirt of red and black stripes with a slit that went halfway up her thighs. Soft black boots over black stockings completed the ensemble.

With her hands holding her upper arms, she turned to go back into the house. But she halted. Coming out of the trees was a man on a horse. Both of them were dark, and against the background of the faraway light, they stood out dramatically.

In an instant, Sophie forgot all her discomfort and stood there staring. In the last few days she'd felt she'd come to know this man, but there'd always been the missing visual of him. Her eyes seemed to devour him. He was the perfect Zorro to match her outfit.

Even though he was high up on the big black horse, she could see that he was tall. A gust of wind plastered the shirt with its big sleeves around him, and she saw well-defined pecs, a flat stomach, arms sculpted by muscle. A wide black leather belt encircled his slim waist, and black trousers stretched across heavily muscled thighs.

As Heather had said, his calves were covered by tall leather boots.

Sophie looked back up at his face, but the

upper half of it was hidden behind a mask and under a wide-brimmed hat. His eyes were concealed but his lips were full and beautifully formed. As he rode forward, he smiled at her, showing even, white teeth.

A flash of lightning struck closer and, just like in a movie, the horse reared. As Reede fought to control it, she heard his deep voice, soft and soothing.

"Down, girl," he said as he leaned forward and stroked the mare's neck.

When he stopped near her, Sophie looked up at him, and for a moment they just stood there in silence, staring at each other, she at his big dark form and he at her barely concealed figure. It took another flash of lightning before he bent toward her. When he put his hand down to her, she didn't hesitate. She stepped up on a low stone wall that bordered a flower bed, took his hand, and let his strong arm pull her up into the saddle behind him.

As he led the horse around, he paused, as though waiting for something, but Sophie didn't know what it was. For a moment she was puzzled, but then she slid her arms around his waist. Reede laughed, a soft, sultry sound. She'd got it right.

He picked up one of her hands and kissed the back of it. "You are beautiful," he said,

139

his head turned so his cheek was near her face. He had a bit of dark whisker stubble, and she was tempted to kiss his neck, but she didn't.

In the next moment he urged the horse forward, its feet clomping on the asphalt road. When the horse yet again lifted its front legs off the ground, Sophie gasped in alarm, tightened her arms around Reede, and put her face against the back of him.

"That's my girl," Reede muttered, and she didn't know whether he meant her or the horse. Nor did she care. She snuggled her face against his back and closed her eyes for a moment. The man, the growing storm, the horse, were all a wonderful fantasy.

They rode down the road for a few minutes, and if anyone came out of their houses to stare, she didn't see them. Sophie and Reede may as well have been alone on the planet.

They soon left the pavement and went into what Sophie knew was the nature preserve that surrounded the little town. Reede expertly led the horse down a rutted road, clicking at it encouragingly when he encountered a deep rut. At one jolt, he turned back to her. "All right?" he asked, and she nodded against him.

Twice she sat up straighter so her breasts

in the undersize corset weren't pressed against him, but both times the horse jerked to the side. In fear of falling, Sophie clung to Reede. She thought maybe he was doing it on purpose, and when he laughed, she was sure.

"Not far now," he said softly after they'd been on the horse for quite a while. Sophie had an idea he'd taken them on a round-about trip through the preserve. For her part she could have continued all day, but it was growing darker by the moment.

When she felt the first drops of rain, he turned to her. "Ready to make a run for it?"

Sophie looked up at him. His lips were beautiful and so very, very close to hers. All she could do was nod.

"Hold on," he said.

Sophie's arms tightened around him.

"Is that the best you can do?" he murmured.

She scooted forward another inch, moved her thighs even closer to his, and snuggled her nearly bare breasts so tight against his back that she could feel his skin through the cloth.

Again Reede laughed, then he moved his heels into the horse's flanks and they shot forward. Sophie wouldn't have thought it

141

was possible, but her arms pulled him even closer.

All too soon, he slowed down. Ducking, he led the horse under an overhang that was attached to a small shed. After a moment's hesitation he slid down and held up his hands to her. She fell forward, her hands going onto his shoulders, his onto her waist.

When her feet touched the ground, he didn't let go of her but stood there, his hands on her waist, almost encircling it. For a moment, Sophie thought he was going to kiss her but he moved away. "We'd better go inside or we'll get caught in the rain."

When Sophie didn't move, he stepped around her. "I better . . ." He trailed off as he went to the horse and removed the saddle. Like all of his costume, the leather was solid black.

She watched while he took the saddle off the horse and made the animal comfortable. Food and water had been left there, so it looked as though arrangements had been made for their arrival. He cares about animals as well as people, she thought.

There was a quick flash of lightning, then a clap of thunder so loud that Sophie jumped.

Reede held out his hand to her. "Let's go," he said.

She took his hand and followed him as they ran out of the shed and down a brick path to a house that was barely visible. Vines grew up trellises on the walls, and over-grown shrubs obscured the windows. She doubted that the building could be seen from the road.

Reede had some trouble getting the door open. It wasn't locked but it was stuck — and he knew exactly where to kick it so it opened.

"It's always been like that," he said as, still holding her hand, he led her inside.

They entered a big room that was open all the way up to the roof. A double row of heavy wooden beams was overhead. There were a few pieces of furniture about, but it all looked old and used. The house had an air of vacancy about it, as though no one had lived in it for years.

Turning, she looked up at him in ques-tion. His eyes were obscured by the mask, but she could see that they were blue and his lashes were long. Dr. Reede Aldredge was a gorgeous man. She wondered why she didn't remember seeing photos of him in college, and if he'd visited Kim, why hadn't she seen him? But then she remembered. He'd said there'd never been anything between him and Jecca, but that wasn't quite true. "Jecca is why I don't remember you," she said.

He looked at her in puzzlement for a moment, then smiled. Dropping her hand, he went around a corner of the big room and into a kitchen. On the old countertop was a big picnic basket.

"You're right. Kim hoped to marry me off to Jecca," he said as he opened the lid and looked inside.

"I'd forgotten that. Every time you visited, I was sent away. But Jecca didn't . . ."

"Marry me?" he asked, smiling. "Tris got to her first."

"Right," Sophie said and suddenly felt let down. It looked like she was second choice.

Reede gave her a long, lingering, full-body look. "I'm glad he did. Jecca can't make a sculpture of me with the children I came to love, she can't make a home out of an old warehouse, and she does *not* look like *you*." He gave her a look of such appreciation that Sophie felt her face turn red.

"Now," he said, "where should we eat?"

Sophie wanted to say "Nowhere," because when they finished they'd have to leave. She wanted to postpone the end. "Is this your house?"

"No," he said, and stepped away from the basket. "But I know it well. Would you like to see it?"

"Sure."

For a moment he was silent, as though trying to decide what to say. He looked at Sophie and smiled. It should have been odd, since they were both wearing masks, but that seemed to add to the intimacy of the moment. "I wanted to buy this house," he said. "It belonged to the family of a friend of mine, and when I was a kid I often stayed here. I —" Suddenly, the rain increased, and the torrent was loud. Reede's eyes widened. "Quick!" he said as he hurried around the countertop and started throwing open cabinet doors. He pulled out a stack of beat-up old pots and held out a couple to Sophie.

She had no idea what he was doing, but then a drop of rain hit her head. "Oh!"

"Right! Oh," Reede said as he ran to the far end of the room and put a big pan on the floor. In the next second a trickle of rain came down and went directly into the pot. Sophie stepped back and put a plastic tub where she'd been standing, and the rain dripped into it. "Where else?" she asked Reede.

"There, in that corner."

It took them minutes of scurrying about, running from leak to leak, to get all the kettles and pots and saucepans down. They ran back into the kitchen — which seemed to be dry — to look at their handiwork.

"Did we get them all?" Sophie asked.

"I think so." He was looking at her with pride. "Thanks for the help, and I must say that it was a joy to watch you run about the room."

She started to say something modest but changed her mind. "Those tall boots of yours are doing it for me."

Reede laughed. "I'll have to thank Sara." He put his hand on the picnic basket. "We could sit at the table and eat."

The way he said it seemed to have a question at the end. "Or . . . ?" she asked.

He stepped back into the living room and looked upward. "See those little doors up there?"

High up, at one end of the tall, open ceiling was a set of louvered doors no more than three feet tall.

"We could sit up there and look out over this room. I've spent a lot of time up there, and the view is good."

She could tell that that's where he wanted to go, and more importantly, she felt that he hadn't shared this place with anyone else. To the left was a staircase and Sophie hurried to it. "Race you up the stairs," she said and started running.

She'd only meant to tease him, but the next moment she heard him thundering across the floor. She wasn't prepared for when he picked her up in his arms and ran with her up the stairs.

"I win," he said when they reached the landing. As he stood there holding her he didn't seem to have any intention of putting her down.

"You cheated," Sophie said, looking up at him. She couldn't help thinking that she didn't mind if he never set her down. She had to resist the temptation to snuggle her head into his shoulder. "I must be heavy," she managed to say.

"Not at all." He was looking into her eyes. In the run he'd lost his hat and she could see his eyes more clearly. "I don't know how I missed seeing you all those years ago. You're so very pretty. And small. But —" He looked down at her body. "So perfectly formed. You're like a pocket Venus."

"A what?" she asked.

But he knew she'd heard him. Reluctantly, he set her down, then stood there, staring at her.

He was doing a great deal for her ego! "So where's the basket?"

Reede smiled. "Left it downstairs. Come

through here." He took her hand and led her past a bedroom and a bath, then into another bedroom.

Sophie couldn't help frowning. Into a bedroom already?! She pulled her hand out of his and turned back toward the door. But Reede went to the far end of the room and opened what looked to be a closet door, then disappeared inside and she heard scraping sounds.

Curious, Sophie went to see where he'd gone. At the back of the closet, which still contained a lot of old clothing, was a little panel. It wasn't really a door, as it had no hinges and didn't reach the floor. Reede had pulled it out of the wall, set it to one side, and seemed to have disappeared into the hole.

Sophie looked inside to see an area about eight feet by three. It was very dark, but then Reede opened the little doors and light came in from the living room below. She stepped into the space to crouch next to him.

"It's shorter than I remember," he said.

She smiled but didn't state the obvious, that he was now taller. It was very intimate in the little space and she liked being so near him. She also liked that she'd been wrong when she'd thought he'd been leading them to a bed.

"Not claustrophobic?" he asked. Above them they could hear the rain, and it made the space seem even cozier.

"No," she answered.

"When I was a kid my friend Tommy and I used to eat meals up here," he said, his eyes looking at her in question.

"I'd love to," she said, knowing that was what he was asking.

"Stay here and I'll get the basket." He started to leave and got one leg through to the closet when he turned back. She couldn't see all of his face, but his eyes seemed to be serious. "Since it's just the two of us, maybe we should remove our masks."

"And ruin the fantasy?" Sophie said. "I was just thinking that I'm sorry the hat's gone."

Reede's smile was so warm, so . . . happy, that Sophie again felt her face turning red. "Go on, get the food," she said and he left.

She started to sit on the floor but then she went back into the bedroom and got four pillows and a quilt that she tossed through the opening and made a sort of couch. When she sat down she saw why Reede liked the place so much. Through the doors was a lovely view down into the living room. She smiled at their pans placed around with the rain dripping into them. For all that the roof leaked and the house was quite dirty, it looked to be in good shape.

"Hello!" Reede called from the floor below and Sophie waved to him. She watched him check on the buckets. The rain was coming down steadily but the containers didn't seem to be filling rapidly.

"See this?" Reede asked as he went to the far side of the room. There was an old iron ladder bolted to the wall and she saw that it went all the way up to the exposed rafters. "When I was a kid I used to climb out of where you are, walk across that beam, and come down this way."

As Sophie looked where he was pointing, she drew in her breath. That was a *very* dangerous walk. It would be bad for an adult, and she didn't want to think about a child up there. "I hope your friend's parents stopped you from doing it," she said sternly.

"They never knew about it," he said. He climbed up the ladder about halfway, then halted. "I've always wanted to try something."

She didn't know what it was about his tone that upset her, but something did. She remembered the framed photo of him that

Kim had hung on their apartment wall. It was a newspaper shot of a man being lowered down a cable into a turbulent ocean to rescue people whose boat had sunk. "My idiot brother!" Kim had said of the photo, but there was so much pride in her voice that everyone knew she was pleased by his heroism.

Sophie watched Reede unfasten something from his belt. She hadn't noticed that there was a whip coiled at his side. "You're Zorro!" she said.

"That's what Sara told me I was." He was unrolling the whip.

"So where's your cape? I was promised a cape."

"I left it at Sara's house. Sorry to disappoint you, but I couldn't handle it. A man has limits."

"Probably didn't want to hide your muscles," Sophie said under her breath.

"What did you say?"

"Nothing. I —" She broke off because he looked to be about to unleash the whip in the direction of the rafters — and she had an idea of what he planned to do. "I'm hungry!" she said loudly. "I'd really, really like to have something to eat. Now. This minute!"

Reede heard the fear in her voice. "This is

151

nothing. It'll only take a moment."

Before Sophie could reply, he'd cracked the whip over the nearest rafter, high above his head. With her hand to her mouth she watched him pull on it to test its strength, then he went flying across the room, swinging on the whip handle. He ended up on the far side of the room and dropped down, grinning like a boy.

"You should have dressed as Tarzan," Sophie said, and she didn't mean it as a compliment. His dangerous little stunt had scared her.

"A leopard loincloth wouldn't hide my muscles, would it?" he said, letting her know he'd heard her previous comment.

Sophie couldn't help but laugh.

Reede retrieved the whip, rehooked it to his belt, grabbed the picnic basket, and bounded up the stairs two at a time.

Within minutes he was seated across from Sophie on her improvised sofa and opening the basket. Inside were lots of little sandwiches, three kinds of salad, and two bottles of wine.

"Did you pack this yourself?" she asked as he opened a bottle and filled two glasses.

"Not a bit of it," he said cheerfully.

She didn't ask, but she figured his adoring staff or even his patients had put it together for him.

"Tell me everything about your life," Reede said as he removed a plate from the straps on the back of the basket.

A montage of everything ran through Sophie's mind: fighting to get to go to college, her mother's death, taking care of her sister, and the icing on the cake: stealing the Treeborne cookbook from Carter.

Reede seemed to understand Sophie's hesitation. "On Monday morning between eight and ten a.m. a FedEx man will stop at Kim's house to pick up your package. I called a friend of mine in Auckland and it'll go to him. He'll send it to Earl."

"Earl?" Sophie asked, then remembered the pseudonym she'd used. "Yes, of course. Earl. I can't thank you enough for this. In other circumstances I wouldn't be so dependent, but —"

"I don't think you're dependent at all. Sophie, that little sculpture you made was beautiful. Your talent amazes me. Why — ?" He cut himself off as he bit into a sandwich.

"Why aren't I exhibiting my work?" She could tell by his expression that he hadn't meant to be so serious, but she didn't mind. "I have a theory."

"And that is?"

"That every person on this earth was

given a talent, whether it's for art or music or . . . or the ability to keep a house clean even when you have young children."

"The clean house gene missed me," Reede said, holding up the bottle. "More wine?"

She nodded. "What makes the difference between people are personality traits. Take you and Kim for example."

"Go on."

"She wanted to make jewelry and you wanted to be a doctor, so you did it."

"I'm not understanding your point," Reede said.

"Kim had an ambition that equaled her talent, so now she has her own shop and a brand-new contract with Neiman Marcus. And you became a doctor."

"I think I see," Reede said. "People let life get in the way and don't follow their visions — or their talent."

"Exactly! When I was in school studying art I met some fantastically talented people, but after graduation I heard nothing about them. There was a young man who wrote a play that awed all of us. Know what he's doing now? Selling used cars."

"Didn't want it enough?" Reede asked, looking at her intently. "Is that what happened with you?"

"I never had the drive of Jecca or Kim. I

—" She looked down at her hands.

"You thought of others before yourself," he said. "I can attest that my sister never let anyone or anything stand in the way of her jewelry making. But you . . . You were needed, so you set your own wants aside."

"That's one way of looking at it." He was making her feel good about herself. For years, when she saw online anything that Jecca or Kim had done, Sophie had felt like a failure. But Reede made her sound, well, almost noble.

She wanted to talk of something besides herself, and she was interested in his world travels. "What's the most beautiful country you've ever visited?"

"New Zealand."

"Really?" she said. "I would have thought someplace tropical, like Tahiti, would be."

"Too much traffic; too many houses."

"Most impressive place?"

"Galapagos Islands, with Petra a close second."

"Scariest?" she asked.

"Tonga, with Easter Island right behind."

"Interesting," she said. "Most surprising?"

"Hong Kong. Very clean, very modern."

"So where would you like to live?" When he started to speak, she put up her hand. "Let me guess. New Zealand."

"Yes," he said. "I have friends there, and I like everything about the country."

"Have you always felt out of place here in Edilean?"

He took a moment before answering. "I think so. It wasn't easy living here as an Aldredge who wanted to be a doctor, but I wasn't *the* Aldredge."

She waited for him to continue.

"See this house?" He waved his hand toward the living area below. "I didn't really like the kid who lived here. He used to make fun of me because I was interested in medicine. But I hung around him because of this house."

Sophie ate in silence, waiting for him to explain.

"It's like Aldredge House, the one Tris inherited. He got the name Tristan *and* the ancestral home."

"And you wanted what he had?"

"I thought I did. But what I think I really wanted was to belong, to have that feeling of being part of a place." He opened a box of cupcakes and held them out to Sophie.

"If your family has lived here for generations I'd think you'd feel that you were part of the town."

"Maybe. I've been told that the Aldredge who settled Edilean was a doctor, but he

156

was also a wanderer, that he rode on horse-back all over the U.S."

"So you're like him," Sophie said as she broke off a piece of chocolate and ate it. The rain was still coming down steadily, and combined with the small space, she was feeling very close to this man. It was a day for revealing secrets. She thought that if they stayed there much longer that she'd tell him more about Carter. She needed to keep the conversation on Reede. "So you'll leave as soon as you can." It was a statement, not a question.

"The very second."

Sophie did her best to conceal her disappointment. This was a man she *knew* was going to leave. Not like her previous boy-friends, whom she'd broken up with, or like Carter who'd shoved her out his front door then run upstairs to call his real girlfriend. At least with them for a while there had been hope that a man would be in her life permanently.

"What's that look for?" Reede asked.

"Just thoughts," Sophie said. "Heather called the party tonight McTern. I haven't heard that name before."

She could tell, even through the mask, that Reede was frowning, and it took him a moment to recover himself. "It was the name

157

of the people in Scotland who founded Edilean. Somehow, the name was changed to Harcourt, but Roan is a McTern."

"You'll look good as Zorro tonight," she said.

"My mother has a different costume for me and I have no idea what it is. This one is for you alone."

She could tell that something was bothering him, but she didn't know what it was, but his good mood seemed to have vanished. "Did I say something?" she asked. "You seem —"

"No, nothing," he said. "Edilean does this to me. I don't think I'm supposed to be here."

"Here in this house or here in —" She broke off at a sound at the front door below.

Reede reacted instantly. He shut the little double doors that opened over the living room, putting them in shadowy darkness.

"What is it?" Sophie asked in alarm.

"I don't know," Reede whispered. "Could be someone I know or —" There were voices below, and Reede put his finger to his lips and eased the door open a bit.

When he saw that Sophie wanted to see too, he motioned for her to move closer. She had to set the basket into a corner and she nearly knocked over a wine bottle, but

Reede caught it.

Silently, Sophie scooted closer to him and he pulled her between his legs, her back to his front. She peered through the opening, but all they saw was an open door, the rain coming down hard outside. She looked at Reede — and saw that he was looking down at the top of her corset.

"The problem is out there," she whispered.

"You are a very distracting presence. I think we should —"

"When are we gonna get out of this hellhole?" came a man's voice from downstairs.

Reede tore his eyes from Sophie's décolletage to look down at the scene below. A short, skinny man, dripping from the rain, was holding the door open.

"Come on!" the man said. "He'll be here any minute."

"Yeah, yeah, I know." Another man, taller, beefier, pushed through the doorway. He had two big takeout bags in his arms that he set on the old dining table. He paused to look around. "How did Pete find this dump?"

"It's just for tonight," the first man said. "And just because of the rain."

"And your driving," the second man said, then halted. "Somebody's been here. Look at those pans catching the water."

When the man pulled a pistol out of the back of his trousers, Sophie gave a gasp. Reede briefly put his hand over her mouth, his eyes warning her to be quiet, and she nodded.

"Did you hear that?"

"I can't hear anything over the sound of my stomach growling."

The second man was moving about the room, his gun held out and ready. "I'm going to check upstairs. This place gives me the creeps."

Reede pulled away from Sophie and motioned for her to stay where she was. Silently, he went to the panel that covered the opening.

Sophie had to work to be quiet when he stepped outside. He seemed to be gone for a long time but she knew it was only minutes. When he returned he put the panel in place over the opening and enclosed them. She couldn't help but think that if the man with the gun knocked that piece of wood away that they'd be trapped. They were up against nothing, as the floor was a story below.

Reede came back inside and looked out the door over the living room, and they sat motionless, in silence. They heard the second man come up the stairs, and listened as he moved about the second floor. Doors opened and closed.

Suddenly, Sophie remembered the mess she'd made of the bed when she took the pillows and the quilt. She picked up one and looked at Reede in alarm.

"I straightened it," he whispered, his lips touching her ear.

It all depended on if the man had seen the room before. If he had, he might miss the pillows and start trying to find out what had happened to them.

When she heard the man's footsteps outside the closet, Sophie held her breath. Reede silently put his arms around her. As the man came closer, Sophie went rigid with fear — and Reede began kissing her ear. At first she was annoyed with him. How could he think of sex at a time like this?

But after a moment she began to relax. His lips soothed her, distracted her from the fact that just a few feet away was a man with a gun.

By the time the man slammed the closet door shut, Sophie's neck was arched backward and Reede's lips were moving downward.

When the danger was past, he gave her a perfunctory kiss by the earlobe, set her

161

upright, opened the door a couple more inches, and looked out. He seemed to be totally unaffected by what he'd just done.

He sat back down and stared across at her. "You don't have a cell phone with you, do you?" He answered his own question. "No room in that thing. You know how bad that is for your celiac plexus, don't you?"

Sophie could only blink at him. What had happened to the man who had been only sweet and kind? "No phone," she managed to say.

"Look in the basket. I doubt if there's one in there, but we can hope."

Sophie quietly rummaged inside the basket, but there was only the remnants of their meal. "What are they doing?"

"They're eating and there are *two* guns on the table."

Reede leaned back against the wall and was glad when the men turned on a radio. It would cover their voices. "It's my guess that they're meeting the man Pete here and they'll spend the night. We may have to stay here until they leave." He gave her a crooked smile. "Are you prepared for a sleepover?"

If he'd asked that ten minutes ago she would have said yes, but his crack about her celiac plexus still stung. "Maybe I'll go downstairs and introduce myself. I've always wanted to be a gangster's moll."

She said it so seriously that he wasn't sure if she meant it. Some women looked on guns as a sign of power. They — He realized she was kidding. Just as seriously, he said, "Think I could use my Zorro whip and knock both guns off the table?"

"You couldn't do that!" she said in alarm, then knew he was teasing. "What do we do?"

"Wait. If we leave here they'll see us. Damn but I wish I could call the sheriff. My gut tells me that these men are criminals on the run. Maybe I should distract them and try to —"

"No!" Sophie said too loudly, then lowered her voice. "We'll just wait. Even if we have to stay here all night. We have food — some anyway — and wine. What more could we want?"

"Safety," Reede said as he leaned back against the wall.

He was doing his best to stay calm and not let Sophie see that he was frightened for her. If he were alone he would make his way across the ceiling beam, go down the iron ladder, and out the side window. He doubted if the lock had been repaired since he was a kid. If he couldn't get out that way, he'd make his way to the side door.

But he couldn't do that now and leave

Sophie behind. He'd already seen that she wasn't exactly adventurous. Not the type to want to go hang gliding. She'd been frightened just by seeing him swing across a room. It seemed that both leaving her alone and getting her to go with him were out of the question.

On the other hand, he'd seen some other things about her too. For one thing, she wasn't like those wimpy women who worked for him. Say one word to them that wasn't kind and considerate and they ran away and hid. But not Sophie. He'd been abrupt with her, and it had put fire in her. When pushed, she snapped back — or poured beer over the person who'd upset her.

He leaned back against the wall and did his best to act as though he were so calm that he was falling asleep. But even with his eyes half closed, all he could do was *look* at her. She was truly beautiful — and built! The corset pulled her waist in so it was tiny, and most of the top of her was above the fabric. She had on a lacy black blouse over the red corset, but little was concealed. As for the bottom half of her, she had on a black skirt that was slit to nearly her waist, and every time she moved, her legs were exposed: slim, well shaped, truly beautiful.

Reede had no idea why his sister had tried

164

to push her other college roommate onto him. Or why Kim had concealed Sophie from him. Maybe Kim had thought he'd be too dazzled by Sophie's beauty to make an intelligent decision. Or, more likely, Kim thought Reede was too bad tempered, too tough, to unleash on sweet little Sophie.

And maybe he was, he thought. And maybe what he was going to do to her in the next few minutes was going to make her hate him. But then, she was already going to hate him when she found out that he'd almost run over her in his car.

Whatever the consequences, he was going to *have* to get her out of this place — and the only way to do that was to walk across the beam. But first, he had to put some backbone, some courage, into her.

He opened his eyes and looked directly at her.

At Reede's look, the hairs on Sophie's neck stood on end. "We have to get out of here, don't we?"

"Yes," he said.

"If we stay here too long, people will come searching for us, won't they?"

"Yes."

"And if someone were to just walk in here, there's a possibility that bullets would be fired."

165

This time Reede just nodded.

Sophie glanced at the doors that looked out over the living room. She didn't want to think about the fact that the only way out was across a narrow beam. It was too dangerous to think about Reede walking across one of those pieces of wood. "I guess our only real hope is for you to sneak out without being seen and to tell someone. Do you think they saw your horse?"

Reede was watching her, and the fear in her eyes was debilitating. He knew from his rescue experience that if they worked together they could do it, but he also knew from one especially bitter attempt that he couldn't carry a whimpering bag of fear. What Sophie needed was some determination. Actually, anger would be good. But how could he make her that angry in just seconds? His first thought was to remove his mask and show her the truth about him. But that wouldn't work. He didn't want her angry at *him*. At least not in that way. She needed to trust him so she could . . . His head came up. She needed to prove to him that she could do it.

He looked at her. "If they'd seen the horse, they wouldn't be so quiet. Sophie, I won't leave you here alone, and the only way out without being seen is for both of us

166

to cross that beam and go down the ladder. But you couldn't possibly do that." He put his head back and acted as though what he'd said was the end of it and he was going back to sleep.

Sophie stared at him for a moment before she spoke. "What does that mean? Why can't I do it?" She was curious as much as anything else.

With his eyes closed, Reede smiled in the most superior, patronizing way that he could manage. "Because you're so short. You can't possibly reach the overhead beam, so you can't hold on, and besides, you're so top-heavy you wouldn't be able to balance. You're not exactly aerodynamically sound."

Sophie blinked at him a few times as she took in what he'd just said. Not aerodynamically sound? What human body *was*? And just who did he think he was to say such a thing? An airplane engineer? "I'm not — ?" she began, but her tongue tripped over itself so much that she couldn't complete the sentence. She glared at him. "I'm top-heavy? You know something, Dr. Aldredge, you're a jerk. A top-of-the-line, first-class *jerk*. I'll have you know that I can balance perfectly well and I can assure you that my arms are long enough to reach the overhead beam."

167

With anger surging through her, she got up and was only vaguely aware that Reede was right behind her. As she stepped out onto the square beam, she didn't look down, she just put one foot in front of the other. For the first steps she could reach the overhead support. It was high above her head, and if she tripped she could never use it to hold her, but touching it gave her balance. She inched along, her mind full of all the rotten things men had said to her in her life. They'd leered at her, followed her places, made passes . . .

She stopped thinking when she got halfway across the beam. Below them, the men were talking over the radio. She became fully aware that if they looked up and saw her, she'd be a target. Panic nearly overwhelmed her.

"I'm here," Reede whispered in her ear, "and you're doing great. Just a few more steps and you're done."

She turned to look at him. His eyes behind the mask were bright and alert, not at all sleepy. "You said all that on purpose, didn't you?" she whispered.

He gave a little smile and said, "I think you're aerodynamically perfect and if you pop out of that thing I'll probably fall backward and break my neck."

Her fingers were like claws on the wood above her head, but she still managed to smile. "Couldn't have that, could we?"

"No." He nodded toward the safety of the wall, then put his hand on the small of her back.

Reede looked down and saw that the two men had moved into the kitchen. They could only see the two people above them if they came around the corner. And they'd turned up the radio, which had started an argument between them.

When Reede looked back at Sophie he could see the fear growing in her eyes. Yet again he knew he needed to distract her. "Sophie," he said softly, "sometimes good people do bad things."

She turned her head slightly to look at him. Had he found out that she'd stolen the Treeborne cookbook? How could he? Maybe he'd assumed it, since she wanted to mail it back to Carter. Maybe —

"Not that a person intended to do anything bad," he said, "but it sometimes happens. Here, put your foot next to mine. There, that's good. Now go a little bit that way. Great. So a person should be forgiven, shouldn't he?"

He? Was he talking about Carter? "I think he should have been honest with me," she said, then her foot slipped. Reede grabbed her about the waist with his left arm and kept her from falling backward.

Sophie's heart was pounding in her chest, but Reede seemed unperturbed by her near fall or even by the fact that they were balancing on a four-inch-wide chunk of wood with nothing below them.

"Honest?" he said, sounding as though nothing had happened. "Maybe he would have been honest if he'd had a chance."

"Are you talking about . . . ?" She had to think to remember the name she'd used. "Earl?"

"Earl? Your ex-boyfriend who is profoundly stupid? Why in the world would I talk about *him*?"

In spite of the circumstances, Sophie gave a little smile. "I don't know." She was moving along the beam by quarter inches and she didn't dare look down or at the end. She kept her eyes on Reede. It was better to think about what he was trying to say.

"But sometimes we need to walk away," Sophie said. Her hands were hurting and her feet were aching. It seemed that she'd been on that blasted beam for days.

"But sometimes a person should be forgiven no matter what," Reede said emphatically. "Walking away isn't always the right thing to do."

She had no idea what he was talking about and she was so frightened, so jittery, that she couldn't think clearly. When her shoulder touched the wall, she almost gave a yelp of relief.

But Reede bent forward and kissed the side of her mouth. Not exactly on her lips but close enough to startle her into silence.

He kept his face close to hers. "Sophie," he said, and his lips were touching her skin. "Be still. They're walking around, and we need to stay out of sight for a few minutes."

Her feet may have been on the beam, but her back was against the safe, secure wall. As for the front of her, that was covered by Reede's big body.

"I need to hide the red," he said, referring to her silk corset as he put his hands on the wall on either side of her head. He was so much larger than she was that she was completely hidden by him. If either of the men did look up he'd see only the back of Reede. But the wall was covered with dark wood paneling, so maybe Reede's all-black clothing wouldn't be noticed.

She didn't know if her heart was racing because she was high above two men with guns, or if it was due to feeling Reede's beautiful body pressed against hers.

"I can take your pulse from here," he said, his lips against her ear.

"I think maybe you're close enough to read my blood pressure."

"Don't make me laugh or we'll both fall."

"I heard a door close. Do you think they're gone?"

"Who?" Reede asked.

"Them! The bad guys."

Reluctantly, Reede turned away from her just enough to look down into the living room. When he saw no one, he turned more fully away. The room was empty. He lost the languorous look he'd been wearing. "We have to go!" he said, then stepped back so Sophie could see the ladder.

It may have been a ladder and should have represented safety, but to Sophie it looked like an invitation to death. The step out into thin air just to get onto the top rung was enough to make her feel faint.

"We don't have time to hesitate. We have to —" Reede began, then said, "Oh hell!" He stepped back, unfastened the whip from his belt, and slung it over the top beam. He pulled on it to make sure it was secure, then to Sophie's shock, he swung out on it to stand on the ladder. He hooked one booted foot over a rung and reached up his arms to her.

172

"You want me to jump?" she asked, incredulous.

"No. You need to fall," he said and his tone was no longer teasing. It was an order.

Sophie couldn't take the time to think about what she was doing or if he could hold her or all the other things that shot through her mind. It was a matter of trust, and this man deserved it.

She put out her arms toward his shoulders and fell forward. As she'd been sure he would, Reede caught her. Instantly, he twisted her around and she grabbed the iron bars.

Reede didn't give her time to think as he started down the tall ladder, Sophie in front of him. Her foot slipped once, but Reede steadied her. When they reached the floor she wanted to cry in relief, but they heard the doorknob turn. Reede shoved her into a coat closet and was right behind her.

The area was tiny and full of old coats so smelly she could hardly breathe.

"I told you I heard something," one of the men on the other side of the door said.

"Will you stop worrying? No one will find out anything until Monday, and by then we'll be long gone."

"I think we should go now. Get out of this town."

"Pete has something else planned."

"What is it?"

"How the hell would I know? If I could figure that out *I* would be the boss."

Sophie and Reede were by necessity jammed together in the little closet and a box started to fall off a shelf. Reede caught it before it hit Sophie's head. He raised his arms to put it back up and when they came down they went around her, pulling her to him.

Under normal circumstances, she would have protested, but as they heard the men moving about and arguing, the radio blaring, Reede's arms made her feel safe. She put her cheek against his chest and closed her eyes.

Reede bent so his head was on top of hers. "I'm going to have to open the door to see what's going on. I want you to get in the back and hide as best you can."

"But if they see you they'll —"

"Ssssh," he said. "I've done this kind of thing before."

She moved to look up at him in question, but he put her head back down.

"When I'm sure it's clear, I want you to follow me."

She nodded in agreement.

"Stick to me as close as my own breath. I

want you closer to me than that red thing you have on is to your glorious body. Understood?"

Again she nodded.

For a moment he didn't move but stood there holding her, one hand in her hair, the other one on her back.

"Sophie, I'm sorry for this. Sorry for everything."

"It wasn't your fault," she whispered.

"Sometimes my anger overrides my common sense and sometimes I don't see what's right in front of me."

She had no idea what he was talking about, but it was obviously important to him.

He put his hands on her shoulders and held her away from him. There wasn't much light in the closet, just what came through a transom above the door, but in spite of the mask, she could see the concern on his face.

"Forgive me?" he whispered.

"For what?"

"I'm about to take advantage of an unpleasant situation," he said as he lowered his mouth onto hers.

Maybe it was what they'd been through together on the beam, or maybe it was the danger they were facing now, but there was a tenderness and a desperation in the kiss that neither of them had ever experienced before. It had the feeling of "the last." The last kiss before a soldier went off to war. The last kiss before a patient went into surgery. The last kiss before the final breakup.

Reede was the first to pull away. "Get in the back and stay there," he said, and she obeyed without question.

Slowly, soundlessly, Reede opened the closet door and peered out.

From behind the old coats Sophie watched him. The radio was so loud that they couldn't hear where the men were. For all they knew they were standing just outside the door.

When Reede opened the door wider and looked out, Sophie drew in her breath and held it.

But Reede turned to her with a cocky grin that told her the coast was clear. When he hand-signaled for her to leave the coats and follow him, she didn't so much as hesitate.

She got to the door, her hand outstretched to take his when, suddenly, Reede shut the door, leaving her alone in the closet. It was so fast she was almost hit in the face. Instinctively, she stepped back into the concealment of the coats. And all she could do was wonder what had happened. Had the men seen Reede? Were the three of them now standing just outside the door? Did Reede have guns pointed at him?

She listened but heard nothing. The music still blared, so she couldn't hear voices. But if the men had seen Reede, wouldn't there be shouting?

Cautiously, she stepped out of the coats and went to the door. Even when she put her ear against it, she heard nothing. She waited and listened, but all she heard was the blaring music. Some cowboy was singing that his third wife had run off with someone else. He couldn't figure out why women today weren't like his mother and put up with anything a man dished out.

Sophie put her hand on the knob. Maybe Reede had left her behind while he went for help. On the other hand, if he'd wanted to do that he could have left her upstairs. Her fear was that he was in trouble and needed help.

Slowly, with her heart pounding hard, she turned the knob.

When shouts came and the music abruptly stopped, Sophie was sure they'd seen the knob turn. She put her shoulders back in preparation for men-with-guns to burst in. But then she rethought the "shoulders back" idea. In that position too much of her popped up above the corset. To be caught while wearing such a ridiculous getup was going to be humiliating. She grabbed an old jacket off a hanger, pulled the mask from over her eyes, then stood up straight and waited.

But the door didn't open. Instead, she heard a man's angry voice. It wasn't the first two men but a different voice. Someone new had come into the house. Was this man the reason Reede had shut the door so abruptly? She put her ear against the door.

TEN

"We'll go when I say we can," the new voice said. "Here, put these on."

Sophie heard something hit a wooden surface, as though boxes had fallen.

"What the hell are these?" the skinny man asked. By now Sophie knew the voices of the first two men.

"Can't you see that they're Halloween costumes?" the second man said.

"So now we're gonna go out and steal candy? From the kids? I like that idea."

"Shut up!" the new man said. He sounded more intelligent than the other two. "We're going to a party."

"What?" the two men said in unison.

"I understand your lack of social graces and that's why you'll have on full-head masks."

"I don't want to go to no party. I want to get out of this two-bit backwater place."

"You will do what I tell you to!" the new

man said. "This town is *rich*! The women here have jewelry dating back hundreds of years. And for this Halloween party they pull it all out of their safe-deposit boxes and put it on. It's the world's most snobbish party, as you have to be a blood relative to get in. They don't trust anybody else — and I know. I've lived here for years and I've never been invited to —" He broke off, sounding as though he couldn't go on with that line of thought. When he continued, his voice was calmer. "I've fixed it so there will be three empty places tonight and we're going to say we're cousins — there are hundreds of them. While we're there we're going to be quiet and talk little. We'll just wander around and eat, but talk to no one. Got it?"

Sophie thought the men probably nodded, but she could see nothing, and with the radio no longer covering every sound, she was afraid to move.

"At ten tonight there's going to be an emergency," the new man said. "And I —"

"What kind of emergency?"

"A fire in town. I've set a device to go off. One of their precious old buildings is going to burst into flame, and the lot of them will run off to fight the fire, us included."

"With the jewels?" one of the men asked.

"No, you moron! The *men* will go fight the fire. This town is like some storybook. The women will stay behind to start cooking to feed the men."

There was silence in the room, as though the two men didn't understand what they were hearing.

"We'll double back and we'll get the jewels. We'll wave some guns around and we'll make the women take their sparklers off, dump them in a bag, then we'll leave. They'll have no idea who we are. On Monday I'll go back to work and I'll be as horrified as everybody else at what happened."

"What do we do then?"

"After the heist I'll give you a map of where someone is to meet you. He'll take care of everything. Any more questions?"

For a few moments there was silence, then the first two men began to speak at once and the man answered. One man said he didn't like his costume because the fur was itchy. "It'll cover your ugly mug." The other man said he couldn't see out of his. "You don't need to see. Just point the gun straight ahead. That's all you'll have to do."

Sophie turned her back to the door and leaned against it. This was *serious*. And this was horrible. A fire was to be started in beautiful downtown Edilean. A robbery of

181

ancestral jewels. Guns waved about by men who couldn't even see what they were doing.

She *had* to get out, *had* to warn people. But how could she do that without being seen?

And even if she did get out, how could she identify the man who was the mastermind? She knew he lived in Edilean and he planned to go back to work and act as though nothing had happened. How did they find someone with just that description?

Sophie looked up at the top of the door. There was a transom with a foggy glass insert. It let in some light, but even if she piled up old clothes to make a ladder, she wouldn't be able to see anything.

When she heard footsteps coming toward her, she drew in her breath. Would one of the men open the door and see her?

But he stopped. "Get that table cleared off," the new man said. "I have a floor plan of the Town Hall."

"Why do we need that?"

"It's where the party is. One of you will go upstairs just before ten and wait for the explosion. I don't want any women or kids upstairs lurking about. You herd them down to me, get it?"

Sophie went down to her stomach to look through the crack under the door. She didn't think she'd be able to see much, but maybe there would be something useful.

All she could see were shoes. One of the two men who'd been there at first had on running shoes that looked the worse for wear. The second man had on scruffy old boots. The new man wore what looked to be very expensive loafers, and she noted that his feet were small.

She was still on her stomach when it suddenly sounded as though hail was coming down. She got to her feet, pulled the jacket close around her, and yet again waited to be discovered.

Instead, the three men began running across the room.

"What is it?" asked one of the first men.

Sophie put her ear back to the door and heard shuffling, as though some things were being moved around.

"Nuts!" the new man said. "Someone is throwing nuts down the chimney."

"Who would do that?"

"Squirrels!" the new man said. "Or kids playing Halloween pranks. How did I get hooked up with idiots like you two? Turn off the lights and follow me outside. I'll give them a thrill they won't soon forget."

"Reede!" Sophie whispered as she heard the men running, then the door slammed shut. Instantly, she left the closet. The house was pitch-dark, and she had to rely on memory to find the door. It took only a few more seconds to get outside, and she was glad that the rain had stopped.

As she ran toward the shed, she didn't look back to see where the men were or if they saw her. When she reached the back of the little building, the mare looked up placidly, unperturbed. Better yet, undiscovered.

The first thing Sophie saw was the saddle on the fence. Great, she thought. Bareback.

Her childhood hadn't included riding lessons with a saddle, much less trying to outride criminals while hanging on to a horse's mane.

"Good girl," she said softly as she walked toward the animal. "We're going to go get Reede and get out of here. Please don't do any of that rearing that you do with him. Pretty please?"

The mare was docile as Sophie climbed up the railing and managed to throw her leg over. But when she got on, she realized that the reins were hanging to the ground. As she slid off, the big jacket she'd thrown over her top got caught on the wood. She flung it off, picked up the reins, took a breath to get her courage up, then remounted the horse.

Her experience in riding was what she'd seen on TV, so she clicked and used her heels to urge the horse forward. Maddeningly slowly, it left the comfort of the stall to step into the cool night air.

There wasn't much light but Sophie could tell where the men were by their cursing. They were to her left, so she went right, urging the horse around the far end of the house. For all she knew there were trees and shrubs blocking the away.

"I'm going to kill those things!" she heard one of the men shout. They were so focused on the roof that they didn't hear or see the horse slowly walking through the mud.

But Reede did. By the time Sophie got to the far end of the house, Reede was crouched down on the edge of the roof and waiting for her.

"What took you so long?" he asked.

"They asked me to tea," she shot back.

In the next minute he leaped. Her eyes widened as he jumped from the low edge of the roof and landed behind her on the horse. She managed to hold the animal steady until Reede was situated.

When she heard him grunt in pain, she

turned to look at him. "Are you all right?"

"Fine, although I don't think I'll ever be able to father any children."

"Maybe you'll just have to work harder at it," Sophie said.

Reede grunted a laugh, reached around her to take the reins, then urged the horse forward. They rode slowly and in silence for a while until they reached deep woods.

"I couldn't get back," Reede said, his voice serious, apologetic. "I never would have —"

"I heard them say that they're planning to rob the McTern party," Sophie said. Against her back, she felt Reede's body tighten.

"Tell me everything they said."

She did. As quickly as she could get the words out, she told Reede all that she'd heard.

"And you didn't see this man?"

"Only his shoes," Sophie said and told how she'd stretched out on the floor and looked under the door.

Reede kissed her neck. "Smart as well as beautiful. I'm going to take you to Sara's house. Her husband, Mike, is a former detective and I want you to tell him everything you can remember. I'm going to go get Colin, the sheriff."

"Do you think you'll be able to find the bomb in time?"

"We'll have a lot of people searching."

The idea of people looking for a bomb scared her. "When it gets close to the time, the people have to get out. They *have* to! They'll understand that, won't they?"

"Yes," he said, smiling at her. "We'll make sure everyone is safe. It's my guess that Mike will bring in some undercover people for tonight. As for you, I want you to stay home. You're not to go to the party. I want you to —"

"I know his voice," she said softly. "I didn't see the man's face, but I saw his shoes, and I heard his voice. I'm the only one who can identify him."

"But —" Reede began. "You can't —" He didn't seem to know what else to say as he urged the horse forward. When they reached the road, they broke into a gallop, and they thundered across the asphalt, then turned into a lane and finally reached what looked to be a very old house. It had been renovated, but the air of age still clung to it.

Reede didn't immediately get down, but held her for a moment, his front to her back. "You look good without the mask," he said. "You're even prettier without it — and I didn't think that was possible."

"What do you look like under the mask?"

"If I take it off my whole body splits in

half. Sophie . . ."

"Yes?"

"You did well tonight. I've never seen anyone more courageous than you were. Walking across that tightrope of a beam, then leaping onto the ladder was wonderful. And I'm sorry I left you alone in that closet. I couldn't figure out a way to get back to you that wouldn't endanger you. I —"

"It's all right," she said, taking pity on him. "If I hadn't been in there I wouldn't have heard their plan."

"That's true," he said. "On the other hand you wouldn't now be facing a bunch of lunatics with guns. I wish I'd shown myself and scared them off."

Turning, she put her hands on his shoulders and looked into his eyes. "You did what was right," she said. "If you'd jumped out at those men, they would have shot you."

"But then the whole town wouldn't be in jeopardy."

So this is how a true hero thinks, Sophie thought. He puts other people before himself.

They locked eyes for a moment and they would have kissed except that the door to the house opened and out stepped a man. He was slim but he had a way of moving that made a person notice him. "You two gonna stay out here all night?" the man asked in a raspy voice. Reede got off the horse and held up his arms to Sophie, and she easily slipped into them. "This is Mike. Sophie." They nodded at each other. "Can I borrow your car? I need to go see Colin and arrange a search party."

Immediately, Mike became alert. "Who's missing?"

"No one, but a bomb has been placed. Sophie knows everything and she'll tell you."

As Mike opened the door wider to let her in, he tossed his car keys to Reede. Sophie started to go into the house, but Reede held her hand and pulled her back. "You'll be careful tonight, won't you?" he said.

"You saw that I'm a scaredy-cat."

"I saw that someone only has to tell you that you can't do something and you tighten up that pretty little mouth of yours and *do* it. Just don't do that tonight, okay? Stay with me, and as soon as you identify this guy, you're out of there. All right?"

"Yes," she said softly, looking up at him. The rain had stopped but the sun wasn't out. It was gray and hazy. Reede gave her cheek a quick kiss, held her hand for a moment, then he was gone.

■ ■ ■ ■

Sophie was doing her best to pretend to be calm, but she wasn't succeeding. Sara Newland was being very nice to her, as was everyone else she was introduced to, but she was still frightened. There seemed to be a dozen young women from Edilean, all of them about her age, going in and out of the room where Sara was adjusting Sophie's costume. She couldn't keep the names straight: Tess, Jocelyn, Gemma, Ariel. Faces and names seemed to run together.

It had been hours since Reede had left, and since then she'd told her story many times. A handsome FBI agent by the name of Jefferson Ames spent thirty minutes going over her story. "We think these guys pulled a bank job in Baltimore about three years ago. They've laid low since then, and not put any of the money in circulation. We figured the leader was hiding nearby, and Edilean is close," Agent Ames said. "Tell me again what his shoes looked like."

Sophie was so busy answering the same questions over and over that it was a while before she paid attention to the dress Sara had her put on. It was green silk, with a low, square-cut neckline. A narrow drape of a dark plum color went over her left shoulder. The dress was high waisted, with an ornate sash that tied under her breasts. Sophie quit answering questions when Sara clasped a necklace around her throat. It was heavy and big.

Sophie put her hand on it, then excused herself to the agent and went to a mirror. "Is this . . . ? Are these . . . ?"

"Rubies set in gold," Sara said. "They're from an ancestor of mine, the original Edilean. We found them in a secret room in this house."

Sophie put her hand on the jewelry. It had a timeless beauty about it that was stunning. She looked at Agent Ames. "These are what they're after?"

"What they want to steal, yes," he said. "The pieces are so unique that it would be hard to sell them, so it's my guess that they'd be melted down. The jewels are superior quality even if they do need to be recut."

The artist in Sophie was sickened at the thought of something so old, so beautiful, being melted down and sold in pieces. Being able to stop something like that gave her courage. "Tell me what I need to do to help you," she said.

Reede didn't return until almost seven,

and by then Sophie was so glad to see him that she had to work not to fling her arms around him. She saw him from the back. This time he had on a suit, but in the style that Jane Austen's Mr. Darcy would wear. It clung to his body, showing off his muscular legs and his trim waist.

She stood still, staring at the back of him, and he turned to her. As before, he wore a half mask that covered his eyes and nose, but left his beautiful lips exposed.

He didn't say a word, just strode across the big room, took her hand, and led her into a bedroom. When they were alone, they stared at each other, their eyes questioning, then Reede opened his arms and she went to them. He held her tightly.

"Tell me what's on your mind," he whispered.

"They don't know what a coward I am. They keep telling me I'm very brave but I'm not. I want to hide under the bed and not come out until it's all over."

"Me too," he said.

"You? But —" She pulled away to look up at him. His eyes were shining so brightly that she couldn't resist elbowing him. "You *love* this! It gets you out of that apartment you hate, and you don't have to stay in an office, and you —"

He kissed her. It was a quick kiss and a familiar one, then he left her sitting on the bed. He picked up a plate that contained a turkey sandwich. "This yours?"

"Yes." She'd been too nervous to eat.

Reede took a big bite of the sandwich. "How much have they told you?"

"Not much," Sophie said as she sat down beside him. "I answer their questions but no one answers mine."

"Someday you and Mike will have to talk about the FBI. I think you two will agree."

As Reede ate he told her what they'd been doing and how the enemy had been set up. With the FBI training ground so near they'd had a lot of volunteers to attend the party and put on the costumes Reede's relatives had planned to wear. "And to put on the all-important jewels," Sophie added. "What do you want to drink?" "Beer," he answered. It took her only seconds to go to the kitchen and get a bottle and open it. She was aware that everyone, agents as well as Reede's relatives, stopped talking and watched her. "I'm the freak of the day," she said when she got back into the room and handed Reede the beer.

"I think it's more likely that they're wondering when you're going to murder me."

"For what? Making me cross that narrow beam? Or for taking me to an abandoned house full of thieves with guns?"

Reede took a deep drink of the beer and didn't answer.

"There's something that worries me," Sophie said. "If this man has lived in Edilean for years, won't he know a lot of the guests at the party? Won't he be suspicious when different people show up?"

"That's why most of the people coming to the party have no idea what's going on."

"But isn't that — ?" She broke off, not wanting to say the obvious.

"Dangerous?" Reede asked. "Yes, but it's worse for you. If these men had any idea that you could identify them . . . Sophie, I don't want to think about that."

He set aside his empty plate and bottle, put his feet up and leaned against the headboard. When he put out his arm, it seemed natural that Sophie should sit beside him, her head on his shoulder.

"Your job will be to talk to every male there," he said. "Only you can identify the voice."

"But you heard the other two. You even saw them."

"Jeff Ames said they'll nab the two we saw in the house right away. We know they'll be in costumes that cover them."

"With itchy fur."

"Right," Reede said. "Agents will put on the costumes so the leader doesn't know they're missing. Jeff said I was to leave you and go identify them, but I told him what he could do with that plan."

Turning, he looked at her and put his hand to the side of her face. "It still startles me how beautiful you are. If we ever get out of here . . ."

He bent as though to kiss her, but Sophie pulled back. "I think it's time you removed your mask," she whispered as she put her arms up to untie it.

Reede reacted quickly. One moment he was on the bed next to Sophie, the next he was standing and looming over her. "I better go . . . uh, check on everything." He left the bedroom.

Sophie sat there, blinking at the closed door. She was almost beginning to think there was something *wrong* with his face. Maybe in one of his heroic rescues he'd been wounded, scarred even. Maybe that's why he didn't like being in Edilean, because people stared at him. Maybe he preferred being in Third World countries because he fit in there. His scars or disfigurement weren't as noticeable.

195

Or maybe he just liked running around in a mask once a year. Sophie stood up, smoothed down the beautiful silk dress Sara had made for her, and went out to the living room. It was showtime.

Three hours! Sophie thought. She and Reede had been dancing and talking to the other people at the party for three whole hours — and it seemed like twenty.

Reede was better at socializing than Sophie was. While holding her hand, he went to every male at the party and said he was trying to guess which cousin was under the disguise. With this game he got each person to talk. Of course they ran into several people who were young FBI agents, and Sophie soon realized that was part of their verification of her as a witness. If she said one of them was the man she'd heard, she would have been discredited. But no one sounded like the man.

At nine-thirty a helmeted man wearing a gladiator costume — which meant he had on very little clothing — took her away from Reede for a slow dance.

"How are you holding up?"

She couldn't see his face, but she'd recognize his raspy voice anywhere. Mike. "You look . . ." He had an incredibly beautiful body!

"Don't say it. This getup is Sara's idea of a joke. Have you heard any voices you recognize?"

"None. Have you found the bomb?"

"Yes," he said.

Sophie gave him a smile of joy. "I've been worried."

"All of us have been, but we brought in some dogs and found it."

"Which building was it in?"

"Welsch House. It's one of the oldest in town. Sara got so mad when she heard where it was I had to send her home." Mike whirled Sophie about to the music, then drew her closer. "So how are you and the doc getting along?"

Sophie glanced at Reede standing by the far wall and talking to a man dressed like Daniel Boone. Nearby was a woman in a Martha Washington costume. "Good," she said.

"That's all?"

Sophie smiled. "Maybe better than that. We get on well and he makes me feel that I can do things."

"Not like home, huh?"

Startled, she looked at him.

"I see things about people," he said. "I

saw you on the day you arrived in town and now you look different. Your eyes have changed."

"A lot has happened in these few days," she said.

"And it's my guess that even more happened before you got here, didn't it?"

Sophie's face drained of color. Mike was a retired detective who had connections with the FBI. Had he been told of Sophie's thievery? When this was over, would he arrest her?

Mike was watching her intently. "I was talking about the beer incident," he said softly.

"Beer?" She had to think to know what he meant. "Oh, right. That." She was so relieved that he wasn't referring to a much more serious matter that she relaxed.

"Sophie, if you need any help on anything — legal, criminal, whatever — let me know. Nothing will shock me."

"Shock you about what?" Reede asked as he cut in between them.

"Sophie had some problems just before she arrived in Edilean. Maybe you heard about her nearly being run over and pouring beer over the driver's head."

"I heard about it," Reede mumbled.

"Have you seen Russell?" Sophie asked.

"He was there that night so he knows who the man is. I thought I'd ask him."

"And he couldn't lie," Mike said, with barely concealed merriment. "I haven't seen the preacher, but Roan saw it all, and he's over there. He's the Viking. Sara had to order the horns for his helmet from Texas. I'm sure Roan would *love* to tell you about the man who almost committed a hit-and-run. And, Sophie, if you find the man and want to press charges, let me know. I can arrange it for you. Reede, you don't look so good. Maybe you better lay off the booze tonight. Ames is calling me, I gotta go."

Sophie smiled at Mike's back as he walked away. "He's a nice man."

"He has a mean streak in him wider than the Shenandoahs," Reede said as he took her hand to lead her to the dance floor.

"Why would you say that?" Sophie asked. "He seems —"

"Let's go talk to that man in the Hobbit costume."

"I'd rather talk to Rowan."

"Roan," Reede said as he led her to the other side of the room. "Roan is a bore and he'll make a pass at you."

Sophie didn't like the proprietary way Reede was treating her and she jerked her hand from his. "And that's okay because

I'm not in a committed relationship," she said.

Reede halted. "If you think that, then you don't understand small towns. My mother has already booked the church for you and me."

His answer was so absurd that she couldn't help but blink at him. "Do I get to choose my dress?"

Reede's face was serious. "Yes. And your china pattern, but that's it. Edilean does the rest."

"And who chooses the mask you'll wear?"

At that Reede laughed. "Who would want to see *me* when I'm beside such beauty as yours?"

She couldn't top that. "Okay, so no Roan the Viking to be competition. Lead me to the Hobbit. But I warn you that if there are any more gladiators here I'm getting back on the horse."

"Any more Vikings *or* gladiators and I'm going to throw you across the horse and ride away. Damned relatives!"

Behind him, Sophie was smiling.

Another hour went by and she was tired and wanted to leave the party. Half the guests had gone home, few of them aware of what had been going on. Since it was after ten and there'd been no explosion, the thief knew his plan wasn't going to work.

"He must be gone by now," Sophie said to Reede. They were standing to one side, watching the few couples who were left.

"Mike says they've been questioning the two guys they caught and they don't know where this guy Pete works in Edilean — or even what his real name is. To catch him, they're going to have to have a lineup that includes every man in town, and even then they probably won't identify him. They're saying . . ." He trailed off.

"Saying what?"

"That they know nothing about a planted bomb and that whoever heard them talking is a liar. Sorry."

Sophie didn't want to look at Reede. Once it was found out that she'd stolen the Treeborne cookbook, her credibility would be gone. No identification she made would stand up in court. "I think I'll go to the restroom," she said and made her way to the back.

When she got inside, she had to resist the urge to start crying. Since she'd arrived in Edilean it had almost been magic. The outside world was full of men like Carter and the man who'd nearly run over her. But as soon as she'd crossed the town line, it had all changed. She'd entered the enchanted town of Brigadoon, a.k.a. Edilean, where everyone was nice and so honest and open. There'd been the welcome from Dr. Reede's three employees. The kindness of the other women — they'd almost begged to go to the grocery for Sophie and to run out to buy pillows — had been so welcoming to her, a Newcomer.

And as for Reede, she didn't know where to begin. He was the sweetest, kindest, most . . . well, heroic man she'd ever met. She'd never believed that there were men like him in the world. No deviousness, no lies, no ulterior motives, just honor and . . . and kisses.

What made Sophie nearly cry was that she didn't have that same honor. She was a liar and a thief. She'd stolen a book that was the backbone, no, the entire skeletal system, of a major company. Nearly everyone in her hometown worked for Treeborne Foods. Would what Sophie had done put them out of work?

She put her hands on the counter by the sink and her head down as she fought back tears. When the door opened she quickly stood upright and grabbed a paper towel. The woman she'd seen before, dressed as Martha Washington, came in, barely glanced at Sophie, then went into a stall and closed the door.

Sophie opened the little bag hanging from her wrist and started to repair her makeup. As she put on lipstick, she looked in the mirror toward the stall the woman had just taken. Had she heard Sophie's sniffling? To her surprise, she saw that the woman's buckled shoes were on backward. It took her a moment to understand. She was standing up in the stall.

Sophie did her best to remain calm. Slowly, she put her lipstick back and waited, but the woman — the *man* — didn't leave the stall. Sophie left the restroom, then stood outside the door, rummaging inside her bag, as though looking for something. After a few minutes the person came out and again looked at Sophie, but this time his eyes showed his appreciation of her cleavage. Under the heavy makeup, she could see what looked to be the beginning of dark whiskers.

She followed him down the short hall, and when they entered the ballroom, Sophie looked around for a familiar face. Mike wasn't far away. She caught his eye and pointed at the back of Martha Washington.

After that, everything happened at once. Reede appeared out of nowhere, his strong arm going around her waist and leading her out of the building. Her job was done and he wanted her out of there.

ELEVEN

Reede refilled Sophie's champagne glass. "You *should* feel good," he said. "If it had been up to me I would have left before Osmond showed up."

They were in Kim's house and Reede's phone hadn't stopped buzzing as Mike kept him informed of what was going on.

"He was an actuary?" Sophie asked as she sipped her second glass.

"Yes, which meant he knew a lot about the finances of people in town. My parents used him for their retirement plan."

She was looking across the kitchen island at Reede. He was still wearing that damned mask and she'd had enough of it. "Off!" she said.

"What?"

"The mask. It's time for the great reveal." When he started to speak, she put up her hand. "No excuses. I don't care if you're covered in scars or if you're the ugliest man alive. I want to *see* you."

Reede put down his champagne flute, then slowly, oh so very, very slowly put his hands to the back of his head to untie the mask. He fumbled with it.

"You want some help?"

"Sure," he said and there was such despair in his voice that Sophie's heart went out to him. Was his face *that* disfigured?

She walked around the counter to him. He was sitting on a stool, so his face was level with hers, and she worked at the knot of the strings. "Who tied it like this?"

"Me," Reede said and his voice sounded like a man standing before a firing squad. "I was afraid it would come off so I double knotted it."

"Triple, quadruple," she murmured. "I think I saw some scissors in a drawer and —"

Reede took her hands in his. "Sophie, I think I should tell you that —"

He broke off because suddenly all the lights went out and they were standing in darkness.

Neither of them moved and Reede kept hold of Sophie's hand.

"Do you know where the breakers are?" Sophie asked.

"In Kim's workroom. You stay here and

I'll check." As Reede made his way across the living room, his phone buzzed and he took it out of his pocket. It was from Colin Frazier, the sheriff. YOU OWE ALL OF US the text message read and it took Reede a full minute to understand.

"Is everything all right?" Sophie asked.

"I'm not sure but I think the power is out for the entire neighborhood."

Sophie made her way to the front door and opened it. Sure enough, there wasn't a light on in any house that she could see. "It's all dark," she said. "All the lights —"

She didn't finish because Reede had crossed the room in a few long strides and his arms were around her.

"You were wonderful today," he said as he put his hands on her shoulders. "You walked across that beam as though you were auditioning for the Cirque du Soleil."

"I was scared to death," she answered as she put her hands up to his face. "It's off," she said and for the first time felt his skin without the intrusion of a mask. She ran her hands over his upper cheeks, across his nose, then to his eyes. He closed them as she ran her fingertips over his eyelids, and up to his brows. "I thought maybe they'd been burned off, that maybe you'd had an accident."

"No," he said softly. "A couple of times I came close to being killed, but I wasn't. Sophie . . ." he whispered.

She knew what he meant. There was a bond between them that she'd never felt before. She'd thought she'd been in love with Carter, but in all their months of dating they'd never shared anything like what she and Reede had been through. She and Reede hadn't known each other for long, but in life experience they'd been through years.

She put her face up to him to kiss. His lips came down on hers. She was smiling, happy in anticipation.

But when his lips touched hers it was as though a bolt of electricity shot through her. She drew back to look at him, but it was so dark she couldn't even see an outline of his face. "Oh!" was all she managed to say.

"Holy crap!" Reede mumbled. "So this is what they meant."

"Who and what?" she murmured.

"Troubadours. All those dippy songs. My cousins who bore me with their stories of having found True Love."

Sophie well knew what he was talking about because she'd felt it too.

For a moment they hesitated, standing there motionless, sightlessly staring into the dark, then all at once they reacted. They were without thought, without even human consciousness as the tore each other's clothes off.

Sophie's low-cut dress easily slid off her shoulders, and Reede groaned when he felt her breasts. It was a primal sound that came from deep within him.

At her urging, the coat fell from his body and his shirt easily came off. The only thing in her mind was that she had to touch him, *had* to put her skin next to his.

Her mouth followed his every garment as she kissed as much of him as she could reach. When the shirt was gone she at last was able to run her hands over his chest, that beautiful sculpted chest she'd seen outlined when she saw him on the horse. Pecs, abs, all of it beautifully cut. As a sculptor, she saw him as a work of art.

"Okay?" he whispered, his lips on her ear.

"I want to make you in clay."

"Fine with me. Clay, in the swimming pool, on top of the kitchen cabinets. Anywhere. Sophie, you are the most beautiful woman I've ever seen."

His lips went to hers and she gasped when he picked her naked body up and placed her on the sofa. When he stretched out on top of her she arched her head back in pure pleasure.

Protection, she thought. She and Carter had always used protection, but now . . . With this man . . . It was the last thought she had as he began to enter her. She put her legs around his waist so he came closer to her.

Reede took his time. His strokes were slow and deep, and she could tell that he was having difficulty restraining himself. That he so much wanted to give her pleasure made her feel even better.

As the crescendo began, all thoughts left Sophie until she was a mass of feeling. There was only this man and this moment.

"I can't hold back any longer," he said.

"Please don't," Sophie said and wrapped her body around his with all the strength she had.

His long, hard, deep strokes took her to new heights of pleasure. She'd never before felt such desire, never felt such a *need* of another human being. Images seemed to flash through her mind. Reede on a horse. Reede on the ladder, his arms up, beckoning her to fall into them. Reede laughing; Reede kissing.

They came together in each other's arms, bodies entwined, united in the most ancient of ways, lips touching skin, feeling breath and heartbeats.

"Sophie, I think I may be . . ." He trailed off, not finishing his sentence.

They both knew that it was too early for words of emotions and feelings.

A minute later she was in his arms and he was carrying her into the bedroom. "Don't tell my sister what I used her bedroom for," he said.

"And what do you plan to do in the bed?" Sophie asked as he put her down and lay beside her.

"Anything I can think of," he said as he rolled to his side and kissed her neck. "First, I plan to give you the most thorough physical exam anyone has ever had. I want to know every inch of your body."

"And what about you?" she asked as she turned toward him and her hand ran down his side. Her fingertips teased along the ridges of muscle.

"Examine all of me you want. I'm yours for the taking." He kissed her again, his hands running over her body, touching, caressing — and driving Sophie to new heights of desire.

It was three hours later when they stopped. Exhausted, fatigued beyond imagining, they snuggled together, sweaty and sated, and drifted in and out of sleep.

"Find us a house," Reede murmured into her ear.

"I'll look for one for you," she said, her eyes closed. She'd never felt so good in her life. This man whose face she'd never seen made her feel as though she could conquer the earth, as though anything was possible. She wanted to stay in his arms forever.

"For us. You and me together."

"Mmmm," was all Sophie could say. Her bottom was snuggled against the bare maleness of him. She wasn't a virgin, but in this she was. She'd never spent a whole night with a man. There'd always been other people waiting for her or she'd had responsibilities elsewhere.

Reede kissed her neck and pulled her even closer. "Roommates if you want."

She was finally beginning to understand what he was saying. "I would like to get out of Kim's house. I feel that I'm encroaching. But us together? No, it's too soon."

"I know it's too soon, but I also know my own mind. When something is right, I know it. There's been a lot of . . . Well, more than my share of women, but I've always held something back."

He didn't have to give his reason, but she knew it. One time he'd given his all to a woman and she'd thrown it back in his face.

It wasn't easy to recover from rejection like that — as she well knew from her own life experience.

"Sophie, you bring out the best in me. You make me want to . . . to be nice to people."

She couldn't help laughing at what he'd said. "But you *are* nice."

"Not really, but that's not the point. I want you to get to know me better. The real me."

"This isn't the real you?" Her voice was teasing as she ran her hand over his bare chest.

"No," he said, and he was serious. "You're going to find out things about me that you don't like."

"I stole a cookbook," Sophie blurted, then put her hand over her mouth.

Reede chuckled. "I don't think shoplifting is a cause —"

"No!" She turned in his arms to face him. It was too dark to see his face but she could feel him looking at her. "Earl's real name is Lewis Carter Treeborne the Third. He's heir to the Treeborne fortune and I stole their cookbook."

It took Reede a moment to understand. "You mean the Treeborne cookbook that the ads say is the basis for all their foods?"

"Yes," Sophie said. Her body had gone rigid and it suddenly seemed too intimate to be so close together. But when she tried to pull away, Reede wouldn't let her. She didn't know why she'd told him and now he probably thought she was a horrible person.

"I guess this was the package you wanted sent back?"

Sophie nodded.

To her disbelief, Reede began to laugh.

"It's not funny!" she said. "I'm a *thief*!"

He tried to get himself under control as he snuggled her down against him. "You told me he said you were . . . What was it?"

"A summer romance."

"I guess that means he had someone else all along."

"Oh yeah. A girl named Traci, and her father and Mr. Treeborne are friends."

Reede lost his humor as he began to see exactly what had been done to Sophie. She'd been used by some rich kid, then discarded when it was time for more serious matters. "I'm sorry," he said. "That shouldn't have happened to you. To anyone, for that matter. Did you make a copy of the cookbook?"

"Of course not!" she said, sounding indignant, then lowered her voice. "Besides, it's written in code."

"Code?"

"That's what it looks like or maybe it's some obscure language I've never seen before."

"Wasn't the woman who wrote it Italian?"

"That's what Treeborne Foods says, but who knows?"

Reede was quiet for a moment as he stroked Sophie's hair. The spread was over them, and it was warm in the room. "Do you think this guy Carter will come after you?"

"If he knew where I was he might. I don't really know him. I thought I did, but I don't."

"I think you know him rather well," Reede said. "He lies without conscience. He's ruled by his domineering father, and he's greedy. In order to get his share of the company he'll court and probably marry whomever will further the business. Does that sound about right?"

"It sounds exactly right," she said.

"So where is it?"

"Hidden in plain sight," she said. "Middle drawer of Kim's desk. I'll be glad when it's gone."

"I'll take care of it."

She smiled in the darkness and his words

comforted her so much that sleep began to take over her. Reede was so warm and he made her feel so safe that she soon dozed off.

Reede held her and he felt her fall asleep, but he was wide awake. His mind was too full of all that was going on in his life for him to be able to sleep soundly.

Sophie had turned his world upside down. A week ago all he could think about was how many days before he could get out of Edilean forever. He complained about Betsy's *x*'d calendar, how she counted the days until Tristan returned, but the truth was that Reede checked that calendar a dozen times a day. He too counted the days. How long was it before he could leave and go back . . . Back to what? To flying from one town to another, from one danger to the next?

There were times when he'd been so lonely, when he'd missed home so much that he'd wanted to leave right then.

He kissed Sophie's forehead, and she snuggled closer to him. She made him feel needed. She made him feel as though he had a purpose in life, a place to go. She made him feel that he belonged.

When Sophie turned over in his arms, he slipped out of bed, opened Kim's bedside table drawer, and withdrew a flashlight. He hadn't told Sophie it was there.

Reede made his way into the living room and removed the torn envelope from the desk drawer. It didn't take him long to dress and slip out the front door. He needed food and he needed someone to talk to.

TWELVE

Reede raised his hand to tap on the window of the diner, but Al saw him and unlocked the door. Many times Reede had been out all night with a patient and had stopped at Al's for breakfast. The diner wasn't open yet, but Al would fry a couple of eggs and toast bread. Reede would sit at the bar and eat and they'd talk while Al made coleslaw for the day.

"What are you lookin' so glum about?" Al asked as he poured Reede's coffee. "Everybody in town knows you spent the night with that little doll Sophie. After they turned out their lights, that is."

When Reede looked up with a doleful expression, Al chuckled. "Let me see if I get this right. You're in love with her but she thinks you're somebody else and when she finds out the truth that you, from what I heard, nearly killed her, she's gonna hate you."

"I think 'love' is a little strong. I only met her a few days ago," Reede said.

"And you two haven't been apart since she came to town. So what mask are you wearin' today?"

"I was thinking of a motorcycle helmet. I'd say the clasp was broken and that I can't get it off." Reede looked at Al as though asking his opinion.

"Ever think of manning up and showing her your naked face and taking the consequences?"

"No," Reede said honestly.

Al shook his head. "I'll give it to you that you two have done a lot in the time you've had. Last night I heard that somebody tried to blow up the whole town. That true?"

"More or less."

"And that your girlfriend stopped it?"

"She was the one who identified the thief. Peter Osmond."

"That insurance guy?"

"He's an actuary, but yeah, that's him. He's in custody now."

Al put a plate of eggs, bacon, ham, and heavily buttered toast in front of Reede. It was all swimming in grease. Not good for you, but the taste was divine.

"I hear you rode down the streets on one of the McTern horses. Had on those girly boots, like in that movie *Pretty Woman.*"

"Not exactly, but close enough," Reede said.

"And you and that girl walked across the roof of the old Haynes house."

"It was inside and on a beam, not the roof, and who told you all this?"

"Who hasn't told me? Those three women you boss around come in here all the time and they don't talk of anything but you. They say you're not like —"

"Don't say it!" Reede half shouted. "I'm not Tristan. Model beautiful, loved by everyone, always patient Tristan. He's so good I don't know why he hasn't been taken directly up to heaven."

Al was unperturbed by Reede's anger. "Same reason the devil ain't reachin' up to grab *you*!"

Reede filled his mouth and calmed down. "So what am I going to do about Sophie?"

"Nothing," Al said. "Nothing you can do. You nearly killed the poor girl. I heard she had to jump into some trees just to keep from being run down by you. You examine her bruised places?"

"No, I didn't examine —" Reede stopped because he knew Al was trying to make him angry. "I like her. I like her a lot. I've not liked a woman this much since —"

"Don't dive into that pool of self-pity again!" Al said as he put a couple of quarts of mayonnaise on the cabbage he'd chopped. That mayonnaise was one of the highest calorie foods known didn't bother him at all — and he had the giant stomach to prove it. "That Chawnley girl did you a favor by dumping you."

"Yeah, I know," Reede said as he put even more butter on the already saturated toast. "If I'd married her and I met Sophie now, it would be even worse."

Al started to say that if Reede were happily married he might not be so interested in another woman, even one as pretty as Sophie. But he didn't say that. Instead, he took pity on the young man. "How bad is it for you?"

When Reede looked up at Al, all he felt was in his eyes.

Al gave a low whistle. "All of you oldies seem to fall so hard for a woman that it eats you up. I'm glad my family is a Newcomer." Al's ancestors had settled in Edilean in the 1880s. "You need to make a plan. Hey! I know what you should do."

Reede looked up with eyes of hope.

"Get a mask tattooed on your face. It'll hide your identity forever."

At first Reede frowned, but then he gave a

low laugh. "I guess I deserved that. I know I'm going to have to come clean eventually and take the consequences."

"That would have worked at first but now you've lied to her for days. My guess is that when she learns how you've humiliated her in front of the whole town she's gonna be pretty damned mad. If she's anything like my wife she'll wait until night and set your bed on fire — with you in it."

"You are a real joy," Reede said. "I'm so glad I came to you for advice."

"You came here for my gourmet cuisine," Al said without so much as a hint of a smile. "The advice is free."

Reede had finished his food, but he still sat there on the stool. "You know of a house I can rent for Sophie?"

"Don't your rich relatives own most of this town?"

"Yeah, but I'm looking for something special. It has to have a place where she can do her sculpture. She makes things in clay."

Al stood there blinking at Reede for a moment. "You mean like an art studio?"

"Exactly like one."

"Old man Gains's wife used to do crafts and he built her a little place out in back of their house. Between you and me I think she was more interested in getting away from him than in twisting all those weeds around wires. But then the tourists seemed to like them."

"Barry Gains? Isn't he — ?"

"In a home in Richmond now. After his wife passed there was no one to take care of him and his Alzheimer's was bad."

"So what happened to the house?"

"It was rented out until six months ago, but that guy moved. It's empty now, and the realty company is supposed to be looking after it but they don't. You wanta get it for your Sophie? Like the pumpkin eater?"

"What does that mean?" Reede asked.

"Peter, Peter Pumpkin Eater, had a wife but couldn't keep her; put her in a pumpkin shell and there he kept her very well," Al quoted.

"You know, don't you," Reede said, "that all those old rhymes are based on truth. Some man probably locked up his philandering wife and some smart-ass made a rhyme about it."

Al didn't blink. "You want the house so your would-be wife doesn't take to philandering? Keep her busy making mud pies?"

Reede started to defend himself but changed his mind. "I want to keep her from leaving town when she finds out the truth about me. And stop looking at me like that.

Desperate men do desperate things. You have the number of the Realtor?"

"On speed dial. My wife is handling the place — and if you're helping on the rent I'm going to tell her to double it because she's got a tenant who will pay anything for a pumpkin shell."

As he got up to leave, Reede didn't protest because being overcharged on rent was the least of his worries.

When he got to his car, he reached under the seat and withdrew the envelope containing the Treeborne cookbook. He'd told Sophie that he'd make sure it was sent to his friend in New Zealand, and he meant to. What he hadn't promised her was that he wouldn't look at it — or make a copy of it. Sophie seemed to think — hope — that the Treebornes wouldn't press charges, that if they got their precious cookbook back they wouldn't tear the world apart looking for her.

But Reede wasn't so sure. They might worry that a copy of the cookbook would be put on the Internet. If that happened the secrets of Treeborne Foods would be revealed. And even if all that was shown was how much oregano was used in the spaghetti sauce, it would kill an ad campaign that was over a hundred years old. They'd no longer be able to flaunt their "secret" recipes when the Internet was plastered with them.

Maybe the Treebornes were trustworthy, but from what Reede had heard, they played dirty. Father and son together had used and discarded a sweet girl like Sophie without even a backward glance.

He drove to his office, made a photocopy of the old cookbook, packaged it, addressed it to his friend, and put it in a drop-off box. Maybe he wouldn't need the copy but it was better to be prepared.

"It's perfect," Sophie said as she looked around the house. It wasn't very big and it needed cleaning and repairs, but it was more than suitable. There were two bedrooms and two baths, a pretty living room with a sunporch to one side. She could see herself sitting in there on rainy days while Reede . . .

She had to look away to clear her vision. It seemed that in just a few days she'd gone from one man to another. All summer her mind had been full of Carter and now there was only Reede.

All the bad that had happened to her seemed to fade. Everything had been replaced by Reede, and it was like she'd known him all her life. What he wanted and needed were of great importance to her, but she couldn't possibly move in with him. Could she? She'd just seen the little studio where she could work, even though she had no idea what she would do. Maybe it could be a shop where she could sell her work to tourists.

She looked back at the sunroom. Who was she kidding? She wanted Reede to leave Edilean, and she wanted to go with him. She'd like to pack a bag and . . . Do what? Reede would need a woman who was a doctor or a nurse, not someone whose only talent was carving things. Of course she could cook and that might be useful.

She knew she was being ridiculous. Reede was going to leave Edilean in two and a half years, and there was no way he'd want a woman with him. Kim had always complained that her brother was a loner, that he got restless after even four days at home with them.

Sophie knew she needed to think about herself. To make plans for her own future. When Kim returned from her extended honeymoon she'd be living in Edilean, and when Jecca finished her training in New York, she too would be living there. It made sense for Sophie to stay in Virginia. She had nothing waiting for her back in her hometown. The Treeborne name was everywhere — and Sophie never wanted to see it again.

And by the time Lisa graduated from college, her world would be different. Sophie very much doubted if Lisa would return to her hometown. So what was there for Sophie? Taking care of her odious stepfather? Watching Carter get married and have children? Would his family come into a restaurant where Sophie was working and she'd wait on them?

The Realtor was looking at her and waiting for an answer. She was a small woman and thin to the point of emaciation. Sophie couldn't imagine her as the wife of the man who owned the diner. His left leg weighed more than this woman did.

"Okay," Sophie said. "I'll take it."

"I have the rental agreement here," she said, "so if you'll sign it I'll give you the keys."

"I don't have a local check," Sophie said and knew that she couldn't use the small amount she had in the bank back home anyway. The Treebornes owned the bank, and they'd see where she cashed it. "And I haven't been paid yet so . . ."

"That's all right. Dr. Reede is vouching for you, so that's good enough for us."

Sophie turned away so her frown couldn't

be seen. She didn't like being dependant on someone, especially not a man. To have slept with him one night and the next day to be renting a house with his help made her feel less than virtuous. If the Realtor had said Reede was paying for the place, Sophie would have walked out. But he was only verifying that she did have a job and that she wasn't likely to run out on the lease. It would be the same if Kim were her reference.

"As soon as I get paid I'll give you the deposit," Sophie said.

"There is no deposit. The owner is so glad to have someone take this place he's waiving that. Rent is due the last day of each month. Send a check to my office or leave it at the diner."

Sophie signed the lease, the Realtor handed her the keys, said congratulations, and left.

For a moment, Sophie just stood where she was. Everything was happening so very fast. Carter, then Reede, then . . . The truth was that she didn't know where things were going. Her mind was still full of the attempted robbery, the masked party, and, well, spending the night with a man whose face she had never seen.

She looked around the little kitchen. It

was nice, not large, but it had a big walk-in pantry that made it usable. She couldn't help smiling as she thought of the meals she and Reede would cook together in the little kitchen. Would they keep the house even if they traveled a lot?

Sophie shook her head at that thought. One night with a man and she was planning their life together.

But as she picked up her purse, her smile wouldn't go away. Sometimes good things *did* happen to people. They didn't seem to happen to her, but maybe her luck was changing.

She went out to the driveway to the rental car and drove back into Edilean. It was just a couple of miles and she thought that it would be good exercise to walk. But not today. Right now all she wanted was to see Reede. That thought made her smile even broader. Actually *see* him. For a moment she had a vision of the two of them laughingly telling people that they were . . . what? In deep like? . . . before she even saw his face. What a truly romantic story it would make.

She parked in the back of Reede's office. This morning she'd been disappointed to awaken to find an empty bed, but she understood. Maybe he'd been called out on a medical emergency. Maybe right now he was saving a life or delivering a baby.

Even though it was Sunday, the back door to the office was unlocked, which Sophie took to mean that someone was there. As she stepped inside, she heard the quiet sounds of someone on a keyboard. It must be one of the women who worked for Reede, part of his adoring entourage.

Quietly, Sophie walked down the hallway and up the stairs to his apartment. Her idea was to make him lunch and have it ready when he returned from wherever he was. The apartment door was unlocked, and she turned the handle silently so as not to warn whoever was downstairs. The women were always so very helpful to Sophie. Anything she needed, they eagerly got for her. But sometimes she felt they were, well, almost invasive. It was as though they were afraid she was going to do something they couldn't control. Such as what? she wondered, but had no real answer. Maybe they just wanted to make sure no one hurt their beloved Dr. Reede.

The door was silent as she opened it, and she tiptoed inside the apartment. To her delight, the first thing she saw was Reede. He was stretched out on the couch, sound asleep, his arm thrown over his face. She smiled down at him and couldn't resist touching his hand. She wanted to curl up beside him.

He had on a T-shirt and jeans and she couldn't help remembering their night together and how well she'd come to know his body. She remembered her hands on his chest, running down his arms and feeling the muscles there. She thought of his mouth on her body and the pleasure he'd given her. Reede was a thousand times a better lover than Carter ever thought of being. Last night she'd felt as though she and Reede were, well, almost as though they were in love.

When Reede moved, he lowered his arm.

It was as though time stood still. Sophie didn't move as she stared at his face. He was quite a handsome man. She knew the lower half of his face well, and if it were dark, she could have identified him by touch.

But it wasn't dark, and the man asleep on the couch was the one who had been driving the car that had nearly run over her. He was the man she'd poured beer over.

They all know, was her foremost thought. *All* of them know. Russell, the Baptist minister, had driven her to Kim's house, and she'd told him she had a job with Dr.

231

Reede. He'd known that Sophie had just poured beer over her boss.

The women who worked for Reede knew. No wonder they'd kept her locked away upstairs and were so willing to get things for her. They didn't want her to go into town, where she might find out the truth.

But why? she wondered. Why had they all worked to keep the secret?

She didn't know the answer to that question and right now she was feeling too humiliated to care.

She gave one last glance at Reede, still asleep on the couch, and left the apartment. Whoever was in the office was still there, but Sophie didn't want to see her. Right now all she wanted in the world was to get out of Edilean and never look back.

When she reached the parking lot, she got into the rental car, and for a moment she put her head against the steering wheel. But she looked up again. If she let herself think too hard she'd start crying and never stop. First, she had to go to Kim's house and get her clothes. At the thought of her "friend" she felt a surge of anger rise in her. Kim must have known about her and Reede, but Kim hadn't said a word. But then Reede was her brother while Sophie was just a college roommate who'd disappeared for years.

She was shaking as she turned onto the road to Kim's house, but then she stopped. The rented house! Just a couple of hours ago she'd signed a year-long lease for a house, a place she'd thought she might share with a man who was a liar of the highest caliber.

Sophie turned left and went to Al's Diner instead. Al's wife had said Sophie could leave the rent checks at the restaurant. Would the woman sue when Sophie tried to get out of the contract? If so, she'd have to get in line behind the Treeborne frozen foods empire.

When Al saw the pretty young woman enter his diner he instantly knew she'd found out. Last night he and his wife had had an argument, something that was unusual for them.

"I think it's disgusting!" she'd half yelled at him. "This entire town is keeping Dr. Reede's identity a secret from that girl." His wife wasn't from Edilean, hadn't grown up there. Al joked that she was too new to even be called a Newcomer, but she didn't find that funny. As a Realtor, she hated not telling people of the two societies in the town, one of them so exclusive that only birth got you included.

She'd been especially angry about Sophie.

Like everyone else in town, his wife had been on the receiving end of Dr. Reede's bad temper. And she'd cheered when she heard of a pretty young woman pouring beer over his head. What had made her angry was when her husband told her Sophie had a job working for Dr. Reede, but she didn't know he was the jerk who'd nearly killed her.

"So how's he planning to keep *that* a secret?" she'd asked her husband, her eyes boring into his.

Al mumbled something about Halloween and masks. He'd told it like it was meant to make her laugh, but she didn't so much as crack a smile. "This town has gone too far," she said.

It had taken all his persuasion to get his wife to show Sophie the little house that had the craft studio in the back. After Sophie had signed the contract, his wife came to the diner and slapped the papers on the counter. "If that girl is hurt by this, so help me, Al, I'll leave this one-horse town for good — and you with it. Enough is enough!" She'd stormed out, anger making her heels click loudly on the floor.

So now it looked like pretty little Sophie had found out the truth — and Al didn't know when he'd ever felt so bad. She looked

234

like her whole world had come crashing down on her head. Had she been a different type of woman she might have been angry, but Sophie looked like there wasn't much fight left in her.

Al's three children were all boys and his wife never stopped telling him that he knew nothing about females, but he could almost imagine what it must feel like to be the butt of a joke made by the entire town. For the first time in his life he was glad he wasn't an "oldie," a descendant of the seven founding families.

There weren't too many customers in the diner, so he motioned to one of the boys to take over the grill. Al knew no one could make a burger as good as his, but now and then he'd let them try.

"What do you need?" he asked Sophie as she stopped in front of the counter.

"A new life," she said under her breath, then looked up at Al. "I wonder if I could talk to your wife for a moment. I'm not sure I have her card, and I need . . ." She trailed off, unable to speak. She kept remembering things she'd thought, things she'd done and seen. When she was at Sara and Mike's house, they'd all been staring at her so hard that Sophie hid out in the bedroom. What was it Reede said? They were all wondering when she was going to murder him. It made sense now. They'd all known that Sophie was being ridiculed by Reede, played for a fool. Used.

Last night he got what he wanted. Would he collect bets now? Had he, rich boy doctor, taken odds that he could get the little country girl into his bed without her even seeing his face?

Al reached for the coffeepot and filled the cup in front of Sophie and she sat down at the counter, but she didn't take a drink. "You can tear up that lease agreement if you want," he said softly so no one else could hear.

Sophie kept her head down and nodded.

Al leaned toward her. "Does it make any difference that the doc was in here earlier telling me he was crazy about you?"

"Started to fall in love with me, did he?" she asked with so much sarcasm — and hurt — in her voice that Al winced.

She rummaged in her bag and withdrew her key ring. She had a key to Reede's apartment and she wanted to take it off, but her hands were shaking so much she couldn't do it.

Al took the ring from her and started to remove the key. But when he looked at Sophie he changed his mind. He put his hand on her arm and pulled her up. "Come with me," he said.

"I —" she began.

"Unless you want the whole town gossiping about your every look, come with me."

Sophie didn't have the strength to disagree, so she followed Al through the door at the back of the counter and into a little office. The big desk had chairs on either side, and masses of papers and catalogs were everywhere. As she took a seat, he shut the door, pulled down the shade, then took a bottle of whiskey out of a cabinet and poured a shot. "Drink it."

Sophie hesitated. Her alcoholic stepfather had made her quite adverse to any form of alcohol, but after what she'd just found out, she needed any courage she could get. She tossed the shot back in one gulp, put the empty glass on the desk, then leaned back in the chair. "You want to hear the whole story about how I was duped by the local doctor? He certainly got me back for pouring beer on him, didn't he? Were you in one of the betting pools?"

Al sat down on the other side of the desk, his hands on his big belly, his apron spotted with grease. His first inclination was to tell her it wasn't like that, that Dr. Reede was really worried and yes, maybe he *was* in love with her. But Al didn't say that. "So what are you going to do now?"

"Get out of this town."

"Good idea," Al said. "Go home to your family and let them take care of you."

Sophie sat there for a moment, blinking at him. She didn't really have a family. Since her sister Lisa was in college, that left only their alcoholic, lecherous stepfather. Her hometown was where Carter lived, home of Treeborne Foods. If she went back there she could possibly be facing a prison sentence.

"Not so good, huh?" Al asked kindly.

"No," Sophie managed to say.

"You have any friends here?"

"Kim . . ." she whispered. "Jecca."

"Ah, right, and they're not here."

Sophie looked down at her hands and shook her head. "I'll be all right," she said.

"What would you *like* to do? Other than run a truck over our bad-tempered doctor, that is? And I can tell you that if you go that road half the people in town will lend you their trucks."

"Bad . . . ?" Sophie asked, her eyes wide. "But I thought everyone loved Reede."

"That is the biggest lie you've been told."

Sophie was so shocked that she couldn't say a word, just sat there and stared at Al.

"I see that you've not been told the whole story."

"I'm the one who wasn't told *any* of the story," Sophie said as she picked up the shot glass and held it out for Al to refill.

She downed the second shot, then listened as Al told her the same story Reede had, all about his good deed of taking over for Dr. Tristan. But when Reede had told it he'd left out how he'd frowned and snapped and made people so miserable that they'd rather be sick than go to him. "Old man Baldwin was having a heart attack and he made his son-in-law drive him to Norfolk rather than have to see Dr. Reede."

"Yeah?" Sophie asked. The two shots of whiskey and Al's story were relaxing her and taking away some of her misery. "But everyone helped him lie to me. If they dislike him why would they do that?"

"You made him smile."

"I did a *lot* of things for him," she mumbled.

Al was looking at her in a fatherly way. "So how much money do you have?"

Under normal circumstances, she wouldn't think of telling a stranger that, but whiskey on an empty stomach was loosening her usual reticence. "One hundred and twenty-seven dollars. I have another three hundred and twelve in a bank, but I can't get to it because if I do they'll find me and maybe put me in jail. How long do you think it takes a package to get to New Zealand and back again?"

Al had no idea what she was talking about, but his main thought was that there was no way on earth he was going to let this young woman leave town in this condition. A very bad joke had been played on her, and he planned to do what he could to make it up to her. "What kinds of jobs have you had?"

"I've done lots of things. Do you need a waitress?"

He almost said yes, but then he had an idea. "You wouldn't like to help me out with a family dispute, would you?"

Sophie couldn't help frowning. In her previous jobs she'd twice been asked to help with "family problems." This had turned out to be a euphemism for "my wife doesn't understand me, but you do."

Al could almost read her mind and he couldn't help being flattered. "Betsy said you can make soup."

"Soup?"

Al patted his big belly. "You saw my wife. She eats two sticks of celery and thinks it's a meal. She told me she wants me to eat more soup."

Maybe it was the whiskey, but maybe it was the way Al said it all, but it almost made Sophie smile. "You want me to make you some soup?"

Al was thinking as fast as he could. What this young woman needed was a way to keep busy, something to get her mind off what the entire town had done to her. And as for that, Al knew that if he used the Edilean gossip wagon correctly he could make the oldies feel so bad that they'd do anything to help Sophie out. The question was, What could she/would she do?

"Yeah," he said. "Make some soup and sell it —" He'd meant to say to sell it in his diner. But from what he'd been told, she made those artsy soups that Druid virgins would like. They didn't really go with the theme of a 1950s diner. As for him, he thought little half-pound burgers were . . . What was that word he hated? *Metrosexual.*

Al looked around his office, searching for a solution to the problem. There were shelves of catalogs, some of them with their pages curling from age. Taped to the wall was a photo of a glass display case that he'd thought about buying but never did. That was when his wife had been nagging him to start selling grilled sandwiches. Something to do with goats and cheese.

"Do you know what a nanny sandwich is?"

"I have no idea," she said.

"Cooked on a grill. Flat."

Sophie blinked a few times. "Panini?"

"That's it." Al looked at her as though she were brilliant. "Can you make those things?"

"A monkey could be trained to make panini sandwiches. You just have to stick it between two hot plates."

Al thought for a moment, then began rummaging through a stack of papers on his desk. "Here it is." He pulled out a fairly clean page and handed it across to her.

Sophie took the paper. It was a printout of an e-mail that read: Why don't you buy that shop from me and serve something that won't kill you with every bite? It was signed Roan.

Sophie put the paper back on the desk. "Is this the Roan who was there the day I . . . ?" She didn't finish. She knew he was one of the people who'd known she was working for the man she had dumped beer on. This man Roan had been at the tavern and later at the Halloween party and had seen that she was there with Reede.

"I see you know who he is," Al said, his eyes twinkling. He was finding that he rather liked taking some of the oldies down to size. "Roan is a McTern." When he could see that that meant nothing to Sophie, he continued. "He's inherited a lot of property around here, and one of the things he owns is a little sandwich shop downtown. He's been nagging me to buy it from him."

Sophie was wondering what this had to do with her.

"The woman who was renting the place moved to Seattle. I think it was for love, but who knows? Anyway, the shop is now vacant and for rent, or for sale to me. If you want it, I can get it for you."

"A sandwich shop?" Sophie asked. "I don't know how to run a restaurant. And I can't afford anything. If I were to stay here — which I shouldn't do — I need a job where someone pays me, not the other way around. I can't keep staying at Kim's, so I don't even have a place to live."

"There's an apartment over the shop. The last time I saw it, it was full of boxes, but I think it could be okay."

"Like Reede's place," she said softly.

Al wasn't going to put up with self-pity. "Naw. This one is better. There are big windows at the front, so you can see out."

"I . . ." Sophie began and she could see a thousand things wrong with this idea. She had no money, no experience, she was the laughingstock of a whole town, she never

243

wanted to see Reede again in her entire life, and —

And this was an opportunity, she thought. Maybe, possibly, this could lead to something else. She had no idea what, but maybe there was something there. And besides, what else did she have to do? Where else did she have to go? Maybe she could turn Dr. Reede's lies into something good.

"I'll do it," she said, and she could feel her heart pounding in her chest.

Al smiled at her with pride. He couldn't feel better if Sophie were his daughter. "Why don't you . . . ?"

"Go occupy myself for a while?" Sophie supplied.

"Tell Ray to give you a burger and fries. You need to eat to get your strength up and you need to plan what you're gonna cook."

There was so much in Sophie's mind that all she could do was nod.

The second the door to the office closed, Al called Roan. "You know that little sandwich place you wanted me to buy?" he said as soon as Roan picked up.

"Damn right I do!" Roan said. "The tenants left me hanging with that thing. I'd sue if I could find them. They —"

"Never mind that now. I need the store rent free for four months."

Roan gave a scoff of laughter. "You've been drinking too much. As Kierkegaard would say —"

"Don't care what any of your relatives has to say. You need to give the new tenant the keys to that shop. My wife will draw up a lease. Four free months."

Roan was silent for a moment. "Okay, you old grease dog, what are you up to and who is this really for?"

"You know the girl who dumped beer on Reede's head?"

"Oh yeah," Roan said in a faraway voice. "I'll never forget that glorious moment. I will die with that image — Hey! Is this for *her*?! The little clone of Brigitte Bardot? The prettiest girl I've seen in years? The —"

"Keys!" Al said. "To the shop. Get them to her. She's going there now."

"I'm on the way out the door."

"Run!" Al said and clicked off the phone. He hadn't thought of it before, but big, good-looking Roan might help Sophie with a lot of her problems. The last time he'd been to see Reede as a doctor Al had been treated to a ten-minute lecture about his weight. If he'd wanted that he would have stayed home with his skinny wife. Yeah, it might be good to introduce Roan to pretty little Sophie. Smiling, Al left the office.

245

Five minutes later, Roan called back. "I'm here and waiting and I want to know what's going on."

Al told him.

THIRTEEN

By the time Sophie had parked her car downtown and walked around half of one of the squares of Edilean, she was sure she was making a mistake. What did she know about running a sandwich shop? There was no way she could do it by herself, so what was she to do for help? Ask one of the citizens of Edilean? The people who'd watched her dancing with Reede while knowing she had no idea who he was? Had they later laughed about the coming scene when she found out? Did they make wagers about how angry she was going to be at him? How amused they must have been!

As she walked toward the shop, she had a wicked thought of hiring the women who worked for Reede. "You owe me!" she'd say to them. She thought of how Heather had greeted her that first day. The young woman had been standing on Kim's porch, just waiting for Sophie to come out. And when she did, Heather practically shoved Sophie into the car. It looked like Heather was afraid Sophie would see someone in town who'd recognize her. Would someone have said "You're the girl who dumped beer over Dr. Reede's head. Good for you! It's what I've wanted to do for years."

As soon as she got to the office the women had pushed her up the stairs. And oh! how they'd lied to her. Every other word was "dear" or "our beloved." And all the while they were just trying to . . . to what? Lock her into his apartment to wait for him?

Sophie was glad for the anger that surged through her because she'd reached the shop. It was narrow, with a door on the left, big windows on the right. DAISY'S SANDWICHES AND SMOOTHIES was in pink lettering. What should Sophie rename it? Lied To? The Town Joke?

"The name's a bit over the top, isn't it?" said a male voice behind her.

She turned to look up at a big, burly man wearing jeans and a plaid flannel over an old T-shirt. She recognized him from the bar and thought maybe it was his beer she'd poured over Reede.

Roan grimaced. "I haven't been looked at with that much contempt since my wife left me. Are you a relative of hers that I don't know about?"

She didn't think what he'd said was funny. "This is a mistake," she said and turned away.

Roan put his big body in front of her to block her path. "I apologize. For all of it. But we all enjoyed it so much that we couldn't stop."

"Enjoyed it?" she said, glaring at him. "Enjoyed humiliating a stranger?"

"Hell no!" Roan said. "It was all about Reede. We all loved seeing you pour that beer over him. Everybody in town's wanted to do that, or worse, but then, we all worried what he'd do to us at our next flu shot. We're all cowards."

"He nearly ran over me," Sophie said, but his sympathy had softened her resolve. Maybe she could just look at the shop.

"That's what I heard." Roan put his hand behind her back, not touching her, but guiding her back down the sidewalk. "Didn't he crush something of yours?"

"My cell phone."

"That's expensive!" Roan unlocked the door to the sandwich shop and waited for Sophie to step inside.

"It was a throwaway." She was looking around the store. It was rather simple, with a tall glass cabinet to the left, a stainless counter behind it, tables and chairs to the right and in the back. It was all small and neat and looked to be in good condition.

"Reede should buy this place for you," Roan said.

"I don't want anything from him," she said. "Nothing at all."

"Yeah?" Roan asked, his eyes alight. He was a good-looking man, with whiskers and thick hair that had a reddish tint. He was looking at her in a way that she'd seen all her adult life — but she wasn't interested. He understood her look. "Okay," Roan said, "that can wait. What do you think of the place?"

Sophie looked at the chalkboard over the counter. It listed six flavors of smoothies and tuna salad sandwiches. "I don't know anything about the restaurant business, and the only cooking I've done is for my family."

"So make some family meals," Roan said as he leaned back against the sides of the glass counter. "Look, Sophie — if I may call you that — from what I gather, you're kind of at loose ends right now. No job, your friends are in faraway places, and didn't I hear that your sister is in some college somewhere?"

Sophie crossed her arms over her chest.

She wasn't about to tell this man more about herself than the gossips already knew.

"All right, so maybe you are the center of interest in this town right now, and I don't blame you at all for being a little miffed."

"Is that what you call it?" she asked. "How about a flaming inferno of rage?"

Roan couldn't conceal a little smile. Damn! but she was pretty. And he really liked her temper. If there was anything he couldn't stand it was a bland female. "And you're right to feel that way. I wouldn't blame you if you left town and never looked back."

"That's my thought too," Sophie said and turned toward the door, but then the old cell phone Kim had lent her vibrated. There was something about a buzzing phone that compelled one to look. So few people had her number that she wanted to know who was contacting her.

She took the phone out of her bag. It was a text message from Reede.

SORRY I RAN OUT. SIX-CAR PILEUP. BE HOME WHEN I CAN. DID YOU GET A HOUSE FOR US? I MISS YOU. REEDE

She knew he was teasing about living together, but for a moment Sophie closed her eyes. If she didn't know what she did, that text would have made her very happy. Get "us" a house? He missed her? Even the thought that he was detained because he was saving lives appealed to her.

But not now. She turned the phone off.

"Reede?" Roan asked.

Sophie gave a curt nod.

"Poor guy doesn't know he's dead meat." Roan said it with so much glee that Sophie came close to smiling.

Again she looked around the small restaurant. Sun was coming in through the windows and showing the dust motes in the air. The glass on the display cabinet was dirty and the wooden floor needed a good scrubbing. Reede's text made her realize that she'd be seeing him every day. "I think this was a mistake," she said and walked to the door.

"Christmas!" Roan said loudly.

She looked back at him. "What does that have to do with anything?"

"Everybody around here, all the way to DC, thinks Edilean is the cutest little town they've ever seen. All of us who live here hate being called 'quaint,' but we've learned to make money from it. Seventy-five percent of our business is from Thanksgiving to Christmas. And all those shoppers get hungry. Make some soup, some fancy sandwiches, charge big city prices, and by the middle of January you'll have enough money to bankroll your trip out of here."

Sophie still had her hand on the doorknob. "I couldn't do this alone."

"So we can get you some help."

"Who is 'we'?"

"The people of Edilean. Al told me he plans to make them feel so guilty that they'll buy three meals a day from you."

Sophie's hand tightened on the knob.

"Okay, two meals, and you choose which ones you want to cook. If it were me, I'd make the menu simple and change it every day. That way you won't get bored. Tell people they have to take what they get. For Thanksgiving you could do —"

"Food in cartons," she said softly. "They could order it all beforehand." She'd seen a butcher shop that did that, and she'd envied people who could afford it. Having to cook a turkey and a dozen side dishes wasn't easy, so it was nice to be able to supplement.

"Did you see the stove?" Roan asked as he went behind the counter. "It's a Wolf. Red knobs. Nice, huh?"

Sophie took her hand off the door and stepped toward the counter to peer through the glass. "I've never used a commercial stove before."

"It has eight burners. The last tenant wanted it and I bought it for her. Cost me a fortune."

"And how did she pay you?" Sophie asked, one eyebrow raised.

Roan gave a laugh. "You got me on that one. Yes, she asked me for an eight-burner Wolf while we were in bed together. I thought she was referring to me, but it turned out she meant a cooking stove."

The tiniest smile crossed Sophie's lips.

"That's better. Don't you think you could stand to do this for two and a half months? Just until after the New Year?"

Sophie went to the end of the counter and looked behind it. There was the huge stove with its cast iron burners, double ovens beneath, stainless steel shelves above. More stainless covered the countertops. The wall had open shelving.

Could she do it? she wondered and tried to envision the little shop full of people. Mothers with overexcited children, carrying half a dozen shopping bags. Locals rushing in at the last minute. Fellow shopkeepers wanting sandwiches to go.

Turning, she looked back at Roan.

"Want to see the upstairs?"

Silently, Sophie nodded, then followed Roan to the back of the shop. As she walked, Sophie couldn't help looking around the place. There were some booths in the back and there were lighter places on the walls where pictures had hung. If there were a lot of tourists coming through Edilean, especially ones "all the way from DC," as Roan had said, maybe Sophie could display some of her work. She used to be rather good at reliefs, so why not hang some on the walls?

If she served breakfast and lunch, no dinner, she'd have the evenings to herself. With no man in her life — and she vowed that there wouldn't be — she'd have time to create things. What a wonderful word, she thought as she went up the stairs, and couldn't help saying it aloud. "Create."

"Did you say something?" Roan asked.

"No, nothing." She opened the door at the top of the stairs and saw the apartment. It was small, as long and as skinny as the store below, but there were windows all along the front, and it had tall ceilings. Facing the street was a living room, the middle held a kitchen, and in the back was a bedroom and bath. There were a lot of boxes that seemed to be full of the last tenant's personal goods and she'd have to remove them, but the apartment could be liveable.

She looked at Roan. "I don't own any furniture, I'd need help in the store, and I don't have any money to pay for anything. I can't even afford to buy a bag of onions."

"What if I — ?"

"No." For the first time since seeing Reede's face, she was sure about something.

"But I —"

"No," she said again and stared up at him.

Roan gave a sigh. "Reede's ruined everything for all of us, hasn't he?"

"If by that you mean men in general, yes. I . . ." She broke off, not sure of what she wanted or needed. It was all too soon, and there were too many confusing thoughts in her head.

All she knew for sure was that it had all been too fast. She'd gone from Carter to Reede in a matter of days. Back in her small Texas hometown she'd seen Carter as her savior. For years, people there had made snide remarks about how Sophie had gone away to a fancy college in the east to learn how to paint pictures. "I learned that in the first grade," some redneck she'd grown up with said, and everyone had laughed. But Sophie had returned to town because her little sister needed help and she'd stayed there. To her, what she'd done was noble.

She'd felt that she was protecting her sister, but the townspeople liked to point out that her uppity college degree didn't help her in her waitressing, or in answering the phone at the insurance agency.

And then along came Carter. That summer had been wonderful. It was great to be picked up in Carter's sexy little Jag. While it was true that they didn't go out to public places often, everyone knew she and Carter Treeborne were a couple.

After about their third date, Sophie began to see changes in the people around her. The teasings were less; the men stopped flirting with her. There were no more comments about how well her uniform fit. Instead, people made a point of saying "good morning" to her.

Was this what she really liked about Carter? Not him as a man but that he was part of the Treeborne family? When Carter had told her it was over, was she angry at losing him or of no longer getting the respect the Treeborne name gave her?

As for that matter, had she latched on to Reede for him or because she'd envisioned throwing a doctor in Carter's face? "See?" she'd say to him. "I *am* equal to you. I *am* marriage material."

"You okay?" Roan asked when they were

again downstairs.

"Just thinking is all. Do you really believe I can make some money with this place? The rent alone —"

"Is free for four months, and I'll take care of the employee salaries for three months."

"You can't —"

Roan's face went from calm to almost angry in seconds. "You know something? You need to get the chip off your shoulder. Everybody needs help at some point in his or her life, and I'm offering it. If it will make that pride of yours feel better, you can pay me back next year, but for right now you need to learn the word 'yes.' "

Sophie's first thought was to storm out and drive away, leave Edilean forever, but then she realized that he was right. "I know," she said. "I'm —" She took a breath and put her shoulders back. It wasn't easy to ask for anything. "I'm broke and I don't have a job and I do need help. Do you have any idea where I should begin?"

Roan gave a little smile out of the corner of his mouth. "So who lied to you the most? Lied flat out to your face?"

"Other than you?"

Roan's smile broadened. "Free rent and paying salaries are my penance. So who else in this town owes you?"

Sophie's lips tightened. "Those three women who work for Reede. When I think of how I spent an entire day scrubbing his apartment and all along they were concealing his identity . . . I'd like to give them a piece of my mind."

"I have a better idea. Let's shower them with guilt." Roan took his mobile phone out of his pocket and pushed a few buttons. "Betsy?" he said. "I'm over at Daisy's." He paused. "Yeah, I've found a tenant and she plans to open it right away, so I want you and the other two girls to come over here and scrub the place down."

Sophie could hear Betsy's voice raised in anger.

"Since when do you think we've become cleaning women for you, Roan McTern? Just because Dr. Reede is out of town doesn't mean we don't have anything to do and we are professional women, not —"

"Sophie is going to run it, and she knows everything," Roan said into the phone.

Betsy took a moment before speaking. "How much is everything?"

"Lies, concealments, the town being in on it. Every last dirty detail."

When Betsy spoke, her voice was meek, apologetic. "We'll need to get supplies."

"Make it fast," Roan said and clicked off

259

the phone. He looked at Sophie. "What else do you need?"

"I don't know," Sophie began, then smiled. "This is like being given wishes."

"Does that make me your fairy god-mother?" Roan asked, eyes narrowed.

"If the shoe fits, Cinderella," Sophie couldn't help saying.

At that insult, Roan turned on his heel and started for the front door.

"I'm sorry!" Sophie said and went after him and put her hands on his arm. "I didn't mean to hurt your feelings. I —" One look at Roan's eyes as they sparkled in delight and she knew he'd been teasing her, and she couldn't help laughing. "I need every-thing! All of it, from furniture to curtains to pots and pans to a sign painter for the windows."

"What are you going to name the place? Sophie's Revenge?"

"How about No Doctors Allowed?"

Roan put his hand over his heart. "I love that name. At least then I might have a chance."

She stepped back from him and put her hands up in defense. "No. No more men. At least not for a while."

"How long?" Roan asked seriously.

"Until . . ." She looked around the little

260

shop. "Until all the walls are covered with my work."

Roan looked at her for a moment. "That's right, you're an artist too, aren't you?"

"I was. I wanted to be."

"I've always wanted to be a writer," he said. "Problem is that I can't write."

"I doubt if that's true," Sophie said. "Surely you can —"

He was shaking his head at her.

"What?"

"I don't think I've ever met a person with a softer heart than you have. You bring out every protective instinct in me and make me feel like some knight of old. Maybe I should show up on a black horse and —" He broke off at the memory, and Sophie's narrowed eyes. "Sorry."

He wouldn't say it, but he now knew what had made Reede agree to wear that ridiculous costume Sara had made for him. When Sophie looked up with her big blue eyes, Roan felt like grabbing a sword and a shield and fighting off any man who came near her.

Too bad, he thought, it wasn't the Middle Ages. If it were, he could challenge his cousin to a joust, with Sophie being the prize. Since Roan was bigger than Reede, he'd surely win.

Alas, it was the twenty-first century and all he had was a cell phone. "Didn't Sara make that red and black costume for you?"

"The one that didn't fit?"

Roan wanted to say that he thought it fit exceptionally well, since most of Sophie's luscious figure was spilling out over the top, but he didn't dare. "Sara knows lots of women who can sew. We'll have curtains for you in twenty-four hours."

"Furniture?"

"From the attics of Edilean. Sara's mother can handle that. She's the town's mayor."

"What do I cook with?"

"You and I will go to a restaurant supply store and fill my pickup."

"I can't —"

Roan held up his finger for her to stop talking.

"But you can't —"

"At!"

Sophie gave a sigh. "Thank you."

"That's all I want to hear. That and the sound of a cash register ringing."

"Speaking of which . . ."

"We'll get one of those too." Roan started punching buttons on his cell phone. "Let me talk to Sara's mom, Ellie, and she'll get everything started. You better open the door."

Sophie turned to see Betsy and Heather outside, buckets and mops in their hands.

"Alice is getting supplies and bringing her husband's shop vac," Betsy said as soon as she was inside. "Sophie, we didn't mean you any harm."

"It's just that Dr. Reede can be such a jerk that we'll do *anything* to give us some peace," Heather said. "And when we met you and you are so very pretty, we hoped that —"

"That's enough," Roan said. "I'm taking Iphigenia here out to do some shopping. When we get back I want this place to be sparkling. There'll be furniture here this afternoon. See that it gets placed correctly."

Sophie was trying to hide her smile over his Iphigenia remark. In Greek mythology she was a young woman who had been placed on an altar to be sacrificed to help others. Whether or not this was carried out differed from one storyteller to the next.

"Ready?" Roan asked Sophie, and she nodded.

Later, when he and Sophie stopped for a late lunch, Roan slipped away to call Reede to tell him that Sophie had found out who he was.

"Who told her?" Reede asked.

That it was hours later and no one from

Edilean had told Reede, Roan took to mean that they were too chicken. "She went to your apartment and saw you sprawled on the couch. I don't know why she didn't drop something else on that ugly mug of yours. She —" Roan broke off because Reede wasn't making his usual protests. "You okay?"

"No," Reede said. "How angry is she?"

"More depressed than angry, but I'm working on her."

"She probably thinks I'm like Treeborne." Reede was standing in the hospital corridor, his white jacket rumpled. There were dark circles under his eyes from lack of sleep, from the trauma of his patients, and from Sophie not answering any of his six text messages, three e-mails, or four phone calls.

"Treeborne?" Roan said. "Like the foods?"

"You didn't hear me say that name. Got it?" Reede said. "Just tell me about Sophie. I was afraid she'd leave town when she found out. That's why I tried to get her to rent a house."

"The old Gains place? Al tore up that lease, although I heard that his wife made him pay a deposit plus the first and last month's rent. But don't worry about Sophie. We're taking care of her."

"What does that mean?" Reede asked.

"And who is 'we'? And what has she said about me?"

Roan had expected to enjoy his cousin's misery as much as he'd loved seeing beer poured over his head. But there was such sadness, such *despair* in Reede's voice that Roan couldn't derive any pleasure from it. At the Halloween party Reede had been the happiest anyone had seen him in years — which is why the town had played along with his prank.

"It's all been Al's idea," Roan said, and told Reede about the sandwich shop.

"She can cook," Reede said in a voice that seemed to have no life in it. "But then Sophie can do most anything. You'll have to see the sculpture she made for me. It's as good as anything I've ever seen in an art gallery."

"So when are you coming back to town?"

"I don't know. Today. Tonight maybe. I have office hours tomorrow. If I could I'd get on a plane and —"

"Run away!" Roan snapped and his voice rose as he spoke. "Like you did when the Chawnley girl dumped you? Only this time you deserve what you got. Listen, I'll tell you what I'll do. I'm going to help you. I'll call some people and see if I can get someone to take over your office here in Edilean.

That way you'll get to run away and lick your wounds for another ten years. And Reede, I want to say that I'm really glad you're going to leave town because I'm going to do everything I can to get Sophie for my own. She and I spent today together and I like her. And unlike you, I am *not* a coward. I'll fight for what I want."

With that, Roan clicked off the phone and shoved it into his pocket. "Idiot!" he said aloud.

The truth was that Roan knew that Sophie was never going to be his. She wasn't interested in him, didn't even seem to see him as a man. Even though they'd spent a day together and he'd worked hard to make her laugh, there was an emptiness in her eyes that was haunting.

They'd spent the day buying necessary equipment for the little restaurant, and try as he might, Roan could never get Sophie to purchase so much as a spoon that she didn't think was essential. Since Roan also liked to cook, they'd talked a lot about food, but Sophie wouldn't speak of anything personal. It was as though she was shutting down, putting a wall around herself — and he hated to see that. Maybe Reede was the main culprit of what had been done to her, but so was the town.

When they stopped for lunch and Sophie excused herself, Roan called Sara and told her what was going on.

"We *all* did this," Sara said. "Not just Reede, but *all* of us. That poor, poor woman. How can we make it up to her?"

"Show her Edilean isn't full of lying, conniving low-life scum?" Roan suggested.

"That would be a start. Listen, keep her out as long as possible and I'll get everyone together to do what we can to make her feel welcome. Kim and Jecca are going to murder us. I have to go. I need to — I don't even know where to begin." Sara didn't say any more but clicked off, and Roan went back to the table to Sophie.

"What else do we need?" he asked her as he slid into the booth across from her.

"This is all too much. I don't know how I'm going to pay you back," Sophie said.

He wanted to say "Forgive us" but he didn't. Instead, "Let me work with you" came out of his mouth. "I took a year off from teaching so I could write a novel, a murder mystery that was going to take the world by storm, but . . ." He waved his hand. "Let's just say that the world is safe. I've been known to cook a bit so maybe I could . . ." He shrugged.

"Help make nanny sandwiches?"

Roan didn't understand, so she told what Al had said.

Roan laughed. "Under a pound of beef and Al would think the sandwich was for girls."

"Maybe I should make a roast beef sandwich that weighs as much as Al — or maybe just his foot. I'd call it The Al."

"With horseradish sauce?"

"Of course."

Roan grinned. "What about his wife? Mrs. Eats-Only-Lean?"

"The Two Sticks of Celery lady? Salad with grilled chicken pieces not —"

"Not a whole breast."

"Of course not. That would be too much. And very, very thin bread. No mayo. Just a little olive oil with a touch of lemon juice. The Mrs. Al."

Roan leaned back in the booth. "You might have something here. Sandwiches for the people of Edilean."

"In that case, should I include arsenic or hemlock?"

"Yeow!" Roan said.

"Sorry. I'm sure they're very nice people and I'm sure they just wanted to help Reede. But when I think of everyone laughing at me because I was working for a man I'd poured beer over, it gets to me. I don't know how I'm going to face them in that shop. How can I serve sandwiches and soup to people who . . . who . . . ?"

"I guess that in Edilean we tend to take care of our own so much that we forget about outsiders. A few years ago a young woman, Jocelyn, inherited the big Edilean Manor, and we kept it from her that her gardener was actually Luke Adams."

"The writer?"

"That's him."

"And she thought he was the guy who planted the petunias? How angry was she when she found out?"

"Not bad, but *all* her anger was at Luke, not the town."

"You're saying that I should understand and be forgiving, aren't you?"

"I guess so. At least give us a chance to make it up to you. Will you do that?"

"I'll . . ." Sophie looked across the table. "Ask me again on the fifteenth of January."

Roan smiled at her. "Fair enough. You ready to go? What kind of sandwich do you think a famous writer would like best?"

"One with *New York Times Best Seller* branded into the bread."

Roan stared at her for a moment then let out a roar of laughter. "Oh Sophie! I'm going to enjoy working with you. And we have to figure out how to make that sandwich for my cousin! Come on, let's go buy a panini press. No, let's get three of them." Smiling, they left the restaurant.

For several minutes, Reede stood where he was in the hospital corridor, unable to move. He hadn't been asleep for a day and a half and he should go home to bed. But the thought of that dark apartment without Sophie was more than he could bear.

How to get her back? was the only thought in his head. Was there any apology that she'd listen to? He doubted it.

As he started to put his phone back into his pocket, he thought of his college roommate. Reede checked his contacts list and pushed the button.

"Hey old man," his former roommate, Kirk, said. "Still trying to get someone to move to glorious Edilean and take over for you?"

"No," Reede said. "I need something else. Didn't your brother get a degree in engineering?"

"Yeah. He works for NASA now. You planning to go to the moon to get away from your hometown?"

Reede winced that he'd made someone think he hated Edilean so much. "Didn't you tell me that when he was a kid he liked to make up codes?"

"Yeah, he did. You planning to become a spy and need some help in your code class?"

"Actually, I am. Sort of."

"Count me in!" Kirk said. "Who do you need spied on?"

"Can't tell you that," Reede said. It was one thing to blab too much to his cousin, but he wasn't about to give the Treeborne name to anyone outside the family. Instead, he lied. "My aunt found her grandmother's old cookbook and she wants to use it, but it's written in some sort of code. Think your brother could break it?"

"If he can't he has the entire space industry to help him. But I can tell you that if it's one of those codes based on the order of words in a book and you don't have the book, there will be a problem."

"It could be," Reede said. "I have no idea, but maybe I could scan it and e-mail it to your brother. Think that would be okay?"

"I just prescribed for his athlete's feet so he owes me. I still have my old e-mail address so send it to me. I'll get it to him."

"I will. I'm in Williamsburg now but as soon as I get home I'll send it to you. And thanks, Kirk. I'll owe you."

"Actually, I've been having hemorrhoid

problems and —"

"Call a specialist," Reede said and hung up on Kirk's laughter.

He left the hospital and drove home. It was late and the office was dark and empty — and his apartment was even worse. Tired as he was, he took the time to scan his copy of the Treeborne cookbook into his computer, then sent the pages to Kirk. When that was done, he sent an e-mail to Al's wife and told her he'd take the house Sophie had seen and he'd be moving in tomorrow. He couldn't bear staying alone in the apartment that Sophie had made into a home.

"Tomorrow," he kept saying as he showered. Tomorrow he'd work on making Sophie forgive him. And maybe helping her with what that jerk Treeborne had done to her would work in his favor. On the other hand, Sophie probably now considered Reede as bad as Treeborne.

When he got out of the shower, Reede pulled all the Treeborne food out of his freezer and threw it in the trash.

"Tomorrow," he said aloud and went to bed.

FOURTEEN

Carter Treeborne felt his father's anger before he heard it. The man was pounding down the hallway so hard and fast that the big vases on the tables trembled.

Carter lay on the bed in his room, the only light being the HD TV. He was drinking a beer — his fifth — and didn't so much as glance up as his father stormed past the open door. A raging father was nothing new or even remarkable, as Lewis Carter Treeborne the Second's anger was legendary. He'd inherited it from his father, the man who started Treeborne Foods right after World War II. One evening he'd said — in his usual tone of anger — "Damned women today don't want to cook, so I'll give them meals to spend their husband's hard-earned money on." It was the beginning of an empire.

Carter's mother used to say the idea had been "planted in rage and fertilized by it."

The first two Treebornes were alike, but the grandson was different. He was like his mother, a gentle, sweet woman who had been chosen for her connections to "society." She used to say, "Your father chose me for my education, my ancestors, and my good taste. Of course he now hates me for those same reasons." Gentle she might be, but she was also a realist.

She'd put all her energy into protecting her only child, her beloved son, from her husband. Even though it hurt her and took away the only thing she truly loved, she sent Carter to his first boarding school when he was just seven years old. But even at that age he understood. If he'd stayed home his father would have had him working in the family business by the time he was nine.

Because of his mother's protection, Carter almost had a life of his own. He was liked at school and invited everywhere, and his mother encouraged him to go. Anything to keep him away from his domineering father.

He and his mother met whenever they could and used every available method to communicate. He didn't let his friends know how much he shared with her, how often he asked for her advice, or how he loved to entertain her with stories of his life.

She encouraged him to do charity work, to travel to faraway places, to see and do. Carter wrote her about all of it, sent thousands of photos, and included her in his life as best he could.

She told him of his father, but Carter didn't realize how much she was sugarcoating everything. To Carter his father was a man rarely seen and to be listened to when he did see him. While it loomed over his head that someday he was expected to return to Texas and take over Treeborne Foods, he didn't think about it much. His father was healthy and still working full-time, and he had no desire to turn over an ounce of his power to anyone else, certainly not to a son he barely knew — and didn't seem to like very much.

The one thing his mother didn't share with Carter was that she was ill. To him, her death was sudden and unexpected. He went tearing back to Texas and was told that his mother had been fighting cancer for years. Long bouts of chemo had left her weak and fragile, but she'd never told her beloved son about any of it.

Carter wavered from being angry at her because she'd cheated him out of seeing her, and angry at himself for not caring enough to figure out the truth. He'd looked to his father to share the grief at her passing, but all Lewis Treeborne had said was, "You can't be a Momma's Boy any longer."

His words made Carter feel some of the legendary Treeborne rage, but he was no match for his father. The day after his mother's funeral, Carter's trust fund money was cut off and he was given an office in the big, ugly Treeborne building. His father gave Carter so much work to do that he hardly had time to breathe. He was told that he had to make up for lost time. What he should have learned as a child had to be taught to him as an adult. The packaging, distribution, and preservation of food took over his life. There were meetings that seemed to last for days. He had to taste new concoctions and decide whether or not to spend millions on them.

Carter wasn't good at the job. What he was good at was hiring young, ambitious people who wanted to learn how to run the business. By his third year with the company, he began to have some time to himself. He had four people working for him who eagerly did his work, and as long as he paid them well, they didn't mind that he took the credit. They knew that someday Carter would inherit the company, and they wanted to be there when that happened.

They knew that he would put them in charge while he ran back to his other life. The only question all of them had was how long they were going to have to wait.

It was that third summer when "the Frozen Boss," as Carter liked to call his father to his private staff, was flying around the country, looking for a place to open a new plant, that he met Sophie. His father had already told his son that he was to marry the daughter of a business rival.

Carter had laughed at the idea. "This isn't the eighteenth century where the parents choose their son's wives. I don't love that girl."

"All that schooling I paid for and you still don't know anything. I don't care whether you 'love' her or not. Her father owns the Palmer canning plant, and I want it."

"Then *buy* it!" Carter said.

"He wants to tie up his daughter's future."

"What the hell does that mean?" Carter was on his third Scotch and soda and it was only 4:00 p.m.

"She's been in trouble in the past and . . ." His father looked away.

"What kind of trouble?" Carter's eyes were wide and his stomach was beginning to hurt.

His father waved his hand. "Who knows?

Who cares? Maybe you'll luck out and she'll be a nymphomaniac. Not like *your* mother, with her pristine, pure bedroom ways and her — Get back here!" his father shouted, but Carter kept walking.

He drove into the little town, hot, dirty, no liquor served anywhere. He thought of driving on but decided not to. After all he'd had to drink he shouldn't be behind the wheel of a car. If something bad happened in the town owned by the Treebornes he'd be forgiven, but the outside world was another matter.

The only restaurant in town had a screen door and ceiling fans. The wooden floor was sandy from the grit outside. He sat in a booth that had names and initials carved on it and picked up a plastic-covered menu, but he couldn't see it. It was one thing for his father to decree how Carter had to earn his living, but who he was to *marry*?! It wasn't possible.

As he stared at the menu his mind filled with arguments that he was sure would make his father change his mind. He came up with reasonable, logical persuasions that would show how an arranged marriage would be bad for everyone.

As Carter planned and plotted, he looked up and saw an incredibly pretty young woman taking orders from four high school boys who were giving her a hard time.

One of them was asking her out. "It's just a dance," the kid was saying. Carter recognized him as the local football hero: big, handsome, with an arrogance that said he'd never failed at anything. He'd probably never before had a female say no to him. "Please. I'll buy you a corsage of any flower you want and Dad says I can have the limo."

Carter knew the kid's father owned the only car dealership in town. His mother worked for Treeborne Foods.

"If you think I'm going to get in the back of a limousine with you, Jason Dailey, I think you need to go back to school. There's a big hole in your education. Now, do you guys want the usual or do you want the escargot and calamari special?"

Carter put his head down to hide a smile. He liked the way she talked, not the local "gonna" interspersed with casual profanity. Who was she? he wondered. For years his mother had kept him informed of the local gossip. She'd established a garden club, a book club, and had brought in a dance instructor. His mother had written him about everything, even that the little girl dancers wanted to name themselves the Chicken Frieds.

Even though Carter had spent little time in the tiny Texas town that was pretty much owned by his family, he knew a lot about the residents. So who was this gorgeous girl who was so deftly turning the lustful teenagers away? He guessed her to be in her mid-twenties, natural blonde, eyes like sapphires — and a figure that should be a pinup.

"Sophie!" one of the boys called out. "Give me extra fries."

"I always do," she answered.

Sophie, Carter thought. Of course. Sophie Kincaid. His mother had written about her. She'd gone away to college and majored in . . . He couldn't remember what it was, but his mother had said Sophie was "talented."

Carter knew that when kids left the town to go to college, they didn't return. Treeborne Foods was the only real business, and they only hired locals for the menial positions. "You can't make a kid boss of his dad who's on the conveyor belt" was his father's reasoning. Carter thought it was more likely that his father liked thinking of the locals as his serfs and he was their master.

Carter watched the girl as she poured the iced tea. When he'd arrived, the owner had come out and asked to serve him, but Carter had said he wasn't ready to order. In this town whatever a Treeborne wanted was law.

Twice Sophie had glanced at him, but he'd put his head down and hidden his face. Wasn't there some tragedy connected to her? What was it his mother had written about her? Something about Sophie's mother. Did she die?

Carter couldn't remember. His mother had written to him of so very many families. What she hadn't mentioned was how extraordinarily pretty this girl was. He couldn't help wondering if his mother's omission was on purpose. If so, had she known that someday her son's wife would be chosen for him? Did she know that her son wouldn't be strong enough to stand up and say no?

He didn't like to think any of those things, but it did seem odd that his mother hadn't told him about pretty little Sophie Kincaid who'd gone to college but had returned home. Had she graduated? Probably not or she never would have returned to her two-bit Texas hometown.

When she got to his booth, he smiled at her, but she didn't smile back. No doubt *all* the men in town came on to her.

"So what will it be?" she asked, her note-pad in hand.

Carter looked at the menu as though considering, then put it down. "What's the sauce on the escargot?"

Sophie didn't hesitate. "Lots of garlic."

"Are they fresh?"

"Pulled out of the cabbage patch this morning."

"And the calamari?"

"Flown in from Italy at six a.m. It was late because of the time difference."

He was trying not to laugh since she wasn't, but Carter couldn't contain a smile. "I hate Italian squid. You'd better give me the burger. Medium well."

"You got it," Sophie said and picked up his menu.

When she bent forward, he said softly, "Thanks. It's been a tough day and I needed a laugh."

She looked startled, her eyes widened, and for a moment it was all he could do to keep from kissing her. Her lips were full and pink and he wanted to put his arms around her and hold her. He hadn't had a girlfriend in over a year.

She gave him a quick frown, as though she could read his mind, then she went into the back of the restaurant. When Carter looked up, the football boys were glowering at him. They seemed to be saying that

Sophie was local and therefore off limits to a Treeborne. Carter turned and looked out the window. He didn't see Sophie again that day, but was served by the owner.

For the next week he went to the little restaurant every day, but she never waited on him. Twice he saw her, but she ran to the back and stayed hidden until he left.

Carter had never had anyone evade him before, not in school and not afterward, and certainly never in his family's town. Maybe it was the novelty of it, but maybe it was Sophie's big blue eyes. Or maybe it was that she wasn't like all the other people who saw him only as the heir to a fortune.

At the beginning of the second week he went there for lunch and this time she came to his table with her little pad. He kept his eyes on the menu so she wouldn't see how much he wanted to be near her.

"So why'd you come back to this town?" he asked.

Sophie didn't answer, just stood there, waiting for him to give her his order. When he did, she went away, and later returned with a tuna melt and fries. She put the plate in front of him, but she didn't leave and he didn't look up.

"My mother died and left my twelve-year-old sister with our stepfather. I stayed here to protect her. I had no choice," Sophie said, then left.

He ate his sandwich, put money on the table with a hundred percent tip, then waited for her to come and take the plate away. "I came back because my mother died and I have to learn the business. I had no choice."

She looked into his eyes but only for a second, then took his plate and left.

The next morning he came again. This time he said, "I hate it here."

"Me too," she said.

That evening he showed up for dinner but Sophie wasn't there — but her sister was. She was taller than Sophie, not nearly as pretty, and looked to be old enough to graduate from the local high school. Carter asked the owner about her, and he was pleased to talk to the Treeborne Prince.

"She's Sophie's little sister and what a handful she's been to Soph. When their mother died, Lisa was twelve but she looked twenty. She was wearing big earrings and half a pound of makeup to school every day." He leaned across the table and lowered his voice. "Nobody knows for sure but we all think maybe her stepfather was . . . you know, trying things with the girl."

Everybody knew but nobody did anything

about it, Carter thought but didn't say. "So what did Sophie do?"

The man shrugged. "Stayed here and took care of everything. Soph worked three jobs and got the girl into shape. There were some loud arguments and Lisa threatened to run away, but Sophie wouldn't let her. She's a good girl."

"So now what?" Carter asked. "After Lisa graduates from high school, what then?"

"Sophie got the girl into State on a partial scholarship. And once Lisa leaves in the fall, Sophie is out of here. No more waitressing for her."

"What did she study in school?"

"You mean in college?" He sounded as though he were talking of an alien establishment.

"Yes. What did she study in college?"

"I have no idea," the man said, then got up and left.

The more Carter heard about Sophie, the more he liked her. She had a college degree but she hadn't abandoned her sister.

That summer his father was often away, and when he did return, his anger was so violent that he appeared to be oblivious to everything around him. All he cared about was getting possession of the Palmer canning plant.

"That bastard," Carter's father, Lewis, said at dinner. "If you knew what he's demanding —" He broke off as he looked at his son. Carter was tall and handsome and looked as healthy as a human could be. And why not? He'd never done drugs, had always eaten well, and played sports. That he was going to be married off to a girl like Traci Palmer was a shame. The girl had been doing drugs since she was a kid. Last year her nose had had to be rebuilt from all the cocaine she'd snorted.

But Lewis knew it couldn't be helped. Old man Palmer was saying that his daughter needed stability, that she'd clean up her ways if she was married to an upstanding, honorable boy like Carter.

Lewis knew that old saw wasn't true, but he also knew that men can become desperate when it comes to their children. His own hope was that a marriage with some conflict in it might make a man of his son. As it was, all Carter wanted to do was read his fancy books and give away the Treeborne fortune. Lewis well knew that his son no longer did any work for the company, but the people he'd hired to replace him were so damned good that he wasn't about to fire them.

"So who's the town girl you're seeing?"

Carter nearly choked on his food.

"You didn't think you could keep a thing like that a secret from me, did you?"

Carter knew better than to lie. "Sophie Kincaid, and I'm not really seeing her. I asked her out, but she said no."

"Did she?" Lewis asked. "When I was a boy there wasn't a pretty girl in town who said no to me."

Carter wanted to say, And I have the half siblings to prove it, but he didn't. "She's just here until her sister graduates from high school."

"Didn't that girl get into trouble a few years back?"

"That's what I heard," Carter said, "but Sophie straightened her out."

"Sounds good," Lewis said and Carter looked at him with hope in his eyes. "Just so you understand that this is just a summer romance. I want you engaged to the Palmer girl by Halloween. Got it?"

Carter knew that he should stand up to his father, but he didn't. He didn't have any money of his own, and he'd never trained for a career. He couldn't see himself working in a shop somewhere and making minimum wage. Living in a fourth-floor walkup, buying his shirts out of a bin, his shoes on sale. No, he couldn't imagine any of that. If he'd been born with a talent or a passion for something, that would be different. But so far he'd found neither of them within himself.

His father was staring at him, as though waiting for a reply.

Carter put his head down. "A summer romance. I got it."

For a second a look of what appeared to be disappointment flashed across Lewis's face. Maybe he wished his son would stand up to him, call his bluff, but Carter was like his mother. Nothing had ever made her lose that cool, aristocratic calm that had at first fascinated him and that he'd later come to despise. "And don't parade her around in public. I don't want Palmer to hear any gossip."

Carter kept his head down and nodded. In a way he knew his father had just given him permission to have one last fling before . . . Carter didn't want to think what autumn would bring. But meanwhile he planned to make use of the freedom that he had.

It hadn't been easy to win Sophie's trust. The evening after his father's marital decree, Carter had been waiting for her outside the restaurant.

"Hello," he said from the dark.

Sophie turned around so fast he thought

she was going to hit him. Instead, she gave him a look that told him to drop dead, then she headed round the corner to the poorly lit parking lot and her car. It was a rattletrap old thing that he couldn't believe even ran.

Later he thought it was an omen that it didn't. She got in, started the engine, but it did nothing. He stood outside in the heat and dark and watched her hit her fist against the dashboard. "Gas or battery?" he asked through the open window.

"Gas. My sister never fills the tank."

"I can give you a ride home," he said and did his best not to sound excited.

Sophie got out of the car and looked around at the empty lot, but not at him. She seemed to be fighting some inner demons. "No thanks. I'll walk to the filling station."

There was only one in town and the next one was thirty miles away. "Don't they close at nine?" He watched as her shoulders slumped and he wanted to pull her into his arms and say that he'd take care of everything. For the last three years there wasn't a second when he'd felt in charge of any situation. It was his father's company, his father's house, his father's money, his father's rule. That this young woman needed him even for something as simple as transportation made him feel good.

"How about if I drive you home and tomorrow you can get your car filled and — ?"

"And the maid will make breakfast?" Sophie said. "If she gets groceries, that is, because there's nothing in the house, and I'm sure neither Arnie nor Lisa went. They —"

She broke off because Carter put his hand on her upper arm and guided her to his dark green Jag.

"Wait a minute!" she said as she pushed his hand away. "You can't make me —"

"Would you stop it!" Carter said, and there was anger mixed with frustration in his voice. "You've been treating me like it's known that I'm some despoiler of women. I've been back here for three years. Have you ever heard even one bad word about me?" He was glaring at her.

"No," she said, "but . . ."

"But what?"

Sophie didn't have an answer for him. "All right," she said at last. "Give me a ride home. Arnie can get gas in the morning."

Carter opened the door for her and she got in. "No," he said. "First we're going to get your groceries." He shut the door.

It had been the best "date" Carter had

ever been on. In college and afterward, he'd been out with girls who expected him, a Treeborne, to give them the best of everything. Wine, food, entertainment. They demanded the top. Maybe this constant expectation was the reason he'd never been serious about a woman. The most he'd ever lasted with one was six months.

Going to the grocery with Sophie had been enlightening. He'd assumed that he'd pay. Actually, he'd envisioned telling her that she could buy anything she wanted. Would she be like those women on the TV shows and grab three baskets and fill them with hams and turkeys? If she did, maybe later she'd be so grateful that they could make use of the backseat of his car.

But when they were inside the grocery and he put some raspberries in the cart, Sophie took them out.

"They're too expensive," she said.

"That's all right," he'd said with a smile, "I'll pay for everything. Get whatever you want."

Sophie gave him a look that was so cold he felt his ears turning red. "I *want* whatever *I* can afford," she said through her teeth.

Carter had been so shocked that he'd just stood there staring at her.

"Why don't you go wait in the car?" she

said quietly so none of the other customers could hear. It was late and there were few people in the store, but they were all curious to see a Treeborne in there. "Better yet, leave and I'll call a taxi."

"I heard he has the flu," Carter said, referring to the one and only taxi driver in town.

Sophie didn't laugh but pushed the cart around him.

He stopped in front of it. "How about if I promise to behave?"

"Can you?" Sophie asked.

"I'll be your slave and you can teach me."

Sophie frowned as she turned away. "Then get half a dozen lemons and a dozen of those apples. No! Not those. The little ones. Don't you read prices?"

"No. Can't say that I do," he said as he took the plastic bag Sophie handed him. "Except in jewelry stores. I have to be careful there. Some of those little stones can bankrupt a man."

Sophie did give a bit of a smile. "That's been my experience too. Get an acorn squash." When Carter hesitated, she leaned across him to point.

"Which one is it?" he asked. "These?"

"No! Those."

"The yellow ones?"

"No, the —" She stopped when she realized that part of her chest was against his side.

Carter gave a shrug of such innocence that Sophie did smile.

They'd stayed in the grocery for an hour and a half. Carter asked questions about products he couldn't have cared less about. All he really wanted was to be near Sophie, to hear her soft voice, to look at her pretty face and body. It seemed that it had been a lifetime since he'd heard of anything except business.

It was at the frozen foods section that he got a jolt. He started to get some, but Sophie told him which ones were good and which were bad. She said that some of the "bad" ones could be fixed by using intricate cooking methods — which the packages didn't explain. But there were others that tasted so horrible she wanted nothing to do with them.

"Anyway, I prefer fresh," she said and kept walking.

Carter looked through the glass doors at the cartons and memorized what Sophie had said.

"How do you know so much about . . . the products?" He'd almost said "our" products.

"Everyone who works for your family knows."

"So why don't *we* know?" He said it lightly, as though it were a joke. They paid a fortune for market research for people to cook the products and taste them.

"You don't hire locals for positions where anyone will *listen* to them. Remember?" She pushed the cart down the dairy aisle.

He drove her home and wanted to carry the groceries inside, but she refused. When he tried to arrange a second date, she brushed him off by saying that she had a lot of work to do and didn't have time for going out. She stepped inside without so much as a good night kiss.

When Carter got home he called his father's chauffeur, woke him up, and told him to take care of filling Sophie's car with gas. "It needs to be done by five a.m."

"Yes, sir," the man said.

Carter hung up, then typed out all that Sophie had told him about the frozen foods. In the morning he called a meeting of the department heads, said he'd been researching Treeborne Foods for months, and this is what he'd found out. He tossed papers on the table and told them to fix the problems. Carter then turned and left the conference room.

Without exception everyone looked at him in openmouthed astonishment. Carter had never before taken the initiative on anything.

For the rest of the week, Carter was waiting for Sophie every day after work.

At first she ignored him, got into her own falling-apart car, and drove away. For days he tried the usual things of flowers, candy, even a gold charm bracelet, but she turned them all down. It was on the eighth night, when he showed up with no gift, that she talked with him. Or rather, she listened.

Just hours before Carter had had a fight with his father. An argument with Lewis Treeborne consisted of his yelling and his victim standing there in submission. "Rather like in a wolf pack," one employee said.

That day Lewis had taken the rage that festered inside him out on his son. There didn't seem to be any reason, just that Carter had been in the wrong place at the wrong time.

Lewis, like all abusive people, felt better after he'd spewed out his venom, but his victim, Carter, was devastated.

He'd driven into town and parked in the lot out of what had become almost habit. When Sophie came out he'd barely noticed her. Usually, he had planned out a speech of why she should go out with him, but that night he couldn't think of anything to say.

Sophie had said good night to him, then got into her car and started the rattling old engine. But then she looked at Carter, still leaning against his car, still staring into the night.

She turned off the motor, got out, and asked him what was wrong.

"Nothing," he said and opened his car door. "Sorry I didn't bring you a gift tonight, but . . ." He waved his hand. "I won't bother you anymore." He had one leg inside before she spoke.

"I need to go to the grocery and I want you to drive me there," she said loudly.

He didn't understand. "Your car quit again?"

"No." She seemed to consider her words carefully before she spoke. "I heard that today your father took out his temper on you. Want to talk about it?"

Carter collapsed into the leather seat as though he had deflated. "Does this town know *everything* about us?"

"If it happens in public, yes we do." She didn't tell him how everyone in the restaurant had laughed about Lewis Treeborne's attack on his son. Everyone saw Carter as a pampered, spoiled wimp. "Too afraid of his old man to stand up to him" was the consensus.

Sophie thought that was probably true, but she knew a lot about being in situations where other people had control. She knew she shouldn't get involved, since this young man was a Treeborne, but he was also a human being, and right now he looked so sad she couldn't leave him alone.

"On I-40 there's a tavern. It —"

"I know the place well," he said. "Get in."

That was the beginning. For the first time in his life, Carter had a friendship with a woman. Over the next few months he told her about his life, about his mother, and how she'd protected him from his father. And Sophie told how she had kept her stepfather away from her sister.

This mutual bond, this sense of sharing, led to friendship, which led to sex, and they led to love. That summer was the best of Carter's life. His father was gone most of the time, there were competent people to run the company, so he spent a lot of time with Sophie.

Her refusal to take money from him was, at first, a problem. Lisa got a job at the local Dairy Queen so Sophie could cut down from three jobs to two, but that still took up too much of her time. Carter began devising ingenious ways to get money to Sophie. Tourists came through and left twenty-dollar tips. The feed store where she worked on Tuesday and Thursday afternoons did so much business her boss gave her a substantial raise.

By the end of the summer she was doing so well that she could afford to take whole days off to spend with Carter.

That they rarely left town, but never went anyplace where Carter might be known, didn't bother Sophie. The two of them spent their hours together in a ramshackle summerhouse hidden on the Treeborne estate. They had a boat, a lake, and a forest to walk through. They spent lazy afternoons together reading, talking, or just being quiet. They made love often, but always quietly and tenderly.

For the first time since his mother died Carter felt that someone cared for *him,* not his money, but for him.

The only blemish in his life that summer was that he knew he was to marry someone else. In September, he tried to talk to his father about what he saw as a life sentence. But Lewis Treeborne wouldn't listen. "You can*not* marry a local girl!" he said in anger, then his face changed to one of concern and he calmed down. "You may think you're in love with her but that's only because you two hide out in the woods together and eat with your fingers. How would you feel if you showed up at the opera with her? Would she fall asleep? Or would she stomp and yell like she was at a figure eight race?"

Lewis put his hand on his son's shoulder, a rare gesture. "I've seen this girl and she's a knockout, I'll give you that, but she's a local and that's all she'll ever be. Believe me, if you married a girl like that, within six months you'd be ashamed to be seen with her. And think about her! All those fancy friends of yours would make fun of her until the girl would want to slit her wrists. Do you want to do something like that to her? Is that your idea of love?"

Lewis gave his son's shoulder an affectionate squeeze and when he turned away he was smiling. Damn! but the boy was easy to manipulate. Palmer was holding out for his druggy daughter to marry "a good, clean young man," and Carter was going to do it no matter what had to be done. If Lewis had to, he'd make the local girl disappear.

Still smiling, he left the room.

As he'd planned, Lewis's words planted a seed in Carter's head and he began to watch Sophie, put her under a magnifying glass. She knew she was being scrutinized and she asked him why. His reply was that he was about to make the biggest decision of his life. Sophie, correctly thinking he was contemplating marriage, looked down to cover her blushes. She had incorrectly begun to believe that she would be the bride.

In the end, Carter had gone with his father. To stand against the man took more courage than Carter had. One night he met with Traci at a formal dinner party put on by her father. He sat across from her and couldn't help noticing that she used a fish knife correctly. And she wore a gown that cost a normal person's yearly wage, and diamonds sparkled on her ears and her wrists. He had a vision of Sophie and him sitting on the summerhouse floor eating barbecued spareribs, sauce all over their faces. How would Sophie do at a dinner like this one? he wondered. Would all the cutlery and glassware confuse her?

After that night he began to pull back from Sophie, but he worked to not let her see it or feel it. By the time what he knew was their last night together came, he had convinced himself that his father was right. But some part of him felt bad enough that he showed her the Treeborne cookbook. Maybe she would tell her grandchildren that she'd seen it. Maybe . . .

What Carter hadn't foreseen after the breakup was how miserable he'd be without Sophie. After he'd spent some time alone with the woman he was to marry, all he did was compare her to Sophie.

It took only days to realize he'd made a big, big mistake. He went to Sophie's house and was told by her stepfather that she'd left town. "Took the car and went away," Arnie yelled. "Now how the hell am I supposed to pay for this place?"

If Carter hadn't been in the same situation he would have told the man to get a job.

Now, after Halloween, Carter was to the point where he hated his life so much that he didn't want to leave his bedroom. The last time he'd seen Traci she'd offered him what she called a "particularly fine line" of cocaine.

When his phone buzzed he almost didn't answer it. But then he thought maybe it could be Sophie.

It was his father calling to tell him to get twenty-five grand out of the office safe and give it to a man who'd be there in thirty minutes. "Can you get off your rear long enough to do this?" Lewis sneered into the phone. He was disgusted with his son's depression, something Lewis had never come close to feeling.

Carter clicked off the phone, tiredly got up, and went to his father's office. The last time he'd been in the safe was with Sophie when he'd shown her the old cookbook. Tears blurred his vision as he spun the dial with the combination.

He counted out the money, put it in an envelope, and sealed it. It was when he looked back at the safe that he realized the yellow envelope wasn't there.

He tossed the cash his father kept in the safe onto the desk, then all the papers. The envelope, the family cookbook, was *not* there.

With his fingertips on his temples, Carter tried to think of when and where. Maybe his father had taken it. Maybe —

Carter knew that only one person would have removed the cookbook from the safe where it had been for decades. That day, that very last day, he and Sophie had made love on the floor of his father's office. Such a violation of Lewis Treeborne's private space had driven Carter to new heights of pleasure. It was as though he was at last defying the man.

Afterward, Carter had carried Sophie to his bedroom and . . .

He put his hands over his face. He'd carried Sophie out and left the safe standing open. She must have returned to the house after he'd shoved her out the front door. He hadn't meant to be so rough, but he was afraid his father would return and see her. He didn't want her on the receiving end of the man's temper.

Carter flopped down in his father's big leather chair. If that cookbook were lost — if the secrets it contained were made public — it could bring down the Treeborne Foods empire.

He stood up, hastily shoved the money back into the safe, and shut the iron door. Right now there was only one thing he knew for sure in life: he *had* to find Sophie Kincaid before his father found out the cookbook was missing.

FIFTEEN

"Hi," Reede said from the doorway of the sandwich shop.

Sophie, her back to him, was going up and down a step stool as she put away the things she and Roan had bought. At the sound of Reede's oh-so-familiar voice, she smiled, but then she remembered everything and it went away. Before she turned around, she had her face composed to be expressionless.

For all that she'd seen him without a mask, he'd been asleep then and she wasn't prepared for the intensity of his eyes. They were deep blue under thick lashes. They would have been considered pretty if not for the depth of them. Hawks could learn a thing or two from him. Her first thought was that she understood why everyone in town was afraid of him. Her second thought was her memory of being in bed with him, his lips, his hands caressing her, touching her . . .

She turned away before he could read her thoughts. "We're not open for business yet so there's no food."

"Could we talk?"

She took a breath and turned back to face him. "Sure. What do you have to say?"

"Will any apology work?"

"No," she said honestly. "But tell me, did you win? You made a fool of the woman who poured beer over you, so does that make you the champion?"

Reede stared at her in shock. "Is that what you think of me? That I'd do something like that?"

Sophie glared at him. "Then why? What other reason did you have for concealing your identity from me?"

"I liked you," he said softly.

"You liked that I cleaned your apartment and cooked for you."

"No, I like that you care, that you listen, that you make me laugh, that you . . ." He trailed off for a moment. "In that first call I didn't know who you were and I confided things in you that I've never told anyone else. I'm sorry about my driving. I'll never again take my eyes off the road. I . . ." He reached into his trousers pocket and withdrew a new cell phone and put it on the counter. It was an unseasonably warm day, and he had on a T-shirt and jeans that hugged his body. "I owe you this."

"You don't owe me anything," she said.

The hostility in her voice seemed to startle him, and for a moment she thought he was going to leave, but he didn't. He looked around at the little restaurant. She hadn't yet had time to do much with it.

Last night when she and Roan had returned from shopping, he'd insisted on going inside with her, even to walking her upstairs, and she soon saw why. While they were out, the little apartment had been transformed with gently used furniture, even some rugs. There was a pretty mahogany bed in the back, complete with blue and white sheets and lots of pillows.

"Guilt offerings," Roan had said.

But whatever the reason, the kindness of the people of Edilean made Sophie smile.

When she looked back at Reede, he was staring at her.

"Do you *want* to open a restaurant?" he asked.

She wasn't going to lie. "No, not really, but it's just temporary. I'm staying here for the Christmas season and New Year's."

"Then what?"

"I don't know," she said. "My life seems to just happen to me. I have work to do, so you need to leave."

Reede stood where he was for a moment, then walked behind the counter to stand near her.

Sophie drew in her breath. It was so strange that this man was so familiar but at the same time she felt that she'd never seen him before. She'd thought his eyes were beautiful behind the mask, but seeing them now made her skin grow warm. "I don't think . . ." she began, but he stepped past her as though she hadn't spoken.

"I'll help you," he said and motioned to the ladder.

Sophie frowned as he picked up a tall stockpot and held it out to her.

She thought she should tell him to get out and that she never wanted to see him again, but she couldn't make herself do it. She stepped up on the short ladder and took the big pot.

"I sent the Treeborne cookbook off to a friend of mine who likes to break codes."

"You did what?"

"I sent the —"

"I heard what you said but what gave you the right to do something like that? I wanted it returned to him. You said —" She broke off when Reede's phone buzzed.

"Sorry," he said as he pulled it out of his

pocket. "I have to take this. When?" he said into the phone. "Did you tell them not to move him? Meet me at Sophie's new place." He clicked off and looked up at her. "It's Heather with an emergency and I have to go. I —" Reede blinked a few times, then reached up and put his hands on Sophie's waist and lifted her down. "You're going with me."

"I can't go with you," she said.

"Please?" he asked. "Let me try to make you believe that whatever I did had no malice in it. If I'd shown you who I was at first you would have slammed the door in my face. You would *never* have gone out with me that first night. You — Damn! I have to go. It's an emergency. Please, Sophie. Go with me."

She was sure she shouldn't, but his eyes were so compelling that she couldn't resist. And she wanted so very much to go with him, to hear him out. She gave only the slightest nod and Reede took her hand, pulled her around the counter, and out the front door.

Outside, Heather was getting out of the Jeep and her eyes widened when she saw Dr. Reede holding on to Sophie with a firm grip.

Since the vehicle floor was quite high,

Reede picked Sophie up at the waist and set her sideways in the driver's seat.

She knew she should hold out and say she wasn't going with him, but the prospect of spending the day putting things away had no appeal for her. And she already knew that when Reede was around exciting things happened. "I'm supposed to drive?"

His look made her swing her legs over the gearshift console and get into the passenger seat. Reede was right behind her.

"I'm no Frazier but you'd better buckle up."

Sophie had no idea what that meant but she did fasten her seat belt. "Wait! I forgot to lock the door of the shop."

Reede gave a scoff of a sound, glanced at Heather, and she nodded. He'd silently asked if his medical kit was in the back. "It's Edilean," he said as he put the Jeep in gear, flipped a switch, and a siren and red lights went off. When he pushed the accelerator, the vehicle leaped forward.

Sophie held on to the armrest on the door with one hand and the seat with the other. When Reede swerved around three cars, barely missing them, she couldn't repress a squeal of fear.

"Okay?"

"Yes." He went over a pothole and she

went flying up to nearly hit the ceiling. She knew she was angry at him, and that she had every right to be, but something suddenly hit her. "So what's the third date going to be?"

The image of her in a red corset, him on a horse that didn't want to obey, and the two of them walking across a beam high above the floor came to him. Date number one. And this was the second. He jerked the steering wheel to miss a dog that was sauntering across the road, then laughter began to bubble up inside him. In the next second they were both laughing as they held on for the wild ride over what had turned into a dirt road.

"Who? Where?" Sophie managed to say over the sound of the Jeep hitting every hole in the road. Even as little as she knew about Edilean, she could see that they were heading out of town and into the surrounding nature preserve.

"Campsite number eight," Reede said. "Some guy hurt himself playing with a bow and arrow. Or that's what I think Betsy said."

"Is it serious?"

"It depends where it went in. Hold on, as it's about to get rough."

"And just when I was getting comfortable," Sophie said, making Reede smile.

But he didn't look at her. "See? Even when the prettiest girl I've ever seen is smiling at me, I don't look away from the road. Oops! Sorry. These roads are bad. Okay?"

"I'm going to need dental work, but I'm fine. Watch that one!" She held on as Reede went onto the bank to miss a six-foot-long rut in the road.

"I'll get the Fraziers to bring a dozer out here. Sophie, I really am sorry about nearly running you down. I saw the papers and heard your phone crunch but I didn't see you. I would never —"

"Left!" she yelled and he jerked the wheel. "I know. But why did everyone *lie* to me?"

"Self-protection. I haven't been too happy about being back here."

"Roan says you're a monster. Or thereabouts."

"Roan would betray his own mother to get near you."

"He's been nothing but a gentleman."

"A gentleman, yes, but did he tell you about his book yet? It's really boring."

"No," Sophie said, her eyes straight ahead. "But he did give me a restaurant free for four months, and he's going to pay my employees' salaries for three months." She couldn't help how pleased she was at the

311

look Reede cut her. Good. Let him be jealous.

Reede drove down the narrow gravel road at what seemed to be the speed of light and skidded to a halt just as another Jeep came from another direction. Out jumped a big man Sophie recognized as Colin Frazier, the town sheriff. She'd met him at the Halloween party when he'd been costumed as an Old West sheriff. Everyone had teased him that he hadn't actually worn a costume but had come as the way everyone saw him. Colin had taken it all so good-naturedly that Sophie had liked him.

Reede grabbed his medical bag from the back, jumped out of the vehicle, and started running. Sophie didn't at first see where he was going, but then she stared in horror. Behind a picnic table spread with food was a man pinned to a tree by an arrow going through his shoulder. Before him was a gray-haired woman, her hands on his shoulder as she stopped the blood from flowing out of his body.

As Reede ran to the man, Colin went to the back of his vehicle to get out a big toolbox. He slung huge metal cutters over his shoulder and ran toward the man and the tree.

Sophie got out of the Jeep, but she didn't

know what to do. She watched as Colin cut the arrow that held the man and Reede caught him as he fell. The woman still had her hands on the man's shoulder.

As Sophie went to the table she heard Reede quietly giving orders to Colin and the woman. It seemed she was a retired nurse and Reede was using her expertise.

Sophie was wondering how the man had been shot. Was it an accident? Someone playing with a bow and arrow? Or had it been with malicious intent?

She looked at the table for a bow. Instead she saw a stack of paper plates and three packages of hot dogs. There were paper cups with cartoon characters on them. Kids! she thought and spun around. Under some trees was a green minibus with the name of a Williamsburg church on the side of it. It looked like they'd taken advantage of the warm day to have one last picnic before cold weather set in.

She walked around the table to stand behind Reede. "How many children are here and where are they?"

Reede looked at the nurse.

"Eight," she said. "They were really scared when Jim was hit and they were screaming, but I couldn't leave him. I told them to hide until I came and got them. But I can't . . ."

"Sophie, could you —" Reede said but she cut him off.

"I'm on it." She was genuinely pleased to have something to do. Turning, she looked back at the woods. They began just a few feet away and the pine trees were so dense she couldn't see but a few feet into them. There were no children in sight.

She wanted to ask their ages but the adults were so busy that she didn't. How could she round them up when she was a stranger? In the center of the table was a bag of potatoes and beside it was an old paring knife, the blade worn down, the handle rough from many washings. There was also a metal spoon with a narrow tip, and she took that. On the ground was Colin's open toolbox. "Could I borrow these?" she asked as she held up a rattail file and a couple of small screwdrivers.

"Sure," Colin said as he looked at Reede, but he just shrugged. He had no idea what Sophie was up to.

She took some potatoes and the tools into the woods. It was cool in there, certainly too cold for the children to be in there alone. There wasn't a sign of any of them. No doubt they'd been traumatized by seeing an arrow that had to have flown across the table, hit the man, and pinned him to

314

the tree. That their other guide, the woman, couldn't get him down must have further frightened them.

Part of her thought she should call out to the children, but then what? Chase them down? Just her and eight kids? It would never work. It would either frighten them more or entertain them so much that they'd make her chase them up the trees.

Instead, she was going to do what she'd done when Lisa was little and would run away and hide.

Sophie found a clearing in the woods, close to the campsite, sat down on the cold ground, and leaned back against a fallen log. She moved slowly, listening, but she heard nothing. She put the potatoes and tools beside her and picked up one of each.

"I'm a sculptor," she said loudly into the silence, and the word gave her a feeling of purpose. It had been a long time since she'd called herself that.

"Do you know what that means? I was given a gift when I was born. I see shapes and I can form clay or stone or in this case potatoes to look just like them."

As she spoke she was cutting the potato by chunks, her hands working quickly.

"I have a sister who is much younger than I am and when she was little I made her laugh by cutting all her food into funny shapes." Sophie held the potato up so if the children were near they could see it. "This is going to be a rabbit. My sister Lisa loves rabbits and she had one when she was little. She called it Annie and she wanted me to make all her food into rabbits."

Behind her, Sophie heard leaves rustling and to her right she thought she saw movement. But she didn't look. She just kept carving as fast as she could. And thinking.

"You should have seen my little sister's plate for every meal. I had to make everything into a rabbit. The pancakes were easy and mashed potatoes were a breeze, but how do you make applesauce look like a rabbit? Know what I did?"

She waited in silence, carving quickly, but not answering her own question.

"What did you do?" a little girl asked.

Sophie looked at the child, saw the fear in her eyes, and smiled. "I made two round puddles of applesauce, put in raisin eyes, and pieces of carrot for ears. But . . ." She paused as another girl and a boy quietly came close to her. Sophie lowered her voice. "I was afraid the bunny would wake up and eat his own carrot ears."

The children laughed. They were about six years old and seemed to be glad to feel safe again.

"Is Mr. Jim okay?" a child asked.

"Yes," Sophie said as she set the potato rabbit on the log beside her.

"Bet you can't make a dragon," a boy said from her left.

"Are you kidding?" Sophie said. "If they gave out awards for potato dragons, I'd get one. Get me some little sticks that look like fire coming out of his mouth so I can make a real dragon."

One by one, seven children tiptoed toward her and sat down on the ground and watched. She finished the dragon, stuck a branched stick in for fire, and the children moved closer.

"Who wants a bear?" Sophie asked, and they all said yes. Finally, the last little boy, the eighth child, came out of the woods and sat down to watch.

When they heard an ambulance with a siren coming down the road, two of the boys started to get up. "Sit!" Sophie said, and her look made them sit back down. Until she was sure there wasn't some crazy killer out there, she planned to keep the children where she could see them — and keep them calm.

The siren got very loud and it wasn't easy to keep the children near her, but Sophie did it. She offered her potato sculptures as prizes to whomever could build the best house for it out of whatever they could find in the woods. Besides, the abnormally warm day was cooling off and the children needed to move around. "But you can't leave my sight!" she said emphatically.

They heard the ambulance doors slam and the siren was turned back on. They all glanced in the direction of the sound but they could see nothing. Sophie wondered if Reede and Colin and the gray-haired lady had gone with the ambulance, and if so when would they be back?

But minutes later Reede stepped around a tree and stood there for a moment, taking it all in. All eight of the children were there and they were busy constructing things out of twigs, leaves, and even rocks. They were all asking Sophie questions by the dozen, such as how to tie things together when they had no string.

Sophie stepped away to go to Reede. "How is he?"

"He'll be fine, thanks to Sue's quick thinking."

"How did it happen?"

Reede grimaced. "Colin thinks it was too much beer and some hunters. He's looking for them now. They might not even know what they've done." He nodded to the kids. "I'm going to take them back in the bus to the church in Williamsburg. I can drop you off in Edilean."

"No," she said, "I'll go with you. We better get them out of here. In spite of the warm day, it is November."

"What are those things on the log that the kids are looking at?"

Sophie smiled. "Nothing important. Just potato animals."

She followed Reede as he walked the few feet to the log and picked them up. There was a rabbit, a dragon breathing fire, and a bear with a pebble that vaguely looked like a fish in its mouth.

"Sophie, these are wonderful," he said, looking at her.

"So who wins?" a little boy asked.

"Everyone," Sophie said. "By this time tomorrow I'll give each of you a sculpture of your favorite animal. Only I'm going to do them in clay so you can keep them forever. Right now we're going to ride back to Williamsburg on the bus and . . . Are you ready for this? Dr. Reede is going to drive! Do you think he knows how to do that? And if the bus starts coughing, what do you think he'll do?"

"Give it a shot!" a boy yelled.

"Some medicine," a girl said.

"Ha!" Reede said. "If there are any problems I'm going to make all of you get out and *push* the bus."

The children looked wide-eyed for a moment, then started squealing and running around.

"Sophie," Reede said softly, "thanks for doing this. If Sue hadn't taken care of Jim he might have bled to death. She couldn't look after the kids at the same time. And if you hadn't been here . . ." He trailed off. "Anyway, thank you."

"I enjoyed it. Doing this made me remember some things."

"Your sculpture?"

"Yes," she said. "It was the driving force in my life when I was growing up, and during college I thought of nothing else. Jecca and Kim and I were like Roan and thought we were going to set the world on fire with our art." She was laughing at herself.

"Instead, you've just set a bad-tempered doctor on fire. Hey kids! Last one in the bus doesn't get to sit next to Miss Sophie."

All of the children started running at once. The two older boys grabbed the potato sculptures without slowing down.

Sophie shook her head at him. "You should have said that the last one in has to sit by me."

"Ha!" Reede said with a derogatory snort. "You have a knack for making people fall in love with you. It's certainly worked with *me.* Hey you two!" he yelled. "Don't eat raw hot dogs. They're full of bacteria." When the children didn't obey him, he said, "And frog guts. Yeah, eat the bread and chips. Carb load." He looked back at Sophie. "I think they found cupcakes. You ready for a ride with eight sugared-up monsters?"

As Sophie walked behind him to the picnic table, she was thinking about his remark about love working for him.

Reede took a cupcake from a box and bit into it. "Make that nine sugar fiends," he said, smiling at Sophie in such a naughty way that she laughed.

They got all the children on the bus, and on the trip back they took turns sitting by Sophie and telling her what animal they wanted. Reede, in the driver's seat, pulled an old notebook and pen out of a compartment on the door and passed it to Sophie. The children's ideas about their carvings had become so detailed she had to sketch them and put the child's name on the picture.

By the time they got to the church and the anxiously awaiting parents, each child had been to Sophie twice. Simple animals had turned into intricate pieces. "And I want its mane to fly out to the back like it's leaping," one boy said of the horse he wanted. "The eyes have to be big and the neck long." A giraffe. "Sweet. Nice," a girl said of a koala bear.

Sophie thought of the restaurant she was opening and that she wouldn't have time to do things like this, but the truth was that she'd rather carve anything than make tuna salad sandwiches.

It seemed that the phones had been busy since Mr. Jim had been shot by an arrow and when they got back to the church all the parents wanted to ask Reede about what had happened. As they surrounded him, Sophie stepped out of the way.

"Did you do this?"

She turned to see one of the mothers, the dragon on her outstretched hand. All of the little critters had sat on the dashboard on the way back. "Yes."

"This is wonderful," the woman said. "I'm Brittany's mother."

"Ah yes, she's ordered a giraffe." Sophie explained her promise to the children and how they'd made their orders and she'd sketched them out.

"And you can make them in clay?"

"Sure," Sophie said. She started to explain about her degree in art but she didn't say anything.

"We went to a zoo this summer and one of the giraffes leaned over the fence, clasped its teeth down on my daughter's ponytail, and pulled. I nearly fainted in horror, but Brittany and my husband laughed. And he got a great photo of it. Since then she's been obsessed. Her room has giraffe wallpaper, a bedspread, and about twenty stuffed giraffes."

"What a lovely image," Sophie said and looked at the little girl. "You have a pen and paper? I'll give you my e-mail address and would you send me a copy of the photo?"

"Yes," the woman said, her eyes alight. Someone called and she waved her hand. "I have to go, but it was wonderful meeting you. We were afraid our children would return traumatized, but all they can talk about is Miss Sophie and the animals she carved. Thank you. I think that what you did blocked out that awful thing they saw. It would give *me* bad dreams, much less a child."

Her words were complimentary, and Sophie realized that it was the first time in a long while that her own actions had made her feel good about herself. For years now it had been men's feelings that had determined her mood. If her male boss was coming on to her, she felt bad. If Carter'd had a fight with his father and was grumpy, she was sad. If Carter's father was out of town and he was happy, so was she. When she'd been alone with Reede in the little room high up in the house, she'd felt great.

"You have an odd look on your face," Reede said as he came to stand beside her. He'd finally escaped the questioning parents. "Care to share your thoughts?"

She wasn't about to tell him that she'd just come to the realization that nearly every woman reaches at some time in her life. "No," she told him. "I was just wondering how we're going to get home. Your car is still in the forest."

Reede knew that wasn't what she'd been thinking about. "Heather called to tell me she and her husband are going out there to get it and to clean up the site. Someone will give you and me a ride home. I'm staying in the Gains house tonight, the one you looked at with Al's wife. Want to stay with me?"

"No," she said and she meant it, not because she was angry at him, but because she had to do some things for herself. She needed to get her feet on the ground before she reconnected with a man. She stood up straighter. "Thank you, but no."

Sixteen

"We have to do something," Heather said into her cell phone as she held onto the door of her husband's pickup. "Really! I mean it. We have to stop this before it begins."

"I don't understand," Betsy said. "Didn't you say that Dr. Reede lifted Sophie and put her into the Jeep? That sounds like things are going well."

"You think so? Roan McTern spent all day with her yesterday and bought her everything she needs for that restaurant. And he's telling people that he's going to be Sophie's sous chef. He's going to be spending fourteen hours a day with her! Roan is a big, good-looking man and if I weren't married —" She broke off as she looked across the seat at her husband, Bill, who was rolling his eyes.

"I'm open for suggestions," Betsy said. "Let me know what to do and I'll do it. The whole sandwich shop thing has been a surprise to me. Did Sophie say anything to you about wanting to open a restaurant? I know she made dinner for the doc, but that's different from cooking on a big scale."

"All I know about her is that the doc is crazy mad for her and that she made that little sculpture out of clay for him. We should have asked Kim more about her."

"Give her what she wants," Bill said.

She frowned at her husband as she said, "Please don't interrupt. This call is important. If those two break up, Dr. Reede will be in such a bad mood I'll have to quit." She went back to the call. "So, Betsy, maybe we can say we couldn't get the apartment together so she has to stay with the doc."

"She couldn't go to a B&B or back to Kim's empty house?" Betsy asked.

"Give her what she wants," Bill said louder.

"Please!" Heather said in frustration. "I'm trying to talk to Betsy about something that will affect all of us." She went back to the phone. "How about if tomorrow one of *us* helps her cook?" Bill stopped the truck at the campsite, opened the door, and got out while Heather stayed on the phone. "We have to come up with a way to get them together so they . . ." As she watched her husband begin to fill a garbage bag with the leftovers from the picnic, she thought about what he'd said. "Betsy, you know where you got that clay for that little sculpture of Dr. Reede?"

"Of course."

"Can you call them and get more delivered to the studio at the back of that house he rented? And some tools? Get whatever kind they use to carve clay."

It took Betsy only seconds to understand what Heather was saying. She looked at the clock. "The store's still open and I know a guy in Williamsburg who'll go there and get whatever we need and deliver it to us. It should be here in two hours, tops."

"This might work," Heather said as she watched her husband cleaning up the campsite. As she hung up she remembered reading somewhere, probably in all the useless info on the Internet, that if a man wanted to turn on a woman he needed to use a vacuum cleaner now and then.

True or not, the memory of the words "give her what she wants" may have been the key to getting Dr. Reede and Sophie together — and those words had come from her husband.

She went to stand on the other side of the table from him.

He didn't glance up. "Hand me those plates, would you?"

When she didn't respond, he looked at her and was pleasantly surprised by the gleam in her eyes. With a one-sided smile he dropped the bag, walked around the table, and took her in his arms. They made love on the cool forest floor. They wouldn't know for a few weeks, but their desire for a family was at last going to come true.

One of the fathers drove Reede and Sophie back to Edilean. The two men sat in the front while Sophie took the back. She wanted to think about what she needed to do, but as she thought, it all seemed overwhelming. What on earth had made her tell eight children that in just twenty-four hours she'd make animal sculptures for them? Out of clay? Why didn't she just stay there and cut some more potato figures for them?

But she knew the potatoes would wrinkle and the children would be upset. So she'd said she'd make more permanent figures for them. After what they'd been through, they deserved them. But where was she going to get the clay? How would she pay for it? Ask Roan for the money? Reede?

He glanced back at her and when he saw the worried look on her face he frowned. A minute later his cell buzzed. He read the message, then handed his phone over the seat to Sophie.

FIFTY LBS OF SCULPTOR'S CLAY AND TOOLS TO BE DELIVERED TO STUDIO OF RENTAL HOUSE. OKAY? BETSY

Sophie read the text three times before handing the phone back to Reede. When he raised his eyebrows in question, she gave a quick nod and turned to look out the window. Just this once, she thought. Just this one more time she'd let herself be taken care of. Tomorrow for sure she was going to regain control of her own life.

When Reede told the man driving the car to take them to the newly rented house, he glanced at Sophie to see if she agreed. Yes. The sooner she started on the sculptures the faster they'd get done, then she could begin making soups and sandwiches.

After the man dropped them off, she and Reede stood there for a moment, not seeming to know what to do next. But then the wind changed and the temperature dropped. Sophie rubbed her upper arms as she followed him into the house.

It was just as she'd seen it the first time, with little furniture, but the late sun coming through the sunroom windows made it very welcoming. The rooms looked to be cleaner, but it still needed a new coat of paint. Three stools had been placed at the open kitchen counter, and Sophie sat on one.

Reede walked around the counter and looked in the refrigerator. It was full of food. "Looks like the girls did the shopping."

"Do they wait on you hand and foot?"

"They do for Tristan but not for me."

"From what I heard, you don't deserve being waited on."

Reede chuckled. "True. At least not until you came, I didn't." He was rummaging in the deli drawer and pulled out packets of sandwich meat. "Hungry?"

"Yes." She narrowed her eyes at him. "Maybe I should look in the Treeborne cookbook and make something."

"Are you going to be mad at me about that?" he asked.

"What makes me angry is your presumption. All I asked you to do was drop off a package and that's what you should have done."

Her tone didn't bother him. "What are you so afraid of when it comes to this Treeborne guy?" Reede was slicing a tomato and at that name his hand clutched the handle hard. "Are you still in love with him?"

Sophie took a moment to answer. "If love can be killed by one sentence was it really love?"

"If that sentence is someone telling you to get lost, then yes one sentence can kill love." He was putting mayonnaise on four slices of bread. "What if this guy . . . Carson?"

"Carter."

"What if this Carter came here and said he didn't mean what he said, that his father made him say it? Would you forgive him?"

Sophie took a breath. "It's almost as though you know him."

"I've met his type, afraid to stand up for what he believes. Afraid of himself and what he might do."

"Like run off with something as low as a town girl?"

"Is that what he said about you?" Reede asked as he put the sandwiches together and cut them on the diagonal.

"He said . . ."

Reede waited for her to finish.

"He said that I'm the type of girl you go to bed with but you don't marry." Sophie looked at Reede with her heart in her eyes. On the long drive from Texas to Edilean, in her mind, she'd heard Carter say those words over and over. She'd looked at them from every angle and tried to see what had been behind them. She'd gone over everything, from her family, the way she dressed, her jobs, to her table manners. While it was true that she hadn't been raised in the luxury he was used to, she'd been to college, and —

The sound of Reede's laughter made her stop thinking. Obviously he thought that what she'd said was amusing. She got off the stool and headed for the front door, grabbing her purse on the way out.

Reede caught her before she got there and put his hands on her shoulders. "Sophie, I was laughing at the absurdity of what he said. From what you've told me about that coward and from what I've read — and yes I did an Internet search — he's ruled by his father. It's my guess his old man has some other girl picked out for him."

Sophie was staring at Reede, still not placated for his laughter.

"Sophie, you *are* the type men marry. This whole town is full of men wanting to walk down an aisle with you."

"That's ridiculous. They may want . . . you know, from me, but . . ." She stepped back from him. "This is an absurd conversation. No man —"

Reede pulled her into his arms and held her. It wasn't a lustful hug but one of comfort. "I'm sorry he hurt you," he said softly. "You gave up everything to help your sister. You walked away from a college education to take on low-paying jobs so you could protect her. You gave up your friends, and most of all, you gave up your passion for sculpting to help someone else. Can you tell me that a woman who'd do something like that isn't someone every man on this earth would want for his wife? To be the mother to his children?"

Sophie couldn't help the tears that came to her eyes. She *had* loved Carter. Against all that she — and everyone in town had warned her about — she'd grown to love his quiet gentleness. Their days in the summerhouse, on his boat, of just being together, had taken away the harshness of her life. Then, in one horrible night to find out that it was all a lie, that he hadn't come close to feeling what she had, had nearly broken her.

She clung to Reede's strong body, her cheek against his chest, and she couldn't stop her tears.

"It's all right," he said as he stroked her hair. "He won't be back and he can't hurt you again. And just because he said that doesn't make it true."

He pulled back to look at her. "But that

doesn't help much, does it? I was very low after some woman told me that she didn't love me and that being around me and hearing of all I wanted to do in life had always scared her."

"That's stupid!" Sophie said. "You got me across that beam when I was terrified. I would trust you with my life."

He took her hand in his and led her back to the kitchen. "I was so afraid she was right that as soon as I got out of school I went to Africa and Guatemala and anywhere else in the world where they'd have me. And you know what?"

"They all loved you?"

Reede smiled. "No. Not by a long shot. But they did *trust* me." He led her back to the stool and pulled the sandwiches toward them.

Sophie went into the kitchen to find the ingredients to make iced tea. "I want to hear more about your travels. You once said that you wanted me to get to know the real you, the one inside that you don't show to other people."

"Only if you agree to do the same for me."

"All right," she said.

He took a bite of his sandwich. "How about if I tell you about the time Kim's husband, Travis, nearly killed me and my donkey? And he destroyed medicines that had taken me six months to get."

"Really?"

"Oh yes. It was in Morocco and it was horrible. There was an international race that day, but the idiots in two of the cars were on the wrong road! Later I found out that they were following each other, some sort of personal vendetta, one-upmanship. The first guy decided to cut a few miles off the course by not going around the village but through it, and the other one, Travis, followed him."

"But what about the people who lived there?"

"Exactly," Reede said. "Someone saw the first car coming so they began to warn everyone and they managed to get out of the way."

"Except you," Sophie said.

"I had a donkey loaded with boxes of medicines and the animal froze, wouldn't move. The first car ran past us, with sand flying everywhere, and the poor creature freaked. Refused to take a step. I couldn't believe it when another car came right behind the first one. It was heading directly toward us."

"What did you do?" she asked.

"I didn't think about anything but keeping the medicines and that terrified donkey safe. I threw myself between the car and the animal."

Sophie stared at him. "That was dangerous."

"Yeah," he said, "but if you had any idea what I'd gone through to get those supplies . . ." Reede shrugged. "Anyway, the guy driving saw us and did a U-turn that scared the donkey so much that it sat down and the boxes split open. I lost everything."

"And Kim's future husband was driving?"

"Yeah, that was him."

"What did he do?"

"Ran off. That race was everything to him and he kept going. Later Maxwell Industries replaced all of the supplies quite generously but still . . ." Reede gave a one-sided grin. "At least he didn't win the race."

"I'm glad he didn't," Sophie said, and Reede smiled at her.

As she looked at him she thought that this moment was more romantic than all the rest that they'd been through. While it was exciting to have a man sweep you away on the back of a horse in the moonlight, it was quite another for him to wipe away your tears. She liked moonlight during the day also.

"Come on and finish your sandwich," he said, and they kept smiling at each other.

SEVENTEEN

Sophie spent the night in her new apartment over the sandwich shop. Reede tried to coax her into staying with him and it was nearly impossible to resist the intensity of his eyes, but she'd done it. She felt like there were other things in her life that needed to be sorted out before there was more intimacy. Now, in the morning, as she lay in bed staring at the ceiling, she realized that something was happening inside her. She wasn't quite sure what it was, but she thought maybe it was hope.

For years now her hope for the future had been tied to when her sister went away to college and she'd no longer have to live in the same house as her stepfather. She'd had hope that her future was connected to Carter, then in just days she'd attached her hope to Reede.

But now . . . Now there were other possibilities. She'd never wanted a restaurant.

She'd learned how to cook because she had to. And because she was a creative person she'd taught herself to do something other than fry pork chops. But perhaps . . .

She had her hands behind her head and was lazing about when the shout of a male voice startled her.

"Sophie!" came the roar from downstairs.

It was Roan, and his voice was as big as his body.

She scrambled out of bed and looked for her jeans as all she had on was an oversized T-shirt.

"Come down or I'll come up," he bellowed, "then I'll have to fight my little cousin for you."

Sophie rolled her eyes. Reede was anything but small. "I'm coming," she yelled back at him.

"Well, get down here! We have work to do. And don't bother putting on makeup. There's no time."

Sophie made a quick trip to the bathroom with an even quicker glance at the mirror. She was a mess! Her hair was a tangle, her eyes sleepy-looking, and she had a crease from a pillow on her cheek. She started to take the time to fix herself, but then thought, What the heck? She was too excited to fiddle with a mascara wand. Besides, this was Roan, not Reede.

Roan was standing at the bottom of the stairs, wearing a frown of impatience. But it changed when he saw Sophie. "Good Lord! Is this what you look like when you wake up? No wonder Reede has become a blithering idiot."

She couldn't help laughing as his compliment was so sincere. She ran her hands through her hair, trying to smooth it. "So what's got you in such a rush this morning?"

"I think we should open tomorrow."

"Not possible. I have to make eight animal sculptures for some kids. They're —"

"Yeah, everybody in town knows about that. The kids saw Jim Levenger get pinned to a tree by a wayward arrow and you rounded them up and calmed them down with potato dragons. And those poor women who suffer through working for Reede bought you some clay so you'd like Edilean and stay here and keep the doc off their backs. Seems that the more sex he gets the nicer he is, and looking at you this morning I understand perfectly."

Under normal circumstances, Sophie would have been blushing at what Roan was saying, but his tone made her laugh. "Did the gossip wagon have any idea how I'm supposed to do eight animals and open a restaurant at the same time?"

"This is Edilean."

"What does that mean?"

"That everybody has an opinion on everything."

"All right," Sophie said. "I have an opinion too. Today I make the sculptures and tomorrow I get groceries and make some soup and the next day I open a restaurant and I'm going to need some help with all of that." She started to say something about the money that she'd need but didn't have, but she couldn't bring herself to mention it.

"It's all taken care of. While you were lollygagging around in the woods yesterday and peeling potatoes, I was working."

"Unpeeled. Makes for better animal skin."

"Right," he said as he opened the front door. His truck was just outside. "Here, hold this open."

She held the door as he went to the bed of the truck and opened the tailgate.

"I brought the fifty pounds of clay and you're going to sculpt and do some actual work at the same time."

"But I —"

"Don't even think of saying that you can't do it. I teach at a university, remember? You kids do your homework while partying to three a.m."

"I'm hardly —" Sophie began but Roan held out a box for her to take.

"Tools," he said. "And I got a few cookbooks so we can decide what we're going to make." Under the back window were four huge shopping bags with the William and Mary logo on them. Beside them were three more bags and four boxes from Williams-Sonoma.

"You've been shopping."

Roan gave a little grin. "Funny thing about women and shopping. I called two women I know who say they are in a . . . What is that disgusting term people use nowadays? A committed relationship. That's it. For months they've been saying they can't go out with me, but when I asked them to help me buy things, they just said, 'When and where?' One helped me buy books and the other one helped me choose cookware."

"All of which you could have done by yourself."

"But who wants to, right?" he said, and they both laughed.

The day was hectic. Roan was used to being in charge of a lot of people, so he came up with dozens of things for Sophie to do at one time. The chaos wasn't helped by the fact that the day before he'd placed an ad in the Williamsburg newspaper.

HELP WANTED IN SANDWICH SHOP IN EDILEAN. CREATIVE, INTELLIGENT, ENTERTAINING, TALENTED, EDU-CATED PERSON DESIRED. COOKING ABILITY A BONUS.

"Are you advertising for a waitperson or a wife?"

"I'm open to opportunity," he said. "Let's see what turns up."

The people who showed up were not what Sophie had in mind to help with the work of a restaurant. Every college kid for fifty miles around who was trying for a degree in some art form answered the ad. Since they recognized Roan's professor attitude, they were drawn to him and sat down at the tables. Soon all of them were into deep discussions about art and philosophy and the meaning of life.

Sophie was left with the work to do. When Reede showed up at one o'clock she was sitting on the floor with a cookbook open beside her, the manual for the big coffee machine Roan had bought in front of her, and a piece of clay that was beginning to look like a giraffe in her hands. Roan and his "students," i.e., the job applicants, were taking up all the tables.

Reede made his way through the mess, looked down at Sophie without saying a word, and offered her his hand. Gratefully, she took it and they went outside.

"Looks like you're getting to know my cousin," Reede said.

"Oh yeah. He has a quote from a philosopher for every thought mankind has ever had."

"Mankind, huh?"

She had the clay in her hands and was moving it about as they spoke. "Another day of this and I'll be calling myself 'one' as in, 'One can only guess at the enormity of the cosmic consequences of one's inner self.' "

Reede laughed. "Sounds just like Roan. Have you eaten?"

"Not for hours."

"Good. Me neither. Let's go to Ellie's for lunch."

"Is she my competition?"

"She's your savior. She owns the grocery, and she'll sell to you wholesale."

"She could give me a ninety-nine percent discount and I still couldn't afford it. I tried to talk to Roan about money, but he was busy."

They'd reached Reede's Jeep and they got in it. "You have to understand that Roan is a McTern."

"Al said he'd inherited some property."

"More than a little." Reede started the engine. They were in the little parking area behind his office. "See the building my office is in?"

"Yes."

"Roan owns that. And the one next to it and that one and that one. In fact, he owns most of the downtown, and we all pay him rent. An ancestor of his, Tam McTern, bought the land and began building the town."

"And it's stayed in the family all this time?"

"Through centuries. He sells some of it now and then but mostly to cousins."

"He wants to sell the sandwich shop to Al. He isn't a cousin, is he?"

"No," Reede said, "but Al's family's been here a while."

Sophie was beginning to learn about Edilean. "A hundred years?"

"Or more," Reede said, his eyes twinkling.

By the time they got to the grocery, she was almost finished with the giraffe. They sat in the car and he watched her as she pushed and pulled the clay. "Could I borrow your keys?"

He handed them to her and she quickly used a point to etch onto the clay a semblance of the giraffe's distinctive skin pattern.

"I don't know how you do that," he said.

"I don't know how you give life to people."

Reede grunted. "This morning I had three cases of hives, one of an 'itchy place,' and a pulled muscle. On a daily basis, it's not exactly an exciting job."

Sophie couldn't help frowning. "But the people need you."

"What they want is my cousin Tristan, who is part therapist."

"You mean that he listens to them?"

"Yeah," Reede said. "He listens. Done?"

She wrote 'Brittany' into the clay and put the little giraffe on the dashboard so it could begin drying.

The grocery was very high end and she was impressed. "I think I'll need a place a little more . . . uh, human than this one."

"Don't worry, Sara's mother, Ellie, owns the store and she'll arrange whatever you need. Hey! I know. I'll get Sara to send Mr. Lang to you."

"I thought you liked this girl," said a pretty, older woman from behind a tall glass deli case. "You can't sic Mr. Lang on her."

"Sara will keep him in check, and besides, the old man likes pretty girls."

"Then he'll like you," she said to Sophie and extended her hand over the top of the counter. "I'm Ellie and Mr. Lang is . . ." She looked at Reede. "How do you describe him?"

"Healthy," Reede said. "I have thirty-year-olds who aren't in as good a shape as he is." He looked at Sophie. "Mr. Lang is over ninety."

"Must come from a lifetime of driving people crazy." Ellie didn't seem to be joking.

"I'm looking forward to meeting him," Sophie said. "He sounds interesting."

"Whatever he is, he grows the best vegetables in the state. If he likes you he'll sell them to you directly." Ellie was straightening the counter as she spoke.

"That sounds like a challenge," Sophie said. "Any suggestions on how to make him like me?"

"Throw a box over him," Reede said, and he and Ellie laughed. "I'll tell you the story later," he told Sophie.

"So what can I get for you two today?" Ellie asked. "I hear you're doing soup and sandwiches at your new shop. How about desserts?"

"No thanks. I have too much to do already." Sophie started to say something about Roan's ridiculous ad but he was their relative so she didn't dare.

But Ellie didn't hesitate. "How are your creative employees doing?"

"I liked the talented aspect," Reede said. "This morning my whole office was giggling about it. Heather said her best talent was doing a backbend over a picnic table."

Ellie and Sophie looked at him.

"I don't think I was supposed to hear that."

"I think not," Sophie said.

"So now to get my foot out of my mouth," Reede said, "we need some butter . . . It's something orange."

Ellie looked at Sophie in question.

"Butternut squash," she said. "He likes that soup."

"What's the name of your restaurant?" Ellie asked.

"I haven't thought of that," Sophie answered, but lying made her glance away.

"Anything to do with doctors?" Ellie asked.

Sophie laughed. It looked like Roan had told what she'd said about naming it No Doctors Allowed. She glanced at Reede. "Maybe I should name it Now and Then."

She and Ellie looked at each other and laughed.

"I don't think I'm needed here," Reede said, but he was smiling.

"You poor thing. You want your usual?" Ellie asked.

"Sure." Reede looked at Sophie. "What sandwich do you want?"

"Brie and cranberries," she said, then looked up. "Oh. Sorry. I keep coming up with ideas for soup and sandwiches. I'll take chicken on whole wheat. And —" Breaking off, she blinked a few times. "Phoenix. I'm going to name the restaurant Phoenix because . . ." She trailed off.

"Rising from the ashes," Reede said as he took her hand and squeezed it.

She smiled at him in thanks for understanding.

"You two are steaming up the glass," Ellie said, but her voice was pure happiness. "I'll get the sandwiches while you fill your carts. Your prices won't be retail and it'll all be charged to Roan."

"Thank you," Sophie said. "Thank you very much."

Ellie looked at Sophie, with a brief glance at Reede. "Thank *you*," she said quietly.

"Hate to break up the hen party but I have to get back to work. Who knows? Somebody may have a paper cut that I'll have to tape together."

"I wish I could find a pill that would sweeten you up," Ellie said, then looked at Sophie as though to say that was her job.

Sophie put her hands up, palms out, and took a step back. Roan had said that she was, well, helping Reede's bad temper, but it looked like it wasn't much.

"See you later." Ellie disappeared behind the case.

Reede got a cart and they went to the produce section. Sophie didn't have a list with her but she knew what she needed to make about four big pots of soup — which should be enough for a day in a tiny town like Edilean.

"How bad are you?" she asked Reede as she put yellow onions in a bag.

"As a doctor? If the case is significant, I don't think I'm bad at all."

"No, I mean your bedside manner."

Reede scoffed. "I'm not willing to sit there and listen all day if that's what you mean. Do you need mushrooms?"

"Yes. Make sure the heads are closed. Why did the people have hives? From allergies? Three people in the same day? Were they related?"

Reede put mushrooms in a bag. "I can't

really talk about individual patients."

"Sure, I understand," she said. "I just wondered because there have been a few times in my life when stress made me break into hives. When my mother died and I realized I couldn't leave town to take my sculpting job, my whole body was covered in ugly red patches. They went up my neck and into my hair. My doctor spent twenty minutes with me while I cried."

"What did he give you for them?"

"I don't know," Sophie said, "but he told me that every day I was to drink a glass of wine and laugh at least once."

"And did you?" Reede asked.

"No. But I wish I had. Where's the dairy section?"

"That way," Reede said and he was thoughtful as he followed her.

"I asked them why the hell they had hives."

"Surely you didn't say it like that, did you?

"I did because I knew exactly what the problem was — or I thought I did. One woman had cat hairs all over her sweater. I've told her three times that she's allergic to cats and to stay away from them."

"But she loves cats," Sophie said.

"Yeah."

"And the other woman?"

"Same, but with strawberries. She dips them in chocolate, eats them, then scratches. When it gets too bad she comes to me."

"What about the last woman?"

Reede was silent for a moment. "She was different. When I asked her what was wrong she burst into tears."

"At the way you asked her?"

"Yeah," he said. "But there was method to my madness. Hives are an indication of something else. It might be something self-caused like playing with the neighbor's cats, or it might be from stress. If it's stress, sometimes they won't tell me unless . . ." He looked at her.

"Unless you catch them off guard."

"Right. She didn't have time to remember her lie."

"What did you do?"

"I can't tell you the details of the case, but I sent Alice with her to a women's shelter in Richmond and I called the sheriff, Colin. He'll take care of the rest of it."

"And you said you had a boring morning."

"Tristan would have —"

She put her fingertips over his lips. "I think what *you* did worked very well."

Somehow their conversation had turned serious and he wanted to lighten it. "Any plans for the third date? I've done some swinging from a cable out of a helicopter."

Sophie didn't smile as she put cheeses in the cart. "I know that walking across beams and people pinned to trees is important and it's very exciting, but sometimes it's nice to be quiet. It feels good to sit together and do nothing."

Reede wasn't sure what she meant, as the two things didn't go together. He hadn't chosen either of the first two events. That first night he'd planned a quiet picnic and — Well, maybe he had dressed in black, worn a mask, and arrived on an unruly horse, but the robbers weren't his fault. Nor was the man with an arrow in his shoulder. On the other hand, Heather had told him a bit of what had happened and Reede had been rather forceful in getting Sophie to go with him.

"Did you and the Treeborne kid sit around a lot?" He hadn't meant to ask that and it came out with more jealousy than he'd meant to show.

Sophie looked like she wasn't sure what to answer, but then she went for the truth.

"Yes, we did." She paused, but before Reede could say anything, she said, "But we were hiding from his father and from the town. I didn't know it, but I wasn't considered good enough to be seen in public." She raised her hands upward. "What I wouldn't give for *normal.*"

When they got back to the shop, Reede wanted to carry everything inside for her but she wouldn't let him. "You have patients and they need you," she said. They set the bags on the sidewalk, he kissed her good-bye, then left.

As Reede drove back to the office he thought about what Sophie had said about being normal. When he was growing up he'd wanted normal. But circumstances — the town wanting "the other Aldredge" for a doctor, the woman he loved dumping him — had changed his life.

When he got back to the office the first thing he saw was the little calendar by Betsy's desk, the one with all the *x*'s on it. His impulse was to take it down and tear it up. Or order her to destroy it. He was sick of being reminded of what Tristan would do.

But Reede didn't do any of those things. Instead, he wondered if he could make her remove it of her own accord.

"So who do we have coming this after-noon? Would you please get me their phone numbers?"

For a moment Betsy just sat there and

stared at him. It was the "please" that was turning her catatonic.

Heather came in the back and didn't see Reede standing by Betsy's desk. He usually hid out in his office. "It's turning cold out there! Did you guys hear that Sophie's opening her restaurant tomorrow? I don't know how she's going to do it with Roan and his worshippers taking up all the seats. Between him and the doc—" She broke off when she saw Reede and her red face told what she'd been about to say.

For a moment they were silent, then he said, "Heather, I want to thank you and your husband for cleaning up the mess in the preserve."

When neither of the women replied, Reede went down the hall to his office.

"I love Sophie," Heather whispered.

"I think we need to thank her. I'm going to start the grapevine that she needs customers."

"Good idea," Heather said, and when she went back to the exam rooms she was smiling.

All afternoon Reede worked on his bedside manner, trying his best to be . . . well, a Tristan clone. Unfortunately, he found that the more he listened the more people talked. By the end of the day he was well behind schedule. He texted Sophie.

LATE PATIENTS. SEE YOU AT 6:30? DIN-
NER?

When Sophie's phone buzzed she was so swamped with work she hardly had time to read. YES AND YES she wrote back.

By four she had the last of the animals done and she set them on top of the big refrigerated glass case to begin to dry. They'd be fragile, not really playthings, but each one had the child's name on it and she'd also put on her initials and the year.

"They're great," Roan said as he came up behind her, then leaned toward her ear. "Not one of these kids would be good for the job. Too much talk and not enough action. I think I'll ask the relatives to find someone."

Sophie was chopping carrots and the look she gave him said it was too little too late.

"Here, I'll help you," he said.

But Sophie could see that he wanted to keep talking with the kids. It looked like he was missing being a professor. "I can do this," she said. "Go on with your new friends." There were only four of them left. "They look hungry, so why don't you take them out to dinner?"

Roan kissed her cheek. "My cousin isn't good enough for you."

"I agree," she said.

Sophie got everything cut up and ready to make into soup but she couldn't cook it yet as she didn't have refrigerator space for the big pots. She'd have to get up early tomorrow and start everything.

As she cut and arranged and planned, some of the parents from the Williamsburg church came by with their children to get the animals. Sophie told them how the dried clay would break easily.

"Don't worry, this will go in the glass case in the living room," a mother said. "And, Sophie, thank you for this. There were no nightmares, just talk of the potato dragon."

At about seven when she was just finishing for the day the Baptist pastor, Russell Pendergast, stopped by.

"Should I throw my hat in first?" he asked sheepishly. She hadn't seen him since that first day when she'd poured beer over Reede. Russell had known that she'd been about to start work for the man who'd nearly run over her.

"It's all right," she said and Russell stepped inside.

"It looks good. Very creatively done by talented people."

Sophie groaned. "Roan and his ad! I think he wanted to lure students to him and he did. I did manage to get them to do a little cleaning while they contemplated how the universe is going to be affected by their own brilliant selves."

"I was never that young," he said.

"Me neither."

"So you still have no help?"

"Is that an opening into telling me that you know someone?"

"I do, actually. Her name is Kelli and she's had a hard time of it. She's young and knows how to work."

"She sounds marvelous," Sophie said. "When can she start?"

"She's on a bus to here now."

"I see. But what if I'd hired one of Roan's kids?"

Russell smiled. "Somehow I knew you wouldn't find anyone through that ad. My wife told me I had to help you. She said I owed you for being a lying, cowardly wimp when I met you."

"Oh my! I think I really like her."

"She keeps me in line." He was on the far side of the glass case and there were two animals left on top. "I've heard about these. You . . . ?"

"I what?" Sophie asked as she dried off

her hands.

"Would you like to teach a sculpture class to our church members?"

"I've never done any teaching and besides, these are just self-hardening clay and they're very fragile."

"I know," Russell said. "But what if I could get a kiln set up for you?"

"Did Reede put you up to this?"

"I have a more important Boss than him. I'm always trying to entice people to come to church, and if my sermons don't do it, I use other things."

Sophie walked around the counter and sat down. She'd been on her feet for many hours and she needed a rest. "I don't know . . . I'd have to think about this. Are you talking children or adults?"

"Both," he said as he took the seat across from her. "We have a lot of retirees in the area and they're used to sixty-hour work-weeks. They need something to channel their interest into besides golf. And there's one man in particular who is nearly desperate to find a good teacher." He smiled at her. "I can see that you're tired and tomorrow is going to be a long day, but think about this. You'd have time around your classes to do your own work, and I can assure you that any equipment you need I can gouge out of my father."

Sophie was a little shocked that a minister would say such a thing.

"Not *that* Father," Russell said. "The one I share with Travis. Randall Maxwell."

"Oh," Sophie said. "Isn't he . . . ?"

"Can afford anything." Russell stood up. "Just keep it in mind and Kelli will be here tomorrow. And, Sophie?"

"Yes?"

"You know the old adage about not judging a book by its cover? That especially pertains to Kelli."

"Okay," she said tentatively, as she had no idea what he meant.

When Reede got to the sandwich shop that evening, no one was about. So much for Roan's ad bringing in help, he thought. The front door was unlocked and he thought he should remind Sophie to lock it when she went upstairs for the night. It was one thing to leave the shop open when she wasn't inside, but another to leave it unlocked when she was there.

The lights were out and he could see that everything was clean and tidy, and in the back he saw something pink. Maybe Sophie had left a sweater downstairs.

But what she'd left out was herself. Sitting in a booth, her head on her arms on the table, and sound asleep was Sophie. He didn't need to be a doctor to recognize exhaustion.

"Come on, baby," he whispered as he kissed her on the temple. She woke enough to slide her arms around his neck.

"No mask," she said dreamily.

He smiled as she nuzzled against him, her face in his neck. "No more masks. Just me, as naked as you see me."

"I like you naked."

"Do you?" He was smiling as he pulled her out of the booth. He knew he needed to carry her up the stairs, and of course he meant to do it the Scarlett and Rhett way, but the stairs were narrow and they'd never fit.

Sophie solved the problem by clinging to him like a child, her arms tightening around his neck. It didn't take much for him to lift her and when he did, she clasped her legs about his waist and clung to him.

The deliciousness of Sophie's body against his was almost more than he could bear.

"I love being short," she murmured as he walked toward the stairs. "I've never figured out what tall girls do with their excess body parts."

Reede could have told her but at the moment he couldn't seem to remember.

"You smell good," she said. As he went up the stairs, her lips were on his neck. "Smell good. Taste good. What about your inner self?"

Reede chuckled. "Better since I met you." He carried her down the hall to the bedroom, bent, and put her on the bed. She instantly turned to her side and went back to sleep.

He stood there for a moment, looking at her curled up, her jeans curving around her bottom, her pink shirt clinging to her upper half. She was shaped like an hourglass, a throwback to a time when women wore corsets to give themselves a twenty-inch waist. But Sophie didn't need a corset to get that figure. Even in modern clothes of jeans and a T-shirt she showed off her roundness top and bottom, with her tiny waist in the middle.

Right now he should leave her. He should close the door and let her sleep, but it wasn't going to be easy. He wanted to snuggle up next to her, wanted to make love to her. Wanted to — She turned over, her face toward his. Without opening her eyes she lifted her arms to him. It was all the invitation he needed.

Instantly he was in bed with her, his arms,

even his legs around her.

"I missed you so much today," he said as he kissed her neck, her face. Her clothes began to come off. "I want you with me all the time. Forever."

She didn't answer, just arched her body against his, enjoying his hands, his lips, his words.

It took him only seconds and she was nude. It was erotic for her to be naked and feel her skin against his clothes, as though they were doing something illicit, almost illegal.

She kept her eyes closed as he kissed her breasts, his big, hard hands on her waist, his thumbs caressing her stomach.

"Sophie, you are so beautiful. I've never seen a woman as perfect as you."

She couldn't help smiling. His lips went lower and lower and when his tongue touched the center of her, her eyes opened in shock. This was new to her, something she'd never experienced before, and it didn't take long before wave after wave of passion went through her.

He brought his face back up to hers. "Okay?" he whispered.

"I never . . . No one ever before has . . ."

"Yeah?" he said. "I like being the first."

"You're the first at a lot of things," she

whispered, her hand on his cheek. She could feel the whiskers, that oh so masculine symbol. She kissed him, felt the whiskers under her tongue.

"I think we should share," she said as she lowered her hand to between his legs. He was ready for her, but she meant to take her time. Button and zipper came open quickly and when she put her hand on his hot skin, he groaned, his head back in the ecstasy of her touch.

She liked having this power over him, liked feeling this large man become hers. His trousers easily slipped off and she felt his skin against hers. Hot, rampant with desire.

For all that receiving pleasure was new to her, the giving of it wasn't. Her lips moved downward slowly, taking her time, her hand lightly caressing him, her thumbs playing along his thighs.

"Sophie," he whispered as she took him in her mouth.

After they'd both found release they could take their time in the joy of discovery of each other's bodies. Caressing, touching, kissing, exploring. It took them a long time until they'd worked to fever pitch and could no longer hold back. Reede lowered her to the bed, onto her back, but Sophie laughed and pushed him down.

"Have your way with me," he said, sounding as though he was submitting to her greater power.

Sophie gave a villainous laugh as she moved on top of him, then lowered herself, both of them groaning in pleasure. "Shall I shape you into a giraffe? Or a bear?" she said as she began to move on him. "Or a hawk to match your eyes?"

His hands were on her waist, holding her, guiding. "Sophie, my love, you can do anything you want to me."

Their lovemaking was slow, languorous, sensual. They held back as long as they could, extending their pleasure as long as possible.

But soon they built to a pitch and Reede pushed Sophie onto her back, her legs wrapped round him. They came together in a blaze of ecstasy, then held each other tightly, neither wanting to let go.

"Sophie," Reede whispered into her ear and the way he said her name seemed to say it all. They clung to each other, naked skin together, warm, glowing.

It was the growling of Reede's stomach that pulled them apart.

"Food is the only thing that takes a man away from lust," Sophie said.

"Lust?" he said softly as he rolled off of her. "Is that what we are?"

She wasn't yet ready to answer that question. "Can I make you a sandwich?"

"Please," he said.

Reede switched on the lamp by the bed and watched Sophie as she got out, nude, and began to dress.

"I feel like I'm putting on a show."

"Yeah," he said, with so much innuendo that she laughed.

When she was dressed she sat on the end of the bed. "Your turn."

As he got out of bed, Sophie watched in appreciation. He kept in good shape and she admired the way the muscles of his chest blended into his hard, flat stomach. "Do I pass?"

"Mmmm. Okay," she said in a way that made him laugh.

"Don't say that to Mike or he'll kill me in the next workout session. As it is, he gives me about fifty burbies to do."

"And what are they?"

"Exercises designed by the devil. How about roast beef with horseradish?"

"Sounds great," she said as they went down the stairs.

In the kitchen he pulled a loaf of bread from under the counter. "Are you ready for your opening tomorrow?"

"Not in the least."

"I wish I could help but my patients are backed up by weeks. I've been busy with other things." He grinned at her.

She told him about Russell's employee who was coming, but she didn't tell him about the teaching offer. "I think Roan misses teaching."

"Can't tell that he's stopped," Reede said. "But it was nice for him to have people to entertain today."

"Is the book he was writing really bad?"

"Truly awful," Reede said as he cut the sandwiches they'd made. He opened the fridge and saw big bowls of lemons and cut vegetables.

"You haven't made the soups?"

"No time," she said. "Besides, there wasn't room to put them in the fridge. The cream in them has to be kept cold. I'll do them in the morning."

"I'll help you."

She knew he meant to spend the night but not yet.

He saw the answer in her eyes. "I understand. When I started practicing medicine I needed to prove to myself that I could do everything. I needed to believe in myself."

"And do you?"

"I did until I came back here to Edilean," he said, making a joke, only it wasn't one. He'd finished his sandwich and stood up. "Sophie, why don't you move in with me? I don't have a lot of furniture, but you and I can go buy some. It'll be your taste, whatever you want."

It was tempting for her to say yes. There was part of her that wanted to let him take care of her, to let herself become half of a whole. But at the same time she wanted to see if she could do something on her own.

"All right," he said, "but I'm here when you're ready." He went to the door. "Lock this behind me and I'll be here in the morning to help you. I don't know anything about cooking but I can follow orders."

"Not from what I've seen," she said, making him grin. "Now go. I need some sleep."

"I could help you with that. I could —"

"Go!" she said, laughing as she pushed him out the door, then locked it behind him.

Once she was alone in the little shop she meant to go straight up to bed, but then she thought maybe she should juice the lemons. Roan had purchased a big commercial juicer and she could try it out. It would probably only take a few minutes to do all the lemons.

Hours later it was midnight and she had

the juicing done, more vegetables cut, and even the utensils set out to start the soups in the morning. As she made her way up the stairs she was staggering with fatigue. She set the alarm for four a.m. She probably wouldn't need that much time to get ready but she wanted to be safe.

She fell into bed and was asleep instantly.

EIGHTEEN

Sophie knew the people of Edilean meant well, but right now she wanted to push them all out the door and lock it. It wasn't even lunchtime yet but she was dizzy with fatigue and her mind was spinning with all the orders she'd had to fill.

At 4:15 a.m. she'd been downstairs making what she'd thought were vats of soup, but if the breakfast traffic was any indication of what was coming at lunch, the soup wouldn't last an hour. At four-thirty Reede called and said he was sorry but one of his patients had gone into labor and he had to attend to her. "And her husband," he'd added. Roan arrived at six-thirty and made the coffee.

When Sophie unlocked the front door at seven, there was a line outside. She'd planned to serve eggs and ham on bagels, but no matter how fast she moved she couldn't keep up with the demand. Roan

371

rang up the receipts, but he loved to talk, and people in line were impatient. Several times during the day Sophie thought of the woman having a baby. Giving birth had to be easier than the chaos of the little restaurant.

All morning Sophie had the big flat griddle filled with eggs and ham and she tried her best to do it all.

At 11:20 when someone said, "Are you serving lunch yet?" Sophie nearly burst into tears. She hadn't had time to clean up from breakfast and she knew there wasn't enough soup.

"Need some help?" came a voice from behind her. It was a voice that was so familiar, and so comforting, that Sophie smiled before she turned around. But then, she realized who owned the voice and saw his face at the same time.

It was Carter.

He was at the head of the line of people waiting for Sophie to take their orders, then make their sandwiches, ladle soup, and serve it all to them.

If Carter had shown up the day before she would have panicked. Just plain gone into an attack of fear. Were the police behind him? Were they waiting to take her away to jail for stealing the precious Treeborne cookbook?

But right now she didn't have time for the luxury of a panic attack. "The cookbook is being sent back to you and would you step aside so I can take these people's orders?" She glared at him, daring him to make a scene. She didn't see any police, so maybe Carter had come alone. If that was true, then all she had to do was say something to Roan and he'd usher Carter out. Probably by the seat of his pants.

"Hey kid!" Roan said. "Make up your mind. You're holding up the flow."

"Yeah," the young man next in line said.

"He's just leaving, aren't you?" Sophie narrowed her eyes at Carter, then lowered her voice. "You're not in Treeborne country now and nobody is going to put you at the front of the line." She couldn't help smiling at that thought. Edilean may have its problems but it wasn't owned by a tyrant of a man who allowed his son to do anything he wanted to anybody.

Carter looked genuinely puzzled, as though no one had ever suggested that he shouldn't be given special privileges.

A lot of words came to Sophie's mind of what she'd like to say to him, to tell him how he'd hurt her, and how she wished she'd never met him. But she didn't have the time. "Go back to where you belong. People work here."

Still looking as though he didn't understand what was happening, Carter moved out of line and Sophie took an order for a brie and cranberry panini sandwich.

She couldn't help but glance at Carter as he walked toward the door. On the drive to Edilean there'd been a dozen times when she'd thought that if he'd shown up she would have thrown herself at him. On one long stretch across East Texas she imagined that he'd so regret what he'd done and would say to her that he'd use the Treeborne resources to tear the earth apart looking for her.

But by the time she got to Tennessee she knew he wasn't going to come for her. And by the time she reached Virginia she was boiling with anger.

Turning, she began to put a sandwich together. She had already apologized fifty times to people because they had to wait so long for their orders. Only two people had complained, and Roan had escorted both of them out the door.

"Anybody else have any comments to make?" he'd asked in a voice that was used to filling auditoriums. No one else had said anything bad.

As Sophie made the sandwich she looked up and saw Carter pulling a white apron off a peg. The sunlight came through the front windows and flashed off his golden hair. She used to like the blondness of him, like his pale skin. But now he looked almost girly.

"What do you think you're doing? You can't —" she began as he took gloves from a box.

"I'm going to help," he said. "Don't you think I owe you that much?"

A shadow came over her and she knew Roan was behind her and waiting for Sophie's decision.

For a split second she was torn. It would feel great to put her nose in the air and tell Carter she didn't need help or anything else from him. She liked the vision of Roan tossing Carter out. On the other hand, there were now so many people in line they were weaving about the tables.

"Soup!" she said, then went back to the sandwich.

She never would have believed it but Carter was excellent help. After just thirty minutes they had established a very efficient assembly line. Sophie took the orders and filled paper bowls and cups with the soup. Carter made the sandwiches and passed them over the counter. Roan took cash and credit cards.

For all that Carter was fast and efficient — which greatly surprised Sophie — he still had that Treeborne arrogance. When some out of towner started giving him orders of no mayo, no onions, double pickles, Carter said, "Do I look like your mother?"

There was something about Carter that made the man back down. Sophie's eyes were wide, as she'd been trained that the customer was always right. She looked at Roan, but he nodded in agreement. He liked Carter's attitude.

The soup ran out by one and at the rate the bread was going it might not last to closing time at two.

Carter yelled, "We're having a twelve-percent-off sale on open-faced sandwiches. Fewer carbs." Nearly everyone took him up on the offer. Only Roan grumbled at having to figure out the 12 percent discount.

At one-thirty Reede came in, and by then most of the customers were gone.

"Hungry?" Sophie asked, her voice full of the memory of last night.

"For everything," Reede said softly.

"This is a family restaurant," Roan said, "so you two cut it out."

Smiling, Reede leaned back and looked at

the chalkboard. "I'll have a —"

"The only thing we have left is ham and cheese. No soup. Sorry," Sophie said.

"I'll take whatever you have." He noticed the man behind the counter and leaned across. "Hi, I'm —" Reede broke off when he saw Carter. He'd seen many photos of him on the Internet and he recognized the Treeborne heir, a man who stood to inherit millions from his family's frozen food empire. The stories about him had all been good, but Reede had held Sophie while she cried, so he had a different opinion.

Carter had heard Reede's flirty tone with Sophie but he was used to that. In his hometown all the males had acted that way toward her. He stepped around the counter and held out his hand to shake. "I'm Carter Tree—"

He didn't finish because Reede hit him with a right cross smack in his face.

Blood spurted from his nose and Carter went down, hitting the floor hard.

Like some predatory beast, Reede stood over him. "Get out of here," he said. "Get out and don't come back. Do you hear me?"

Sophie, still behind the counter, was stunned. She'd seen no evidence of violence in Reede and hadn't expected this. She had to admit that part of her liked — no, *loved*

— that Reede had hit Carter. She'd certainly wanted to do that to him.

But the larger part of her was civilized.

"No," she said softly, then louder, "No!" She put herself between the two men, Carter still on the floor, blood pouring from his nose. As for Reede, his fists were clenched, ready to do more hitting. He was a great deal bigger than Carter, and right now he looked like some knight of old.

She put her hands on Reede's arms. "He helped me today and you have to look at his nose."

"Out!" Roan yelled to the remaining customers, who were staring with great interest.

"But my —" one man began.

"Come tomorrow and you'll get a free soup," Roan said as he cleared the place, locked the door, and turned back to the others.

Reede was still standing over Carter, his fists clenched, and the smaller man was on the floor, looking as though he didn't dare get up.

Roan got his phone out of his pocket and sent a text message to Reede's office that his medical bag was needed. SOMETHING FOR A BLOODY NOSE, he wrote.

"Reede," Sophie said and looked at him

half in pleading and half in command.

It took him a moment to recover, then he held out his hand to help Carter up. Hesitantly, the smaller man took it, sat down in a chair, and put his hand to his nose.

"Don't touch it," Reede snapped.

Carter put his hand up in protection, as though Reede was going to strike him.

"He's not going to hurt you," Sophie said. "At least not again, are you, Reede?"

"No," he said. "Put your hand down and let me see your nose."

"Are you crazy?" Carter asked.

"He's a doctor," Sophie said.

"You've got to be kidding. No doctor would —" Reede's look cut him off, and Carter dropped his hands to his side.

There was a knock on the glass door and Roan opened it to let Heather in. She was out of breath from running with Reede's heavy medical bag.

"What happened?" she asked, looking at Carter's bloody face. "You look like you ran into the side of a building."

"Reede hit him," Roan said proudly.

"Not possible," Heather said. "He wouldn't —" She looked at the doc. "You hit him?"

"Temporary insanity," Reede said as he gently examined Carter's nose. Heather and

Sophie went to get some hot water and clean cloths.

"I take it Sophie told you what I did to her," Carter said softly.

"Oh yeah," Reede said.

Roan was hovering in the background, watching the two men. Carter Treeborne was as blond as Reede was dark, as gentle-seeming as Reede was intense. It looked like the second time around Sophie had chosen a different direction.

Sophie and Heather returned with cloths and water, and Reede stood back as Heather cleaned Carter's face.

Sophie put her hand on Reede's arm and nodded upward. He followed her up the stairs.

The instant they were alone, he started apologizing. "I'm sorry. I've never hit anybody. At least not since I was in grade school. I know I have a temper, but this was —"

He stopped talking because Sophie kissed him. It was a sweet kiss and he couldn't help feeling that it had more meaning than the more intimate times they'd shared together. "What was that for?"

"To say thanks. I've never before had anyone do something like that for me. It was wrong, of course, and you shouldn't

380

have done it, but thank you."

"It was a gut reaction and you're right, I shouldn't have. As a doctor I took an oath to —"

"I know," she said. "Come in the kitchen and I'll get you something to eat."

He followed her and sat on a stool and watched while she pulled leftover chicken and salad out of the fridge. "Why is he here?"

"I don't know," Sophie said.

"He wants you back."

"That's a nice thought."

"What?!"

She smiled as she put the plate before him. "Every woman dreams of the man who dumped her begging her to return. Do you think he'll go on his knees to me?"

"Excuse me if I don't find any humor in this."

"Roan said I'd turned you into a blithering idiot but I didn't believe him until today."

"My cousin talks too much." He bit into the chicken. "You have to tell him to leave."

"I'm not going to," Sophie said.

Reede nearly choked on his food. "You can't . . ." He trailed off. "But maybe you want him. Maybe you want to go back to Texas and live with some kid who's going

381

to own a mega corporation. Maybe you —"

"If you're trying to make me angry, you're succeeding," she said.

Reede stopped talking.

"Carter was good help today, and I need that."

"You said that Russell is sending someone."

"I know." She told him of Russ's offer of a job teaching sculpting.

"But that's great! You can set up a studio in the craft house."

"Run that and this place too?" she asked.

Reede looked at her but said nothing. He knew what *he* wanted. Since he'd met Sophie he'd felt strongly about her. From their first phone call when he'd poured his heart out to her he'd felt the connection. On the surface it looked as though they hadn't known each other long, but he knew that what he felt was timeless. He'd loved only two women in his life.

When the first one didn't want him he'd been so devastated that he'd almost taken his own life. For years he'd been only half alive.

The truth was that he'd only truly revived after he'd met Sophie. He'd told himself that he'd never again feel that deep bond with another woman, but he'd felt it with her.

He liked everything about her, from the look of her to the way she was afraid of things but didn't let that stop her.

But now, facing this situation of dealing with this man who had hurt her, this man whom she'd loved, was terrifying him. In Africa he'd once faced a lioness on the hunt. He'd been alone, with no weapon, and no cover, but he'd stood his ground and she'd walked away. Later, Reede's legs had given out from under him and he'd collapsed, but he knew what he'd faced.

That day and that lioness were nothing compared to the thought of Sophie being alone with her former lover.

He remembered Al quoting Peter, Peter, Pumpkin Eater and that's exactly how Reede felt now. He wanted to grab Sophie and lock her away. He didn't want to do anything to risk losing her.

He took a deep breath. What he was about to say was the hardest, most courageous thing he'd ever said in his life. "Sophie, what do *you* want to do?"

"What an extraordinary thought," she said as she turned away. Her first impulse was to say that she wanted him, Reede, but then she remembered quiet times with Carter.

No walking across beams, no dealing with men pinned to trees. Every moment she'd spent with Carter had been good — up until the very last, that is. If it was true that he'd come back here for her, didn't she owe it to herself to find out what *she* wanted? Reede? Carter? Or maybe she'd get a job as a sculptor at some movie studio in LA and work on the next Hobbit film.

When she turned back to Reede she was smiling. "I don't know."

"You look like that's a good thing." There was no smile on his face.

"I have choices," she said. "Wonderful choices and I'm going to take my time deciding what I want to do."

"But —" he began.

"First of all, I'm going to talk to Carter. Alone. I'm going to see what he's after, whether it's me as a woman or me as a thief. For my own peace of mind I need to get the cookbook problem settled."

Reede sat down on the couch in the living room and watched her. This was a Sophie he hadn't seen before. But he liked her. "And what if he's here for you?"

She looked into Reede's eyes and thought about lying, but she couldn't do it. "I'll have to see about that. I don't know if I genuinely loved him or not. He's a Treeborne in a town owned by that family. I think that had a lot of influence on me. To go from high school boys making lewd remarks to me to the same kids holding doors open for me was heady. It felt so good it changed me. Changed how I felt about myself. Does that make sense?"

"I understand what you're saying, but the people in Edilean hold doors open for you because you're a fellow human being."

"I know," she said. "I've seen that. But they've also done things for me because of *you.*" Her face changed to pleading. "I want to see if I can do things on my own. Is that so difficult to understand?"

"No, it's not," he said as he stood up and looked at her. "I grew up here but I needed to find my own place in the world. Sophie, I'm going to tell you the truth. I love you. I've been in love with you almost from our first conversation. If I were a pirate I'd kidnap you and hold you prisoner until you said you loved me too. If this were medieval times I'd offer your guardian a cartload of gold for your hand."

She couldn't help but take a step toward him.

"But I can't do any of those things, so I'm going to wait. And I'm going to do anything I can to help you. But first —"

He took a step toward her, pulled her into his arms, and kissed her. He kissed her with all the longing, all the desire, and most of all, with all the love that he felt for her.

Her knees went weak, her arms limp at her side — and Reede dropped her. He just flat out let her go, and she fell down onto the couch.

"But I warn you that I don't play fair," he said as she stared up at him, still unable to catch her breath.

She sat there blinking as he left her apartment.

NINETEEN

Heather came up the stairs, tiptoeing quietly. "Are you okay?" she asked Sophie, who was still sitting on the couch and blinking.

Sophie nodded.

"I have to go back to work, but do you need anything?"

"A cold shower," Sophie murmured.

"Oh yeah? That sounds promising. I'm sorry about your lack of help today. Maybe tomorrow we can get someone. If you want to stay here, that is."

"Yes, I do," Sophie said, and it was the first time in a long while that she was absolutely *sure* of a decision. She got off the sofa and headed toward the stairs. "What kind of soup do you think I should make for tomorrow?"

"Cream of broccoli. That way you have fewer vegetables to chop."

"Good idea, thanks." Sophie was beginning to recover herself. What had Reede meant when he'd said that he didn't play fair?

"That man, Carter . . . Is he really Tree-borne Foods?"

"Heir apparent. If his father doesn't disown him because of me," Sophie said but didn't explain.

"He says he's waiting to talk to you. Want me to send him up here?"

"No!" Sophie said. Her apartment was too intimate, too . . . too personal.

"Are you in love with him?" Heather asked and she looked like she was expecting the worst.

Sophie hadn't known Heather long enough to confide in her, and besides, right now she wasn't sure about anything. "I think I better talk to him."

"If you don't want to be alone with him, I could stay."

Sophie thought that was an odd offer, as Heather was Reede's only nurse so he needed her. But then Heather had gone to a lot of trouble to keep Sophie from finding out who Reede was. "No, but thank you. I need to talk to him by myself."

"Okay, but if I can be of help with any-thing . . ." Heather trailed off, not seeming to know what to say. Turning, she left the apartment.

Sophie took a moment to refresh her makeup and comb her hair before going downstairs to face Carter. Her mind was ringing with the awful things he'd said the last time she spoke to him. That was when they'd made love and when she'd sneaked back in to steal the cookbook. Right now she wished she'd remembered to ask Reede what he'd done about that book. He'd said small things but she'd never heard the whole story.

For a moment Sophie stood at the head of the stairs, and it took all her strength to make herself go down.

Carter was wiping the stainless counter and when he saw Sophie he put down his cloth and went toward her. He seemed about to do their usual greeting of a cheek kiss, but she stepped back.

"Sorry," he said. "Habit. Can we talk?"

"I don't have a lot to say." Her back was rigid, her eyes unforgiving as she stared at him.

He nodded toward a booth in the back, but she took a seat in front of the big window to the street. They sat down, across from each other. While Carter leaned forward, his arms on the table, Sophie sat upright in the chair, which was a foot out from the table.

"I think I should tell you what my father is trying to do to me," Carter began. "Maybe if I explain the horrible, medieval thing —"

"Carter, I have to make lots of soup for tomorrow, so I really don't have time to hear about what your daddy is doing to you. Besides, whatever it is, I'm sure I can top it. What I want to know is what you're doing about the cookbook I stole."

Carter looked surprised at her words. "Nothing."

"What does that mean exactly?"

"I'm not doing anything about the cookbook and I don't plan to. Is that what you wanted to hear?"

Sophie wasn't sure she believed him. "That's the Treeborne cookbook," she said. "It's worth everything. Your family never shows it to an outsider. They —"

"The whole thing is and always has been a publicity gimmick. Yes, my great-grandmother had a cookbook and —"

"In code."

Carter smirked. "Yeah. A code made up by her. She had a drunken husband who sold everything she owned, so she made it useless to him."

"Do you know what it says?"

"Yes I do, since she told her son when he decided to go into the frozen food business

390

and it's been passed down to me."

"So the ads *are* true, and when your father sees that the cookbook is missing he'll —"

"Do nothing," Carter said. "Right now all he can think about is merging with the Palmer cannery. That's why he wants me to marry the owner's daughter. She's a serious druggie."

Sophie glared at him. "Is this where I'm supposed to feel sorry for you? Poor you. Married to make a deal. Sounds like the title of a book."

Carter looked at her for a moment. "You don't seem like the woman I knew."

"The one who had to be nice to local football heroes in the hope of getting a tip? Or the one who had to give up a career and stay in a town run by Treebornes? Or maybe you mean the one who was swept off her feet by the son of the town tyrant for a summer fling?"

Carter couldn't help a smile. "Whoever she was, I liked her." He lowered his lashes and his voice. "No, Sophie, I loved her. In fact, I've come here to ask you to marry me."

While she stared at him in astonishment, he reached into his pocket and withdrew a ring box, which she recognized as a design

391

created by her friend Kim. "I stopped in a little jewelry store when I got here yesterday and I bought you a ring." He went down on one knee and as he opened the box he said, "Sophie Kincaid, will you —"

She got up from the chair, walked to behind the counter, and put on an apron.

Carter, his face red with embarrassment, got up, closed the box, put it on the table, and went to her. "Sophie?"

She was scrubbing the clean countertop.

"Sophie, please talk to me."

When she looked at him, her face was furious. "So that's it?" she said through clenched teeth. "You walk in here and expect me to say yes to a marriage proposal? Then what? I throw my arms around your neck and all is forgiven? Do you even remember what you said to me before you shoved me out the front door?"

"I didn't mean to be so physical, but I was afraid my father would come home. If he saw you there he might have said some really cruel things to you."

"Cruel? Like what *you* said to me? Your father couldn't have hurt me as much as you did. To be able to do that you have to know a lot about a person — as you did about me. All those months when we were together and I'd confided so much to you!

You used every bit of it to cut me down."

"I didn't mean —"

"Don't try to make me think you didn't mean to hurt me. You meant every dagger slash. And you know what? You had thought about every bit of it, planned it. You *did* mean it!"

"You're right," Carter said, "but my father —"

He broke off because someone had knocked on the door. Standing outside was a short, stout man with gray hair, and he was holding a two-foot-square piece of plywood with a plastic covered lump on it. Over his shoulder was a big canvas satchel.

"Not now," Sophie mumbled. "We're closed!"

The man gave a sad, pleading look at Sophie and gestured toward the object he was holding. It was familiar to her. She knew it was a sculpture he was in the process of making and he wanted her to look at it. Critique it.

"Come back later," she said, then looked at Carter.

But he'd gone to the door and was unlocking it.

"I'm —" the gray-haired man said, but Carter cut him off.

"Sophie, this is Henry," Carter said.

393

There was a split second when the older man looked surprised, and he gave Carter a hard look, as though trying to remember him, but then he recovered his equilibrium and looked back at Sophie.

"Henry," Sophie said, her voice angry, "now is not the time for this. I'll look at what you've made later."

Carter took the platform from the man and set it on a table. "Should I . . . ?"

"Sure," Henry said, looking from him to Sophie and back again. "I'm sorry to interrupt, but the pastor said you were here and that you'd know what to do with this. It's not quite right, but I can't figure out what's wrong with it."

Carter unwrapped the plastic to expose a foot-tall clay sculpture of a Revolutionary soldier. He was leaning on his rifle and looking as weary as a man at war would be.

"That's great," Carter said enthusiastically. "Really wonderful. You are a man of enormous talent, and your technique is beyond anything —"

"Stop it!" Sophie snapped. "Really, Carter, just stop talking about things you know nothing about. This figure is out of proportion. If he were real he'd be five feet on the bottom and six feet on the top." She was so angry at Carter that she didn't think about what she was doing but grabbed the legs of the clay man and squeezed until she was almost down to the steel armature underneath.

"This is what you always do, isn't it, Carter? You look at something — or someone — and think it's absolutely perfect. You're fascinated with it. But then when you spend time around it, you begin to see that she isn't what you thought. Get me an ice pick."

"What?"

"Get her an ice pick," Henry barked, and Carter ran to search through drawers until he found one.

Sophie dug the pick into the clay to make an adhesive surface. She glanced pointedly at Henry who was watching her with an intensity usually reserved for brain surgery. "Is that bag empty?"

Quickly, he set it on the table, opened it, and pulled out a lump of plastic-wrapped clay, and unrolled a canvas carrier full of plastic and metal sculpting tools. She grabbed the clay, pulled off the wrap, and began to knead it into the legs. Her hands worked with lightning speed as she rearranged the clay. She was greatly hindered by the steel structure underneath but she was able to add a half inch length onto the man's legs.

"What did young Treeborne do to you?" Henry asked.

"He told me I wasn't the kind of woman a man married," Sophie answered. "To bed, yes. Wed, no."

Henry gave Carter a look that said he was an idiot.

"He thinks because his family's rich and mine isn't that we're different classes. He thinks that I wouldn't know how to act in the Treeborne mansion. I guess I'd hang the laundry in the front hallway."

"Like Mrs. Adams," Henry said, and Carter and Sophie looked at him. "When she moved into the White House it kept raining so she hung the laundry in the East Room."

Sophie didn't know what that had to do with anything. She took a plastic tool out of the roll and began carving away at the upper body of the clay soldier.

"Why'd you say such a stupid thing?" Henry asked Carter.

His face turned red. "My father . . ." Carter glanced at Sophie.

"The Palmer deal," Henry said.

Carter nodded.

Sophie looked from one man to the other. "Oh great. I have two of you from the same world. This is my lucky day."

"I used to be in that world," Henry said.

"But now I'm in yours." He watched as Sophie began to work on the soldier's face. "Is that ring from you?" He nodded at the box on the table as he looked at Carter.

Carter grimaced. "I asked —"

"I saw you on your knee," Henry said, "but I was hoping that you'd dropped something. A proposal is a serious matter and needs some planning. It shouldn't be done in front of a window where everyone can see. And not wearing everyday clothes." Henry smiled at Sophie.

"Let me guess. You've been married to the same woman for thirty-two years."

"Thirty-four," he said, his eyes twinkling.

She looked back at Carter. "I think you could learn a lot from this man. Now, if the two of you will excuse me —" She turned to leave the room but Henry caught her arm.

"I haven't stayed married all these years by leaving a lady to stew in her own anger. Let's take a walk."

Sophie gave him a look of I-don't-know-you.

"We can walk to the church, in plain view of everyone, but I do think you need to get out of here. And besides, young Treeborne here can vouch for me."

"He is —"

Sophie didn't so much as look at Carter. All she knew is that she very much wanted to get out of the restaurant. "I'll get my coat," she said and hurried up the stairs.

Minutes later, Henry was holding a door open for her. As they went out into the fresh air her mind began to clear. "I'm sorry about that in there. Especially about your sculpture. It does show talent. It's just that your armature was out of proportion and that made everything off. Your teacher should have caught it."

"Don't have one," he said.

"I'm sure the local colleges have art courses and you could take one."

"I've had too many years of being the boss to be able to stand there and listen to some kid talk to me about form versus line versus perception." He waved his hand. "Besides, in a college classroom I'd be called 'the old man' and my ego couldn't stand that."

"Better than being too low class to marry," she said before she thought. "Sorry. Carter showing up today threw me. Usually, I have rather nice manners."

"That makes one of us. I have three daughters, all of them about your age, more or less, and you should have heard what I said to the last boy who played with my third daughter's heart. His ears will be stinging when he's ninety."

Sophie couldn't help smiling. "You sound like a good father."

"If I was, it was because my wife made it clear that no matter how successful I was in the business world, at home I was to help with the dishes and the diapers." He chuckled. "I used to spend the day making multimillion-dollar deals with Tokyo, then on the way home I'd have to stop and pick up half a gallon of milk."

"And was it all worth it?"

"My daughters are sane and sensible, and my wife still loves me. What do you think?"

"I think you're a very lucky man."

They'd come to one of the town squares and there was a bench under a huge oak tree. "Want to sit for a while?" he asked.

She hesitated. There was a lot of work to do before tomorrow and she needed to get busy on it.

Henry reached into his jacket pocket and pulled out two fat little red-and-white-striped bags. "I have peanuts."

She smiled. "In that case, how can I refuse?"

They sat next to each other on the bench and for a few minutes they shelled peanuts and ate them in silence.

"So, Sophie, what's *really* wrong in your

life? You seem to be more agitated than young Treeborne could have caused. Is there someone else?"

"Maybe," Sophie said hesitantly. She didn't know this man, but at the same time there was something about him that inspired confidence. From the way Carter had been in awe of him she was sure that Henry had been some very high powered man in the business world.

She wanted to pour her heart out to him, but since she'd graduated from college her life had been one long series of people wanting things from her. "What do you want from me?" she asked and couldn't help narrowing her eyes at him. "You showed up complete with a sculpture and two bags of peanuts. This isn't a coincidence."

Henry smiled. "If you're an example of this generation, it's good I got out. You're too clever for me."

"I doubt that. So what is it?"

He took a moment before answering. "My wife's sister lives in Williamsburg. I wanted to retire to a place of endless sun, but it was either come here or lose her."

"She's a good bargainer."

"Tyrant, is more likely," he said. "So anyway, I hate golf, can't stand country clubs, and I don't know what to do with myself."

"You're the man Russell mentioned."

"That's me. When I was a kid I used to make figures out of mud. I wanted to go to art school, but my father sent me to study business. Back then I was as bullied by him as young Carter is by his father."

"But you seem to have survived."

"I guess business was in my blood," he said. "But then I early on learned how to look at a deal as though it were an art form. Was my opponent a Gainsborough or a Pollock?"

"Or a Mondrian?" she said, amused.

"If I figured out his style I knew how to deal with him."

"So what was on the walls of *your* office?"

Henry laughed. "I had my daughters' drawings framed."

"Ah yes. Family. Everything for them. Did anyone ever figure you out?"

"Not until this moment," he said.

"Which brings us back to my original question. What do you want from me?"

"A teacher. No, actually, I want an art buddy. As much as I love my family, I miss the office — and my wife dearly wants me to get out of the house."

"An art buddy? And you're thinking about me for this?"

"Russell Pendergast gave me the idea. You know who his father is, don't you?"

"Randall Maxwell, isn't it? Colleague of yours?"

"Off and on. I can't say we're friends. When it comes to business he's a Robert Motherwell."

Sophie had to laugh. Motherwell's paintings were a white canvas with huge, rough-edged black slashes and ovals, sometimes with a vivid splash of red. Very dramatic. Unforgiving. "Did you beat him?"

"Only once."

"Is this Edilean preacher like him?" she asked.

"More than he knows. After all, he's trying for a merger between you and me. He said you want to be an artist and that you've done a lot of bronzes. He also told me what you did for your sister."

"I guess he learned all this from my friend Kim?"

"I think so."

While the idea was appealing, Sophie didn't think it would work. "The problem is that I've never been good at teaching. You saw that in there. A teacher needs to have patience and to . . . well, *teach*. But I just grabbed your sculpture and tore it apart. That's not the way a teacher should be."

"I can get those on every street corner. I like the other half of that saying 'those who can do and those who can't, teach.' "

"I don't understand," Sophie said. "I can't sculpt for you, now can I?"

"No, but when you're doing your own work I can learn by watching."

"I don't know," Sophie said. "I'll have to think about this. Think about everything."

As Carter stood in the little restaurant and stared at Henry and Sophie walking down the street, he couldn't help grimacing. He was sure Sophie didn't even know who she was talking to, a man who made his father look like a pauper. It looked like what his father had said about Sophie not fitting in with "people of our sort" wasn't true. But then, Carter had learned long ago that whatever his father did was for his own purposes.

Carter went to the big refrigerator on the far wall and opened it. While Sophie was upstairs Henry had said he was to make the soup. "Like I'm the damned maid," he said aloud. "Like I'm not part of Treeborne Foods, like I'm not —" He stopped when he saw that the refrigerator was nearly empty. How was he to make soup — which he didn't know how to make anyway — if there weren't enough groceries? Was he supposed to go buy some?

He shut the door and looked around the place. All Sophie's questions about that damned cookbook had made him think about his family's so-called legacy. His grandfather had been an unpleasant old man, angry at the shrapnel in his body that would always cause him pain, angry at his own father for leaving his family. That his father had died when a boiler blew up made no difference. To his grandfather's mind, the man had still abandoned his family. Most of all, he was furious because his exhausted mother made all four of her children spend their childhoods in a tiny restaurant. He went away to war saying he never wanted anything to do with food. But when he got back with a body riddled with metal pieces, he saw an opportunity and took it. He Americanized their family name and Treeborne Foods was created.

As Carter looked around Sophie's little restaurant he knew that the one his grandmother had run was about the same size. Little more than a sandwich shop really, and she'd served skimpy plates of food — but she'd sprinkled her secret ingredient on top of everything. She'd been so successful that she'd managed to support her family after her drunken husband died, and she'd helped relatives come over from the old country.

"And now I'm supposed to carry on the family tradition," Carter said with a sigh. He was supposed to step into the giant beast that Treeborne Foods had become and —

He had to stop his wallow in self-pity because someone was tapping on the door.

"Who's this?" he muttered. "Someone else who wants to marry Sophie? Another man who wants to hit me?" Frowning, he opened the door. A young woman was standing there. She was dressed all in black: boots, tights, shirt, leather jacket. Her hair was cut straight at her chin line, with thick bangs at her brow. It was so black against her white skin that her hair had to have been dyed. She had a tiny silver dot pierced in her nose, and the edge of a tattoo peeped above her collar.

"You're not Sophie," she said, looking at him as though he'd just lied to her.

"And you're not Sophie, either," he responded.

Her blue eyes looked him up and down, as though assessing him, then she seemed to dismiss him as she walked into the restaurant.

"You'll have to come back later," Carter

said, annoyed that this girl had pushed past him.

"Russell said I was to cook today." Her tone was almost belligerent, as though she were challenging him.

"I have no idea who Russell is and you don't look like any cook I've ever seen. We don't do greaseburgers." He looked her up and down just as she'd done to him. "And no vampires or werewolves come here."

"Then how did *you* get in here?" she shot back at him.

Carter could only blink at her. Maybe what Sophie'd said about his being spoiled was true. No one — other than his father, that is — had ever spoken to him like that. He couldn't help it, but he smiled.

She didn't smile back but kept staring at him.

"So you came here to cook?" he asked, the anger leaving him. His mother used to say that he'd inherited the ability to get angry from his father, but her genes made it so Carter couldn't stay angry very long.

The girl turned toward the door. "I think I better come back when this Sophie is here. Tell her I'll be at Russell's house."

"Wait!" Carter said and put himself in front of the door. "I'm supposed to make some soup for tomorrow."

"So make it." She reached out to the door, but Carter didn't move.

"I could spin straw into gold as easily as I could make soup."

"This woman hired you as a cook but you can't even make a pot of soup?" She again reached for the door.

"It's not Sophie's fault. I came here to ask her to marry me and she told me to leave, but I wanted a second chance so I stayed to help. Then Henry showed up and took her away because she remade that ugly little toad of a sculpture of his. So Henry is the one who told me to make soup. Sophie knows I can't cook. I'm heir to Treeborne Foods but I hardly know a potato from a carrot. Ironic, isn't it?"

She stood there staring at him for a long time, looking as though she was trying to figure him out.

Carter thought she had on too much makeup and he couldn't help thinking that without it she'd be quite pretty.

"How'd you get the eye?" she asked.

He put his hand up to the side of his face. "Sophie's boyfriend doesn't want me here. He's a doctor."

She blinked at this a few times. "Do you think that making some soup will impress your girlfriend enough to get her back?" She hesitated. "To make her *marry* you?"

He gave a little half smile. "No. I can see that that's not going to happen. But I'd really like to make her forgive me. I did something I regret and —" He broke off because she'd turned her back on him and gone to the refrigerator to open it.

"Not even I could make soup out of this. Where's the wholesale market?"

"Don't look at me, I just got here. I live in Texas."

"Ah, right. You're Treeborne Foods. The freezer kings." Her tone was condescending.

Carter couldn't help groaning. "I guess you eat only what you buy at the local farmers' market. You turn your nose up to anything that was picked longer than two hours ago, and I'm sure you'd starve before you used anything that had ever been frozen."

"For the last year I've been working at an inner-city homeless shelter and we used anything anybody gave us. People look in their pantries, see a can of beans that's been in there for three years, and give it to us. They think they're doing a good deed. Treeborne Foods's fancy frozen packages would have been a step up for us. You have any more elitist remarks to make to me or you want to go find a grocery and make some soup?"

"Soup," he said and couldn't help his smile.

She stood by the door. "Well?" she said and he had no idea what she meant. But she was waiting for him to open the door for her. Carter rushed forward and opened it wide.

Once they were outside, he hesitated. "I don't have a key to get back in. Sophie will probably be back, but . . ." He didn't seem to know what to do.

"This doesn't seem to be a town of rampant thievery," she said, looking up at him. "Do you have a car? Or did you come with a driver and a limo?"

"It's a rental and I drove it from the airport all by myself."

"Congratulations. You're on your way to being one of the people." They walked a block to where his car was parked and she let him open the door for her.

"Kelli," she said when they were both inside. "Kelli Parker."

"Lewis Carter Treeborne the Third," he said. "Better known as Carter."

"Is that what Sophie calls you?"

"Not at the moment," he said. "Do you know where the grocery is?"

"The bus passed it on the way in. Turn left here. I want to know everything that's going on."

"Well," Carter said, "my father is trying to make me marry some girl to seal a deal, but —"

"So you came here and tried to get Sophie to marry you because then you'd be safe. Gee. Can't imagine why she said no."

Carter couldn't help grimacing. "In the Texas town where I live everybody works for Treeborne Foods. And everybody . . . well, treats me with courtesy."

"And here you have to earn it. Poor you. Turn here. Tell me about this restaurant you've been left in charge of."

"It's not like that." He pulled into a parking space, turned off the engine, and looked at her in speculation. "Why did you come from wherever you came from that took a bus to get here just to work in some two-bit sandwich place? I bet there are higher paying jobs back there, wherever it is."

"Chicago," Kelli said.

He was incredulous. "You couldn't get a job slapping ham and cheese on rye somewhere in Chicago?"

"If we're going to make soup I think we need to get started." She pulled up on the door handle but Carter pressed the button

410

and locked it.

"Who are you and what are you up to?" he asked.

"Look. I just met you thirty minutes ago. My life is none of your business, so let me out of here or I'll start screaming."

Carter didn't move. "Trouble with the law? Were you working in a homeless shelter for community service?"

Kelli just stared at him, but the slight flushing of her cheeks gave her away.

Carter leaned back against the door, smiling. "So what did you do? Hot-wire a car? Threaten someone with a gun? Lewd sexual behavior?" On the last one he looked hopeful.

"I borrowed some tart pans! There. Now will you let me out?"

Carter, intrigued, unlocked the door and followed Kelli into the grocery. The last time he'd been in one had been with Sophie. He leaned on the basket and guided it as Kelli tossed produce into it. They were silent for a while.

"Did this preacher, Russell, bail you out?"

"More or less," Kelli said.

He moved along the aisle. "So why did you steal the pans?"

"You're a pest, you know that?"

"Sophie thinks so and my father would

411

agree wholeheartedly, but my mother rather liked me. So why'd you steal the pans?"

"Because my boyfriend ran over mine with his motorcycle and I had to bake six tarts to try to get a job as a pastry chef at a major hotel."

Carter waited for her to continue.

"I'd been working for a jerk of a chef who took credit for everything I did and I wanted to get away from him. Two days before I was to show up with examples of what I can do, my boyfriend and I had a fight. The next day while I was at work he cleaned out my bank account and ran his bike over every piece of cooking equipment I owned."

"So you 'borrowed' some more."

"That's right. That's what I did."

"But you got caught?"

"He was stalking me," she said.

"The boyfriend or the mean chef boss?"

"Boyfriend. He followed me, saw what I was doing, and called the cops. The mean chef pressed charges. The judge thought it was all ridiculous, so he sent me to help at a homeless shelter."

"And that's where the Edilean pastor met you."

"Yes, he did, and he called me for this job, even bought my bus ticket."

"You're a pastry chef but you came all the

way from Chicago to take a job in a sand-wich shop?"

When Kelli didn't answer, he stopped and stared at her. "If you want me to help you, you need to tell me the whole story."

"What else is there to tell?" They were in the spice aisle and she was buying the big-gest, cheapest containers she could find.

Carter didn't reply but picked up a ten-pound bag of King Arthur flour. "When I started working for Treeborne Foods three years ago I suggested that we branch out into baked goods. Give Sara Lee a run for her money. In front of everyone my father told me to sit down and shut up."

Kelli seemed to be deciding whether to tell the real reason why she'd come to Edilean. "Russell said that the sandwich shop used to sell pastries and that there's an empty building next door."

Carter instantly saw what she was getting at. "You want to tear through the wall to make a work area."

Kelli nodded.

Carter's eyes lit up. "I can get all the bak-ing equipment you need, including hun-dreds of tart pans, from a rock bottom wholesaler."

"Just mention the Treeborne name?"

Carter grinned. "Just mention the Treeborne name."

Understanding passed between them. Maybe, just possibly, Carter was seeing a way around his father's rule. If he could come up with a line of pastries, things that could be frozen . . . He'd do something labeled as healthy, as that's what sold. Healthy, high fiber, low carb. All the catch words of the industry.

He held the bag of flour aloft. "How many do you want to start out with?"

"Five ten-pounds bags should hold me over for a day or two."

When Sophie got back to the restaurant, she was shocked to see Carter and a girl she'd never met up to their elbows in flour. There was a wooden box of apples on the floor, and every burner on the stove was covered with big pots. The shop smelled wonderful.

She and Henry had walked to the church and she'd heard his ideas of building a studio on his property.

"My wife and I own five acres outside Williamsburg. Right now I'm working in a three-car garage, but Sophie, I could build us a studio. It would be two stories high, open to the roof, with windows on the north. It could have triple doors so any big

414

bronzes you — or maybe we — made could be moved in and out."

What he was saying was like a dream come true. All through school it was what she'd imagined having someday. She and Kim and Jecca had spent long evenings talking of their possible futures.

For Kim, everything she'd wanted had come true. She had her own shop and it was possible that she was going to go national. Jecca hadn't become a painter as she'd wanted to be, but she did have an art career before her.

As for Sophie, she felt that even though she was twenty-six years old she was just starting life. Her own life, that is.

"Are you Sophie?" the young woman behind the counter asked as she wiped her hands. "I'm Kelli Parker."

The name meant nothing to Sophie.

"Didn't Russell tell you about me?"

"Yes, he did." She was looking at the kitchen. If she'd been in the restaurant longer, if she'd begun to feel that the place was hers, she would have been resentful of this stranger taking over. But this morning the deluge of customers had shown her how her lack of experience had come close to being a disaster.

She saw that this pretty young woman was

looking at her anxiously, waiting to see what Sophie was going to say. "What are you doing?"

"She's a pastry chef," Carter said over the tall glass counter. "She's going to fill this cabinet with . . . I don't know . . . pastries, I guess."

"Could you just get back to work and let me tell her?" Kelli said, then looked back at Sophie. "Oh, sorry, you're the boss so you should tell him what to do."

Sophie didn't smile. "If I told Carter what to do it would involve boiling oil and foul language."

Carter's groan echoed around the room, but he didn't stop working.

Sophie looked back at Kelli. "I think pastries would be a great idea. What can I do to help?"

TWENTY

It was almost Christmas, Reede thought, and he had no idea what he was going to get Sophie. If he had his way it would be an engagement ring, but he didn't dare do that. He didn't think he could live with her telling him no.

In the months since she'd arrived it seemed that his life fluctuated between perfect and horrible. He was glad that she was settling into the community of Edilean, but at the same time he knew he wanted to leave the little town — and he wanted Sophie to go with him.

He'd loved seeing her excitement of the last few weeks. It was as though everything she'd ever wanted was at last coming to her.

Reede hadn't been too happy about Carter coming to town, although he admitted that he shouldn't have hit the man. Afterward, the manager of Kim's jewelry store, Carla, had called Reede at his office, saying that it was very important that she speak to him immediately.

"I just heard what you did," Carla said. "You know, when you hit that guy."

"Yes, I do know," Reede said with a sigh. "I shouldn't have —"

"But you *should* have," Carla said. "The whole town knows you and Sophie are meant for each other. On Halloween half the town was peeping through the curtains to watch you two riding through the night. It was the most romantic thing this town has ever seen. At least it was the best thing to happen since Dr. Tris went after Jecca, and of course there was the way Luke nearly killed Rams over —"

"Carla!" Reede said. "Is there a point to this call? I have patients."

"Oh yeah, sure. I thought you might like to know that I sold that big pink diamond ring Kim made. It was by far the most expensive piece in the store."

Reede knew there'd been some trouble between his sister and Carla, something to do with the sale of a sapphire ring, but he thought it had been settled. "Do you want me to take charge of the money?" Reede asked with as much concern in his voice as he could manage. "The new me" he thought of himself since Sophie had arrived. Patient,

418

understanding, sweet tempered.

"Are you saying I can't be trusted with money?" Carla asked loudly. "Because if you are, then —"

"Cut it out!" Reede snapped. "Just say what you're avoiding telling me."

"The man you hit bought the ring. He said it was for his engagement."

"Treeborne?"

"Is that his name?" Carla asked. "He isn't part of those frozen foods, is he?"

"I'm sure you know more about him than I do," Reede said. "Carla, unless you have anything else to tell me, I have to go."

"Don't let him take her away from you," Carla said, her voice frantic. "Just because he's rich and gorgeous shouldn't scare you away. Sophie is Kim's friend and you two are beautiful together. Forget that you nearly ran her over with your fancy car, and don't think about how she poured beer all over you, and definitely don't think about how you and everyone else in this town lied to her about who you are. I still think you two should be together. Don't let a flawless pink diamond scare you away. Sophie can —"

"Good-bye, Carla," Reede said and hung up.

For all that he'd told himself that Sophie

would never go back to Texas with a guy like Carter Treeborne, Reede had difficulty concentrating that day.

As soon as he saw his nurse, Heather, he knew that Carla had told her about the ring. Heather's eyes were so full of rah-rah encouragement that he half expected her to tell him to keep his chin up. "You *can* do it" might have come out of her mouth if his glare hadn't prevented her from speaking.

But for the whole afternoon Heather had hovered over Reede, watching him with every patient. Twice she suggested tests that Reede forgot to order for people.

Old Mr. Felderman put his hand on Reede's shoulder and squeezed. "I proposed to my wife eight times before she said yes. Hang in there."

Reede had to clamp his teeth together to keep from making a sarcastic remark.

When he stepped out of an exam room at four, the three women who worked for him put on a show for his benefit. They pretended they were just casually chatting but they were so loud he could have heard them in Virginia Beach. Underwater.

"And Sophie has been sitting on a bench with this man for hours?" Heather half shouted.

"For a long time, anyway," Betsy answered

at the same ear-blasting level.

"And he's old enough to be her father?" Alice shouted.

Reede had been about to step forward and tell them to be quiet. The last thing he wanted to hear was how Sophie had spent hours with Carter. But who was the man "old enough to be her father"?

Reede opened a file folder and pretended to be reading it.

"So who is he?" Heather asked, her voice lowered somewhat, since there didn't seem to be any danger of Reede not hearing.

"The old man or the young one who bought Sophie an engagement ring?"

Reede's hands tightened on the folder. Right now he certainly wasn't regretting hitting the guy.

"Both!" Alice said, pretending she didn't know that Dr. Reede was standing just a few feet away.

"The new preacher has something to do with the older man," Betsy said. "And the younger one must be an old boyfriend."

The women were silent for a moment, not sure what else to say to warn him about what was going on. Dr. Reede had been much nicer since Sophie had come to town, and the women had done everything they could think of to keep the two of them together.

Just then the four-thirty appointment came in and she looked from the women to Dr. Reede standing in front of a door, his head bent over a folder. "Are you talking about the new sandwich shop?" she asked as she signed in.

The women nodded.

"I was at the grocery and that blond guy who helped Sophie out this morning was there with some dark-haired girl — never saw her before — and they filled four carts full of food. Not that I was looking, but it was a lot of flour and butter and cream. Then later I took my daughter to her dance class and I saw the two of them in the restaurant and it looked like they were making pies."

"Where was Sophie?" Betsy asked.

"I saw her coming down the street. She doesn't know me but I said hi anyway. She went inside and later when I picked up my daughter she had on an apron and was sitting at a table peeling apples. Not that I was spying or anything."

"No, of course not," Alice said.

"Where was the blond guy?"

"Behind the counter and standing *very* close to the dark-haired girl."

"He wasn't near Sophie?" Heather asked.

"No. In fact it was like she was staying away from both of them. Do you think they're going to start selling baked goods? I wish I could buy the cupcakes for my daughter's school party here in town."

None of the women answered because they'd all turned to stare at Reede.

He knew he shouldn't let his pleasure, relief, and all-round happiness at hearing this show, but he did allow himself a small smile.

In return the women grinned at him.

Reede turned away but he was feeling much better. When a young mother brought in her toddler who had nothing at all wrong with him, Reede spent thirty minutes listening to her fears. His prescription had been to tell her about a playgroup his female relatives had formed. "Motherhood shouldn't be a lonely business," he'd told her.

The patient must have said something because later, Heather smiled at him so warmly it was embarrassing.

In the ensuing days it hadn't been easy for Reede to deal with Carter. There was something primitive inside him that made him want to challenge the guy to a fight to the death.

Mike Newland, Sara's husband, had understood so well that he'd taken Reede on in the boxing ring. Mike's new gym was being built out of town, but it wasn't complete yet so he was still using the old clothing store. Sara's former fiancé had once rented that place.

"Think it's a coincidence that I took this place over?" Mike asked in his raspy voice. He was letting Reede know that he understood about wanting to protect the woman in your life.

But modern American society wouldn't let Reede do what he wanted to. He couldn't demand that Sophie throw Carter out, to never see him again.

Besides, Carter and the girl Kelli had freed Sophie up enough that she could spend more time with Reede. When he'd told her he didn't play fair he'd meant that he'd take up her time. But he didn't have to "take" anything, for she seemed to want to be with him as much as he with her.

They talked; they made love; they went places together. It hadn't taken long to find out that they preferred each other's company to anything else they did.

By Thanksgiving they had a routine that Reede picked Sophie up by six and they made dinner together. She was very interested in the countries he'd visited and she liked to try to re-create the food. They scoured the Internet for recipes and ordered little out-of-print, local cookbooks on the regions Reede knew best. Several times Sophie served foreign soups in her shop. The yam and raisin had been a big hit, the lamb and garlic less so.

"Well, I liked it," Sophie said and he agreed with her.

After they'd had dinner with Colin and his wife, Gemma — their infant son was being babysat by his brother, Shamus — Reede and Sophie took their advice about buying furniture. The next Saturday they went to a big warehouse and spent a day choosing everything from cookware to a sofa.

But no matter how involved they became, Sophie didn't move in with him. Every night she stayed in her apartment. He knew he'd made it clear that he wanted her to live with him, but she said she needed time to think about her life and what she wanted to do with it.

They spent a lot of time talking, telling each other things they'd told no one else. It took some work on Reede's part, but he got her to talk about her stepfather.

"Sometimes I think he leered at Lisa just to make me stay there and take care of everything. I cooked, cleaned, and kept a job. And I think Lisa was grateful for someone to use as the bad guy. While I was in college she got mixed up with the wrong crowd and didn't know how to get free. When I got there she told them I wouldn't let her go out with them. One of the kids very angrily told me that I'd threatened to send Lisa to juvenile detention if she didn't stop seeing them."

"Did you?"

Sophie smiled. "I said that's where she was heading if she didn't get away from that gang. The town gives me credit for straightening her out, but I had three jobs. I didn't have *time* to do much in the way of discipline."

"Maybe your sister saw what you sacrificed for her."

Sophie was thoughtful for a moment. "You know something? I don't feel that I did sacrifice, not as though I gave up everything anyway. I was never like Jecca and Kim, where my career was everything to me. I tried to be, but it wasn't all that difficult for me to give up that first job offer and go home to my sister. I think that if Jecca couldn't spend her life doing some form of art she would have jumped off a building."

"And I can assure that my sister is the same way," Reede said. "As much as she loved Travis I think if he'd said that it was him or jewelry she would have chosen the diamonds." Reede looked at her. "But you know, Sophie, you might feel differently once you get back into your sculpture. This man Belleck might open some doors for you."

"Ah yes, Henry," she said.

Two afternoons a week she worked with Henry in his garage. The man was a scholar of the American Revolution and he wanted to do figures of the most important people.

Sophie made sure his armatures were correctly proportioned, then forced him to really *look* at the portraits of the men and women. She taught him to see tiny differences in facial features. He would form George Washington's face in clay, then Sophie would show him why it didn't look like the man. With a few pushes with her thumbs, a scrape of a knife, a bit of clay added, in seconds she changed it to look like the former president.

Henry marveled at her talent. "I don't understand why you didn't pursue this."

"There are things more important," she told him, and Henry had looked at her oddly.

Later she'd told Reede about it. They were snuggled on his new couch together, a big bowl of popcorn between them, and watching a DVD.

"What's more important?" he'd asked while pretending that her answer wasn't of utmost concern to him.

But he didn't fool her. "I haven't figured it out yet," she said and looked back at the movie.

Reede had figured what was important to him right after he'd met Sophie, but he couldn't help a sense of déjà vu because he'd felt like this before. He'd been a teenager when he'd first seen Laura Chawnley, and he'd decided right then that she was for him. He'd felt the same way since he'd seen . . . no, since he'd talked to Sophie. There was a vulnerability about her, a feeling that she, well, maybe she needed him, that appealed to him.

He would never let her know it, but her story about the cookbook had shocked him — not because she'd stolen it, but because she was probably going to be in serious trouble. Treeborne Foods was big. Huge. Nationwide. Reede didn't think they'd smile and say her theft was justifiable revenge for the way the heir apparent had treated her.

Reede had admired Sophie's sense of remorse and he'd liked her idea of returning the cookbook via a foreign country. But he didn't trust the Treebornes — which is why he'd gone to so much trouble to keep a copy of the book and to have it decoded — something he was still waiting on.

The night after Carter came to Edilean, Reede asked Sophie about the cookbook, and she'd told him what Carter had said, that there'd be no prosecution.

Reede urged Sophie to push Carter further to make absolutely *sure* there would be no retaliation. The next day Carter had called the family housekeeper and asked her to tell him when the package arrived. A few days later Carter told Sophie that the cookbook was now under a pile of papers on his father's desk. "He'll never know it was missing," Carter said.

Still, Reede wasn't satisfied. He called his former roommate again and asked how his brother was doing with the decoding.

"Broke his leg skiing, but I'll see that he gets right on it. The book, not his leg," Kirk said.

Reede didn't tell Sophie that he was still working on the deciphering, and she didn't ask, and later when Kirk called and said his brother had reported that the code was probably based on a book, Reede didn't tell Sophie that either. He didn't want to worry her.

For Thanksgiving they went to Sara and Mike's old house, and Jecca and Tris came home for the long weekend.

"How miserable are you in New York?" Reede quietly asked his cousin Tristan.

"If I start to tell you I'll weep like a baby," Tris said. "Not a pretty sight."

Reede didn't miss the irony that Tris hated being out of Edilean as much as Reede disliked being in it.

Although Sophie had helped calm Reede's restlessness, and had made him more content, he still itched to leave, to travel, to *go*.

It was at Thanksgiving dinner that Tris's nine-year-old niece Nell handed Sophie a lump of modeling clay and asked if she could make a centaur.

Sophie smiled. "A centaur, huh? Like in Harry Potter?"

Nell, her beautiful eyes serious, nodded. To her, her aunt Jecca was a true artist, but Jecca said that 3D was Sophie's field of expertise. "She can make anything."

Sophie'd always loved horses and had made many of them in several media, so that was easy.

By the time she'd formed the animal, every child who could walk was around her and staring with wide eyes. Sophie stopped when she got to the man part of the creature and held it up.

"So who do you think looks most like a centaur?"

Instantly, every face in the room, over twenty people, looked at the sheriff, Colin Frazier. He was a huge man, his body covered with powerful muscles.

Everyone, and especially Colin, laughed.

After that, Sophie got no rest. She was asked to sculpt every adult male there into an animal. Tristan was a gazelle, Ramsey a bear, Luke a scholarly-looking badger, while Mike was a fox. Reede came last and she put his face onto a lion.

Sara took all the figures and put them into a glass-fronted cabinet. She wouldn't let the children touch them, but Mike gave them a flashlight so they could look at them.

After the dinner cleanup, Reede caught Sophie in the hallway, pulled her into his arms, and kissed her. "That was very nice of you. The kids really appreciated it."

"I enjoy doing that kind of thing. The kids in the forest and now these."

"Better than Henry?"

Sophie laughed. "Oh yes! He is so very serious about all of it. He wants to win awards and prizes, and I think his goal is to have a piece of his work put in a museum."

"And what about you? You don't want

431

awards?"

"I —" She broke off because the children had found her. Nell was trying to herd them around the house but they were escaping her.

"Miss Sophie!" one of them yelled, as she was now their favorite person on earth.

They grabbed her hands and pulled her away with them.

Sara came out of the bedroom, one of her twin baby boys in each arm, and handed one to Reede. "You should keep that girl."

"I'm trying," he said.

"Whatever you have to do, you should do it," she said to him, and there was no humor in her eyes. "You're not exactly a man who falls in and out of love easily. If you lose Sophie you'll be an old man before you recover."

"Thanks for telling me what I already know," Reede said.

"Any time," she answered as she went back to the kitchen.

Every day Reede and Sophie grew closer, their lives intertwining. It quickly got to the point where Reede couldn't imagine a life without Sophie.

But Roan had told him that Sophie was staying only until the middle of January. "Think you've changed her mind?" Roan asked. "Think you've talked her into moving into your house and the two of you settling down in Edilean? What are you going to do when Ariel comes back and Tris does? Aren't three doctors too many for little Edilean? Or are you hoping for a spread of cholera?"

Reede glared at his cousin. He didn't have an answer to any of the questions. Ariel was Sheriff Frazier's sister, and as soon as she finished her residency in California she was going to return to Edilean and work with Tristan — when he got back from New York, that is. Ariel was married to Mike Newland's best friend, and the two men planned to open a big gym that would have members from Edilean to DC.

It was all family, Reede thought. It was all cozy and warm and friendly. And it was maddening to Reede! Just last night he'd seen a TV show about a doctor who equipped a boat as a hospital, and he went to remote areas of the world to help people.

If Reede could get the funding he'd love to do something like that. But what kind of life was that for a woman? And by that he meant Sophie. How could she do her sculpture while moving around the world?

And then there was her growing love for Edilean and the people in it. They'd accepted her quickly. And why not? She was kind and thoughtful. If someone told of a favorite sandwich, the next day it was on the menu.

Sophie had become friends with the young woman Kelli. They were an unusual pair, Sophie so pink and blonde, Kelli so dark with her heavy eye makeup.

Sophie had shown him Kelli's sketches of her plans to cut into the building next door and make a real bakery. Since Roan owned both buildings, it was all up to him. Sophie laughed at how Kelli was working hard to make desserts to please Roan. Pears with almond cream and chocolate. Apples with a rice custard, orange with cardamom. There were savory tarts of pumpkin with garlic, potatoes with ham on puff pastry.

"Kelli takes them out of the oven and hand feeds them to Roan while he's at the cash register," Sophie said, laughing. "One day I thought Roan was going to faint in ecstasy over Kelli's apricots and cream, and he asked where she came up with all the things she made. She said" — Sophie grinned at Reede — "Kelli said she had an old cookbook from her French grand-mother. Carter and I looked at each other and burst into laugher. Kelli and Roan knew we were laughing about the famous Treeborne cookbook but, as you know, there was a lot more to it than that."

She smiled at the memory. "But what's *best* about it all is seeing Carter's face get red with rage every time Kelli feeds Roan. Personally, I think Carter's anger is why she does it."

Reede turned away so Sophie wouldn't see his frown. He couldn't help the jealousy he felt. She'd gone from hating Carter to laughing with him. Every time she said, "Carter thinks we should . . ." or "Carter says . . ." Reede had to swallow his jealousy. She was spending most of the day near him.

One evening after dinner and a couple of glasses of wine he said, "I thought you were angry at Carter. Hated him, even."

"I *was,*" she said. "I was furious. When I drove to Edilean I was so angry I could have torn a bronze statue apart with my teeth."

"Sounds interesting," he said, smiling, preferring to hear this than whatever Treeborne had said at work that day.

"No, I'm not kidding." She paused for a moment. "I *know* Carter cared about me. I was sure of it, and when he talked about having to make the 'most important decision of his life,' I still think he meant *us.*"

"Probably did," Reede said but didn't add his opinion. He wanted her to go on.

"But it all changed in one evening. Instead of having what I had seen as my glorious future, I ended up with a dead car and a stolen cookbook, and standing in the middle of a highway trying to get a cell signal. Then some jerk ran over the phone and the cookbook." She looked at Reede with wide eyes. "Sorry. Maybe not a jerk. I'm sure you —"

He was coming toward her with the eyes of a predatory animal. "Say all that again."

Sophie backed away from him and there was a look of almost fear in her eyes. "Reede, I didn't mean anything bad. I thought you *were* a jerk. I'm sorry I said that but —"

"Not that part." He was advancing toward her. "About the highway and the phone."

She didn't understand what he meant. "I was trying to find a signal."

"And where were you?"

"On the way to Edilean." She backed up more. "I told you that." Her back was against the kitchen counter; she could go no farther.

"You just said 'There I was, standing . . .' And what was the rest of that sentence?"

Finally, she understood, and she tried to keep her face from turning red. She moved to duck out from under his arm, but he wouldn't let her. "Well, maybe I was . . . uh, sort of . . ."

"Standing in the middle of the highway?" His face was nearly touching hers. "A busy highway with vehicles doing sixty miles an hour and you were smack in the middle of it trying to get a cell phone signal? Is that right?"

Sophie's pretty face lost its look of fear and was replaced with guilt. "Well, you see, my car had stopped and I really *needed* to call someone and my phone —"

"The one I ran over?"

"Uh, yes. It didn't work and I *had* to —"

Reede turned away.

As he'd hoped, her guilt made her shower him with kisses. Their lovemaking that night had been special. Reede hadn't realized it but he'd been carrying a heavy burden of guilt about nearly having run over someone. While it was good that the incident had shocked him into changing his driving, he still felt bad about it. Sophie's confession relieved him of that guilt.

From now on he had something to balance out the fact that he and all of Edilean had lied to her. In fact, the next day Heather had referred to the beer-pouring incident.

"She was standing in the middle of the highway to get a signal for her phone,"

Reede said as he looked at a chart.

"Did you just find that out?"

"Yes," he answered.

Heather had smiled. "So now you have something to get back at her. That's the way all marriages work." She left the exam room before Reede could reply.

Three days before Christmas everything changed. At five Heather said, "There's some man here to see you. He says it's personal." She was frowning as though she didn't like the man.

Reede looked into the waiting room and there was his old friend Tyler Becks. They'd spent years together in school, had played soccer and drunk many beers together. Tyler was tall, blond, blue-eyed, and always had a long list of girls' phone numbers that he never minded sharing. At the time Reede had been so attached to Laura Chawnley that he'd felt almost fatherly as he watched the others arguing over who got what number. In Reede's mind he might as well have been a married man.

Reede smiled at Tyler and led him back to his office. Once they were out of sight of his nosy employees the two men hugged in the way of old buddies.

"Sit down," Reede said. "How have you been?"

Tyler practically collapsed into a chair. "If you'd asked me that a month ago I would have said I was in heaven. I had a wife, I was in partnership in a growing practice, had a big house, and was thinking about starting a family. What about you? I bet you have at least three kids by now. Home and family as well as saving the world one village at a time?"

Reede didn't smile. It had been years since he'd talked to Tyler and they'd shared news about their lives. "No wife, no kids."

"Right. I forgot. That girl you were so faithful to dumped you, didn't she?"

"That was a long time ago," Reede said. "Since then I've done a lot of traveling, but now, as you can see, I'm back here in my hometown. Are you just passing through? This area is beautiful at Christmas. It —" He broke off because tears had come to Tyler's eyes.

Reede grabbed some tissues from the box on the desk and handed them to him.

"I'm sorry," Tyler said. "I have no right to —"

Reede went to a cabinet along the wall and pulled out a bottle of forty-year-old single malt McTarvit whiskey and poured them both a glass.

Tyler downed his in one shot. "Sorry," he

said again. "It's been a bad few weeks. My wife told me she wants a divorce. We've only been married three years, but she wants out."

Reede sat down across from his friend, sipped his whiskey, and was silent. He knew from painful experience that what a person in this much agony needed most was someone to listen to them.

"Seems she and the partner in my practice have been having an affair for the last two years." Tyler downed another shot. "The bastard! He gave me a sob story about how perfect my life was while his was so empty. If we had a late patient or an emergency I was the one who went. He used to beg me to give him time to try to find a woman half as good as my Amy."

Tyler looked up with red eyes full of his misery. "He didn't want a copy of my wife, he wanted the original."

Reede was beginning to see where this was leading. Tyler was one of the many people he'd called and offered the job in Edilean to. He'd told of his situation in the most glowing terms he could come up with. Edilean was practically a paradise on earth. Great for families; great for single men looking for a family. Reede had also talked of how he wanted . . . no, needed . . . to go back to being an itinerant doctor, traveling around the world setting up clinics. Some doctors had politely listened; some had nearly hung up on him. But all of them had said no. Tyler's reaction had been laughter. He'd said that everything in his life was so great he couldn't think of changing anything.

Reede leaned back in his chair and listened to Tyler tell about his current horrible situation.

"I was ready to start a family. Babies. I was talking to Amy about it but she kept putting me off, saying she wasn't ready yet. Her job as a receptionist was too 'important' for her to think about having a baby. What woman doesn't want a *home*?! Answer me that. Walls, roses over fences, kids running around? But my wife —"

Reede's mind went to Sophie. Not long ago she'd been about to marry Carter Treeborne. She would have had a huge wedding and a home that was a mansion. All that would have happened if Carter hadn't been such a coward.

But now Carter was growing a backbone. Every day Reede had to listen to Sophie tell him of ideas Carter had, of plans he was making. For all that Treeborne told Sophie that all he wanted from her was her forgiveness, Reede thought the guy was working hard to win her. He wasn't blatant, but was subtle with his jokes and talks of a future line of baked goods for Treeborne Foods.

Each day it was getting more difficult for Reede to compete with Carter. If he were to accept what Tyler was leading up to asking, if Reede were to go back on the road, he knew he'd lose Sophie forever.

"And then I thought of your call," Tyler said. "Six weeks ago the idea of leaving my practice was a laugh, but now —"

"The salary is abysmal," Reede said. "I can hardly feed myself, much less support a wife and kids."

"That's all right. My brother is a lawyer, and he said that by the time I get through with the . . ." Tyler swallowed. "With dissolving the partnership I'll have enough to live on for ten years. Right now I just need somewhere quiet to live and work, and your little town looks to be as quiet as it gets in this country."

"Yeah," Reede said, "but we're far away from everything."

"Are you kidding? Williamsburg is just next door. And there are some great places here in this town. And of course there's year-round sports in the preserve. This place is paradise."

Last night Sophie had said almost exactly the same thing, that Edilean was a little paradise.

"So when do you want to leave?" Tyler asked.

"Later," Reede said. "Now I . . ."

"Right. I get it. After the new year. I've got a lot to do before then." Tyler stood up and held out his hand to Reede. "Do we have a deal?"

"I don't know," Reede said.

Tyler dropped his hand. "I understand. My whole life is upside down. How about if we talk again on the fifteenth of January?"

That was the date Roan said Sophie was planning to leave, Reede thought. "That's a good idea," he said, and the two men shook hands. Reede asked him to have dinner with him and Sophie but Tyler said no. He knew some people in the area and they'd invited him out.

Tyler stopped at the door and looked back. "I feel good about this," he said, then left.

"That makes one of us," Reede murmured as he collapsed onto his desk chair.

TWENTY-ONE

"What are you doing for Christmas?" Henry asked Sophie.

They were in his big garage working on a three-foot-wide sculpture of the Battle of Bunker Hill. The two of them had found a way to work that consisted of Henry trying to form the clay to look like some photo he'd found on the Internet, then he'd step back and Sophie would redo it for him.

In the last weeks she'd come to know Henry well. For all that he was a quiet man, he was a powerhouse. She could see how he'd been able to rule a couple of very big businesses.

He surrendered only to his small, round wife.

"Henry! If you don't get that mess out of my garage you're going to find yourself living alone," she'd said one day.

The next time Sophie went to their sprawling estate, construction on a huge studio had begun.

"Now you'll be able to do your own work," Henry told Sophie happily. "Come and see what I did yesterday."

He'd made an ugly little man sitting on a horse that had one leg a half inch shorter than the other. Worse was that if the man stood up he'd be a foot taller than the horse. Henry's ambition was much larger than his talent.

Repressing a sigh, Sophie tore Henry's work apart. She tried to be gentle, but her bad mood wouldn't let her. She pushed and pulled at the clay, then picked up a stainless steel tool and started gouging.

Henry, rather than being offended, laughed. He was a man who knew how to delegate. "So what about Christmas?" he asked again.

"I don't know. Reede and I put up a tree and we went shopping and bought his family and friends gifts. It was fun."

"What are you getting him?"

"He showed me some pictures of his travels and I'm going to make a sculpture of one of them. I'm hoping to have it cast in bronze, but it won't be ready before Christmas."

Henry was watching her as she rearranged the clay man he'd made. He could always

445

see when his sculptures were wrong. He just couldn't figure out how to make them right. "You're upset about something."

"No, I'm . . ."

"I have three daughters, remember? I know when things aren't right."

Sophie wiped her hands on a cloth. "Yesterday a man came into the restaurant. Seems he'd been sent there by Reede's nosy threesome."

"The women who work for him?" Henry was careful to keep his opinions to himself. If he'd learned nothing else from raising daughters it was that if he spoke against someone, they would take the opposite side. His middle daughter had almost married a kid with a record for armed robbery because Henry had talked to her "for her own good."

So Henry stood in silence and waited for Sophie to tell him whatever she wanted to. His personal opinion was that Reede Aldredge was suppressing Sophie's magnificent talent. That she was wasting her time in that dreary little sandwich shop bothered him. His plan was that for Christmas he was going to offer her a full-time job. She'd have a good salary, benefits, and a great place to work. No more spending her days making tuna salad sandwiches.

"His name is Dr. Tyler Becks and he wants

to take over Reede's practice," Sophie said.

Henry had heard a bit of the gossip around town, how Reede had given up his flamboyant, daredevil career to return to Edilean to help his friend. But then, Reede had been trapped here. "What did Reede say?"

"Nothing," Sophie said and there was frustration in her voice. "He didn't even tell me about this doctor. Roan did. But then, I *never* know what Reede is thinking. We practically live together but I don't know any more about him today than I did months ago."

"Everybody in town says he's mad about you," Henry said softly.

"I guess." Sophie looked away for a moment. In the distance she could hear the thump of a nail gun as the men framed Henry's new studio. She had an idea that he was going to offer her a job in it, and she didn't know what she was going to say.

The truth was that she had no idea where her life was going. Roan teased her about leaving on the fifteenth of January as she'd said she was going to do. But where could she go? Lisa was quite happy at college now and was even planning to spend Christmas with friends. She no longer needed her big sister. Sophie knew she couldn't go back to her hometown. To what? The only person she really cared about there was Carter, and he was here in Edilean.

Sophie knew Reede was deeply jealous of Carter and there was a part of her that liked that he was.

"Does any of this have to do with young Treeborne?" Henry asked.

"No, Carter's fine. I think he's falling in love with Kelli."

"The baker? The one with the . . ." Henry motioned around his eyes.

"That's her. She's a really good pastry chef, and what I like is that she doesn't take anything off Carter. I used to be so aware that he was a Treeborne that I treated him like a prince. I was in awe of him."

"But Kelli isn't?"

"Not by a long shot. She acts like his being a Treeborne is something he needs to overcome."

Henry smiled. "That sounds good for him."

"It is. It's how I should have treated him."

"What's really bothering you?" Henry asked.

"This man, Dr. Becks . . . The three women sent him to me. Not pointedly, they just strongly suggested that he get a sandwich at the Phoenix shop and ask for

Sophie."

"Have they done that before?"

"No, so I knew it was important, and I sat down with him to talk. Poor man. He's a mess. His wife has been having an affair with the other doctor in his practice and she wants a divorce."

"And he wants to come here to little Edilean to heal his wounds?"

"Yes. And I think it'll be good for him. The locals will match him up with somebody, and by the time Tris returns he'll be in recovery." She stepped forward to make some more changes to the ill-proportioned sculpture Henry had made.

"It all sounds like a good thing," Henry said. "But you don't seem to agree."

"I think it's wonderful," Sophie said. "I know this is what Reede wants. He wants to return to his charity work. That's where his heart is. At least I think so. It's not as though he's ever actually told me so. A few weeks ago there was a piece on the news about a doctor who owned a big boat that was set up as a hospital ship. He went around the world to places where people had never seen a doctor in their lives. You should have seen Reede's face! It lit up like a light had been turned on."

"What did he say about it?"

"That's it!" Sophie said. "Reede didn't say a word. He just got up and went to the kitchen to get a beer. I went after him and asked him if he'd like to do something like that. You know what he did? He laughed. He said, 'Do you know how much something like that would *cost*?! I'd never get funding for something as big as that.' I tried to get him to talk about it, but he wouldn't say another word."

"Funding, huh?" Henry said. "If he did get the money for such a project, then what? Would you go with him?"

"What could I do? I'm not a nurse or know anything about health care. I'd just be in the way. Reede climbs down cables on helicopters. I'm terrified of walking across a roof beam."

Henry couldn't help smiling. "So am I, but I don't think that means I'm useless. Sophie, you have a wonderful talent. I'd think you'd want to use it."

"I do," she said. "I mean, I think I do. But sometimes, I . . . I don't know. All I know is that Reede didn't tell me about the doctor who wants to take over his practice. I dropped about a thousand hints, but Reede didn't take them. He was quiet all night. I'm afraid . . ."

"Of what, Sophie?" Henry asked.

"That he'll stay here because of me and give up his dream. Or maybe he'll take this doctor up on his offer and I'll be left behind. Either way, one of us is going to be miserable."

Henry could see that she was on the verge of tears and he did the same as he did with his daughters and pulled her into his arms. Over her shoulder he saw his wife, but she turned away, sympathy on her face. She knew that her husband was very good with crying women.

When any of their daughters fought with one another or their mother, one by one, wife included, they went tearfully to Henry, and he solved the problem.

"Let me talk to some people," Henry said as he released her. "I know some businesses that could afford to fund a doctor who wants to save the world." He smiled. "And when he comes home you'll be waiting for him."

"Good," Sophie said and as she looked at Henry she knew that this was a bargain. A business deal. If she would give Henry what he wanted, which was a private teacher and a shot at placing his work somewhere important, he would fund Reede's mobile clinic.

She took a breath. This is what she'd

wanted, wasn't it? What she'd trained for. And now everything she'd studied for was right in front of her. Henry, this man who'd come into her life like a fairy godfather, was offering her a beautiful studio and endless supplies. No doubt through Henry she'd have fabulously wealthy clients who could afford a life-size bronze sculpture in their gardens. All she had to do was work with Henry, who was an easy man to be around.

And as Henry said, she could stay there in Edilean and probably live in the house Reede had bought and wait for him to come home when he could. He could send her photos and call often. She could show him her work, tell him of her success. They could adjust to a life that was separate as well as together.

It was all great. A perfect solution. So why did she feel like she wanted to crawl into a hole and pull a cover over her?

"Fine," she said at last. "I'll talk to Reede about it all."

That night she and Reede were both quiet.

"Is something bothering you?" she asked him.

"No, nothing. What about you?"

"No problems," she said, lying as much as he was. If he didn't want to tell her about Dr. Becks being willing to take over the practice, so be it. She wasn't going to ask him. And if he was already making plans to leave, that was his right. But then she did *not* want to hear him tell her that she couldn't go with him because she'd be useless. What could *she* do with sick people? Shape their pills into unicorns? Compared to what Reede did, her profession was frivolous. No, she didn't want to hear him tell her — kindly and with gentleness, of course — that she wasn't needed in the very important business of what Reede did.

The next day it was too busy at the shop for Sophie to think about her own problems. It seemed that half of Virginia had put off shopping until the last minute, and they'd all decided to do it in cute, quaint, adorable little Edilean.

Carter and Sophie made sandwiches, Kelli ladled soup, and Roan took over the pastry cabinet. His booming voice and persuasive manner made even the skinniest of people try the tarts that were dripping with cream.

As for the cash register, a woman in her thirties took it over. She had belatedly answered Roan's ad. "I didn't see it until I changed the bottom of the birdcage," she told Roan when she'd arrived early that morning. "My name is Danielle, Danni for short. I think I'm intelligent, I've been known to be creative, and I have some talents, but I am not and never have been entertaining. Sorry. However, I used to work in a restaurant." Her eyes were alive with merriment as she said this.

She was a pretty woman, with dark hair and eyes, a bit too much on her hips, but her large top balanced her. She was immediately likable.

Sophie, up to her elbows in soup making, left it all to Roan, but when Carter nudged her shoulder, she looked up. Roan, big, gruff-looking, was staring down at pretty Danni in silence.

Sophie grabbed a dry cloth, wiped her hands, and went around the counter. "Can you run a cash register?"

"Yes," Danni said, her voice calm and pleasant.

"Then you're hired. Roan tends to argue with people over money." She looked up at him, and he was still staring at Danielle. "You have pastry duty today," she said softly, then when he didn't respond, she raised her voice. "Roan! Pastries?"

"I like them," he said.

Shaking her head, Sophie went back to her soup and Carter caught her eye. "I smell love in the air," he said.

"Yes, you and Kelli do make a good pair."

At that, Kelli laughed and Carter's face turned red.

When Kelli went to the back to get something, Carter whispered, "Is it that obvious? I mean, can everyone see that I like her?"

Sophie thought about making a joke but she didn't. "Your father won't approve of her."

"Yeah, I know," he said, and for a moment he kept slicing cheese, but then he stopped. "You know something? I don't care anymore. Sophie, my fear of losing Treeborne Foods made me do something I'll always regret. I lost you."

She stepped back from him. "If this is —"

"No. That's not what I'm saying. Even if my father hadn't interfered I don't think you and I would have been good for each other."

"Are you referring to the fact that I was in awe of you?"

"No, I liked that part."

With a laugh, Sophie hit him on the shoulder. "Some prince *you* are!"

"That's it," Carter said. "I could never have lived up to what you thought I was. I saw it in your eyes and when I was with you I felt that I was a great and powerful being."

"I never thought *that* about you."

"I was always afraid that you'd see the coward that I actually was. I've been terrified of my father all my life."

"There's a whole town afraid of him," she said.

"But I'm not anymore."

"Because of Kelli?"

"Yes or no," Carter said. "Mostly no. I see now that I can earn my own living."

"What you make here isn't going to supply you with what you've grown up with," she said.

"I have some money from my mother, and I plan to use it to open a bakery. And I think I'll see if I can get some backers for frozen baked goods."

Sophie looked at him for a moment. "The Treeborne ambition is alive and growing."

"Maybe it is," Carter said.

"What about your father? What does he say to all this?"

"Ha!" Carter said. "I walked out in pursuit of you and I left no note, nothing. When I called the housekeeper about the cookbook, I asked her if Dad had asked about me. Not a word. I am a dispensable person to him."

He said the words lightly, but Sophie knew the pain behind them. "You can stay here in Edilean with Kelli and start your new business here."

456

"I think I will," Carter said. "And what about you? Your boxing doctor ask you to marry him yet?"

"I . . ."

Carter stopped slicing and looked at her. "You what?" When Sophie said nothing, he said, "I just poured out my heart to you, so I think you can tell me what's going on with you. If this doctor has done anything to hurt you, I'll —"

"No!" Sophie said. "It's just that —" She broke off because it was eight a.m. and Kelli had unlocked the front door. In an instant the little restaurant was full of customers, all of them hungry.

TWENTY-TWO

At Christmas eve lunch, Lewis Treeborne showed up in the sandwich shop. He just walked in, ordered soup and a sandwich, then stood there and waited.

Sophie recognized his voice and froze in place — and all her fears came back to her. Were the police with him? Would she be taken away in handcuffs?

Carter, a bowl of soup in his hands, held it out to her. "Hey, Soph! Wake up. People are waiting."

She nodded toward the register, where Mr. Treeborne was paying.

Carter hesitated for a moment, then put the bowl down and turned his back on the man.

"Shouldn't you go to him? Or something?" she asked quietly.

"I'm not afraid of him anymore," Carter said softly. "He found me here, so if he wants more he knows where I am."

Sophie nodded and had to work to keep from hurrying to the man to ask what he wanted. She reminded herself that this was Edilean and that the Treeborne family did not own *this* town.

But she couldn't help watching the man sitting alone at a little table, eating slowly, never once glancing at the people behind the counter.

"Why are you two whispering?" Kelli asked Sophie and Carter. "What's going on?"

"That's Carter's dad," Sophie said, nodding toward the man.

"Yeah? Ol' Treeborne himself?"

"The monster in the flesh," Carter said with a grimace.

Kelli looked from one to the other. "You two are cowards."

"You know us well," Sophie said.

Kelli rolled her eyes as she went to the big glass counter full of her freshly baked pastries and began to fill a plate full of slices.

"What are you doing?" Carter asked.

"Taking an opportunity," she said. When the plate was full of samples, she got napkins and a fork and took them to Lewis Treeborne's table. "Your son and I are thinking about using his connection to the Treeborne empire to start a line of frozen pastries."

Lewis didn't look up as she set the plate on the table and turned away.

Sophie and Carter pretended they weren't looking, but they were. And when Lewis picked up his fork and took a bite they drew in their breaths.

"What's going on?" Roan asked and Kelli told him.

Even though there was a line at the register, Danni left it to ask what they were looking at, and Roan explained. By that time everyone in the shop had caught the tension and had stopped to look at the man with the big plate of desserts.

"Does he like coffee?" Danni asked Carter.

"Yeah, sure."

She poured a big mug of it. "Sugar? Cream? Milk?"

"No," Carter said. "Black."

The crowded restaurant was quiet as Danni took the mug of coffee and set it on the table beside the man.

He took a sip.

"Good, huh?" Danni asked.

"The coffee or the pies?" Lewis asked.

"Both."

He took his time in replying. "Not bad." As he stood up, he didn't say which one he meant, but he'd tasted each of the pastries.

The whole restaurant was silent as Lewis Treeborne walked to the front door. He didn't look at any of them, but paused, his back to all of them. "Eight tonight," he said loudly. He opened the door. "Both of you." He left the restaurant.

It took a moment for everyone to release their breaths and start talking at once. Roan, used to crowds, tried to answer the questions shot at them, while Carter, Kelli, and Sophie went back to work. But the three of them exchanged looks that were full of hope — and questions.

"Where will the meeting be?" Kelli asked.

"Williamsburg Inn," Carter and Sophie said in unison. It was the best in the area. Old World elegance.

"You have to go with us," Kelli said to Sophie, then looked at Carter. "But then, maybe your dad meant Sophie when he said 'both of you.' "

Carter and Sophie looked at each other.

"No," Sophie said. "I'm of no use to him."

"She's right," Carter said. "He wants you and your magic hands."

Sophie stepped away from the two of them. The looks they were giving each other said everything. As she went to clear a table she couldn't help looking at the two couples. Carter and Kelli had their heads together,

461

whispering and planning. She heard them talking about what Kelli could cook to take with them that night. At the other end of the store Roan and Danni were quietly talking and working in such unison that it seemed they'd always known each other.

Sophie had to look away. She envied them very much!

Just before closing, as she thought he'd do, Henry came in. He had a big manila envelope with him and she knew what it contained: his proposal. The others took over while Sophie sat down with him.

"I thought I'd bring this by now and not interrupt your Christmas." He pushed the envelope across the table toward her.

She didn't open it.

"It's all in there," he said. "It's a job offer and I think it's a good one. The studio will be done by April and you can start then. Sophie, you can do whatever you want. You can teach classes or you can work on your own projects. The salary is enough to live on, and you can supplement it with sales of your own work. Does that sound good?"

"Perfect," she said but she didn't smile.

Henry frowned a bit as he continued. "And there are benefits, health and dental. If you should marry, the plan extends to your husband. And Sophie —"

"Yes?"

"The plan will cover him wherever he is in the world. I saw to that. If he needs to be airlifted out of some godforsaken place, that's covered too."

"Good," she said and managed a weak smile. "What about funding for Reede?"

"It's all in there. I have several men ready to help with this. If your young doctor wants a fully equipped medical ship, he can have it. If he wants mobile clinics or to open a hospital somewhere, he can have that too."

Henry put his hand on hers and squeezed. "Anything he wants I will do my best to get it for him."

"Thank you," she said and tried to smile.

He leaned back in his chair. "And, Sophie, if you two should get married I negotiated that every year all expenses will be paid for you to have two visits of two weeks each. You can meet anywhere in the world. And of course he'll come home to you often."

"He hasn't asked me to marry him," Sophie said.

"He will. The whole town says so." Henry smiled broadly. He'd been worried at her glum expression and was afraid that his offer was what was making her sad. But it looked like her unhappiness was caused by her lazy boyfriend. Henry squeezed her

463

hand again. "I'm sure he will ask you. Maybe tomorrow, for Christmas, he'll get down on one knee."

Sophie picked up the envelope. "I'll go over all this with Reede and let you know. It's a very generous offer and I thank you for it."

"It's my pleasure," Henry said, but he was watching her closely and trying not to frown. He wished he knew her better so he could reassure her.

On the other hand he wasn't sure how Dr. Reede would react to the offer. If Sophie gave him the packet, saying that his trips would be funded, what would that mean to Sophie? Would he give her a kiss, say "Thanks, babe," and run away?

If he did, Henry thought, he'd make sure the young man lost his future funding. Sophie was a nice girl and she didn't deserve being treated like that.

After Henry left, Sophie went back to help clean up. They'd be closed for Christmas Day, so they wanted everything especially tidy.

Kelli and Carter were talking quietly about what they were going to do at the meeting with his father, and their excitement filled the air. At the other end of the restaurant Roan and Danni were sitting in a booth and talking. They seemed to be planning where they were going to spend Christmas.

An hour later the four of them left, wishing Sophie a very merry Christmas. She made herself a pot of tea and sat down to go through the packet Henry had given her. It was, indeed, a very generous offer. There was no specific amount for the funding but seemed to be open-ended. However much whatever Reede chose to do cost, that's how much would be available. She couldn't help but wonder how many favors Henry'd had to call in to get such a generous proposal.

As for her, what he offered was equally generous. She'd be paid for working in a fabulous studio, and she could supplement her income in any way she could imagine. The insurance benefits were excellent. All in all, the plan couldn't be better. Nothing had been left out.

So why did the sight of it depress her?

She went through the documents one by one and took out everything that had her name on it or pertained to her and Reede as a couple. For all that he wanted her to move in with him, he'd certainly never mentioned marriage. It would be embarrassing to hand him papers that referred to their marriage as though it were a done deal.

When Reede picked her up at five she did her best to be cheerful, but it wasn't easy. "We're going to Sara's tomorrow?" she asked as he was driving them to his house.

"Sure. Unless you don't want to. We could go into Williamsburg and see the programs there. We can do whatever you want."

"When were you going to tell me about Dr. Becks?" she asked softly.

"Nothing to tell," Reede said.

"That's not what he told me. He's offering to take over the practice so you can leave."

"It's more complicated than that," Reede said. "I need funding. I let every business contact I had drop because I was here. It would take me months to reorganize everything. By that time Tyler will be gone."

Sophie took a breath. "I have something to show you. It's something that you're going to like very much."

"So that's it?" Colin asked. It was Christmas Day, and he and Reede were in the back parlor of Sara and Mike's old house. They could hear carols on the other side of the closed door, and people were laughing and talking, but it was relatively quiet in this room. "You have it all now. Funding, someone to take over the practice, and you and

Sophie are mad about each other. What else is there?"

"I don't know," Reede said. There was a blaze in the old fireplace, and Sara had a little Christmas tree in the corner. "Sophie has everything. It took me hours last night before I could get her to tell me why that guy Henry was offering me all this. He gave her a fabulous job." He told Colin the details, even down to the dental plan.

"She can't turn down something as good as that and leave with you," Colin said softly. He'd been through this problem with Tris and Jecca. Her job was one place and his another. "What are you going to do?"

"Stay here," Reede said. "As Sara said, I don't fall in love easily. I lost the woman I love the first time; I'm not going to do it again."

"But you hate it here."

"I'm adjusting," Reede said. "It's certainly more pleasant now that Sophie is here. And I can't bear to lose her! That idiot Treeborne spends every day with her. If I left town he'd be after her in a second."

"From what I heard he wants that girl who bakes."

Reede shrugged. "That's only because he thinks he can't have Sophie."

Colin couldn't argue with that, as he felt

the same way about his wife, Gemma. To him she was the most beautiful, desirable female on earth and he was sure every other male saw her that way. "Have you told Sophie yet?"

"I will tomorrow. I hope it cheers her up. She seems pretty down about it all. But then when I think of leaving her I feel bad too."

"So she gets the job she's always wanted, but *you* get stuck here in Edilean." Colin shook his head. "For you to turn down an offer like this must hurt a lot."

Roan groaned. "More than you can imagine. It's what I dreamed of for years. I was planning to hit my new brother-in-law up to fund something like it. At least now I won't have that embarrassment. And there's always Sophie's job. She really is the most talented person I've ever met. She deserves to be known in the art world."

"I agree. I saw that little sculpture she made for you. By the way, what did you get her for Christmas?"

"A camera. I figured she could use it to photograph her work."

"Maybe you should visit Kim's shop," Colin said, referring to the beautiful little jewelry store.

"Yeah. Right. I'll get Sophie a ring and ask her to marry me. It's just that . . ."

"Afraid she'll say no?"

"Terrified of it. I . . . I mean I . . . She's . . ."

"I know exactly what you mean. Over-whelming, isn't it?"

"She's more important to me than any-thing else," Reede said. "And I'd do any-thing for her."

"Even to giving up an offer that you've wanted all your adult life?"

"Yes," Reede said. "I'd give up everything for Sophie."

"As far as I can tell that's exactly what you *are* giving up. Everything."

"That's not the way I see it. I'll have Sophie and she'll be able to create. It's what Kim and Jecca wanted so much that they were willing to give up the men they loved. I know that if I leave here I'll lose her."

"Maybe she could —"

Reede knew what his cousin was going to say. Maybe Sophie could go with him. "I'm not even going to suggest it," he said, "because she might agree to do it. Then what? Follow me around the world? And never use that talent of hers? I couldn't ask that of her. It would be like her asking me to give up medicine. I'll stay here and do some volunteer work at some free clinics."

"Great," Colin muttered. "Half your

patients will be drug addicts, not people who desperately need you."

Reede shrugged. "I don't see any other way, do you?"

"I think you should talk to Sophie and tell her the truth."

Reede got up and went to the door. "And have her sacrifice everything for *me*? No thanks. I don't want to live with a martyr." Reede left the room, closing the door behind him.

"So *you* are going to be the martyr," Colin said after he left. He went out to join the others but he couldn't bring himself to smile at Sophie. She was such a pretty little thing and part of him was glad that Reede had found someone to love. On the other hand, he hated that she'd changed Reede's three-year sentence into a lifetime of unhappiness. Colin well remembered when he'd visited Reede in the field. That man — dynamic, energetic, forceful, and above all else, *happy* — was not the man he saw in Edilean. Trapped in an office all day, dealing with people who came in with splinters in their fingers, wasn't what Reede wanted to do with his life. Tris loved it, loved the people and their problems, but Reede couldn't bear it.

But now, because of this young woman

who'd come to town and made Reede fall for her, he was going to spend a lifetime doing what he hated.

When Sophie, laughing at something one of the children said, looked up at Colin, he didn't smile back at her. He tried to keep his expression even, but he couldn't. Reede was his cousin, his friend, and this woman was ruining his life. He wished she'd never come to Edilean.

TWENTY-THREE

Carter was about to lock the shop door, but three women threw it open and burst inside. It was two weeks after Christmas and quite cold out but they didn't have on coats and they looked like they'd been running.

"Sorry, but we're closed for the day," he said. "If you want something special maybe we can make it tomorrow." The women just stood there blinking at him. He'd seen them around town but couldn't remember where. One was older, one middle-aged, and one was young and pretty. "Dr. Reede!" he said. "You work for him."

"We do," said the middle one, "and we need your help."

"If this has to do with the doc's boxing lessons, leave me out."

"No, it's about Sophie. I'm Betsy, this is Alice, and this is Heather. She's expecting."

For a moment Carter wondered what she was expecting to happen but then he under-

472

stood. "Congratulations." The women just stood there staring at him, as though waiting for him to do something, but he had no idea what it was supposed to be. If this was about Sophie maybe they thought Carter was trying something with her. After all, Dr. Reede hadn't popped the question yet.

Two days ago Roan had asked Sophie about that. "I've only known him a few months," Sophie said.

Roan put on his professor face. "In this case I think it's a matter of experience that precludes time. He didn't ask you and you turned him down, did you?"

"Not that it's anyone's business, but no." Sophie left the room. It was obviously something she didn't want to talk about.

Carter was sure that half of Edilean — and probably Sophie — knew that the day after Christmas Reede had bought a ring with three diamonds on it. Since his sister owned the shop he hadn't done it over the counter, but her assistant, Carla, had told everyone of the deal.

But Sophie kept showing up at work with no ring on.

Carter looked at the three women standing in front of the door and couldn't help putting his hands up, as though for protection. "I'm involved with Kelli and we're working on a deal with my father. He wants me to return to Texas, but I told him no. I need more time to stand on my own feet before I get eaten up by the Treeborne machine. Besides, Kelli and I like it here. We're thinking of opening a branch of the new business here. We'd be giving jobs to the people of Edilean."

The women were still standing there and looking at him pointedly. The older one, Alice, shifted her weight from one foot to another, but they didn't speak.

"I take it you're not concerned about Sophie running off with me," he said, smiling a bit at his own ego.

"We're dealing with real love," Heather said quite seriously. "*True* love. The kind that lasts forever. Look, we only have forty-five minutes for lunch and if I don't sit down I'm going to hurl."

Carter grabbed a chair off a table and set it on the floor. "Please." As he got down two more chairs he realized he was nearly joyous that the women hadn't come there to berate him. Ever since he'd arrived in Edilean he'd felt he had to prove himself. After Dr. Reede hit him — and his nose was still a little sore — all of Edilean had found out why and Carter'd had to answer a lot of questions.

"I don't have any coffee made but the refrigerator's working," he said. When the women looked blank, he added, "How about sampling some new pastries Kelli made and telling me what you think? If you can stand them with milk, that is."

For the first time the women smiled at him, and Carter grabbed a tray as he went to the fridge.

Minutes later, they were still sitting at the table, three empty pie plates in front of them. The women hadn't eaten entire pies but most of them. Heather had been nearly insatiable. She'd licked her spoon so hard Carter was afraid the design was going to come off.

"So you want me to find out what's really going on with Sophie?" he asked.

"Exactly," Betsy said. "You're the only one who knows her well enough to talk to her. Her friends, Kim and Jecca, aren't here, so that leaves you."

It was on the tip of Carter's tongue to say that he didn't know Sophie either. Not *really* know her. The frightened, overworked young woman he knew back in Texas wasn't like the Sophie he'd met in Edilean. For all that she'd never run a shop before, she was good at it. A natural organizer.

"Comes from years of managing two jobs

and a household of people who thought 'Let Sophie take care of it' was a way of life," she said when he complimented her.

"And you put yourself through college," Roan added. "That wears out the students."

But since Christmas things had changed. Sophie'd told them about her new job offer and that in April she'd be leaving to become a full-time sculptor.

"That's cause for celebration!" Roan said. "Carter, go buy some champagne and make sure it's cold."

"No!" Sophie said. "Really. No. It's a job and I . . ." She didn't seem to know what else to say. "We need supplies for tomorrow so I . . ." She grabbed her handbag and left the shop.

"Be careful what you wish for," Roan mumbled and went back to clearing out the register.

After that no one mentioned the new job, but they all saw that Sophie wasn't happy about it. At first they thought it might be because she'd be working with Henry, but Sophie seemed to genuinely like the man.

One afternoon as they were closing up and Sophie was away, they all decided that she was upset because Reede hadn't asked her to marry him.

Danni spoke up. "Yesterday I had to go to

him for the burn on my arm and he looked miserable. Those two are *very* unhappy people."

They'd spent the few minutes speculating on the cause of the misery, each person having a different opinion.

"Bad sex," Danni said. "If the sex isn't good, no matter how much you love someone, it's not worth it."

"I agree," Kelli said.

Carter and Roan looked at the two women with eyes full of concern.

"Are we . . . ? I mean . . ." Carter said to Kelli.

"Baby, we're great!"

He sighed in relief and so did Roan when Danni kissed his cheek.

"So what's the problem between Sophie and Reede?" Danni asked. "What's making them the two unhappiest people on earth?"

Not one of them could come up with an answer, but now Dr. Reede's three employees were asking Carter to help them.

"You see," Betsy said, "we sort of made a vow that we'd do whatever was necessary to make the doctor happy. We were the ones who kept the secret of who he was."

"And the corset was us," Heather said.

"But Sara helped with the horse," Alice added.

"And the doc's costume, of course," Heather said.

"We had nothing to do with the robbers, but Mike took care of that. He's been a real asset to this town," Alice said.

"So you see," Betsy said, "how hard we've worked."

"And it's paid off as Dr. Reede's temper has greatly improved since Sophie came to town," Alice said.

"But now he's so glum that —" Heather began.

"That's too mild a word," Betsy said as she looked hard at Carter. "The truth is that Dr. Reede is so depressed that he's barely functioning. And we think Sophie isn't much better."

"They are *very* polite to each other," Heather said. "The day I'm polite to my husband is the day I'll ask him for a divorce."

The three women stopped talking and stared at Carter.

"Ladies," he said slowly, "I have *no* idea what you're talking about. Not a word of it."

Betsy looked at the clock on the wall. "We have to get back to work or we'd stay and explain. But it all boils down to the fact that *you* have to talk to Sophie and find out

478

what's going on between her and Dr. Reede."

Immediately, Carter saw a thousand things wrong with that idea. Kelli, for all that she pretended not to be, was quite jealous of Sophie. "This past summer?" she'd asked. "Just a few months ago you were thinking of marrying Sophie and now you want me to believe that you're completely over her?" Nothing he'd said had made her believe Sophie was in the past — the recent past.

Besides that, Roan and Reede glared at him, and the giant who was the local sheriff stopped in often and looked at Carter as though he were a criminal he had to keep close watch over. Although, since Christmas, the sheriff had seemed to be looking at Sophie with less than affection.

As for Sophie, she still moved away when Carter got too near.

"Really and truly," Carter said, "I don't know what's going on."

Betsy stood up and the other women followed her lead. "That's just the point. No one knows what's going on but *you* are the one who has to find out."

With that, the three women left the restaurant. Carter locked the door behind them then flopped down onto a chair. At this moment the thought of returning to Texas and the little town that was virtually owned by his family appealed greatly to him.

He looked around the empty restaurant. Everything was clean and no one was there. Kelli had gone to get supplies, and Roan and Danni were . . . Wherever lovers went in Edilean. Sophie was upstairs in her apartment, where she often went in the afternoons now. No more staying downstairs and helping clean. Since Christmas Sophie looked as though she would never smile again.

Part of Carter wanted to flee, but the bigger part of him knew the women were correct. Right now, in this town, he was the closest thing Sophie had to a girlfriend.

With a sigh, he started up the stairs. She probably won't see me, he thought. She'll probably —

He knocked once and Sophie opened the door.

"Oh. I thought you were Reede. Sometimes he gets off early."

Carter stepped inside and closed the door behind him. "We need to talk."

"Carter, if you and Kelli have had an argument and now you want me back, it's not going to happen. I —"

"No argument. I came here to find out what's wrong with *you.*"

"Nothing," she said. "You need to leave. You saw what Reede did the last time he got jealous."

Carter's eyes widened. "Sophie, is that what's wrong with you? Is he horribly jealous? Does he . . . Has he hit you? I can get you some help. I can —"

Sophie plopped down on the sofa. "Of course he hasn't! Reede couldn't be kinder. He's very sweet to me. Very courteous."

Carter sat in a chair across from her. "Sophie, you're driving us all *crazy*! You look miserable but no one can figure out *why.* What is wrong? You have a fabulous job coming up, some doctor is mad about you, you have friends, and —"

"Reede won't leave. I can't get him to go."

"You want to break up with him?" he asked with sympathy.

"Heavens no! Where did you get that idea? I want to marry him and get pregnant immediately. Don't you think Reede was made to be a father?"

Carter ran his hand over his face, then looked at her with eyes full of pleading. "Sophie, help me out here. I was told to talk to you and find out what's wrong between you and Dr. Hit-First-Talk-Later but all I hear is good."

"I did tell you," Sophie said. "What's

wrong is that Reede won't leave."

"Last I heard, if the man leaves no babies are made."

Sophie looked at the windows to the outside. She desperately needed to talk to someone. The last two weeks had been hell. Reede had been so resolutely cheerful that she wanted to strangle him. Instead, she'd smiled back at him as sweetly as she could. But several times when he'd thought no one was looking, she'd seen the look of . . . well, fatalism on his face. She could see that the happiness he tried to show her was only skin deep.

"Okay, Sophie," Carter said, "I know I'm failing the girlfriend test but I really don't know what the hell you're talking about. You want to marry him; you want him to leave. Make up your mind."

Sophie shook her head at him is disbelief. "You are failing as a girlfriend. Carter, I want Reede to leave and I want to go with him."

Carter still didn't understand. "So go. Now, is the problem solved?"

"No, Mr. Rich Boy, the problem is not solved. Reede can't leave to go save the world because he has no money for funding. I can get the money but only if I stay here and work for Henry. But Reede won't accept the gift and leave because I can't leave."

Carter blinked at her for a moment. " 'The Gift of the Magi.' "

"Right," Sophie said. " 'The Gift of the Magi.' "

They were referring to the O. Henry story where the very poor couple who were deeply in love wanted to buy each other gifts. He sold his gold watch to buy her combs for her glorious hair; she sold her hair to buy him a fob chain for his watch.

Sophie looked up at him. "I'm considering telling Reede I'm actually in love with you so he'll take Henry's offer of funding and leave town. I want him to go do what he's meant to."

Carter turned pale at that idea and involuntarily put his hand to his nose. "Please don't do that. What about your sculpture? You're so very talented."

Sophie stood up, walked to the windows, then turned back to look at him. "I think maybe everyone on earth is given a talent."

"Not like yours."

"Maybe not," she said, frowning, "but to succeed I think a person also needs . . . I don't know, drive. Ambition. Something to propel a person forward. I've heard people in churches sing better than people who sell

483

millions of disks. So why aren't the best singers being given the money and applause?"

"I have no idea."

"Because it takes more than talent to succeed. Kim and Jecca were driven. All through school all the two of them did was create. Anything. They cut out paper stars at Christmas."

"What about you?" Carter asked. In all their months together he'd never seen a hint of this Sophie.

"When I was given a choice between a job that could have put me on the ladder to success and going home to my little sister, I took family. And I cut off all contact with Kim and Jecca because I didn't want them to find out that I wasn't like them. I'd already lied to them about where I was from."

"Texas embarrassed you?" Carter was smiling.

"No, Treeborne Foods embarrassed me. I'd learned that people thought it would be great to live in a town owned by one company. I didn't want to explain that Treeborne is ruled by a man who doesn't believe in hiring locals for management positions."

Again, Carter's face drained of color. "I'll change that," he said softly.

"I think you should."

"So you don't want to be a sculptor?"

"I don't want to spend my life making twenty-foot bronzes for rich people to put in their fancy gardens. When I was in school some snooty kid in law school said I should build a cup holder into every one of my sculptures. He said that way they would be *useful.*"

"Yeow!" Carter said. "Even I know that's not good. So you want to go with Dr. Reede? Roan said something about Reede setting up a clinic on a boat. You want to raise children on a boat?"

"Why not? Who said that a three-bedroom, two-bath home is what's best for kids? Couldn't they — ?" She cut off as she sat back down on the couch. "It's absurd to think about any of this. Reede would never agree to my going with him, even if he got the money from somewhere else. What could I do to help him?"

"Shall we see?" Carter asked.

"What does that mean?"

"It means, my dear friend, that Treeborne Foods will fund it all. The trips, the clinics. Everything that Henry Belleck has offered, Treeborne Foods will match."

"Carter, you can't do that. Your father will —"

"Screw him! I've been scared of my father all my life. Terrified of him. But when Kelli and I had dinner with him two weeks ago, I realized that I'm all he has. If my father dies, what happens to his precious Treeborne Foods, which he loves more than any human? It'll fall apart without someone who cares about it to hold it together. Who will that be? His right-hand man? That guy would sell in a minute. Can my father disinherit me? How will that look in the ads that brag that we're a family business?"

Sophie was staring at him in silence.

"Look, Sophie, since that horrible day when I pushed you out of my father's cold, empty mansion because I was afraid of him, I've done nothing but think. I now know what I'm going to do. Kelli doesn't know it yet — or maybe she does — but I'm going to marry her and we're going to open a line of baked goods that will probably double the size of the company. And it's all come about because of you, Sophie. If I hadn't come after you —"

"Because I stole your cookbook."

"Right." He smiled at her. "If you hadn't stolen the cookbook, I wouldn't have met Kelli, wouldn't have stood up to my father, and wouldn't have known that I do like working with food. And I wouldn't know how much I like living in a town where I'm the crown prince."

Sophie couldn't help laughing at the last part.

"Sorry, but that's my ego. I'll see to it that Treeborne Foods funds whatever Dr. Reede wants to do. Besides, I can write off the expense and use the whole thing in publicity."

"You *are* a Treeborne."

"I had no idea I was, but I think maybe I am down to my very toes." The two of them exchanged smiles and it was the first time he'd felt that maybe Sophie could possibly forgive him. When he'd first become involved with her he hadn't done it with bad intentions. That things had turned out badly had been due to Carter's fear of his father. "By the way, Sophie, about that cookbook . . ."

"I'm sorry about that. It's just that I was so very angry at you, and —"

"And you had a right to be. But I think I owe you the truth, after all I've put you through. The reason the cookbook is written in code and why it's kept locked up is because great-granny put cocaine on everything."

"What?"

"It was legal back then and it made you

487

feel good. Coco-Cola was named for its secret ingredient."

Sophie was looking at him in shock.

"You see now why I was so frantic when I saw that the cookbook was missing? I wasn't afraid someone would publish our so-called secret recipes on the Internet. I was afraid that if we were found out we'd be laughed out of the industry. We have Granny's photo on every package."

"And she doused the food with cocaine?"

"She sprinkled it over everything. And just to let you know, if the code were broken and the recipes made without the coke, they're awful. She used lard and pig jowls, whatever was cheap, then she dumped it all over hard little noodles. Without the coke on top nobody could even chew the stuff. My great-granny was a marvelous business-woman, but a cook she was not."

It took Sophie a few minutes to absorb this information, then she began to laugh. And Carter joined her.

"Your grandmother was —"

"An addict," Carter said.

"Treeborne Foods, a family business."

"Right," Carter said.

"And the code?"

"Based on an old book she had. It's in the safe too."

Sophie was smiling, thinking about it all. The great family secret that she'd almost exposed.

"So will you think about my offer?" he asked.

"To fund Reede?"

"No," Carter said, "to fund *both* of you. And Sophie, as for what you can do to help, from what I've seen of you in Texas in managing your hellion of a sister, then coming here and charming an entire town —"

"I didn't do that. Reede —"

Carter held up his hand. "This is my speech, so let me finish it. Sophie, you have changed people's lives, and I think *that* is your real talent. Sculpting is just a sideline. And as much as I'm not a fan of your doctor friend, he sees the truth. Now that he's met you he'd rather give up his dreams than lose you. And he's smart to see that."

He put his hands out to her, and she took them. "I want you to go find him and talk to him. Really talk to him."

"Henry —"

"I'll take care of Henry," Carter said. "He'll understand and I'll find him another teacher and someone else to fund. Now go! Right now, this minute, go find your doctor and tell him what you need to."

"Carter, I —" she began, sounding as

though she was going to protest, but then she broke off. Instead, she kissed Carter's cheek. "Thank you. I . . ." She didn't know what else to say as she ran out the door.

Sophie ran down the stairs and out the front door without bothering to grab a coat. She ran the short distance to Reede's office, and as soon as she stepped inside, she hesitated. The office was so full of waiting patients that she thought she should wait until later this evening to talk to Reede.

But Betsy saw her, nudged Heather, who caught Alice's arm, and in an instant all three women were surrounding Sophie. Heather slipped between Sophie and the door so she couldn't leave.

"Carter talked to you, didn't he?" Betsy asked, her face serious.

"He did and I have some things to talk to Reede about, but he's busy. I'll see him later." She turned to the door, but Heather was blocking it.

Betsy put her arm around Sophie's shoulders. "Does anyone object to Sophie talking to Dr. Reede?" she asked the waiting patients.

"I'll wait!" said a woman with two children.

"I can come back next week," a man said eagerly.

"I just have bronchitis," a woman said as she repressed a cough. "Had it before, no big deal."

"My stitches can come out tomorrow," said a young man.

"See?" Betsy said, smiling, "no problem at all." She took Sophie's arm and half pulled her into the hall at the back of the office, Alice and Heather close behind.

Betsy knocked, then opened a door. An older woman was sitting on the end of the paper-covered exam table, wearing a hospital gown. Reede was on a stool before her and he was examining her foot.

"If you'd just stop cutting your nails this short you wouldn't get ingrown toenails," Reede was saying in a grumpy tone. "I told you this the last time you were —" He broke off when the door opened, then his eyes widened at the sight of Sophie, as she was practically encased by the three women.

"I told them that this can wait for later," Sophie said. "I didn't mean to —"

The older woman lithely jumped off the table. "It's all my fault and you told me it was. See you later," she said as she ran to the door.

Seconds later, Sophic and Reede were

alone in the room.

"What in the world is going on?" he asked. "Sophie, are you all right?"

"Fine," she said. "Physically well, but I have something important to say to you." She motioned for him to take a seat on the end of the exam table. "Remember when I made the potato animals for the children that day in the forest?"

"Of course I do."

"Those children were traumatized — and rightfully so. An arrow had come sailing over their heads and pinned a man to a tree. No one knew if it was an accident or a madman was after them. I can just imagine the way the woman had to have warned them. She must have been nearly hysterical. She had to hold the man up to keep his wound from tearing, and she was trying to protect the children as she was calling for help, all at the same time."

Reede had no idea where Sophie was going with all this, but from the look on her face it was very important to her. "But you calmed the children down," he said, smiling. "When I saw you, you looked like some woodland goddess surrounded by children who were looking at you as though you were rescuing them from certain death."

"Some of them were certainly scared,

weren't they?"

"Not with you and your dragons there. And at Thanksgiving the kids thought you were an angel. Sophie, you have a way with children that's downright magic."

"I like to feel needed. I think it's why I chose going home to Lisa rather than accepting a sculpting job. I didn't feel the world *needed* spoons with the heads of the presidents on them, but Lisa was a mess. She was a teenager with no mother, an insufferably lazy stepfather, and she needed an excuse to get away from a very bad group of people."

"And then there was Carter," Reede said quietly. "He needed you too."

"Yes he did. His father is the biggest bully on the planet."

"But what does all this neediness say about me?" he asked, smiling. "I'm pretty self-sufficient. I run businesses, clinics, take care of a whole town's medical problems, and about half of their psychological problems. I've never told you — or anyone else for that matter — but I practically run a dating service. One time I —"

He cut off because Sophie was laughing. "You self-sufficient? Are you kidding? You've got to be the neediest person in the world."

"Me? Sophie . . ." He couldn't help feeling hurt that she knew so little about him. "You know that here in Edilean I have employees but when I'm on my own I —"

"Get nearly run over by race car drivers."

"That was one time," Reede said and couldn't help frowning. "Sophie, what are you trying to say to me?"

She took a deep breath. If she said what she truly and deeply felt, told him what she wanted, what if he said no? What if he laughed at the idea of her going with him? "Carter and Treeborne Foods will fund your hospital ship and I want to go with you."

Reede looked at her, blinking. "But what about your sculpture? And the fabulous studio Henry is building? With his contacts he could set you up in the art world. With your talent, you could become famous."

"I'm not like Jecca and Kim. I'm not driven to succeed in the art world." She took a step toward him. "I felt better helping those children with the potato animals than I did after anything else I've ever made." She took another step toward him. "Is there a place in what you do for a woman who can deal with traumatized children? Do you think you *need* someone like me in your work?"

"Sophie," Reede said, and there were tears in his eyes. "Yes. *I* need you. And the world's children need you."

She was standing in front of him, her face close to his.

"Sophie, will you marry me and go with me to . . . to wherever the world needs us?"

"Yes," she said. "I'd very much like to do that."

He pulled her into his arms and kissed her — and outside the office they heard people cheering. It looked as if someone had been listening at the door. Within three minutes, the fire department set off its alarm, Colin turned the sirens of both sheriff cars on, and the bells of all three churches were set to ringing.

Reede pulled away from Sophie to look at her in surprise, then the two of them started laughing. "I think they agree with us."

"Yes," Sophie said. "Yes and yes and yes."

ABOUT THE AUTHOR

Jude Deveraux is the author of more than forty *New York Times* bestsellers, including *Moonlight in the Morning, The Scent of Jasmine, Scarlet Nights, Days of Gold, Lavender Morning, Return to Summerhouse,* and *Secrets.* To date, there are more than sixty million copies of her books in print worldwide. She lives in North Carolina. To learn more, visit JudeDeveraux.com.

The employees of Thorndike Press hope you have enjoyed this Large Print book. All our Thorndike, Wheeler, and Kennebec Large Print titles are designed for easy reading, and all our books are made to last. Other Thorndike Press Large Print books are available at your library, through selected bookstores, or directly from us.

For information about titles, please call:
    (800) 223-1244

or visit our Web site at:
    http://gale.cengage.com/thorndike

To share your comments, please write:
    Publisher
    Thorndike Press
    10 Water St., Suite 310
    Waterville, ME 04901